EMPEROR!

EMPEROR!

A Romance of Ancient China

LANNY FIELDS

iUniverse, Inc.
New York Lincoln Shanghai

EMPEROR!
A Romance of Ancient China

iUniverse books may be ordered through booksellers or by contacting:

iUniverse
2021 Pine Lake Road, Suite 100
Lincoln, NE 68512
www.iuniverse.com
1-800-Authors (1-800-288-4677)

Because of the dynamic nature of the Internet, any Web addresses or links contained in this book may have changed since publication and may no longer be valid.

While some characters and events may be historically accurate, this book is a work of fiction.

ISBN: 978-0-595-40852-8 (pbk)
ISBN: 978-0-595-85216-1 (ebk)

Printed in the United States of America

Emperor has taken a long time to birth, and I owe deep-felt gratitude to those who aided in its journey. The idea for writing a novel about China's first emperor came from a holiday gathering with my parents, Bruce and Betty, along with Carolyn Han. The first draft flowed in eleven weeks and was hand written. Many have read it and encouraged me through numerous revisions: Linda Stockham, Diane Halpern, Nancy Hahn, and Jason Crosson. Linda Burgess read it twice and offered invaluable advice and encouragement. Karen McChrystal gave it a careful editing and her support. Donna Stone provided rock-solid support through difficult times, and she gave the manuscript close readings, too. It would take another lifetime to repay her. Any mistakes are my own responsibility.

My wife and partner, Kathryn Leeman, provided the magical space and encouragement to see *Emperor* through to publication. Environment is all. Bless you, Kat.

I have taken liberties with the history of China when its empire came into being (221 BC and after). This "history" is, of course, fictional. Indeed. I also Romanized for the non-expert reader (Chin rather than Qin or Ch'in, Su Ma rather than Sima Qian, and so on). We know little about crime and gangs in that era. Enjoy your own journey into *Emperor*.

When a writer calls his work a romance, it need hardly be observed that he wishes to claim a certain latitude, both as to its fashion and material, which he would not have felt himself entitled to assume, had he professed to be writing a novel. The latter form of composition is presumed to aim at a very minute fidelity, not merely to the possible, but to the probable and ordinary course of man's experience. The former—while as a work of art, it must rigidly observe itself to laws, and while it sins unpardonably so far as it may swerve aside from the truth of the human heart—has fairly a right to present that truth under circumstances, to a great extent, of the writer's own choosing or creation.... The point of view in which this tale comes under the Romantic definition lies in the attempt to connect a bygone time with the very present that is flitting away from us.

Nathaniel Hawthorne
Preface to <u>The House of the Seven Gables</u>
As seen in
A.S. Byatt
<u>Possession</u>

LIST OF CHARACTERS

Su Ma (c. 145–84 BC)—Han-dynasty historian

King Jeng (Ying Jeng, 259–210 BC)—King of Chin, emperor of China

Marcus (Marcus Lucius Scipio, 263–180 BC)—Roman traveler, friend of King Jeng

Sariputra—Buddhist monk from South Asia, friend of Marcus

Du Fu—Half-Chinese traveling companion of Marcus and Sariputra, translator for them

Old Juang—Chief of the Reds, one of the gangs in Chin's capital

Tao—Orphan and member of the Reds

Lee Su—Key administrator of the Chin warring state, eventually Chancellor of the Chin empire

Lee Bu—Son of Lee Su and administrator in Chin

Ming Tian—Chinese nun and later partner of Marcus, academician of the Chin empire

Mother Lo—Abbess of the Great Mother Temple on Mount Hua

Shu Wei—Minor aristocrat of the Chi warring state

Lotus—Shu Wei's first wife

Bing—Merchant-industrialist from the state of Chi

Liao—Intellectual-strategist who served the Chin warring state

Old Liu—Peasant in southern China (warring state of Chu)

Chen—Wife of Old Liu

Dr. Wu—Imperial physician and friend of Marcus

Meng Tian—Commander of the imperial garrison

Jing Ko—Palladin and assassin

General Wang—Famous general of Chin

Black Bear—Shaman from the area north of China

Shu Tung—Nephew of Shu Wei, academician of the Chin empire

Jin Mi—Master thief of the Reds and friend of Tao

Bo Lo—Abbot of the Green Dragon Lodge and sometime companion of Marcus

Academician Hu—Member of the imperial academy and friend of Academician Ming

Fu Su—Eldest son of Emperor Jeng

Hu Hai—Youngest and favorite son of Emperor Jeng

Feng Ping—Former officer in the Chin army and outstanding administrator in the imperial government

Hung An—Wife of Feng Ping

Jing Ling—Mine owner and widow in the commandery of Ba

Han Yu—Female official of the Chin empire

Jo Jing-Jeng—Commander of the White Panthers (White Tigers) and head of the imperial academicians

Feng Jie—Imperial secretary of the Chin empire

PROLOGUE
SU MA, FORTY-FOURTH
YEAR OF THE MARTIAL
EMPEROR OF HAN
(98 BC)

Su Ma lay atop the castration table with his brown robe hiked up above his navel and his undergarments removed. He knew that the grizzled castration official had used the saw and knife for two decades. A white-haired head witness assumed a dignified pose, his wispy goatee quivering, as he explained the procedure. Words faded into the shadows.

Su Ma's limbs recoiled protectively. Padded restraints clutched his arms and legs. With a metallic flash, the surgical blade descended. Su Ma's abdomen contracted as if he'd been kicked in the groin. Another convulsion brought wetness and the scent of fresh blood.

When the castration ended, Su Ma got off the table and attempted to stand alone. He fainted and awoke in the dark completely disoriented. A friend helped him home.

Two weeks later—a full twenty days—Su Ma lounged on his own bed. The succeeding days had blurred as infection ravaged him. Today, however, he felt well enough to contemplate his unfinished history of China. The bamboo strips upon which it was written were neatly stacked against the wall. It was time to finish the monumental work that Su Ma's dying father, grand historian for the Han court, had charged him with completing. That unfinished task had prompted Su Ma to choose castration over suicide—the prescribed punishments for enraging his emperor during a court debate. Now, he thought, he must fulfill his father's wish.

Su Ma fingered the lacquered medicine jars. The four-legged one was an ebony piece shaped like a crouching red dragon, and the flat-bottomed red one portrayed a phoenix rising from an inferno. The study's main lacquer piece, a massive clothes chest, guarded the door. Su Ma sighed.

The waiting history drew him, just as the lodestone doors at the entrance to the throne room drew iron. Su Ma reclined on his teak bed, arm resting on the woodblock headrest. A sparrow scolded outside. Drool trickled down Su Ma's hollow chin as he recalled the bird-filled wicker trays in the Western Market. Deep-fried, the birds melted in his mouth.

Su Ma had succeeded to his father's court position at thirty-seven years old; he lived with his family and servants in quarters provided by the state. Dismissal from his state post, held in the family for decades, should have brought eviction, but the Son of Heaven for some reason had commanded Su Ma to join the inner court secretariat—a place of real power.

He lifted the teapot, purchased at the Green Temple. The old one had broken, and he refused to spend a great sum on another. He'd bargained hard that day, but Orchid scolded him for paying too much. He had winced after trying to make amends for dropping the ancient pot, her brother's wedding gift to them.

The barley tea was tepid, but Su Ma needed something to sip while contemplating the Chin annals section. Over one hundred forty years ago, King Ying Jeng had ascended the Chin throne at age thirteen. Ying Jeng had become emperor twenty-five years later, after uniting China. His state, Chin, conquered the six other warring states of Jao, Wey, Han, Yen, Chu, and Chi. What had Ying Jeng looked like? As a eunuch, Su Ma would have access to the library of the inner court. Perhaps there was a portrait.

Research and writing invigorated Su Ma like an icy bath.

He mused about the Chin warring state. Over 250 years ago, Chin had been a woefully weak state, until Lord Shang forged mighty armies and an efficient administration. Yet, Lord Shang had offended the Chin crown prince, who then had the hapless minister torn to pieces.

Su Ma regarded the stacks of bamboo slips. Though incomplete, the draft already had 500,000 words. He poured another cup of tea. Shadows lengthened in the deepening stillness.

King Jeng had united China and become emperor. What had that transition been like for aristocrats and peasants? Had crime ceased? How had officials governed? What had foreigners thought?

The diminutive historian reached for his ink block and dish. He hobbled to his mahogany desk and ground down the block. After adding water and stirring, Su Ma dipped his brush in the dish and began the section on King Jeng, who would become the first emperor of China.

PART 1
UNITING CHINA
(238–221 BC)

CHAPTER 1

KING JENG (238 BC)

Dawn unfolded a pastel tapestry with pinks, mauves, and light blues. The morning star winked. Rosy fingers stretched from the horizon and caressed distant peaks. Southeast of the Ganchuan Palace, maroon shades yielded to orange and then to golden yellow.

Rays invaded the palace, sifting into his corner room. Ying Jeng preferred eastern rooms. He threw off the autumn-colored spreads. The restful night had recharged him. Never had he felt healthier.

Two months before, the cold had frozen homeless people huddling in the capital's alleyways. Birds had dropped from the sky like icicles. King Jeng was pleased that the princesses—his half sisters and cousins—had started a relief fund.

The king's face clouded as he contemplated his upcoming capping ceremony; he would soon rule on his own. The Regency Council had finally agreed to a date. The young king's forehead wrinkled like fingers left too long in water.

Lee Su, head of the king's spy system, stalked enemies like a ferret. King Jeng considered putting the wily Su in charge of all intelligence operations but remembered the sage advice about placing too much power in a single person's control.

Morning rays highlighted a brown medicine chest with gold writing delineating each compartment's contents. Ying Jeng had wanted to trust the old physician who'd kept him alive the last eighteen years … yet, "trust no one" had been his father's dying words.

Forehead wrinkles reworked their patterns. Jeng choked back bile at the memory of his father's death stench. The mausoleum complex where Jeng himself would be interred had been under construction since he had succeeded his father eight years ago.

Jeng's companion stirred, and Jeng lightly caressed his naked back. As the king grew hard, he rolled the young man over.

Later, Jeng pranced to the stables to meet the equipage officer—a stocky, muscled man.

"Good morning, Your Majesty," said the bowing official.

"I'll ride now. Saddle Midnight!" the king commanded.

The burly man said, "I beg to inform the Son of Heaven that she came up lame yesterday. I have Rising Sun. He's spirited and will complement Your Majesty's character."

"Prepare the horse. I'll depart at once. Pick three escort riders; we'll ride in the great park near the Western Highway."

Jeng chortled as his horse galloped across the lush meadow near the exotic-animal enclosure. He spied a lumbering elephant. The cold snap had only killed three beasts, thanks to the newly installed heated animal rooms.

The stallion bolted when a covey of birds exploded from their cover in the underbrush. The king fought the reins—both broke. As he leaned forward to grab the horse's neck, the action spurred the stallion. Animal and clinging man galloped toward the highway.

He heard pounding hooves and saw a hand reach for the reins. They missed. After another fruitless effort, Jeng's grip slid down the stallion's neck. Fingers crossed his vision, seized a jewel-encrusted rein, and tugged. As the pull tightened, the wild-eyed horse slowed. A final jerk halted the heaving animal. Jeng tumbled to the thick meadow grass and inhaled its sweet scent. He heard ants march to their nest and the wind caress the wings of a hawk.

A pungent scent filled Jeng's nostrils. His eyes opened to a hairy face. Blue eyes stared back at him from a mass of red, wavy hair! King Jeng watched as each of the beast's hairs writhed in wild abandon. The being's complexion, sun-darkened and leathery, heightened his alien hue.

Hoof beats grew louder, and Jeng's eyebrows narrowed at the thought of his escort. The barbarian loomed as the king called to him. "Who are you? You've saved our life." The stranger looked puzzled. "I'll reward you," Jeng continued. "Are you deaf?" As King Jeng's head shifted, he saw two riders: one was purplish black, and the other seemed normal.

"Of course … you're a barbarian and can't speak," King Jeng mused. "We must make you understand!"

The bearded one extended his hand. The escort members, who had just arrived, drew their swords.

The Chinese rider spoke. "Please forgive us, Your Excellency. We are ignorant travelers in your glorious land. I'm Du Fu … this is Sali … and he's Maku. We're at your service." Du Fu pointed at the dark-skinned man and the hairy one in turn.

The escort leader shouted, "The barbarians' behavior is disgraceful, sire! I'll teach them proper manners!"

"Halt!" Jeng commanded. Then he spoke to Du Fu. "Your furry companion saved me. We are King Jeng of Chin."

The Chinese man spoke to his companions, who nodded. Their awkward ways brought a royal smile. Du Fu had a wispy goatee and wore a thick, black leather jacket. The dark man wore an orange robe with a bag slung across his chest. He was hairless. Was he a eunuch? The furry one wore brown pantaloons with a matching jacket.

Jeng turned to the Chinese man. "Please tell Ma ... that since he saved our life, we will reward him."

Du Fu translated the bearded one's reply. "Maku said that he's honored, but desires no reward."

"Maku? What's his full name?" asked the king, who eyed his escort through his peripheral vision.

The travelers conferred. "His name is Lu-shi-su Ma-ku-su Shi-pi-o," said the translator, who looked like a hunting falcon.

"The name's impossible. We'll call him Ma. The reward is ours to give, not his to refuse! You will stay at our palace as guests."

The Chinese man answered, "Yes, Your Majesty."

"Where did you learn to speak?" asked the king.

"My father comes from a land east of here. I plan to visit his birthplace and my ancestors' graves," Du Fu said.

"What about your companions?" The king picked a blade of grass and chewed it. He realized that it had been singing to the morning.

"The dark one on the horse lives in a faraway place southwest of here," Du Fu answered. "The one who saved you comes from the far west, Your Majesty ... Rome." Du Fu mopped his brow with a blue cloth.

"Enough! Let's return to the palace," the king commanded. Jeng walked to his sweat-soaked horse. Examining the reins, he realized they'd been cut halfway through with a knife. "Nasty accident. Let's depart. I'll take your mount and send a party for you," the king told the escort leader in a commanding tone.

Jeng had another escort rider lead Rising Sun. The foreigners recovered their supply animals, and the tiny party rode off.

Arriving at the royal stables, King Jeng summoned bodyguards to arrest the escort soldiers and the equipage officer. Jeng seized a guardsman's sword and hacked furiously at a cringing member of the escort. After severing the man's head, both of his arms, and a leg, the gore-splattered monarch threw down the sword.

As the foreigners warily dismounted, the king, flanked by guards, ordered a servant to prepare quarters for his guests. He bade them farewell and strode away.

In the days that followed the rescue, King Jeng often summoned the travelers. Tales about other countries astonished him, and he asked about weaponry, strategy, and tactics.

Marcus (Maku) was rewarded in the Ganchuan Audience Hall, which dwarfed anything the three travelers had seen. King Jeng presented him with a white jade scepter and a golden bowl. The Roman also received an annual income from the produce of five hundred households, along with the post of inspector of the royal gardens.

The investigation of the assassination attempt revealed by the sliced reins continued. Under torture, the escort leader named three lackeys associated with Marquis Lao Ai, a member of the queen mother's entourage.

Lee Su handled the principal investigation, and King Jeng verified stories. Five days before the capping ceremony, three top officials were arrested, and the king shifted the ceremony to distant Yung, an ancient ceremonial center. He would be capped in the Hall of the Royal Ancestors. King Jeng wondered if he would survive to see it happen.

CHAPTER 2

OLD JUANG (238 BC)

The dwarf crept into the modest dwelling topped with a brown-tiled roof on the edge of the Southern Market in the Chin capital. Midlevel officials occupied this warren of homes; some called it the Little Lords' District.

The spring air was mild. Less than six weeks ago, scores of people had frozen to death. Old Juang recalled the five ox-drawn carts jammed with blue corpses. At least city officials had moved efficiently to prevent a worse disaster.

One of the tiny man's sources had sworn that rare jade pendants were in this dwelling. Ordinarily, Old Juang would have entrusted an underling to steal the valuables, but the pieces might be worth a fortune. Besides, he believed it wise to test his skills occasionally. Best not have his gang members suppose he was growing soft. A wicked smile brightened Old Juang's face.

The central room smelled wrong. The dwarf sniffed. He walked over to the bed, lifted a corner of the coverlet, and gagged. Old Juang had seen the bodies of plague victims, and these corpses bore the familiar signs. His first instinct was to flee; instead, he found a taper and lit it. Shadows swirled in sinister shapes, and the dwarf took three steadying breaths. Old Juang settled into himself and located the cache of jade in the pantry.

As Old Juang caressed the lustrous pieces wrapped in gold-threaded brocade silk with a firebird motif, he heard a sound. He unsheathed his polished iron dagger—taken from a dead soldier twenty-six years before—then turned to see a slender lad of about seven or eight poking his head from a rainbow-colored quilt in a corner of the room. The child coughed as Old Juang advanced.

The boy raised himself on a bony arm, eyes opened wide. "Who … who are you?" he stammered.

"Shut up!" The dwarf raised the dagger. Then he spotted scattered bamboo writing strips covered with a childlike scrawl. The thin strips lay curled on the floor like worms and insects. Old Juang lowered the knife.

"Did you write this?" Old Juang asked with a thin smile. His free hand scratched his ear.

The little boy, who had a nervous facial tic, nodded solemnly. "My father taught me until he and Mama got sick. I'm thirsty."

Shadows transmuted to a light gray hue, and the room shimmered. "I should kill you as a mercy!" the dwarf said gruffly. But he sheathed his dagger. A gang member who could read and write would give an edge over the Greens. The lad had survived the plague; although weak, he appeared as if he'd recover.

"What's your name?" Old Juang asked, scratching his armpit.

"Tao, sir," said the boy quietly, rubbing his eyes.

Old Juang guessed the boy's mind had been challenged more than his will or body. And yet, the lad remembered his manners.

"No need to 'sir' me, except when my men are around. You'll get to know them all."

"Yes, sir," the boy said.

Old Juang slapped him. The boy gasped as his cheek reddened. "Shut up! When I tell you something, you'll obey me … or I'll kill you. Understand?" When Old Juang scowled, his eyebrows were warring caterpillars. The boy stifled a sob and nodded.

"Follow me," Old Juang continued. "I'm taking you out of here. Do as I say, and you'll be fine, you little bastard." Juang turned away and permitted himself a smile as he dipped a cup into the half-full water barrel, handing it to the boy. Tao greedily guzzled the water. With his long ears, Tao resembled an elf or some kind of woodland creature in a tale told by the fire.

The two crept out into the dawn, and the dwarf led them a circuitous route, doubling back and retreating—not merely to confuse the boy, but also to watch for someone tailing them.

Tao bowed to a gruff man who had been told to spare no effort in seeing that Tao mastered reading and writing. Both of Tao's cheeks were red from the teacher's slaps. In the weeks since he had been taken to the Reds, Old Juang's gang, Tao had quickly learned to suppress his anger, frustration, and tears.

The filthy study was dark except for a huge taper held in a bronze bear's paws. Dank smells steeped the shadowy room, among them the acrid stench of urine. The ceiling was black with soot, and dusty cobwebs shivered when the door opened.

"I said, read this sentence!" the teacher bellowed with his hand poised for another slap.

The boy slowly exhaled. "The Dao that can be spoken of is not the real Dao. The name that can be named is not the real name."

"Not bad," the man said with awe in his voice. "That was a sight translation of a difficult passage."

"What does it mean?" Tao asked as he rubbed his cheek.

"Never mind, you little turd! Let's go on to this passage and see how smart you are." Bamboo strips placed side by side contained a mix of familiar and new characters. Tao sight-read the passage.

Old Juang raised his eyebrows at Tao's acute perceptiveness. Then the dwarf flicked a bamboo rod at the blindfolded boy in an effort to confuse him, raising a welt on his shoulder. Tao was naked except for a clean loincloth hiding his private parts. His knees were relaxed despite the pain.

"Don't even think about flinching or crying." Despite his harsh tone, Juang was impressed by the lad's newfound mastery of interacting with the world of the senses. "See with your ears; listen with your nose; sample the air with your tongue. How will you survive while asleep? You must be fully aware moment to moment! How many times must I repeat myself?"

The boy inhaled and resumed a slow-motion dance through the booby-trapped room. He halted before the broken glass.

"Good! Now you are seeing with your toes. Open your mind and body; permit the room's energies to be revealed. Turn to your right." The dwarf deliberately praised the lad to cloud his mind. He saw Tao shake off the compliment and back away from the dead scorpion. Old Juang smiled. The worth of the boy had doubled again.

CHAPTER 3

MARCUS (MAKU) (238 BC)

While court intrigues moved toward a decisive confrontation, Marcus, the Roman, Sariputra (Sali), and Du Fu toured the palace. One large room contained pieces of exquisitely carved jade. Marcus walked over to a pyramid-shaped black piece three hands tall. Close inspection revealed a miniature mountain with tiny roads and trees. Nearby was a mauve jade orchid. Marcus could even see the veins in its leaves and petals. Another room was decorated with bronze sculptures. There were three large bird candle stick holders. They were phoenixes, the favorite symbol of the young king. Vases and urns graced tables, and many had inscriptions incised on their sides. Marcus vowed that one day he would read the inscriptions.

Specialist Bo, their guide—a middle-aged, average-size man with a strong body odor—regaled his charges with commentary on the labor quotas, which mandated that each village supply five adult males, each of whom worked for thirty days without payment. Under special circumstances, the thirty days could be extended to forty-five days. The five-family heads supervised the labor draft from the village side.

"What are the five-family heads?" Marcus asked as Du Fu translated for him.

Specialist Bo stroked his bushy, black beard. "All people are divided into groups of five families. Each unit selects a head, who maintains a census record, collects taxes and duties, supervises obedience to laws and ordinances, and fills the labor quota."

"It sounds like a military organization," Marcus said, idling beside an open window that looked over the city. People hurried by, intent on their business. One man carried two loads of firewood in baskets strung from the ends of a thick pole. The pole rested across his shoulders. Man, baskets, and pole all swayed in a graceful dance of color and sound.

A delicate incense wafted from a bronze tripod. It reminded Marcus of frankincense, and he inhaled deeply. Specialist Bo mopped his brow. "Perhaps you are correct. The minister who established the system was an army officer."

"What if someone in the group committed a crime?"

The official's dark eyes bored into the alien interrogator. "Crimes happen rarely. Should they be serious, the whole group would be put to death."

"Even if they were innocent women and children?" Marcus asked. The cumbersome translation process frustrated him.

"Of course! No one is innocent in the mutual-responsibility system. Everyone knows everyone's business. If you leave your money on a restaurant table, it will be there when you return. Criminals are apprehended before they commit crimes; inmates are a labor resource. As a great minister once said, 'When the laws are regulated by harsh punishments, all will be educated to obey.'" Specialist Bo proudly stood at attention.

Du Fu rested before the next question. Marcus spoke, fanning himself. "In my land, we have few police and some crime. Yet, our senators would not tolerate innocents being punished."

Du Fu asked Marcus to give another word for senator. The Roman substituted "aristocrat."

The official smirked. "Chin's aristocrats tried to resist this system. They were eradicated!"

Marcus frowned. "A land without nobles! My land wouldn't survive. There'd be no senate … no officers for the legions … no effective government. They are our memory. Our heroes are highborn!" After a sharp intake of breath by Du Fu, the translation commenced.

The Chin official gathered himself. "You are an honored guest who saved His Royal Majesty. For that I—we—thank you. Please know crime is rare. Know, too, that between the labor obligation and the convicts, all construction needs are met."

Marcus steered the conversation in another direction as he absently stroked a sheer silk scarf. "The walls are smooth and beautifully painted. Do the laborers also paint them?"

Specialist Bo barely suppressed a smirk. "Peasants have no talent. They are simpleminded. Painters from the mural guild paint them. Jade workers, bone carvers, and goldsmiths work thus."

"How are they paid?"

"They work for the state. Everything is furnished," Specialist Bo said as sweat dripped from his tiny nose. "They work nine days a week. And, of course, they have the usual holidays. The great reformer insisted on it."

In response to a query from the Roman, Du Fu explained that the Chin calendar used a ten-day week. Marcus scratched his cheek. Chin differed from Rome. Fortunately, he didn't have to spend the rest of his days here.

CHAPTER 4

OLD JUANG (238 BC)

Old Juang gazed at his chiefs seated around a highly polished cedar table, indulging in a luxury the crime boss permitted in the conference room. This was their weekly meeting, when they examined the previous week's gains and losses.

One-armed Chi peered at Juang without fear or hatred. Chi did not aspire to higher posts (night master or day master); nor did he covet the boss position. Chi knew his limitations and could be trusted; he and Old Juang had worked together for over twenty years, guarding each other's backs when chaos or death threatened. Chi had foul breath; he savored spicy and fermented foods. More than once, Chi had laughed as he voiced his preference for old dogs over puppies—even better if they had been dead for a day or two.

Shifty-eyed Pa seemed dissatisfied with his lot as day master, the third highest post in the gang. He aspired to Old Juang's position. He even looked like a boss, with his large frame and gigantic belly. Others called him "Porker"—but not to his face. Violent and cruel, Pa was the enforcer when merchants or clients got out of line. Juang guessed that Pa had killed around 120 people, often with his bare hands. Lingering deaths were his favorite—because, Pa claimed, he drew their life force into his own. Old Juang was skeptical.

Lefty Lu seldom let emotions show. The night master could be a dangerous foe, but Old Juang had made a point of rewarding Lefty Lu. He was also given the most difficult tasks. The night master sneezed and wiped his bulbous nose on the inside of his grimy, green robe. Lefty's square face and wide forehead were covered with pockmarks from his youth.

These three were effective, and loyal to Old Juang, their boss—at least outwardly. None had ever, to the boss's knowledge, made jokes about dwarves. They respected or feared him.

Old Juang crossed his arms over his chest and began. "Well, how was our haul in the last ten days? You first, Lefty."

"Boss, we pulled in over sixty gold pieces, three hundred forty silvers, and twenty three thousand bronze coins from our night jobs. We also brung in twelve jade necklaces and bracelets. Boss, you was right to suggest we hit the big house of the old silk merchant. This is the best week in the last three years."

"Good, good. And what about the whorehouses?"

Lefty flinched. It was barely perceptible, but Old Juang had been trained to see what was in front of him, rather than what he thought was in front of him. Missing clues could be costly.

"They earned one hundred twenty seven gold, one hundred forty one silver, and eleven thousand eight hundred seventy bronze," the wizened man said. "No jade or other valuables." Sweat dotted Lefty's forehead just below his receding hairline. Lefty rued his hair loss and was rumored to have tried dozens of potions and incantations to restore it. At least two women who had promised a hair-restoration program had vanished. Old Juang tried not to think about how they died.

"OK, and how about information?" the dwarf asked quietly. He seldom spoke in a loud voice; the softer one spoke, the more attentive were one's listeners.

"A shipment of silk leaves for Central Asia next third day ... twenty camels, each with twenty-five bolts of heavy brocade fabric. The young king may last long enough to be crowned. His rival, Lao Ai, will try a coup, but betting money is on the king. Lao Ai may be good at fucking the king's mama, but he's not a threat. Some rat's always giving him away." Sweat stung Lefty's eyes.

Mentally, Old Juang made plans to have Lefty followed for the next month. Out loud, he merely said, "Excellent, my friend. Information is more precious than life. Remember that we stay out of politics unless sought out by top officials. No meddling, any of you. Clear?" All nodded.

Other reports showed a growing flow of hard coins and information. The Black Gang was ensnared in the current political struggle, having backed Lao Ai. Old Juang smiled inwardly, imagining that his Red Gang would inherit new territory and four whorehouses when the Black Gang was destroyed by the king's officials. Whorehouses were gold mines and fecund sources of information. Officials and merchants bragged to impress their women, little knowing that all reported to the night master and some directly to the boss. It was best to have many sources to check—tedious, but necessary.

CHAPTER 5

MARCUS (238 BC)

King Jeng invited his rescuers to his capping ceremony. Two days prior to the festivities, a heavily guarded procession marched to the ancient city of Yung. That night, they camped at a fortified garrison. The march resumed just after dawn.

Marcus pulled his horse up to Sariputra. "My friend, all troops seem ready for a fight. What's happening?"

"It could be the weather, but something causes tension," Sariputra observed. "Their faces appear normal ... but observe their arms and hands. Regard the skittish horses: they easily pick up their riders' tensions. Watch a person's body, my friend. It can tell you more than words or facial expressions. Listen to the tone of a voice. See the hands ... or, even better, the fingers. After your unfortunate incident in Bactra, your fingers danced like a troupe of performers to your hair, to your mouth."

Mention of the horror in Central Asia awakened the absentminded fingers.

"Trust your feelings, Marcus," Sariputra added. "You haven't meditated in a long time."

Marcus gazed at a massive thunderhead. The underside of the cloud formation was gray, but the sun backlit the crown—a cloud mass like the purest snow. Soon a tempest drenched the procession. Marcus sniffed the fresh air and the odors that wafted from the earth. All transported him back to childhood revels in Rome.

Late that night, they arrived at Yung. In the flickering torchlight, objects cast eerie shadows. Lightning flashes limned the massive outer wall. Heavily armored soldiers met them.

The following day dawned unseasonably cool, yet Marcus felt snug within the heated inner room. Subterranean heating units housed massive fireplaces tended by two shifts of slaves; the heat swirled through ceramic conduit pipes under the floors.

Marcus looked up from studying Chinese characters and noticed a cylindrical enclosure made of ceramic material. He had learned that it kept food chilled in the summer; ice blocks retarded spoilage. Each palace also had cool quarters, with extra long window overhangs and overhead carved wooden fans with blades shaped like giant seashells.

The next day was the capping ceremony. The foreign guests were awakened before dawn and transported to the Altar of the Red Sovereign, where crimson-robed officials waited. The courtyard bore festive red banners and pennants.

Drums kept a solemn beat, and a white stallion with a red-dyed mane was led in. A squad of scarlet-uniformed men marched toward their king, who wore a crimson robe. Glaring gold dragons gamboled on the red garments.

When the marchers halted, an official who resembled a large rat crept forward and intoned a proclamation. Then, about two dozen women wearing silk gowns began a slow but stately dance. Near the end, the ladies broke into a songlike chant, swaying like slender willows in a zephyr. When the women retired, a towering official bearded with a scarlet goatee marched to the altar, bowed, and proffered a golden goblet to his king. The king raised the chalice and drank. The white stallion was then led to the king, who stepped aside as the horse's forelegs were secured with red cords. Another man carrying a short sword encased in a gold-studded, scarlet scabbard bowed to the altar, to the king, and to the horse. At that moment, a reddish orange sun lifted over the distant peaks, and a shaft of reddish orange light pierced the courtyard. The audience roared appreciatively. The official grabbed the horse's neck, then thrust the sword into its chest.

The retracted sword sliced the horse's throat, silencing a loud, piercing whinny; gushing blood streamed into the golden chalice. The emperor drank from the goblet, red rivulets coursing down his chin. The ceremony complete, the audience moved to the Altar of the White Sovereign.

The remaining offerings and sacrifices were brief and subdued. In each case, a horse with a mane dyed to match the sovereign deity's garments fell to the sword. After each death, officials chatted amiably. Marcus stared numbly. Not even a sympathetic smile from his companion could soothe him.

That night, while Marcus and Sariputra chatted, Du Fu burst into the room. "There was a revolt yesterday! Hundreds tried and failed to overthrow King Jeng. One million dollars in cash is the reward for the leader's capture!"

Marcus and Sariputra exchanged looks. Du Fu frowned. "Don't you care about what's been happening?" Du Fu asked them. "Can you be so stupid?"

Marcus breathed deeply. The arrogant man had sneered at them since they'd entered Chin. "We knew something must have been planned. Too bad many died. I pity their families."

Du Fu gestured wildly. "Shut your mouth. Don't let King Jeng learn of your treasonous talk. Remember what he did to that man on the day you saved his life. You are crazy; that much has been obvious since you beat and castrated that man who was having a little fun. Barbarians!"

Marcus's hands clenched, then opened like flower petals. "I pity anyone who dies in war. I have seen dead bodies strewn like downed trees in a forest." Marcus muttered the words through tight lips.

"What greater honor than to kill an enemy? The fighting spared King Jeng ... whose life you saved. Or have you forgotten? He rewarded you, and you sympathize with his enemies." Du Fu snorted.

"I'm happy to be alive, and I'm grateful to King Jeng, but I feel pity for those who perished. What about you, Sari?"

"I renounced the taking of all life when I became a monk."

Pivoting, the Chinese man rushed into the corridor. "Going out to celebrate. Back late."

CHAPTER 6

TAO (238 BC)

Old Juang and Tao awoke early and wandered the streets of the capital. The false dawn had passed, and its deep purple was yielding to mauve in the eastern sky when they reached the Western Market.

"Look at the merchants preparing for the day," Old Juang said to the round-faced boy, who trailed the dwarf at a respectful distance. The immense market-place spread out with makeshift stalls; booths from which to sell meats—camel, goat, pork, beef, puppy, pony, and yak, just to name a few—were being erected.

Tao sniffed the blood-steeped air as the butchers unpacked their meat. The lad was intrigued by the slightly different scents: the sweetish scent of pork, the wildish cast of the camel, and the sour odor of the fermented beef.

The dwarf led him toward the vegetables and fruits, sorted by color and by quality. Soon, shrewd servants of the officials' houses would begin the singsong bargaining process. They knew merchants believed that a successful first sale determined one's good fortune for the day. The sellers grumbled, but accepted lower prices if the buyers earnestly began walking away.

"See that merchant?" Old Juang pointed to a vegetable dealer dressed in a blue and silver silk robe. "What do you notice?"

Tao squinted and waited before he offered his perspective. Although he could size things up in a glance, Tao did not wish to miss anything. Besides, he didn't want the dwarf to see how quickly he could work.

"His eyes are shifty, though that alone means little. Look how he fondles the weighing scale. I would bet that he has a crooked scale to cheat his customers."

"Good! What else?"

"He's counting out silver coins … unusual for a vegetable seller. He must be preparing to bribe a market superintendent."

"Excellent deduction, Tao," Old Juang said. "See what's there. Look at everything, and see reality," the tiny man added.

Tao climbed up to the entrance of the Ministry of Law and looked over the market; Old Juang ambled amiably behind. Tao took in the unfolding panorama of bustle and ordered chaos: the great marketplace of the world. Thousands of stall owners and countless customers went about their gathering of foods and stores to feed the clients for the coming days. Tao inhaled the bustle, the noise, the swearing, and the bargaining chants. This was the heart of the teeming capital city—a city geared for war, but one that had to eat and fart and shit.

The pair strolled by the stalls. Tao was amused by Old Juang's leisurely pace, but experience had already taught him to accept nothing for its face—to remain on guard. As they approached the area where caravans arrived, a strong stench engulfed Tao. Deep growling alerted him to a line of camels. Most of the two-humped, giant beasts patiently waited to be unloaded. One camel opened its mouth, displaying a deadly set of teeth that looked like medium-sized, stubby knives.

Tao walked toward a massive, ancient, brownish bull. The camel stayed aloof from everyone and everything like a great lord; its musky scent pervaded the area.

"Don't get close to the old master; he's a vicious bite and a lethal kick. If he didn't carry the heaviest loads, I'd have killed him long ago. He's a devil, that one."

Tao regarded the speaker, a deeply tanned man wearing a dark red turban characteristic of a western tribe. The man's face was covered with scars and boils, yet his fingers each sported a thick, gold ring, and a gold tube necklace hung heavily around his neck. Three chins quivered.

Tao cared little for gold. He continued toward the beast. Old Juang's breathing slowed. The camel's massive head lowered. The great neck stretched, and the massive lips pulled back. Old Juang stifled a cry.

Tao never took his eyes off the camel; its eyes fixed on him. Slowly Tao raised his arms, which encircled the camel's neck, gently pulling it down. It lowered to its foreknees with a belching grunt. Tao placed his face next to the camel's face and scratched its ear. Its back legs also bent into a settled mode, and its neck and head rose slightly to accommodate the boy. A low rumbling began in the camel's throat.

"You're either the bravest or stupidest boy," the camel driver said as he slowly exhaled. "I have never seen that bull so gentle, except maybe with that little girl at the Black Oasis. You, boy, have a gift."

Tao cradled the old bull's neck and scratched the other ear. The camel's heart beat slowed. He'd had luck with animals, but not with ones this gigantic. The camel's eyes closed. After a time, a reluctant Tao released the camel's neck. The camel's eyes opened and serenely regarded the boy. Tao knew he should rejoin

Old Juang, but it was difficult to break the spell. He whispered to the camel and turned away. The great animal moaned.

The two, Tao and Old Juang, walked silently to the Reds' headquarters, a rickety building of two stories. From the front, it looked like an abandoned whorehouse; inside was a hive of activity, with people arriving and leaving via guarded underground trapdoors. (One only entered after giving the correct number of knocks; the codes were changed weekly.) They walked by the building. Old Juang affected a jolly, carefree manner, but his eyes darted furtively. When satisfied, Old Juang ducked through a broken-down wooden fence, with Tao following. They disappeared behind a bush thicket, and Old Juang rapped on a door that led underground.

CHAPTER 7

MARCUS (238 BC)

Marcus and Sariputra immersed themselves in the Chinese language; they learned phrases as quickly as they could, practicing five to six hours daily. They conversed with servants to improve their pronunciation and learn new words and idioms. Tones troubled Sariputra, who often mispronounced words, and ended up swearing or mislabeling things.

The written language had its peculiarities; each character had to be memorized for its number of strokes and the order in which the strokes were written. Marcus loved the language that sometimes painted word pictures; the character for mountain was a peak with two lesser summits. Though the Roman had learned that the brush must be held in the right hand, he used his left.

Hour after hour, black Chinese characters filled the rectangular boards. Child-like scrawls evolved into balanced and compact characters. Intently writing Chinese was meditative.

King Jeng invited his foreign guests to see an irrigation project. As the group rode out, Jeng recounted that eight years ago, a neighboring king had plotted to exhaust Chin's resources by suggesting a massive irrigation project and sending a hydraulic engineer, Guo, to beguile the Chin court.

In succeeding years, one half month was added to the laboring obligation of peasants, and convicts were drafted too. When Chin spies discovered the plot, King Jeng initially arrested Guo, who proudly announced that Chin would soon have sufficient grain to supply Chin's armies for the upcoming unification wars. King Jeng realized that Guo had switched his allegiance to Chin and thereby rewarded Guo. Chin agents began offering land and tax exemptions to immigrant farmers.

The royal party arrived at the Guo Canal. Villages nestled on verdant farmlands. Marcus recalled his own farm. His had been a life to savor: working soil, weeding plant rows, and gathering harvests. The Roman stared at a man and his plow horse; a harness straddled its chest, using far more of the animal's pulling power than the neck collar used in Rome.

King Jeng spoke. "Farm tools are cast of iron instead of bronze. My father gathered agricultural experts to advise him on the use of such materials. We rent tools to people."

Marcus discerned the essence of the king's remarks. Du Fu's translation confirmed his guesses. The Roman replied, "Your Majesty, I must imagi ... think tools cost much; to loan or ... rent them ... good."

Du Fu sneered at the labored effort, not realizing that King Jeng was watching him. The king spoke slowly. "We regard agriculture as basic. The black-headed ones work hard and stay loyal."

Marcus glittered like a multifaceted jewel lit by sunrays. His speech shifted to Greek; Du Fu improvised. "You have a strong government, helping toilers and treating them as friends."

Sariputra whispered, "Marcus, your mouth's wide open. Are you hunting flies?"

"Sari, these methods surpass anything in Rome. Here, the government takes an active role."

"Perhaps the king would allow you to purchase land."

The scent of the rich, watered soil kindled an urge. Marcus slipped into labored Chinese. "Your Majesty, you use the term 'black-headed people.' Why?"

"As you see, farmers use black turbans and have black hair," King Jeng answered. "Black means power; this accords with our farmers, without whom we could not prosper."

The afternoon sun amplified a compelling odor: night soil. Two farmers toted an earthen jar filled with human and animal waste products, while a third ladled the liquid which was used as a fertilizer.

Canal water lapped at the bank, and its bluish gray surface stretched to the horizon. Swaying willows charmed the eye. A young woman dipped a bucket, then a second. As she bent under her balanced burden and straightened, she smiled. All watched the waddling dance.

Marcus looked down at his sandals and asked the king, "Your Majesty, may I purchase some farm land here?"

King Jeng peered into the Roman's face and replied, "You wish to own farm land? Why?"

"I tended my own farm in my homeland, and I loved working with the soil. I felt peaceful and free," Marcus sweated profusely as he labored to express himself.

"I see," said the king. "I'll consider your request."

"Thank you, Sire," Marcus bowed at the waist.

The party returned to the western gate as the horizon swallowed the sun. A collective shout drew the Roman's attention. An army unit drilled beside the wall. *Women! An Amazon force!* His head buzzed with questions.

Back in his palace room, Marcus sipped a cup of iced juice. His unfocused gaze rested on a silk hanging that depicted a unicorn. That night, he dreamed he was weeding between grain rows. Quintus, his son, played with a black-haired child. In the distance, Marcus saw King Jeng holding leg irons.

Early the next day, Marcus visited a Chinese acquaintance, Lee Bu, who worked in a drab, three-story office building in the northwest quadrant of the capital. Marcus had often talked with Lee Bu, who permitted Marcus chances to practice his Chinese.

The green-tiled office roof sloped gracefully. Dust added a dark brown hue. Inside, Marcus saw Bu poring over a disorderly pile of bamboo strips. Bu's loose black robe had a frayed collar and a faded cast. The Chinese man looked up. "Good afternoon, Ma-ku-su. How are you today?" Bu's hands were small, with slender fingers; his nails were bitten to the quick.

"I'm well, thank you. By the way, shouldn't you have said good morning?" Marcus queried. It was hard to speak while trying not to breathe too deeply. The room reeked of mold.

The dignified man chortled. "Time has little meaning here."

Eyebrows knitted, Marcus asked, "Do I speak correctly?"

"Perhaps you should teach me Chinese. I will be your pupil."

Marcus smiled and changed the subject, pressing forward in his awkward Chinese. "Yesterday, I saw a female fighting force. Black uniforms. How?"

Bu brought his right hand to his nose and absently sniffed a finger. Reaching for a capped vase, Bu offered juice. The men moved to two brown rush mats. "Ah, you saw the Black Panthers," Bu said. "My state is the only one to allow women to fight. The most successful female fighters enter officialdom; those high ranks include about fifty, at last count. I have found them to be hardworking, conscientious, and bright."

Marcus followed Bu's meaning, but that became more difficult as Bu grew animated. A dog barked, but Marcus took no notice as he worked hard to construct a sentence. "In my home, women do not fight. Chin is unique."

"Your Chinese is good." Bu smiled. His teeth were yellow.

Marcus wished to speak with Bu more often. His clear and distinct enunciation facilitated understanding. "You give kind words. I try to speak in your tongue, and people laugh."

Bu scratched his hairless chin. "My people believe that one tongue is all one needs. Let the bar ... er, foreigners ... learn ours. About women warriors, there is a tale. Would you like to hear it?"

Marcus replied, "Yes."

"Long ago, a warrior wandered the land, looking for a ruler to make him a general. As a test, one king ordered the office seeker to train the royal concubines ... er, wives." Bu paused.

"The warrior took the ladies to the training area, lined them up, and gave them commands. The ladies laughed and made errors. The warrior realigned them. They laughed and turned many ways. The same thing happened yet again. The warrior ordered two favorites of the king to kneel, then ordered an officer to cut their heads off. No one laughed. When lined up again, no woman turned wrong. Soon the ladies were fierce fighters; the war leader was hired." Bu sipped from his cup.

Marcus coughed. "When I rescued the king, he grabbed a sword and killed a man, severing his head and limbs."

Bu tugged at his ear. "Our sovereign did that? I have heard my father say that the king always stays in control."

"While he seems calm, he is volatile. I wanted to run."

"He was in the midst of a life-and-death struggle. Someone tried to assassinate him. Perhaps he struck back in fury and frustration."

"The king treats us kindly. I'm certain that it was unusual. Thank you for the information and the chance to speak. I hope we'll meet soon," Marcus said as he bowed and left.

CHAPTER 8

MING TIAN (238 BC)

The Black Panthers held the most citations in the army. Although men directed operations within the Chin command structure, Panther officers handled tactical matters.

Women volunteered for the Panthers. Weapon mastery was a top priority. As one Panther said, "Anything in a room or on the ground may defeat the enemy." The Panthers' quarters included sleeping and cooking facilities. Once a month, they observed a day of silence. The officers, who maintained a distance from the regulars in public, mingled with their sisters in the barracks.

Two volunteers were escorted by Chen Lan and Chen Ban. Chen Lan, the elder twin, chatted amiably. "Here's the kitchen. We share cooking duties; two prepare meals for five days. Our diet is meatless, and we fast once a month. We hire women to buy and ready the food. Our cook is a clumsy, lazy oaf."

A savory aroma wafted from a giant kettle. The obese assistant grimaced at Chen Lan's words. "Don't heed that gas pot," the assistant said. "She blows from both ends and is the worst cook of the lot."

Chen Lan whined, "Lies. You've mixed us again. I'm the master chef; this one"—she pointed to her twin sister—"can barely boil water." The younger sister feigned a sulk. Chen Lan smiled. "Let's go to the courtyard."

Seven Panthers sat quietly before a wooden pavilion topped with a tile roof and open on all sides. Jasmine scents wafted as Chen Lan spoke. "The vial atop the altar contains water and air representing the Great Mother, creator of life. Water yields, yet erodes. Air caresses cheeks and topples trees."

Chen Ban chimed in: "The short sword and four colored stones represent Nu Gua. When the four pillars that held up the sky collapsed, and beasts devoured humans, Nu Gua came from heaven and slew the animals. She caught a giant turtle, lopping off its feet for support pillars. See the tiny jade turtle."

Chen Lan interrupted. "She forgot to mention how Nu Gua gathered reeds and ashes to stem floods." Chen Lan lifted a leather totem pouch from her black

25

robe, then lovingly held it in her hands. It contained lucky items given to her by friends and family. It had kept her safe for years.

"The small spear represents Fu Hao," the younger one continued. "She was the greatest warrior more than fifty mothers past. Partner of the king, she ruled her own domain and commanded armies. She always triumphed; she once captured an army intact."

The tallest volunteer, Chi, spoke. "Men are beasts. On hunts, they surround great areas and slaughter all animals. They despise civilians. They pillage, rape, and murder. Men bind their daughters to other men. To be weak is to be dominated."

Chen Ban whispered, "Our father spared Mama from beatings, but enjoyed five concubines. He prized sons. In poor families, girl babies were often drowned, though our government forbade it."

The twins shepherded the new women into an attached building, where Panthers practiced throws, blocks, and blows. As one officer with gray streaks in her mane nearly reached the floor's end, three screaming attackers charged. A whirlwind of defense repelled them. As each panted in a crumpled mass, the older one offered encouraging words.

The women reached a bright red doorway. Inside, two Panthers danced atop an arrangement of clay soup bowls spread over a large table. Four bowls were placed face-down, with a fifth wedged face-up in the center. Two Panthers mounted the bowl pyramids, then sprang from one to another. Soon a bowl broke, and a nasty gash opened on one Panther's ankle. She finished the routine despite the wound; then a senior officer tended the wound.

"She was courageous to finish the form," said Ming Tian, the other volunteer.

"One undergoes mind stilling before stepping up there, Sister Ming," Chen Lan said. "The awake mind must be overcome, because it is impossible to think and move from bowl to bowl. Find the mind of the Great Panther."

"Still, one might have serious blood loss." Ming Tian wished to make her point. Sweat mingled with the fresh blood, resulting in a sweet and sour odor.

The elder twin interjected, "Iron discipline means life over death. Success is all."

Sister Ming shrugged at the gangly Chi, who nodded as they entered another room, this one with three life-size effigies. At a command, three Panthers reached into their hair for three-prong spikes and hurled them. The ornaments bit into their targets. At a second command, the women probed their sleeves, found daggers, and threw effortlessly. A third order unlocked their waistbands, which were tossed at the effigies. Weights dangled from each end.

Later, the newcomers chatted in their room. Sister Chi hugged herself. "What a place! I'll become invincible."

Sister Ming sat quietly. "Why so eager to slay?"

"Women must rule, sister. Are you too dense to realize that elementary fact?" Chi's eyes glowed in the candlelight.

"Does life only mean murder and power?"

"If we don't grasp the sword, they'll always be over us. Like my father … I'll kill him, I swear. I'll kill him!"

Sister Ming peered at the fresh-cut lilies in a vase. Like every other piece of furniture in the room, the table on which the vase rested was carved of aromatic cedar—an appealing Panther trademark. Ming sighed. "Hate devours your heart. Death stalks you."

Chi snarled, "Don't you hate them?"

"I long for a time of love and nurturing."

"Would you have us defenseless?" Chi spat.

"No. I came to serve people and to escape an arranged marriage. I desire sisterly company … but not here." Ming shivered.

"Stay! We can unite and slay the beasts!" Chi shouted.

"There must be another way. Tomorrow I'll go to the Hua Mountains, where nuns teach soft martial forms."

Chi fumed. "Education's useless. Weapons give true power … not wooden strips covered with writing."

"Education's the peaceful path to service. Following that path, I can help change the old ways," Ming murmured as she watched a feathery moth circle the flame.

"I can do the same through the Panthers."

"Tomorrow, sister, I leave for the mountains."

Chi extinguished the dying flame.

CHAPTER 9

OLD JUANG (238 BC)

The crime boss sat in his accustomed seat at the table's head. Three muscled enforcers stood behind him. The three chieftains kept their heads down, their eyes tracing the stained whorls of the wood grain.

The dwarf left the room without a glance at his longtime comrades. After several minutes, he returned with a scowl etching his aged face. "How shall we deal with traitors, Lefty Lu?" the master asked, his scowl giving way to a mirthless smile.

"Pardon, master?"

"Now, now, Lefty. How many times must I tell you never to call me master? Old habits are difficult to break, though I haven't heard that title for years." The smile transformed into a mocking leer as the day master wrung his hands.

"Mas ... ah, what did you say?" Lefty asked.

"How should one deal with traitors, Lefty!" the dwarf screamed in the henchman's ear. "Answer that simple question!" Suddenly the anger in his words was transformed into the icy tone of death itself—the hissing whisper of the undenied one.

"Kill 'em," Lefty answered. "Kill 'em all ..."

"Kill them how, Lefty?" Old Juang whispered. His quiet question had the others straining and sweating.

"Hang em ... gut 'em ... feed 'em to the beasts and birds!" The answer burst from him in a wail; he sounded like a whimpering mutt.

"How about a scorpion's sting?" Old Juang grabbed a cloth bag and pulled out a black scorpion, then another, then another, dropping them down Lefty's shirt.

"Oh! Oh ... oooooh!"

"Don't worry, Lefty. It will take an hour or so for the poison to stop your heart ... at least, that's what the poisoner told me. She's never been wrong."

"What?" the bearded subordinate gasped.

"Lefty, I've had you followed for weeks. Not only have you been skimming off hundreds of golds a month, you've also been consorting with the Black Gang," Old Juang whispered.

"Oh! Ooooh!"

"Fear not, Lefty. The one nearest the base of your skull will do the job; the rest are nuisances. Heh, heh."

"But master, I didn't ..." the chieftain blubbered.

"Silence! I have checked and double-checked my sources. Do you think I execute you on a whim? While I punish petty thefts, betrayal to a rival gang is unforgivable!" Rage shattered the dwarf's self-control.

After a time, Lefty's eyes glazed. He'd whined and sobbed to no effect; finally, he realized he would die. "Yes, master, I told the Black Gang leaders our plans. They paid good for the information, and they promised me the night master post. They found out that I had a daughter ... I couldn't bear to see the little girl hurt. All the money I saved for her. Master, don't hurt her. She's a good girl. Give her a life. Please.

"The Black Gang's safe house's in the silversmith ghetto. Though they blindfolded me when I was taken to the day master, I heard hammering on silver. I apprenticed to a smith, and there's a queer sound when the metal's hot.

"From their talk, master, they mean to hurt us bad. Yes, they know about this house. It's coming ... but I don't know when." Lefty fought the poison. "Please, master, help her ... she's all I have. In my backyard, there's a gnarled, ancient pine. Two paces north of the trunk, there's a stone, black as night. One pace under's the gold. Help her."

"How touching. Yes, I know about the girl. After the Black Gang's destroyed, I'll sell her to the Yellow Gang's whorehouse—the one off Third Avenue. You know how they treat their whores; they last two, maybe three years. If she's a virgin, she'll bring a good price for some old gentleman. Someday, you and your daughter will meet in hell, Lefty."

Lefty slumped with a look of utter despair.

The leaders watched their partner die. At a nod from Old Juang, both left the room.

CHAPTER 10

MING TIAN (238 BC)

Young Ming Tian walked the royal highway with a large family that was relocating in the south. When Ming reached a village at the foothills of the majestic Hua Mountains, she asked for directions to the Great Mother Temple. An innkeeper sneered, then indicated a narrow trail. "Why go alone? It's an evil place with tigers, bears, and devils. People never return."

Ming drew up to her full height. "I've business there."

His deeply recessed eyes narrowed. Large hands like bear paws gripped the blood-splattered butcher's block. A wicked-looking carving knife hung on the wall, companioned by an array of knives and meat cleavers. One mitt pointed to the peak. "It'll take two days, and you'll cover rough ground. Be wary, little lady."

Ming inhaled, choking on the stench of stale vomit and bad body odor. "I travel alone. Does the trail have a place where one may sleep, or must I chance the open sky?"

Slabs of meat dangled from the ceiling, and red drops filled terra-cotta bowls. *Blood pudding tonight*, Ming thought. The proprietor's upturned lip curled. "Two cottages, but you'll have to hurry, 'less ya plan to leave the morrow. Purify yourself at the first rest place—don't eat no meat, and take a ritual bath. Otherwise, the purple devil'll possess ya. Ain't ya just a wee bit fearful?"

Ming Tian knew he feigned a coarse demeanor but did not care to wonder why. As words drifted her way, his widened lips revealed brown, mottled teeth. Instinctively she shifted back, bent her knees, and relaxed. Calm pierced the bullying facade. "I carry no harmful feelings, and only fear the cats," she said.

The bully's right eye twinkled as he sold her oil and sandalwood powder. Since she'd eaten little meat in the last year, forgoing it presented no inconvenience. After selecting dried fruit, nuts, and a preserved cabbage, Ming set out.

Fortunately, a path had been marked. By late afternoon, she reached a pine cottage nestled within a thick grove of oaks and aspens. Ming had made excellent time, although she regretted striding so quickly through the lovely glen of dancing daffodils. The cabin door, undecorated in the manner of forest dwellings, creaked open. Laying her knapsack on an oak bed, Ming looked around. A small window permitted air and light. Cobwebs stretched everywhere.

With the golden sun swimming to the horizon, Ming decided on a brief excursion. She loved the sober pines, and she inhaled the vanilla scent of a giant tree trunk. After hugging a narrow side path laced with protruding tree roots, Ming reached an overlook, where a mountain updraft tousled her topknotted hair strands. The plains spread below her large, calloused feet. Irregular light-and-shadow patterns crisscrossed the lush landscape. Ming had not realized that she'd climbed so high. Birds darted to catch the ebbing day's last insects. If only she could join their airy romps. Warmth enfolded like a mother's hug.

Hurrying back in a race against the deepening shadows, Ming stubbed her toe, then limped to the cabin. Cleansing materials lay beside the bed, and her food was on top of the bunk. She ate rapidly. The gentle twilight back glow outlined the trees, sharpening the landscape. *A magical time*, Ming thought.

Ming's monthly flow began and, although the amount was manageable, withering cramps followed. A crone had once remarked that having babies would end the pain. Ming smiled ruefully as she recalled being forbidden to join the family rites. Her father had said that her period polluted the ceremony. Humiliation had gripped her until an aunt explained that the flow should be treasured. Ming reached for the soaked strap. Tomorrow, it'd be washed out. Ming went outside, climbed a boulder, and listened to the night.

Dawn tiptoed along the treetops. Ming shivered in remembrance of the morning's rite. Hopping from bed, she stretched, coiled her hair, and bound it behind her head. She shed her garb and raced outdoors, where chilled air raised goose bumps, and the cold mountain stream glistened. Ming found a pool, lay her bloody strap on a stone, and then waded into the water. A tiny, red rivulet running down her inner thigh decided her. Scrambling up a boulder, Ming peered into the dark gray pool and dove. As the water received her, the jolt triggered furious paddling. When the icy grip relaxed, Ming gazed up at a blue patch peeping through the verdant foliage. She paddled to a rock resembling a hunchback and retrieved her pad, immersing it with a scrubbing motion. She left the water, lathered her body and hair, and then dove anew.

Ming toweled off, and the rubbing suffused her skin with a pinkish glow. She dressed, then remembered the cleansing oil. Screwing up her face, she undressed once again. Wet clothes were flattened on a clean boulder as she coated her limbs with the oil. Then Ming dressed, ate the simple meal, and departed.

Along her way, a family of deer bounded through an open glade, halted at a tree line, and stared. Ming wistfully smiled at twin fawns nursing at their mother's breast while a sassy squirrel scolded from a cypress.

Although she would have to reach the next cottage before dark, Ming paused for lunch. As she reclined on the grassy knoll, a wild animal cry startled her. She heard a brief, snarling fight. Three deep breaths relaxed her, and she finished the dried peaches.

The afternoon was uneventful. As the shadows deepened, Ming padded across a brown pine-needle carpet to the second cabin. After depositing her gear, she hunted a stream. Two animal trails yielded nothing, but a third led to a bubbling brook.

Even though twilight approached, Ming meditated, resting her back against a towering pine and imagining her own roots penetrating the earth. She inhaled and exhaled deeply. In minutes, she soared to the Western Mountains, where she met the queen mother. After a chat, Ming Tian sped to an ocean and alighted on an incandescent beach. A ball of brilliant, blue light flashed her way as a dark-skinned man in shining indigo robes extended his palms. Light shot from the left straight to her heart. He was a spirit guide. She'd wanted a female, not this black barbarian.

Ming opened her eyes as pines crooned their cleansing melody and sun shafts danced over the needled floor. As her eyes accustomed to the twilight, Ming Tian saw a gorgeous, tawny mountain cat sleeping beside her. Perhaps the meditation transformed her fear of such cats. She placed her ear on its chest, then rubbed its massive head. A chasmlike yawn revealed a full set of white fangs. The animal rose, stretched, and stalked away. Cramped legs bent, and needled flesh throbbed.

After another meal, Ming slept dreamlessly. The next morning, chattering squirrel sounds and birdsongs filled Ming's ears. A dreamy smile crept over her face as she snuggled under the blanket. Morning. If only she could tarry. Morning. The coverlet flew off, and Ming bounded to a meal of pine nuts and dried cherries.

By afternoon, she stood peering at a closed wooden door that snuggled into the stone wall of the nunnery. A mossy, wood-tile roof overlaid the structure. A knock brought muffled steps and an opened door. The silver-haired woman who answered seemed unsurprised. The wooden floor—oak, Ming guessed—creaked as they walked to the end of a corridor. The guide tapped at an unpainted door, and a voice granted entrance.

Seated at a writing table was a woman of an age impossible to discern. Jet black hair highlighted her fair skin. When the woman smiled, her shiny white teeth—with three incisors missing—showed. She was aged, yet amazingly young.

"My name is Mother Lo, and I'm seventy-five, if you must know. And your name and age?"

"Ming Tian, and I am sixteen."

"No need to be formal or hide your confusion. Age matters little. One may be old at sixteen or young at seventy-five. I savor each year, each day, each moment. It matters only how well one's years are lived. People long to live forever. Better to treasure each day as if one were to die the morrow."

The guide departed, and Ming took in the room, furnished with the modest writing table at which Mother Lo sat cross-legged. The woman's comments jolted Ming. "I hadn't really thought."

The older one chuckled. "Welcome to the Great Mother Temple, where we honor life's creator. We dedicate ourselves to the inner quest and aiding others. You may stay until you've found your path. Then, it's back to the human world to serve. A lifetime of spiritual contemplation can be as stunted as a life of decadent pursuits. Our library's the best. We offer martial training as you desire, but we offer it for the purpose of strength, not violence. Weapons are not permitted, so you'll have to surrender the knife. Meals lack meat … but, by your aura, that's not a problem. We raise vegetables and gather fruit and nuts. We trade for grain. You perform labor every fourth month: cooking, gathering firewood, repairing, or cleaning. You'll find solitary time. We're sisters with different abilities, skills, and training. We're all teachers, all learners. We also speak sparingly."

Ming chuckled. Mother Lo's eyes twinkled mischievously. "Our library has books by women and men. Histories, myths, diaries, poems, letters, essays. In fact, we choose not to categorize, unlike the librarians in our capital. Knowledge is universal and overlapping. We love a poem, painting, quilt, or meal. Beauty can be personal or a shared love. Sisters and mothers are honored. We preserve their ways not out of hatred of men, but for wisdom. Oneness is neither male nor female—it simply is. Enough with words … Welcome! Tell me about the tiger later!"

CHAPTER 11

OLD JUANG (238 BC)

The leader of the Reds reviewed his plan to strike the Black Gang. From Lefty, he'd learned the location of one safe house, but he had to believe that they had two, perhaps three. Old Juang grimaced at the crumpled paper and growled. He'd taken precautions and weighed possibilities, but one never knew how a campaign would end. One planned for the worst.

The plan included informing the subdistrict police chief—a risky strategy, because one could never count on officials to do one's bidding. Old Juang smiled at the notion of using the state's vaunted mutual-responsibility system to control crime. It worked in rural areas, but not in cities. People were always moving to the city and falling outside the system. Cities were difficult to manage. Old Juang lit a candle and pored over the musty paper.

Chief Hui was a reliable bribe taker … yet, one could never be certain. Street theft was a minor problem for the police. Old Juang limited it as a part of his deal with Chief Hui. That left plenty from the whorehouses, gambling dens, and lenders.

Old Juang scanned the list of names and addresses of three whorehouses of the Black Gang while scratching his armpit. The police would raid each house. The losses would shrink the enemy's funds. That was the first step; the second was the Red Gang's raid on the safe house. Old Juang decided on a midnight raid after learning that the day master used the house to plan the next day's operations. An impending strike by the Blacks forced haste. Old Juang preferred to act with the new moon's cloaking darkness.

The crime lord rose from table and lit incense before the Red God. He loved the smell of sandalwood. Old Juang chanted,

Great Master be with us tonight
and keep us in your care.
We do this for you and ourselves.
Hide us from watching eyes,

guide us through traps and snares
through sealed doors and
windows bare. Keep us safe
and in your sight.

He opened the leather bag, pulled out a bloody dog's liver, and gingerly placed it on the altar. The Red God demanded fresh meat.

The crime lord took the tattered cloth and slowly wiped his hands.

CHAPTER 12

SHU WEI (238 BC)

Shu Wei woke. Overwhelmed by the musky, sensual odor, he fondled a milk-swollen breast, then remembered the summer solstice, when the Superior Man banked his desires. The female yin force began to wax; without restraint in one's appetites until the equinox, grain might wither. Shu Wei had to curb his diet and close his ears to music. Restraint was crucial because of Little Mouse. His son would become a famous scholar and minister. Yin sapped the adult male's yang force—and, what's more, that of Little Mouse.

The supple body rested beside him. He stood erect, donned his robe, and bolted.

Servants wove garlic bulbs, onions, and shallots through bright red cords. The colors belied the somber ceremony, in which cords would be strung across major corridors. Others would be placed around grain fields. Large fires became taboo, charcoal burning ceased, and smelting metal slowed until autumn.

The day's highlight was the ceremonial offering to Shu Wei's ancestors. This year, Little Mouse would be presented along with the clouded wine and spiced pork. The baby wore a red silk gown, and his mother proudly carried him to Shu Wei, who felt sincere in resisting lust. Today he would elevate Chrysanthemum as his second wife. Spring Lotus's family would be upset, but it was his house. Besides, she had produced no children in their nine-year marriage.

Later, at the autumn equinox, Shu Wei banqueted his friends. A suckling pig was gutted; its belly was stuffed with dates, and the carcass was wrapped with straw, then plastered with clay. After the pig was cooked for four water levels, the skin was removed, cleaned, and deep-fried, then served with pickled beef. Pheasant, mutton, steamed carp, and sautéed vegetables complemented the entree. Wei could not recall feeling so contented as he paraded Little Mouse before his guests.

The men adjourned to the library for wine, and conversation shifted to the current moral decline. All lamented the resolution of the crisis in Chin—Chi's hated enemy. A thin, severe-looking man, Shu Wei's closest friend, spoke.

"Chancellor Lu, the second father of the current king, has been retired to his estate." A snicker ran through the men, because they believed that the old merchant was King Jeng's real father.

Shu Wei asserted, "Lu receives ambassadors and assembles paladins and others. A second power center weakens Chin."

A tall and elegantly attired guest who was a friend of a friend spoke. "Yes, but the young king seems to have the situation under control. He smashed the plot of the queen mother's lover, Lao."

Shu Wei addressed the man. "I reply, sir, that two centers can weaken that barbaric state. It would be time for Chin to collapse. All it needs is a nudge. Isn't the king sickly?"

The unfamiliar courtier rejoined. "Current intelligence suggests that the king is healthy. Paladins will never stand up to the Chin army. The last decade has been a lull; soon, war drums will beat." As wine cups emptied, the conversation lightened.

Later, Wei staggered to Chrysanthemum's room and felt the rising urge. He fondled the heavy breast. A sip would be just the thing.

CHAPTER 13

OLD JUANG (238 BC)

Old Juang and Tao walked through the ruined whorehouse. Scorched wood and bricks lay everywhere; it appeared as if a giant had torn down the house and set the timber ablaze.

"What do you see?" Old Juang asked the lad, who had grown rapidly in the last months.

"I ... think the fire was deliberately set. See the burned rag and the shattered vessel?"

Old Juang squinted in the direction Tao pointed. After a stretching silence, Tao continued. "Look at the tree. Part of the trunk was scraped away, and that black mark was painted ... some kind of bird."

Old Juang nodded, because he had missed the raven. Tao looked at the old man; seeing agreement, he went on. "It seems to be a message that if we don't stop, more will follow. There's another blackbird."

Curiosity teased Old Juang; the boy's perceptiveness astonished him. As usual, silence drew people out; most could not stand a vacuum of sound and thus rushed into the emptiness.

"I, uh ... think that something will happen soon to a place like this, or somewhere else. You ... we need to be more watchful, or perhaps strike first," Tao said. Despite his precocious ways, he still hungered for approval.

"You have done well, my lad," Old Juang said. "You see beyond the surface. Even though the attack on the Black Gang succeeded, someone found out about us and has retaliated. I must eradicate them." Ash and soot were everywhere. Fortunately, a whore had smelled smoke and screamed, and the women had rushed out. They were the key assets.

Old Juang's shoulders slumped from the difficulty of planning alone. Since the affair with Lefty, the Reds' boss had been loath to trust anyone. He planned everything and told the others only at the last moment.

Tao looked at the dwarf. "Perhaps something can be done."

"What did you say?"

"I was alone on Fourth Street yesterday, coming home after the lesson in sums. I saw a man with a blackbird on his arm. I like blackbirds and followed him ... slyly, so he didn't know. Sometimes I can hide in the shadows or make myself not seen. He walked down the alley behind the old teapot shop and back out, reversing himself. He almost caught me, but I managed to hug the shadows. He finally went into the house in the block where the new officials in the Law Ministry are being put up. I walked on by, but I could find it again. Seeing the blackbird brought it back."

Old Juang started to pat Tao on the head, then caught himself. "You have done well. That's another safe house. If we hit it and one more, we can shatter them. You say the man you followed had a blackbird on his arm? It's a raven, by the way."

"Yes," Tao replied.

"Was it a tattoo or on a sleeve?" Juang asked.

"A tattoo. I wouldn't have seen it, but he reached for a coin that had fallen on the road, and his sleeve pulled back." Tao saw a light in the old man's eyes. The dwarf's feet began a dance.

CHAPTER 14

SHU WEI (238 BC)

The aristocrat received an invitation to a banquet in Linzu, the bustling Chi capital. The host was Bing, an industrialist and member of the lowest class. Refusal, however, meant missing a marvelous party with willowy, dancing girls. Besides, Shu Wei's expenses had increased, and Bing's interest rates were the best.

Linzu, a city with several hundred thousand people, had walls six paces tall that rested on a four-pace-thick base. The city sprawled in a grid layout. Wei's carriage stalled in the heavy traffic as soon as it entered Linzu's famed west gate. As the scarlet conveyance wove through the marketplace, Shu Wei noticed surly idlers near the Longevity Wine Shop. Sporting jade green robes and yellow officials' caps, most were scions of rich families. Wei cursed them as common criminals.

The carriage halted in the clothing-guild quarter. Silk clothed the elite, while commoners wore hemp. Robes tipped with silk or fur advertised a wearer's social standing. Wei bent slightly to enter his favorite shop, the venerable Sparkling Stream store. Faded characters embellished its signboard. Three generations of the Shu clan had done business here.

Then Wei scurried to a furrier—the Dapper Fox. The sign's calligraphy was done in gaudy black characters quoting an insipid platitude from Confucius. Wei entered despite his frown because the Dapper Fox had the best furs in the northeast. He sighed as he selected a sable coat and a silvery fur for Chrysanthemum, who'd been deliciously submissive recently.

Guilt drove Wei back to the Sparkling Stream, where he purchased a nondescript silk brocade blouse for his first wife, Lotus. His next stop was the bronze workers' guild. A gift for Bing should put him in the mood to grant a loan. Wei emerged from the Bronze Giant store carrying a shiny wine holder molded in the tripod pattern characteristic of the ancient Yin dynasty. Wei admired the single gilded character, "metal," elegantly painted over the shop door.

The carriage rolled up before Bing's two-story, dust-stained building. Wei dismounted, inhaled deeply, and entered. The front office partially muffled the manufacturing din at the rear. Bing's booming voice erupted into a roar of curses; the language scalded Shu Wei's ears.

Informed that a gentleman wished to see him, Bing finished a withering scolding of an overseer and walked up front. "Ah, it's you, Wei. Honored to have you here. What can I do for you?" The merchant-industrialist bent slightly. The two men formed a study in contrast: the fashionable, jasmine-scented noble and the smelly, soot-blackened, muscled industrialist.

"I wanted to inform you that I accept your dinner invitation and have decided to see your place of business. You seem busy."

Bing's blackened hand cupped his chin. "Yes, a military rush order on top of a request for a thousand plowshare tips. I'll stay open for the holidays. Expansion is becoming necessary as well—I must buy the building next door and knock down the dividing wall. How about a look around? You might appreciate the new casting process. We get a more flexible iron strip with a life twice the older pieces."

Wei's nostrils moved like a rabbit's. "Another day. I have to buy a toy for my son. Any suggestions?"

Bing stiffened. Black-streaked sweat dripped from his smooth-shaven skin. "Try the Golden Kitten, near the Western Market. Someone said the owner bought a load of stuffed bears ... or were they cats? How's your son? Handsome and talented like his old man?"

Shu Wei gingerly probed his robe sleeve and extracted his favorite golden silk handkerchief with a phoenix motif. "Thank you. He's teething and fusses a lot but eats well."

"Spoken like a proud father. I hope to see him soon."

"Yes, yes," the aristocrat said politely. "Why not stop by for some snacks next week? My cook is an expert with stuffed dumplings—crab, shrimp, pork."

"I'm honored. This day next week?"

"Yes," replied Wei.

"We can settle the time tomorrow evening," Bing said. "I'll leave here early. Even if there's a crisis, my manager can handle it. Don't tell him that, or he'll ask for higher wages. Ha, ha!" Bing's eyes screwed up as he chortled merrily.

Shu Wei looked away in embarrassment about Bing's coarse manner. "I spied the Green Gang in the market. Damned juveniles have no shame," Wei said, wiping his forehead.

"Haven't bothered me, but I've heard they harass old-timers. Police are helpless because of the family ties. At least Chin cleaned out its gangs."

"By the way, I brought this replica from an earlier age," Wei said, pressing the bronze piece toward Bing. "I was wondering if ... ah ... you would loan me five thousand ... until the harvest's in. Extra expenses with the boy, you know." Wei bent slightly.

Bing's eyes twinkled. "My cash is a bit tight now."

The noble's face imploded.

"Wait," Bing said slowly. "That's right, the money for the last big order of sickles came in. I can cover you. The usual percent?"

A broad grin wrinkled the aristocrat's face. "Indeed. Don't forget to stop by next week. I've got to get the present for the boy. Thank you, thank you!"

CHAPTER 15

TAO (238 BC)

Young Tao skipped along the street. He seldom had leisure time in his new life, but on his way home to and from lessons, he would play, be silly, or just feel thankful to be alive. The capital's streets sizzled with drama. Often, Tao saw accident scenes with shouting, blood, or broken limbs. He would take those occasions to see what was really there—what was underneath.

Once he had seen a pony beaten by an enraged man. The tiny cart the animal had been pulling lost a wheel and overturned, spilling out scissors, shears, cloth, pins, and shoes. The street was muddy from a passing storm, and the peddler was furious. Tao saw the man's rage and the pony's terror. It had been beaten regularly.

During that debacle, Tao had seen a street urchin slip two pairs of scissors into his ragged coat and calmly walk away. He saw that same pickpocket lifting valuables from onlookers; the man had rubbed his hand down and under a woman's buttocks. Distracted by the scene, she had absently brushed away the hand.

As a city watchman had approached the accident, Tao realized the peddler had been drinking; his walk was unsteady. The pony kicked at its assailant, which stoked the man's fury. The peddler was reaching down for a stick when he spied the watchman. Gathering the fallen items, he stopped when he noticed the loss of the scissors, shook his head, and howled in frustration. Tao walked away, humming a childhood tune.

CHAPTER 16

SHU WEI (238 BC)

The aristocrat arrived at Bing's just before sunset, because he'd heard about the panoramic view from the western garden. Earlier, Wei had admired himself in the bronze mirror as his women and servants praised him. Little Mouse, bathed and covered with sandalwood powder, was carried out to his beaming papa.

The sunset sprinkled muted rainbow hues into the sparkling conversation. At dinner, Wei counted three separate fry dishes, including the rich fry of pickled lamb daintily scattered over beds of millet and steeped with melted fat. Forgetting himself, Wei ate four helpings. A similar fry included pickled beef—which was fried, then tossed with barley and enriched with fat sauce; and the steeped fry, made with veal sliced wafer thin, steeped in plum wine, and lightly fried. One ate it with pickle and vinegar.

After two water-clock measures, the guests idled on rush mats while a troupe of women danced. One slender lovely with flowing, black hair caught Wei's attention. Five blind musicians, including two flutists, one harpist, a bell ringer, and a lutist, wove melodies around the dancers. The harpist dominated two pieces, then soloed. Lilting chords lifted Wei to an endless steppe with romping horses. A distant figure waved at him. Neighing caught his attention, and Wei saw a black stallion mount a light brown mare. The music stopped, and the aristocrat shuddered.

The beauty floated over the mats, in her mauve gown with extended sleeves. Bing watched Shu Wei. When the dance concluded, the host motioned the dancer to sit by Wei. She panted lightly; beads moistened her brow. Wei offered alcohol, and one cup followed another.

The women were dismissed as the men adjourned to a library. Wine, nuts, dried fruit, and fried chips filled translucent white bowls. Bing had obtained a copy of the Spring and Autumn Annals of Chancellor Lu from Chin, and Bing threw out some of its ideas for discussion. Many supported combining the best ideas of different thinkers into a grand synthesis.

Shu Wei countered that mismatches meant confusion. "For example, follow-ers of the Dao argue that learning and culture, not to say government, are useless … yet Confucius and Mencius said education is everything, and properly ordered government is vital to civilization. Without learning, we are no better than the barbarians." Wei preened his mustache.

As agreeing murmurs sounded, Wei licked his lips. "Culture makes us human. We must know the proper way to love our parents, to correctly order our fami-lies. Each has a defined place; otherwise, there's chaos. Wives should neither rule families nor governments. The natural order demands males on top."

Chuckles encouraged Wei. "What if children ruled their parents? No, my friends, education and culture are the natural order." He plunged deeper into his argument. "Master Mo says that rich people live lavishly, and governments waste on music, art, and architecture. If his followers ruled, there'd be no banquets such as this. Should we love strangers as we love our parents?"

A stranger interrupted. "Including the king? Does one love one's parent more than his monarch? If your father rebelled, would you support him?"

The clear, caustic voice stiffened Shu Wei. "Confucius said that children who love their parents also love their kings. They would never betray them," he replied.

The antagonist's hooked nose reminded Wei of a raptor's beak as he spoke. "Reasoning which answers nothing. If your father plotted against the Chi mon-arch, would you support him or the king?"

Shu Wei blushed. "I'd support both. I'd convince my father that his rebellion was wrong and would halt it."

The inquisitor's hairless pate reflected candlelight. "Humbug! Adherents of Confucius glorify the Cultured King, the Martial King, and the Duke of Jo, all of whom rebelled against their rightful king. Did the sons of the Cultured King sup-port their father or their true monarch? Traitors all! Did not Mencius say that it was justified to kill one's sovereign? Chi cowers before Chin, because followers of Confucius and Mencius are in power, favoring their relatives. When the law is weakened, the state withers. Master Han Fei is correct: followers of Confucius and Mencius are vermin."

Shu Wei's face flushed scarlet. "Any fool knows that the Shang Dynasty's last ruler was a tyrant prompting Heaven to withdraw its favor. Read the Classic of Documents!"

"Bah. The Classic of Documents was written by the winners. Would they call the king they threw out a good lord? History distorts events; it's fiction. In my homeland, followers of Confucius undermine my state's will to fight. Mark my words, aristocrat: Chi will be swallowed by Chin."

With a nod to his host, Liao stomped from the library. At dawn he was on the road to Chin, the warring state he admired for its clear laws, strong army, and contempt for Confucians.

CHAPTER 17

MARCUS (238 BC)

The Roman dreamed he strolled in a forest glen surrounded by majestic pines and traversed by a bubbling brook. It was the same place he had seen during his youth. A moss-covered boulder nestled comfortably beside a tiny stream.

"Master." The gentle word opened his eyes to the dream world. That face ... the one of his childhood reveries. "Master, you're wanted by the abbot." Marcus peered down at the stilled water of the pool. A Chinese face looked back!

Marcus awoke to blackness; then he remembered saving King Jeng's life. He recalled Du Fu. He remembered Sari, the gentle man who had taught him Buddhism. The three had set out on a journey.

And before that, he had deserted from a Roman legion—the Eleventh—after a battle with the enemy Gauls (no, really, it had been more of a slaughter), including women and children. He had been injured, but his wounds were mild; he had been knocked out while killing an old man who came at him with a kitchen knife. He had impaled the man, who was utterly naked in the Gaul fighting way. The killing blow had caused Marcus to stumble and crash to the street.

Marcus shivered, his mouth dry as he recalled the macabre scene of his awakening in the Gaul village. Night and dying flames had cast eerie shadows. He stumbled across bodies broken during the slaughter and saw the girl—face-down, legs splayed. As he turned her, he saw the matted blood and her slit throat. Raped and ravaged by a Roman legionnaire!

Marcus had buried her, wishing he had time to bury all of the Gauls. He placed a rag doll under her folded arms and lay a cloth gently over her body. He prayed. He thought about the Roman gods, but their betrayal of his trust had caused him to turn to a deeper wisdom found in the stillness of oak trees. After a time he found wildflowers: blues, yellows, reds, and whites. He placed them on her grave.

Marcus had searched for food, placed items in his knapsack, and set out. He had headed home as a deserter, a coward.

Coming back to himself, Marcus wept quietly in the deep, still, lonely night.

CHAPTER 18
LIU (238 BC)

In the village of Wanshi, a dominion of Chu (the southernmost warring state), peasant families celebrated the Cha Thanksgiving Festival. A pig roasted in the fire pit, seven chickens baked, and two pinstriped ducks broiled (along with four types of fish). Leeks, bamboo shoots, cabbage, water chestnuts, oranges, and papayas covered tables—accompanied, of course, by mounds of steamed rice.

Drinking occupied the men who had gathered at the wine jars containing rice or plum liquor. Callused hands dipped plain bamboo cups. That morning, offerings had been made to the Farming Sovereign and to the Queen of Fertility. The village head, a man of about sixty years, presented three peppered rice balls to each deity. A morsel of pork also rested atop the cat shrine, and a larger piece of pork rested on the tiger altar. These spirits deserved offerings for devouring grain-eating rodents and crop-destroying boars.

Autumn and winter were for repair: roofs, tools, and dykes. Men mended. Women wove. During the growing season, women weeded, plowed, or harvested, and tended their households. Colder months meant taxes and rents: a head tax on adult males and a land tax consuming 30 to 40 percent of the harvest. One could work thirty days in winter or serve two years in the army.

Much Wanshi land belonged to a Chu prince and was worked in common by the villagers, with 50 percent of the crop owed. Although six-tenths would not have been outrageous, custom dictated half of the harvest.

Liu, an emaciated man whose black beard blew gently in the breeze, considered the last year. The dry midsummer unnerved him until the blessed rains came. Two years ago, a five-week drought had scorched the tender shoots. Cha had been canceled.

A liver pain reminded Liu of the death of his frail seven-year-old son. A large swig of wine dulled the ache.

A sigh welled up from his heels. Chen, a plump woman with large, almond-shaped eyes and the longest black hair, was a scold. She made his life a trial. He should beat her, but spanking the little ones was hard enough. His two sons loved him; the three of them would amble to the river and fish.

He saw Chen gassing with four females, telling tales and laughing until she wet herself. The village women admired her—the fat one who cocked her head like a rooster. Chen's shrill shriek knifed through his ears.

Liu tottered down the lane. On the way, he detoured to a wine jug and tripped, spilling alcohol on his straw shoes. Another slip convinced him not to trust the ground. The thirty-year-old man squatted on his haunches and sipped the dregs. Finally, peace—from her, from toiling, and from his cares. He sat alone with the smiling moon.

Liu sniffed the breeze. *Rain, tomorrow or no later than the day after.* Winter would be cold; animals were storing supplies and had thick coats. War devoured simple folk; young Bo had returned a cripple. A shadow passed over Liu's head, and he trembled. He fell and muddied his trousers. She'd be angry, his personal demon. Liu sighed and returned to the revelry.

CHAPTER 19

LIAO (238 BC)

Liao, who'd deflated Shu Wei at Bing's party, arrived in the Chin capital on a bleak day. Grain fields wore dull brown and black hues. Gray clouds smothered the sky.

One evening in a dirty restaurant that served delicious fried millet, Liao recalled that his friend, Han Fei, had mentioned a classmate, Lee Su, who served Chin. Liao called at the Lee estate the next day. By mentioning their mutual acquaintance, Liao got an interview with Minister Lee. They shared a congruence of views, and Minister Lee promised to speak with King Jeng.

Eleven days later, Liao received a royal summons. At the palace gate, Minister Lee escorted Liao to a throne room. A smiling young man wearing a modest gold crown hurried down from the elevated dais. King Jeng wore a deep blue robe and a golden sword. The sweet-sour scent of incense steeped the chamber.

"You are Liao of Wei," King Jeng said. "You write that All Under Heaven be united. These are exactly our sentiments. What brings you to us?"

"Your Majesty, I come to your great land because it is the most modern within the four seas," Liao said. "Chin will unite the world. Alas, the sole reason you have not done so is that you lack one element. I humbly submit that I have a comprehensive solution."

King Jeng drew closer. "What is it?"

"Military strength, agricultural prosperity, and evenhanded application of the law are significant ... but the key is in the other warring states. Chin agents should bribe their officials."

Jeng's eyes widened as Liao continued. "To corrupt and employ these men will be expensive ... at least half a million gold pieces. Weaknesses must be exploited. If money is no problem, you can corrupt people in each court. I suggest that Your Majesty target midlevel officials with promising futures. The plan may take a decade, but subversion and sabotage are worth a million brave warriors."

"Splendid! Money and lives are of no matter. When will you begin? The commander of the armies post is to become vacant."

"Your Majesty, I'm honored. If I fail, you can have my life."

King Jeng smiled. His reaction told Liao that his pledge would come true at the slightest mistake.

"I have contacts in the states of Chi and Chu, as well as a lead on a courtier in Jao. My own state, Wei, will be easy," Liao said.

CHAPTER 20

KING JENG (238 BC)

The monarch informed Liao that he would be given quarters. Then he dismissed the petitioner and turned to Minister Lee.

"Your Majesty. Liao's brilliant plan might bear fruit. It's simple," Minister Lee said cautiously.

King Jeng clapped his hands twice and gazed at a giant tapestry commemorating the Changping massacre. King Jeng studied a detail of the work: a triumphant Chin warrior holding a severed general's head. "Fools complicate things, while visionaries simplify," the king mused. "Lord Yang developed three things: law, agriculture, and the army. Liao's appointment will bring a flood of office seekers who won't aid other kings. Your memorial about using aliens was to the point. Fresh ideas from the likes of you or Liao help us. Your petition echoed our thinking."

"Liao must be watched ..."

"We know our duty! I'll assign someone to watch Liao. Even if he's another hydraulic engineer like Old Guo, we'll get a good canal out of him. Don't undermine Liao too soon. And don't put Bi on his tail; that man couldn't find his own ass."

"Your Majesty?" Lee asked.

"Yes?"

Minister Lee drew in a long breath. "Intelligence shows that former chancellor Lu gathers paladins and other vermin. Lu even received a Jao envoy. We must defang the old man."

"Continue."

"Since Lu harbors traitorous ambitions, I propose that he be exiled. Perhaps we can persuade him to commit suicide."

"And if he resists?"

"A fatal accident can be arranged. The boil must be lanced."

"Work up an indictment."

Lee's tongue swept over his lips. "Yes, Your Highness."

"All vermin must be eradicated. Now leave us!"

King Jeng regarded the tapestry. *We will have war, conquest, and the long-dreamed-of unity of All Under Heaven. History will proclaim us the greatest ruler ever. Liao and Lee, our hounds, will lead us to victory. Marcus will be our pet, keeping us sane.*

CHAPTER 21

MING TIAN (238 BC)

She swept the oak floorboards, once again admiring the whorls of the polished grain. Her eyes followed the endlessly flowing parallel lines. Eddies of dust scooted across the wood and rested in dark corners. Dust motes danced and swirled in the air, which was pierced by sunbeams. Ming loved simple tasks like these, though it was difficult to keep her restless mind focused on the chore at hand.

Suddenly she was home on that terrible night when her father crept into her bedroom and began fondling her. Ming awoke to his heavy breathing, with his hands groping her breast and groin. Pleasurable sensations evaporated when she realized what was happening. Ming moaned and pleaded for him to stop. The rubbing grew more insistent. He lifted her robe. Something broke within her, and she lashed out with her left hand, driving it into his swollen penis. He gasped and bent over as she hurled herself from the bed and bowled him over, fleeing in a panic.

A tiny stone that Ming absently swept skittered across the corridor and struck the base of a plain bronze lamp. The sound shattered Ming's vision, and she sagged to the floor, weeping freely. The morning after her father's assault, Ming had left home for good. Her family told neighbors that she was fleeing an arranged marriage. Her mother and elder brother stood in the doorway, begging her to stay. Her father was not in sight. Ming had bowed her head and adjusted the knapsack on her back. She had enough food and money to reach the Chin capital by foot. It would take three days of hard going in all, but Ming didn't mind. It was important to get away from her father.

Ming came back to herself and the sound of mountain jays scolding something. She reached for the handkerchief in her tattered brown robe sleeve. Her mother had embroidered tiny golden butterflies along the handkerchief's border. It was the only keepsake Ming permitted herself. She rubbed it over her cheeks and then dried her eyes.

Why had her father done such a thing? Had she encouraged him? Ming dabbed her eyes and frowned as she traced the needlework. Were all men animals? Why didn't she despise them? Ming shivered away the questions and rose. She had to complete her chore. She reached for the broom and began to sweep. A childhood tune about sparrows came unbidden to her lips. Her mother had often sung it to her at bedtime. Ming gently laid down the broom and slowly walked, head bent, to Mother Lo's office.

CHAPTER 22

OLD JUANG (238 BC)

The leader of the Reds sat with his subordinates in the dimly lit room. It was the reporting time of the month, and he had brought Tao. None of the others had known about the lad, and Old Juang wanted to let his men see the boy, and for him to see them. Tao watched from behind Old Juang.

The dwarf began, "First, I'd like to update you about the Black Gang. They turned Lefty against us. After dealing with the traitor, I worked out a successful plan to hit first.

"The Black Gang hit back by torching one of our houses. Tao here identified and followed a Black leader to a safe house. When we raided the headquarters, we nabbed two leaders and found a ledger detailing some of their operations. We found and destroyed their safe houses. All their operations have been taken over. We've won!"

The bosses grinned and nodded vigorously. More territory meant more money, and more money meant happier Reds.

Pa, the night master, spoke first. "Congratulations! That gang was a worrisome bunch, I can tell ya. They'd poach on our turf ... nothing serious, mind ya, just testing the waters 'til I threw 'em back. We coulda helped ya if ya'd told us about this. We was wondering about all of the sneaking."

One-armed Chi, the day master, spoke. "Yeh, congrats ... That gang was trouble. The new whorehouses will bring in lots, 'cause they're located in higher-class places."

Deng, the enforcer, cleared his throat. "You know, I agree with Pa. You should have let us know, so's we could have helped. More money and happier people all the way around. When are we going after the other gangs?"

Old Juang paused, then raised his hand to his cheek and brought it outward, palm up. "After Lefty's betrayal, I used extra caution. I'm sure you all appreciate that." Heads nodded.

"The operation was a close thing," Juang continued. "The Black Gang had key contacts and information sources. But we got their leaders, and the rest fell into our hands. It's time to consolidate the new holdings and assets; then we'll think about other gangs. Now, to your reports."

The exchange of information dragged on for two water marks. Then Old Juang and Tao walked to the boss's home. During the day, Juang operated a modest silk store and maintained a residence behind the store. He was certain that no one except Tao knew of his other life as a storekeeper.

When they reached the modest reception room, Old Juang asked, "What did you see, little one?"

The lanky teen replied, "They're uneasy and unhappy about being left in the dark. Each is genuinely happy about the result, however."

"Go on."

"The one-armed man is nervous, though he hides it. Deep down he feels that he'd like to move higher but doesn't dare. He fears you!" Tao's eyes grew glassy; it seemed as if he were speaking from another world.

"And ..."

"Pa is unhappy about something ... probably personal, rather than something about the Reds. Deng is the most dangerous. His eyes, while shifty, are dead; they don't reveal what's going on inside. Most people reveal their thoughts and intentions through their eyes. Shifty Eyes could strike without warning, though he does tend to tense before he speaks or moves."

Old Juang filed away the information. He felt odd about providing Tao with such confidences, but the lad was unusually perceptive.

"So, I'll have no worry with this bunch for a time?" The boss smiled as he probed.

"Difficult to say. There's much new money and information. It'll take time to absorb the Blacks' operations, especially the houses. No one is likely to strike at you before the settling out of things." Tao looked almost sleepy.

"What makes you say that?" Old Juang asked. He was curious about how one so young would guess that.

"Houses have lots of people, and all must learn the new ways," Tao answered. "Also, some may not like the new system. That's when you need to be watchful. May I go to bed now, please?"

Old Juang nodded amiably and thought about his own exhaustion. He had one more task before bedding down.

CHAPTER 23

MARCUS

As the autumns drifted past, Sariputra traveled to other cities to assess his chances of converting people to Buddhism. He told Marcus that people had rudely remarked about his dark skin or had stared. The monk related to Marcus that he had gradually lost hope.

Before undertaking one extended journey to the south, Sariputra had asked Marcus to join him. Marcus declined, mentioning his upcoming trip to visit King Jeng; Sari journeyed alone. The next day, Marcus learned that a farm for him had been located.

Marcus's estate included a spacious four-room house, a pigsty surmounted by a lavatory, an unused chicken coop, a toolshed, and a stable. Surrounding the farm buildings was a pounded-earth wall, two paces high. The five-acre farmland was connected with the irrigation system. Living a mere six miles from the capital, Marcus could easily reach his palace quarters, or the king could pay a visit.

The Roman hired two servants and four field hands. After consulting nearby farmers, Marcus decided to plant millet. A small plot would be reserved for experimental farming.

One day, as Marcus looked over the verdant landscape, he marveled at how different it seemed from his homeland. Although the weather tended toward aridity in Chin, irrigation water wrought a wondrous transformation. Marcus stooped to scoop a handful of soil. It had the consistency of loam rather than dust. He had to learn the names and properties of the plants that dotted the metropolitan region. Who might he ask?

CHAPTER 24

KING JENG (230 BC)

As commander in chief Liao's long-term plans matured, the Chin state gathered supplies and soldiers for the long-promised wars of unification. When the army finally mobilized along the frontier with the Han warring state, King Jeng reviewed an elite detachment. Two thousand soldiers knelt before their sovereign, who climbed a specially constructed platform. All of the Sixth's soldiers had volunteered from other units. Each wore light torso armor over a specially fitted battle robe. Iron pieces sewn loosely into the fabric deflected sword blows but permitted maximum flexibility.

King Jeng proudly surveyed the massed troops. Pikemen were forward, along with martial experts. Screened behind the pikemen were crossbow archers. The new Chin crossbow fired two bolts without reloading, unleashing a lethal torrent of metal.

Although senior officers stood at the head of the division, they would stay at the rear in actual combat. Army units had red, blue, white, and black banners. Movements of units were partly directed by the drummers and horn blowers.

King Jeng shouted, "Men! Tomorrow we attack Han, whose treachery knows no bounds. Its bandit king must be punished. What say you?"

The massed soldiers began a chant. "Yes ... Yes! Yes! To Han, to Han, destroy Han. Yes! Yes!"

King Jeng permitted the roar to subside, then added, "First Han, then the other bandit states. Punishment and victory. Victory to Chin!"

The Panthers launched a preemptive strike by infiltrating the Han army's general quarters and slaying a general and four staff officers. The hapless Han army surrendered two days later. Twelve Panthers died, and the unit was honored with the coveted vermilion banner. Han was annexed.

In the year after Han's collapse, Chin armies turned to Jao. The brutal campaign lasted two years. The Panthers suffered heavy losses, including their commander (and the elder twin), Chen Lan. Sister Chi volunteered for dangerous missions, winning promotions.

At last, the Jao King was escorted to Chin, where he was presented to King Jeng, who had him executed, one severed body part at a time.

After each conquest, the Chin army compiled lists of the prominent nobles, merchants, and officials. They and their families were removed to the Chin capital's metropolitan region or to remote commanderies.

As the occupying army moved across Jao, King Jeng secretly visited the Jao capital, where his father had been a prince hostage. The city was also the native home of his mother. Accompanied by an aide who had served the hostage prince there, King Jeng combed the lists of key Jao people. One hundred forty people who had known his mother were rounded up, taken to a pit, and tossed in. A special detachment buried them alive.

On his first night back in the Chin capital, King Jeng slept dreamlessly. The military unit that carried out the secret operation was Commander Liao's creation. The special unit handled assassinations and sabotage. The distinctive feature of the unit was a white uniform that symbolized death. Led by Jo Jing-jeng, they were known as the White Panthers.

CHAPTER 25
OLD JUANG (228 BC)

The dwarf studied a map with markings outlining each gang's territory. The Red Gang's territory had doubled in recent years, as each enemy gang's territory and members were absorbed. Two other gangs, the Blue and the Yellow, remained.

The Blue Gang, headed by the mysterious tattooed man, was a formidable force with fierce and wily members. Old Juang had long tried to penetrate the gang. Blues specialized in contract murders, loan sharking, and prostitution. It was rumored that the head of the Metropolitan Police Force was on the gang's payroll. What else could explain the murders—usually one every week or two? Merchants, caravan drivers, and ward headmen turned up dead, with blue scarves knotted around their necks.

The Yellow Gang was ruled by the scarred man; unlike his Blue counterpart, the scarred man traveled the city in a private carriage, daring authorities to arrest him. He was rumored to have many allies, including a subminister of the imperial household. The Yellows specialized in smuggling, prostitution, and extortion. Unlike their boss, the Yellows kept low profiles, avoiding crimes that attracted public attention.

Old Juang frowned. Both the Blues and Yellows controlled more territory than his gang. Furthermore, accidents had begun to claim the lives of many Reds, including agents, messengers, managers of whorehouses, and loan sharks. Government raids netted whores and their clients on a regular basis—too regular for Old Juang.

Old Juang turned to Tao, who also gazed at the city plan. Now lanky, he sported a ragged mustache that needed quite a few more lip hairs to reach adult growth. Tao had apprenticed as a thief for a year as a way to learn from the bottom and to sharpen his skills. Old Juang remembered his foray into Tao's family house … a mission to hone his own skills … a mission that had proved its worth many times over.

"What do you see?" Old Juang asked Tao.

Tao knitted his brow and waited. He was gangly; he still had some growing to do. Despite his slightly boyish appearance, in the last year he had managed the Golden Cock, the most profitable whorehouse of the Reds. Old Juang had wished to see how Tao would respond to sexual opportunities and how he would manage women as well as finances. As it turned out, Tao had a knack for increasing revenues and educating the whores in eliciting information. Men confided in the women, and Tao taught them how to learn the most from clients, praising and pumping them.

Tao had appointed a crone, Old Mu, to chat with the whores every third day. Old Mu would listen to their information and pass it on to Tao. She could write as well as do sums and had served the Tao family. Old Juang preferred to completely separate Tao from his past, but the lad had been persuasive. Old Juang employed the crone as a temporary hire. Tao showed Old Juang the record book every week—or sooner, if the information warranted immediate consideration.

"I see two threats," Tao finally answered. "That's obvious, but what I also see is the possibility of the Blues and the Yellows combining against the Reds ... against us."

"Go on."

"There's the common boundary between them ... quiet for the last nine moon cycles. It could mean anything, and yet ..."

"Go on." Old Juang clasped his hands behind his lower back. As he swayed from side to side, his eyes never left the teenager's pockmarked face.

"I think ... no, I believe the two gangs fear our growing power. They plot to destroy us before we absorb them. That's what I would do. Our recent problems signal a campaign to eradicate us."

"I agree. Yet, what we should do? We've been successful, but the game grows subtle. Do we attack? If so, what or who is our target? If we defend, how is that accomplished? What do you think?" Old Juang wiped his brow. Their room was shuttered, and the heat of the day smothered the room. The serious situation unnerved Old Juang.

Tao looked up from the map and studied his boss. "Perhaps a plan can be developed to strike at the weaker of the two. Or, perhaps, to sow dissension between them."

"Perhaps, as you would say ... but which? At times, I feel alone in thinking and planning for the Reds ... my gang, my men. And yet, what else can I do? It all began with that damned Lefty Lu. Since then, I had to assume the sole burden. Sometimes I feel so weary." Old Juang hated to reveal himself, but Tao was the only one he trusted—slightly, to be sure, but that was enough.

"I think we should sow dissension and attack."

"Yes, that might work. We could strike at the Blues and make it look like the Yellows. Of course, they will deny everything, but we'll strike again and again, leaving clues."

"And at the same time, we might corrupt someone in the police or higher to do our work, so that we would not be seen as being behind this campaign," Tao added. His arms dangled loosely. He looked away from the old man, appearing to contemplate the three bear-held candles arrayed at strategic points around the map table. Two had new tapers; the other was guttering out. Tao walked to the corner where the replacement candles were stacked.

"I have an ally—a district police chief who was reassigned to the Yellow turf. Big Wu knows some Blues, and he's clever enough to kill one or more, making it look like a Yellow operation. This must be planned carefully and thoroughly," Old Juang muttered.

CHAPTER 26

KING JENG (228 BC)

After his return from Jao, King Jeng visited his mother, who had been placed under palace arrest in distant Yung and elsewhere for the last ten years. Occasionally, remorse ruled the king; she had once listened to his complaints, his fears, and his troubles. He had loved her ... but she'd betrayed him with surprising treachery.

King Jeng looked at a royal portrait of her and sighed. Her brooding eyes dominated the painting, and her plump upper lip reminded him that she had been a concubine to the merchant Lu. From physicians' reports, he knew she'd not live long.

As King Jeng rode through the repainted and refurbished palace gate to see her, he admired the pleasant surroundings, which boasted many birds, flowers, trees, and servants. He was a good son; he had provided for his mother even in her punishment. Each palace wing extended in a different direction from the center structure: east, south, west, and north. Silver-tinted guard railings contrasted with the azure background of the walls. The inner courtyard had been replanted with chrysanthemums—her favorite flowers.

King Jeng hurried to his mother's sickroom. A phoenix candleholder proudly guarded her door. He stopped and took a long breath, then pushed in. Waves of stench and incense assaulted him. Her sickbed, surrounded by green silk hangings, lay in a far corner. He dismissed all the hovering attendants.

With trembling hands, King Jeng walked toward the bed, but stumbled over a medicine-table leg. He grabbed at the nearest sash to regain his balance, ripping the delicate fabric. Sheepishly, he lifted the curtain.

Emaciated skin sagged off her cheeks, yet her eyes burned bright. White hair and a toothless mouth collapsed in a maze of wrinkles. Words erupted huskily, as if from a long-dormant volcano. "So, you've come at last. My son acknowledges his mother."

"Jao is mine. Your enemies are gone! They won't ever trouble you again."

Surprise and then disgust gripped her face. "Trouble me? How could they trouble me? Of course, I smarted from their ostracism when I married your father, but I expected that. Did you know that I married him? I caught his eye one night at Lu's mansion in Jao. My chance to marry royalty. I had heard from Lu that he'd be king one day, so I'd be his queen. Why do you look surprised?"

The king looked away. "Mother, don't talk like ..."

The veins in her hands and forearms rose like purple rivers over a crevassed landscape. "Why not? I've been dead for ten long, boring years. Wait! You murdered them because you thought they knew about Old Lu and me."

The king's tension-etched face stared at the dying crone. "People have said that ... that ... he was my father."

She looked at the sun-washed mountain peaks visible through her window. "That fool?"

King Jeng's jaws clenched. "People have said that you were pregnant by him ... and that when my father married you, the news was hidden from him. Am I a merchant's son?"

She paused, then glared. "No, damn you! Your father was a Chin prince. You murdered all of them? The only real way would be to kill all in Jao. The rumors will outlast those you killed." She watched as the death mask covered his features. "You'd kill all of them, wouldn't you!"

"Mother! Please ..."

"You conquered Jao. Han also?"

"Yes, two years back." He flushed.

"Men ... needing to fight, win, dominate." She sagged on the bed and gazed out the window.

"I'm fighting to end wars. When I've united All Under Heaven and punished the bandit kings, I'll give a lasting peace."

She smirked. "Punish bandit kings! Do you fancy yourself to be Heaven itself? Your peace will last a few years—if that—then more fighting. Our land's well watered by blood. If peace truly lasts, I'll salute you from the grave." A laugh burst from her. "What about Lu? How'd he react to the fall of his former homeland? At least he had a sense of humor."

"Dead, killed in an attempt to topple me."

She sagged again and reached for a cup of water.

King Jeng wiped his tongue across his lips. "He was implicated in the plot of Lao ... indirectly, of course."

Her expression turned wary. "How so? Perhaps you think he involved me with the younger one to cover his tracks. I attracted Lu after your father died. Don't look shocked. Why shouldn't I? Your father, the king, enjoyed other women. He rarely saw me ... and why should he, with all the young things? Why shouldn't I have fun? Lu imagined that he seduced me. The younger one too!"

Teeth-grinding noises could be heard as the king looked away.

"Let me give you advice: be wary of Lee," she said. "I never liked or trusted him. He'd say or do anything for favor."

The king's eyes widened. "He denounced Lu twice."

Her gaze softened. "I bet he whispered all sorts of things in your ears to rise in power."

"He serves because I find him useful. He longs to be chancellor, but I don't plan to give him that kind of power."

She regarded her son. "Despite all the battles you fought against disease, you've won. You look healthy. Ruling suits you."

"Father advised me to trust no one. I trust only the barbarian—a simple-minded boy at times, and at others, an insightful man who saved my life and only wants to farm when he could live like a king. Why did you plot with Lao against me? How could you?"

"Lao loved me for myself. Lu introduced us and made certain that I knew about his giant cock ... as if that mattered. I'd much rather be held or snuggled than stuffed. Men seldom see that. Lao asked what I liked. The best times were sunsets or moonlit nights when we played music and composed poems. Yes, there were two sons. I always birth boys; their arrival changed things. Lao lusted for the throne. I thought it harmless. Then I learned of a deadly scheme. He left me for long periods ... but it wasn't for that. I couldn't permit him to harm you, my firstborn. All the trials and hardships we'd come through together. I was the one. I warned you about the plot."

"You? How?" The king's face collapsed.

A smile crept across her cracked lips. "Remember when the palace servant, Wang—the one with the fish-eye squint—came to you? I had told him to tell all. Lao lusted for power; he'd harm you. I'd never permit that."

"But you loved him and the boys ..."

"An impossible choice. I didn't want anyone harmed, but I couldn't let you be killed."

The king smashed his fist on the medicine table, scattering jars, pouches, and vials over the teak floor. "Impossible!"

"You're puzzled because you think like a man. Do you want to hear something strange? If I had to do it over, I wouldn't change a thing." A hysterical laugh swelled into a shriek.

He stared at the skeletal fury of his mother—decaying, yet radiant. He shivered, grabbed a pillow, and placed it over her face. She fought, scratching and kicking, but he pressed down until she went limp. He waited for a time, then lifted the pillow. Her eyes stared, and her mouth was a rictus of surprise. King Jeng closed her lids and fussed with her covers. Then he walked through the door and called for the attendants.

"My mother has died. Attend to her."

He left the palace and rode to the capital.

CHAPTER 27

TAO (228 BC)

Tao strolled down a side street, munching on a fried wheat-flour wrap filled with pork, onion, and garlic. These days, he always seemed hungry. Tao scanned the milling people. His days as a thief had taught him to watch out for the face that reappeared.

Today, he threw away caution. He had the best news tidbit: the government planned a raid on the Reds—on the Golden Cock itself. He'd seen the report from Old Mu, who'd stayed up all night to tell him. And now he headed for Old Juang's safe house.

Tao looked back out of habit. The man with the hood who stood at the top of the stairs had been in an alleyway four streets back. Tao looked left. A man with a harelip examined a brass mirror. He had been outside the shop where Tao got his sandwich.

Tao picked up his pace as his heart sank. He was going to be killed or taken, and he wasn't certain which was worse. He reached into his robe-sleeve pocket and fingered the dagger. Tao saw a group of foreign merchants. Two were drinking something—probably fermented mare's milk. Tao darted through the group and ducked to his left. The harelipped attacker had already swung his club, just missing Tao. Seeing the man off balance, Tao kicked backward and heard the crack of a rib as the man screamed. A second attacker lunged from an alley; his knife thrust at Tao's chest. Tao rolled to the street surface, curling into a ball and ending back on his feet. He lunged at the assassin, punching him in the back near the right kidney. The man screamed and fell.

Tao darted around people, avoiding alleys. He had seen others, but they seemed to have been left behind.

Tao shook his head. He could assume nothing. He saw a blind man with a cane. That man had also been outside the food shop. Tao reached for the dagger and threw desperately. The point failed to turn in time for the kill, but struck the assassin just as he raised his cane.

Tao looked to his right and left. He chanced an alleyway and bolted into its darkened entrance, uttering a prayer to the god of thieves. His luck held, because the alley was empty—and hopefully not a dead end. The way curved right, and soon Tao saw light. He slowed and exited into the waning sunlight. He walked for a water mark, doubling back and waiting before he tried the safe house.

CHAPTER 28

OLD JUANG (228 BC)

Old Juang looked from the medical man to Tao.

"He has bruised ribs and a slight cut on his neck. I put salves on both, to prevent infection and help healing ... and to ease the pain. The lad's strong. He'll be fine."

"He'd better be, for all I pay you. He's too valuable to ..." Old Juang stopped as he saw Tao's look. The meaning of the stare was difficult to read. To the medical man, he said, "You may go. Mind that you keep all of this to yourself. Wouldn't want you to have a fatal accident." The warning was unnecessary, because Bi had served the Reds for three decades.

As the doctor left the room, Old Juang turned to Tao. "Tell me again what happened."

"I was coming home with news and saw a familiar face in the crowd ... and then another. Just as I was preparing to speed along my way, a man struck ... then another ... and a third, a fake blind man who fooled me. I didn't see him correctly." Tao's head sagged.

"A lesson is all. Could have been fatal, but your thinking and actions saved the day," Old Juang interjected. "What do you think? A theft? A murder? A kidnapping? What?"

Tao raised his head. "I'm uncertain." Tao paused, took a deep breath, and began anew. "I believe that it was an attack by a gang. They know of our connection. Perhaps there is another informant. They must have knowledge of my martial training, because they sent three or more. Many tailed me; that was why I had such a time recognizing the trap." Tao sighed, almost as if in relief, and Old Juang knew the boy was beginning to understand that he had not been careless. "I took care in seeing that I was not followed after I escaped their net. I wandered, doubled back, and watched from the shadows. I knew not to lead them here."

"We must assume that our houses are known. We need to pull back to our second-line houses immediately."

Tao nodded absently. "We need to hit back. If we do nothing, they will grow more bold."

Old Juang smiled. "My thoughts exactly. It's time to call in our ally at the Metropolitan Police. Any ideas about the informant?"

"Someone with a grudge or someone with ambition."

CHAPTER 29

MARCUS (228 BC)

Winter banked the Roman's farming energies. The serious summer drought had devastated crops in unwatered fields, but his plants had been large and numerous as a result of plentiful irrigation waters. Marcus felt guilty for planning without regard for the amount of rainfall. Less fortunate peasants suffered losses and still had to pay taxes or rents. They faced a difficult winter.

The royal land grant exempted the Roman from labor duty, military duty, and taxes. Marcus enjoyed access to advanced agricultural technology. He marveled, for example, at the iron-tipped plow blades. A mucuslike substance applied to the metal tools retarded rust formation.

During the winter, Marcus repaired the weathered toolshed door with borrowed saws, hammers, and planes from the government storehouse. His favorite tool was a calibrated, adjustable measuring device.

When the weather cooled, he picked a day to finish the stable door. After repairing the broken latch and replacing a rotted baseboard, he turned. Before him stood a fevered Sariputra.

"Sari, you're back! What's the matter?"

The unshaven monk had a thick mane on his head and a beard to match. His face was gray. "Glad to be h … ere." He collapsed.

Marcus carried his friend into the warm house. He rested his palm on Sariputra's feverish forehead and decided to send for a physician. He wrote to the king, describing the emergency. He bound the handwritten bamboo strips with a thong and dripped on the wax, affixing the phoenix seal given to him by King Jeng. The missive was given to a servant, who was ordered to ride to the palace.

Soup arrived, and after a few gulps, Sariputra lay back.

The day had been cloudy and somber. That night, a knock resounded through the house, and Marcus opened the door to a corpulent man wearing a bushy black beard. "I am Wu, His Majesty's physician. I was commanded to treat a sick man. Am I to stay out in this cursed weather all night?" An icy blast chased them inside.

"Forgive my manners. I am Ma-ku-su. My friend is ill."

The physician's eyes darted about the room. "Describe the sleep. Does he moan? Cry out?"

Marcus groped for words. "He moans."

The doctor strode into the bedroom after discarding a heavy fur coat. He felt the Indian's forehead, reached for his left arm, and firmly placed his fingertips along the inside, an inch above the wrist. The physician lightly felt the skin's texture. Next, Sari's mouth was forced open, and his teeth, tongue, and throat were examined. A fat digit pressed the monk's gums and traced his lips. Sariputra's eyes opened. "That's all right. I'm Wu, personal physician to His Majesty." And then, to Marcus: "Does he speak?"

Marcus nodded affirmatively.

"Please answer some questions," commanded the doctor.

Pain-scalded eyes widened. "Fire in belly. Leave me."

"What kind of dreams have you had?"

"... ships, water. Drowning." The monk shivered.

"Do you fear death?"

"Used to be unafraid ... now terrified." The Indian's parched lips were flecked with blood. "Water."

"How about when you pee?"

Sariputra's eyes drooped. "Fiery ... dark yellow, almost brown."

The doctor continued. "Aches?"

"Bones, knees, ankles."

"How about your hearing?"

Strained words came in spurts. A wind-whipped tree branch struck the outside wall. Wu strained for the soft replies. "Noises like waterfalls ... running water in ears."

"Would you pass urine? I have a vase that I'll insert your penis into. Some say it's just like a vagina." The light-brown terra-cotta container was lifted from a large, black bag and placed over the flaccid penis. The doctor chatted, and a swishing sound accompanied the Indian's grimace. The container was removed, and the physician wafted it under his nostrils. He turned to the prostrate man. "Please rest. I'm going to the outer room for a while. Don't worry, you'll get better."

Dr. Wu smiled at the dark-skinned barbarian. When the Indian sank down, Wu signaled for Marcus to leave. Outside, the large man explained, "The man's gravely ill. He's drained from a lack of willpower. Yet he traveled here. I'll use acupuncture and moxibustion. The bladder meridian must be opened so that energy flows freely. The most serious problem is the will. Touch him and send determination through your fingertips. I have herbs that must be ingested."

"I gave him some soup with vegetables and chicken pieces. Actually, my friend is a holy man who refuses meat, but I thought he should have energy."

Wu stared at the lamp nestled in the corner. It was a finely worked Spring and Autumn era piece. "You were stupid. Give him vegetable soup unless he specifically requests chicken."

Marcus stared at his winter shoes—thick-soled hemp lined with rabbit's fur. Anger choked off a retort. For Sari's sake, he spoke. "What about salt? He craves that."

The doctor's fat-enfolded face bore a trace of scorn. "No. Taste is but a symptom. Ask me before you do anything."

Wu reentered the bedroom, reached into his bag, and extracted a packet of thin needles. He retrieved a green pouch filled with dried leaves. A acrid scent emerged when the pouch was opened. A blue silk bag stuffed with dried plants was placed on the wooden bedside table. The urine container was gingerly passed to the Roman. Marcus left and returned to find his friend lying on his stomach, back exposed.

A pile of dried leaves rested at midback. Wu ignited it and watched it burn to the skin, then placed a cup over it. Marcus's mouth watered at the sweet aroma, and he shook his head in anger. The physician tapped on the cup to test the suction and appeared satisfied. Next, he inserted three needles along Sari's spine. Marcus looked away as the doctor twisted the upper silver needle between his thumb and forefinger. The doctor extracted the needles and re-covered the Indian, then motioned for Marcus to step out of the room with him.

"Would you kindly enlighten me? I come from a barbarian land where the doctors aren't skillful. I would like to know."

Wu relaxed. "As I said, your friend's symptoms indicated a bladder infection. His aura was dark blue shading to black, meaning an advanced affliction. It was good that you summoned me."

The Roman looked stupefied. "What do you mean by aura?"

"The color of a person's face and the surrounding cloud. With careful observation, one can see auras."

Marcus seemed dubious. "Why check his hair and mouth?"

Wu paused for a swig of liquor. "I was determining how dry he was. Brittle hair's one indication, and the dry gums confirmed the other symptoms."

"What else?"

"The groaning and aching bones supported the initial diagnosis. But I had to rule out a kidney disorder, and the deep pulse gave the vital clue of a bladder imbalance." The doctor swallowed another handful of snacks.

Marcus scratched his arm and picked up some smoked beef. "What's the deep pulse?"

The doctor chewed a chicken bone, sucking the marrow into his gullet and spitting the remains into a bowl. "In the arm, seven pulses may be detected. Each has a signature. The pattern of the sick man indicated the bladder. Each case is a puzzle. I became a physician because I love to solve mysteries."

The Roman reached for the teacup. "And the dreams?"

"Water, ships, dying, fear, traveling. All suggest a water-based illness. Five forces—water, earth, fire, metal, and wood—govern the body. Your friend's problem was water related, being connected with blue, the salty taste, the cold, the north. The disease peaks between the third and fourth afternoon segments. Is that when he collapsed? It's simple, actually."

"A group of Greeks ... er, barbarians ... believed that the universe was composed of four elements: earth, air, fire, and water," Marcus said while pouring another cup of tea.

Wu frowned as he reached for another chicken wing. "I know nothing about four elements. The five-force perspective aids us."

"What's the role of the needles and of the burned leaves? Sari seemed in pain. Isn't it cruel to injure an ill person?"

Dr. Wu chuckled. "You think I'm torturing your friend. His pulse indicated a serious obstruction in the bladder meridian, and the needles broke the roadblock. Energy must flow unimpeded. I frontally attacked the blockage. Once the energy flows, recovery hastens. Your friend had one major wall and three lesser ones. I burned leaves at the serious obstruction and used the needles for the others. Your friend felt little pain. Most people proudly display their moxibustion scars."

"How'd you know where to burn and where to stick?"

"I've studied medicine for ten years ... followed my father and his father. I memorized the key meridians. The bladder line extends from the left eye over the skull through the neck and down the left side of the spine, then loops around and up the other side. This single meridian has fifty-two points. By the way, one needle was to ease the barbar ... er, your friend's pain."

"You mean that you can stop pain? Would you show me?"

Dr. Wu swilled the liquid over his tongue. "Acupuncture is not a game."

"I have a sore finger. It hurts in the cold times."

The proffered digit had been broken and never reset. The irregular mending had created conditions susceptible to arthritis. "I'll give you a demonstration and a salve to ease your ache. I'll also show you an exercise. You should have told me earlier."

"I didn't know you. Would I disturb the king's physician?"

The doctor chortled. "Well, you managed to get the king's doctor to leave his warm, comfortable quarters, take a wild night ride, and stay away from his beloved court for three days!"

Although foggy from the drink, Dr. Wu lifted his ever-present bag and ordered the cook to boil water, into which he immersed the needles. Retrieving them from the roiling water with a pair of chopsticks, the physician lay them on a clean cloth. The burly man inserted two needles in Marcus's arm, far from the painful area.

Marcus thanked his guest. "Why didn't you stick the finger?"

"The acupuncture point is far from the finger. I'll send you a copy of the charts and some books too. Do you read?"

Sariputra recovered slightly. Dr. Wu instructed him to drink liquids and said that recovery might be hastened by eating chicken, but the monk refused to forgo his diet. On the third day, Sariputra left the bed to urinate.

Dr. Wu cautioned him. "You abused your body in traveling. Now you'd better pamper yourself … just like pampering a concubine."

The monk's face shriveled. "I've never known a woman."

"What, a virgin at your age! No wonder you're so tight."

That night, Marcus had a long talk with the physician about the abstinence from sex that governed the lives of Buddhist monks.

A chastened Dr. Wu stayed two extra days. Marcus learned that Chinese medicine had originated with the Yellow Emperor, who had lived thirty centuries earlier. Dr. Wu mentioned that the two closest medical centers could be found on Hua Mountain. The male branch was the Heavenly Way Temple, and the female branch was the Great Mother Temple. Since he'd stayed at each place and personally knew the heads, Wu offered to write letters of introduction for Marcus. The possibility of traveling, if only for a short distance and a brief time, thrilled Marcus.

Books and charts arrived the day after Dr. Wu left. Each new visit to the capital included stops to see Dr. Wu. Once, Marcus accompanied the physician to the royal library's excellent medical collection, which held over a thousand volumes.

Marcus returned home to find a bronze miniature replica of the human body. Acupuncture meridians were engraved upon the form, with the pressure points indicated. A set of silver needles lay beside the bronze statue. He loved this gift from his friend, King Jeng.

CHAPTER 30

TAO (228 BC)

Young Tao lounged against a wall, looking at the modest house. The Reds' spy had said the Blues used it as a safe house. Tao could see no light or movement inside or outside. A sliver moon smiled down on the raiding party. The time was about two water marks before dawn ... payback time. Old Juang had ordered all to dress in Yellow Gang garb. Tao fingered the hem of his colorful coat. A piece would be left at the scene. Underneath his coat, Tao wore a light armor vest; Old Juang had commanded him to wear it. One never knew where a stray arrow or sword might land.

A bird whistle sounded. Furtive shadows crept toward the house. Weasel Pi snuck up and slit the lookout's throat, and Big Lu came to the door with a weighted hammer. He swung once ... twice ... and the door exploded. Five men rushed through the door frame, with Tao behind, carrying a short sword.

Half-dressed men rushed out of rooms, but they were immediately killed. The narrow halls and small rooms lent themselves to brief, brutal fighting.

As Tao headed down one corridor behind two of his own men, the wall beside him exploded outward. A large man shook off the dust and debris, then swung a war hammer. Tao ducked and sliced downward with his sword, catching the burly man in the calf. The sword sheared through skin, muscles, and tendons. The man screamed and fell. Tao drove his sword through the man's ribs. Dust filled the air.

Tao stepped around his victim and continued down the hall. He brushed dust from his robe and hair. Bodies lay crumpled in the next room. The Reds had been efficient; two were military veterans. Tao saw one cut the throat of a dying Blue.

Tao heard a whining voice interrupted by shouts; a leader had been apprehended. The Reds had strict orders to take alive any leaders. All had been cautioned to watch for secreted poison capsules—it seemed unlikely, but one never knew about the Blues. Tao saw the leader. Already his left eye was swollen, and his left arm hung helpless.

"Get up, ya bastard! I'd just as soon gut ya as look at ya," Pigeye said. His right eye had been lost in a fight. Pigeye was one of the most fierce and trusted of Old Juang's henchmen. He and two others would escort the Blue leader to the Reds' lair (a mansion, used as a last resort).

Many were taken; none were left alive. The Blue looked at Tao and looked away. He had been one of Tao's assailants. So it had been the Blue Gang that attacked him on the street. Seemed they knew his route back to the lair.

A small man rushed up to Pigeye. "The house is clear and secure. Fourteen dead and one escaped. We let him think ..."

"Not now," Tao said. The Blue leader couldn't be allowed to overhear anything, even if he was already a dead man. The midget glared, but his face cleared when he glanced at the Blue lord.

"Let's go. Never know who might show up. Check that room, lad." Pigeye glanced at the room from which the leader had been taken.

Tao obeyed. Light thrust toward a far corner revealed a loose wallboard. Lowering the light, he found a secreted bundle, untied the binding, and skimmed the writing.

CHAPTER 31

MARCUS (227 BC)

In the spring, rain painted the fields lush green. As the days lengthened, Marcus decided to visit the medical schools on Mount Hua. He instructed his farm manager to use irrigation water if the rain stopped for more than six days.

One muggy morning, Marcus and Sariputra left. Following a farewell to the king and to the physician, who gave them letters of introduction and a treatise on tropical diseases, they departed. As Chin envoys, they enjoyed the benefits of the official travel lodges. They soon reached the Mount Hua foothills.

In the following days, they stayed at two cottages along the mountain path and rested pleasantly. Marcus loved the scent and swooshing sounds of the pine forest enveloping the second hut. Although those woods seemed vaguely familiar, he realized that the mountainside was not his dream place.

They decided to meditate. Marcus left his body and met a beautiful woman whose semitransparent gown revealed more than it hid. Marcus awoke refreshed but puzzled.

The next day, Marcus and Sariputra found the Great Mother Temple. They were led to Mother Lo, who perused the letters of introduction. "We are fortunate to receive this medical tract. Of course I can write to Wu, but I'd like you to convey my delight with his gift. Is he still terribly fat and insulting?" Twinkling eyes scanned the pair. Mother Lo pointed to Marcus. "So you are here to learn about the yin medicine. And you, master monk?"

"I accompany my friend. I'm also curious about your medicines, which saved my life. In my homeland, I attended physicians." Sariputra relied.

The abbess looked pleased. "I, too, am a student. There's much to unlearn or remember. I suggest you look at our library's section on diet and deep breathing. They will help you avoid bladder infections like the one that nearly killed you."

"How'd you know?" Marcus exclaimed.

Her eyes shone playfully. "By his aura and the way he dragged his left foot. We'll talk later. We can have you for four weeks, and you'll follow our rules. Most of those rules, Sari, will be similar to those of the monks in your land. You may use our library. It isn't as large as the royal library, but it is more specialized. You may converse with women, but if they choose not to speak, do not press." Her eyes bore into Marcus.

"I am here to learn," he assured her. "I pledge to obey your regulations."

"You concern me. Remember how friendly you were with that voluptuous woman yesterday. She's a demon, and you fell for her trap. You'll know soon why I caution you."

Marcus looked away. "I will obey. It is an honor to be here."

"Good. I'll summon your guide, Sister Ming. Please wait."

The men regarded the sparsely furnished room. The door opened, and the abbess entered, followed by a dark-complexioned woman with wavy hair.

"I have the pleasure of introducing Sariputra ... and Marcus. Please know one another," the abbess said.

"Please, tell me about the altar items," Marcus requested.

Sister Ming moved to the altar. "These represent the Great Mother, giver of life. These colored stones symbolize Nu Gua, who fused giant stones to prop up broken pillars that supported the sky. These stand for the queen mother of the west, who gives medical knowledge. The pine tablet represents Banpo, a place of peace where women ruled."

Questions raced through the Roman's mind. "Banpo ... peaceful? Near my homeland was a place where women ruled ... warriors. Here I saw a unit of black-robed females—the Panthers, as I recall."

Sister Ming's dark eyes glistened. "Here places ruled by women follow peaceful ways. It's true some are warriors, but the character of the female is peaceful."

Marcus could not hold Sister Ming's gaze. "Once, I was a soldier and killed a man in self-defense. When I saw the battlefield carnage, I ran like a coward. For me, peace is best."

Sister Ming escorted them to their quarters. On the way, they passed a flower-bedecked courtyard. As Sariputra wandered off, Marcus asked Sister Ming if she'd visited the royal library.

"No." Ming took a tiny fan from her sleeve and cooled herself. She looked away.

"It's an amazing place with hundreds of works about medicine. If there are works you need, I'll have copies sent," Marcus said.

A green songbird in a nearby oak tree serenaded the azure sky. "You are kind, Ma ... please forgive me. I have trouble with your name." The fan waved faster.

He stooped to a blade of grass. "It's Ma-ku-su. When you practice, you can say Ma-ku-su, Maku-su. Makusu ... Marcus."

After the men reached their quarters, the monk lay down. Marcus accompanied Sister Ming to the courtyard, where a mauve rose bobbed elegantly. Bees buzzed lazily, while a squirrel chattered noisily from a pine. Sister Ming swept her hand. "It's wondrous in moonlight."

Marcus started; she had read his thoughts. Ming broke the silence. "Don't worry, Makusu ... I feel what you feel. Our bond is so strong that I can already finish some of your sentences."

Her elegant fingers plucked a grass blade as they idled on the marble bench, located so that it lay always in the shade.

He spoke. "It's hard to understand your words, Sister Ming. My heart has known you. All's ancient, yet new. My friend, my love ... how can I say these things to a nun?" He fidgeted. "You're the reason I'm here! I don't mean just here in this place, but in Chin. Think how far I've come in miles—thousands—or, in your measure, li—tens of thousands. Of all the places I could have gone, I'm here because of you." Energy suffused his body.

"No, Marcus. *You're* the reason you're here," Ming replied. Her thin lips curled. "Once, we've been mother and daughter." She tugged at a loose strand and tucked it behind her ear. Her mouth curved in a perfect arc as she smiled.

His memory could not locate that lifetime, but somehow he knew the bond of which she spoke. "Another lifetime you were a man, and we quarreled and parted. I'm sorry ... how I've wished to say that."

"No need," she replied, smiling mysteriously.

His enraptured gaze dropped like a frost-stricken orchid. The songbird's liquid melody melted him. "Merely something to be said." His paw groped for Ming, then recoiled as if from a fiery bush. *Friend, lover ... abbess!* "We must've been close." The sun, framed by a silvery white cloud, warmed them. "This is like reaching home after a tiring journey."

Ming glowed. "I, too, feel serene. Somehow, there will be a time to come ... a time for hellos, good-byes, and all the in-betweens."

"Sister Ming, I hope we'll have time to talk and walk." As her body shifted, they touched. Marcus edged closer.

Ming drew away. "Ma-ku-su, I am fearful of us." She spoke haltingly. "I'll be here the morrow, after the noon meal."

His hand brushed her face, and he saw that her eyes were slightly averted. Sweat covered her brow. She seemed tormented by something, but he hesitated to ask. When the sun moved behind a cloud, Marcus smiled and left.

CHAPTER 32

OLD JUANG (227 BC)

As the Reds' leader admired his garden, he imagined himself a giant land tortoise moving slowly in search of some delicacy. He absently regarded a lilac bush. Pruned last fall, its buds threatened to burst into bloom overnight. Old Juang felt comforted by the fact that greenness always returned.

Tao, who had been walking by the old man's side, paused. His face was a mask again. Old Juang asked, "What do you think?"

Tao turned slowly. "About?"

"The documents uncovered in the raid. Information can be gleaned from them. What do you think?" Old Juang watched his apprentice and shook off a sentimental thought.

"I think the Blue Gang has strength in numbers of members, allies, and wealth. They must be destroyed."

"And?" Old Juang pursed his lips—watching, waiting.

"A weak spot exists. We'll know when the Blue leader breaks."

"What is the Blues' flaw?" Overtaxed by worry, Old Juang sank into a soporific state. The late-morning sun caused his eyelids to droop.

"Their assassination-contract system. We have several contracts. They are evidence for our police allies." Tao preferred "police allies" to "stoolies" or "underlings," terms employed by others.

"Several murder mysteries can be solved, and the documents will assist the career or careers of our inside people," Old Juang said. "But the police may think the documents forged or otherwise corrupted." Old Juang picked a lilac bud. It was nearly open as it twirled in his stubby fingers. There was no scent.

"I think they will see such opportunity to improve their careers that possible forgeries will not be a problem. The question is how to reveal the information in a timely manner." Tao watched his boss.

"We have a junior police official who can be persuaded to pass the documents to his superiors. Of course, he'll have to explain how he came across these incriminating documents."

"Isn't he the one with the street informants?" Tao asked. He picked a lilac bud and slowly crushed it.

The gesture did not go unnoticed by Old Juang. He frowned, wondering where Tao had learned about Officer Chu's informants. "We'll tell him to imply that an informant sold him the information. There are other documents. I left a stack on your bed. Write a report detailing your findings and conclusions. You did well in the raid, lad. One day, this will all be yours—if you live that long." Old Juang chuckled as he watched Tao's pimply face grow an unguarded flicker of hope—tinged with greed.

CHAPTER 33

MARCUS (227 BC)

The forty days in the nunnery's library seemed like a day to Marcus, who discovered that "yin" meant "water," "life-giving," and "vital," as well as "nurturing," "helping," and "guiding others." Yin was the cooling shade; it yielded to nature's way, receiving what was offered.

Some female-authored texts railed against men; more ignored them; others gave balanced assessments. He saw the value of using yin/yang diagnostic assessments. Fevers meant an excess of yang; the preferred treatment was to give a yin remedy like hot soup to induce sweating.

Another discovery was the link between diet and health. A meatless diet seemed best to some. Others believed that occasional helpings of fish strengthened a person. Soups, especially those made with chicken, benefited people. Most believed that sickness came from imbalance or disharmony.

Marcus devoured an essay linking good health to regular exercise and understood why the nuns of the Great Mother Temple were purposively active. Most moved in patterns resembling slow-motion dancing. Marcus discovered a book on deep breathing. One inhaled from the diaphragm area, filling the lower lungs first, then the upper lungs. Then one cleansed by mentally guiding the breath through the body. Energy followed intent.

His free time was spent with Sister Ming. Sariputra was not surprised that they had known each other in past lives. Marcus and Ming recounted their lives and discussed their dreams, spiritual beliefs, and political viewpoints. Marcus heard her perspective that marriage perpetuated male control. He hoped for a world where people didn't have to control one another.

Once, Sari told Marcus that women could not attain enlightenment.

"Why not?"

"They lack the necessary religious feelings, my friend. The best they can hope for is to be reincarnated as men."

"How are men superior?"

The Indian folded his arms and lowered his head. "Men wrote the religious books and started the religions of my land. They are the gurus. No one goes to see a woman."

Marcus stepped closer. "What about the women here—the abbess, Sister Ming? Aren't they enlightened?"

The monk tensed, and his head drew back. "These women seem advanced, but they're nothing like our spiritual adepts, who fly and walk through walls. It is impossible for women to rise as high. I feel compassion for them, but they'll never go far."

Marcus's face screwed up like a dried plum. "How do you know that the abbess can't do things like your arhats? She sees the past—what I meditated about—and she cautioned me about Sister Ming, whom I hadn't even met. Your religion holds women down."

"You are a man! I've seen you change here. You want to 'free' women. Who are you to tell these people what is right? A family headed by a man is natural. Look at animals … is the female dominant? What do you know? We have nuns. If you insult Buddhism, I'll not speak." The Indian stomped out of the room.

Marcus related the argument to Sister Ming. "Sari was angry and refuses to talk. He defends men dominating women."

"What do you expect? Many of China's ways came from men too. They have written essays and destroyed our writings. That's why our temple is precious."

"Are there ways that were started by women?"

"Yes. Some follow the teachings of the great queen of the west. Come to think of it, men aren't allowed into our rituals."

"Will men and women ever understand each other, Ming?" Marcus asked, then became silent. The month was closing. He lightly measured her hands with his own. "I hate to leave," he finally said.

Ming sighed and stretched like a cat. Her sinewy arms drew into the folds of her garment, then thrust out of her sleeves. She rolled her head three times right, then left, as Marcus gazed at her neck. "There is no other way now, my love."

His head snapped up. "Love! You love me?" Tears came. "I, too." They touched in the forest glen—their special refuge.

Marcus's heart fell into an abyss as he left the temple.

Weeks later, however, back at his farm, the claims of the farming life, medicine, and court life made the days in the Great Mother Temple a blur. But Sister Ming was not forgotten. One day, they'd meet.

CHAPTER 34

OLD JUANG (227 BC)

The room was dark and filled with smoke—some kind of incense, perhaps sage. Old Juang opened his eyes and looked at the shuttered window. His beard itched, and as he lifted his hand, a sharp pain stabbed his left side. Then he remembered.

After Tao's mishap, Old Juang had insisted that gang leaders be guarded. Two trustworthy fighters shadowed him. Despite the extra security, the attack scene had rushed in on him. Four men had emerged from an alley and run the short distance to him. As the bodyguards drew their weapons, Old Juang reached for his stiletto. Both guards fell to the attackers, but only after the guards had mortally wounded three of those attackers. The fourth man, who resembled a weasel, had circled behind, and Old Juang had realized that three were decoys.

Juang had faced his man, who balanced lightly on his feet after he came to a stop. He grinned, but whether it was from glee or just a facial mannerism, the Reds' boss could not say. The weasel struck with blinding speed, and Old Juang barely managed to deflect the killing blow. As the weasel thrust again, Old Juang parried, looking for an opening. People gathered.

The weasel had licked his lips and come in again with less speed—but with grim determination. Old Juang had not known if he could take much more. He felt the sharp bite of the blade. His metal chest protector had deflected the savage thrust, but the glancing blow had sliced into his side. Old Juang's dagger caught the assassin in his unprotected abdomen. None had fought back so tenaciously.

Old Juang heard the clanging of the police alarm, and he saw the assassin rise for a final slash. The Reds' leader stepped to the side and then into the surprised assassin. Juang slashed the weasel's throat, and bright red blood sprayed his face. The effort overbalanced the crime lord, who fell into blackness.

Now, he lay back on the bed, his side burning. The door opened. Tao seemed to have aged in the last days and weeks. Worry lines covered his forehead. "What do you see?" Old Juang croaked as he coughed up a ball of phlegm.

"I see an old man who is sore and exhausted. A man who barely escaped with his life and who wants to get out of bed and resume his duties." Tao spoke softly.

Old Juang strained to hear his protégé's voice. "Speak up. And?"

"You'll live, but you will be sore for weeks. That's what the physician said. There was no poison on the blade."

"Where am I?" Old Juang coughed until his chest hurt. The incense was cloying, but he refused to complain.

"In a house I located a year ago. The Blues and Yellows do not know of this place." Tao's voice grew stronger.

"You … a house? Where did you get the money?"

"One of the whores from the Golden Cock owed me a favor. She told me of this place, owned by her brother. I took money from the receipts of the Golden Cock and bought it for a good price … a steal, someone might say."

Tao's even tone unnerved Old Juang. "Why did I not know?"

"I thought it best to keep the house a secret. Did I do wrong?" Tao spoke in a pleading tone and lowered his head.

"No, it was a good idea. But you should have told me."

"There's an informant. Too many safe houses have been attacked. If I kept this a secret, its location would never be known to our enemies. Did I do wrong?" Tao whined.

Old Juang smiled. "How did I get here?"

"I had you followed. Two men who work at the Golden Cock agreed to tail you. I thought it best to be sure that you were well guarded. I was right, wasn't I?"

"Yes, I see. I should have had men watching your back. I commend your thoughtfulness. Too bad they failed to help me."

"I questioned them. They had hung back, and the attack came so swiftly that they could not intervene fast enough. They only had time to carry you to a nearby alley and away from the scene. Even at that, it was close." Tao's eyes caught and held Old Juang's.

The dwarf had cheated death once again; perhaps he'd retire to allow Tao to take over the gang. "How long have I been here?"

"Six days." Tao looked away.

"Six days!" Old Juang exclaimed. The exclamation brought on a headache that reached from his chin to his crown.

"You fell, hitting a cobblestone. I visited the crime scene to see for myself. I found nothing except for some hair … yours, I believe." Tao held up a tuft of hair: gray with a smattering of black, and tied with a tiny thong.

"Interesting trophy. I'll keep it as a souvenir." Old Juang took the proffered piece, which fit snugly in his hand.

CHAPTER 35

MARCUS (227 BC)

Sariputra grew listless. Dr. Wu examined his patient and recommended rest, along with herbal strengtheners. He confided to Marcus that he worried about the monk's idleness. The Roman mulled over the doctor's words in his verdant fields.

The millet stalks and leaves were robust, causing Marcus to surmise that his presence on the farm was unnecessary. Still, when he walked among the rows or weeded the fields, his unease receded. Marcus bent and scooped up some loamy soil, peering at a wriggling earthworm. Chin soil surpassed Rome's. *Just add water and watch.*

In the following weeks, as Sariputra and Marcus walked, talked, and shared silences, the Roman realized the monk missed his home. One summer day, when the weather cleared after three rainy days and when the sky shimmered a cobalt hue that would satisfy even the most forlorn soul, they lounged by the brook.

"I'll never return, Marcus. I'll die in this unfriendly land. My message falls on arid soil. The Buddha left his family to begin his journey; here, the family is paramount. Family ties—our enslaving attachments—are the essence of one's identity here. In my homeland, attachments interfere with the greater, spiritual search. Our speculative, abstract thought patterns don't appeal to Chinese minds. Don't even mention the language barriers.

"Another disheartening thing is the wars," Sari continued. "Fatherless children, wives without husbands, childless parents, trampled crops ... these recall the Kalinga War that sickened my own Emperor Ashoka. Yet, he had the consolation of Buddha's truths."

"Let's return to Bactra and head south," Marcus suggested. "It would be better to do so next spring, but we could depart within weeks. Gather your strength, Sari." The brook gurgled, nearly drowning Marcus's words.

"I appreciate your offer, but I must travel alone. I'll return a failure. If things weren't hopeless, I'd stay." A cloud engulfed the weary monk. "If I can survive winter, Marcus ... the cold, even the thought of it, is killing me. My homeland's hot … or, at worst, mild. Cold here seeps into my bones and devours me. It stays long and returns early."

"Next month, I'm going, no matter how much you protest," Marcus said. "I won't wait until you refuse me twice and then agree at the third offering in the Chinese manner. I'm going."

Sari smiled through tears. "We'll talk. Now I must return to the farmhouse and sleep. I despise my ever-present dizziness."

"We'll leave in a month. I'll begin preparations tomorrow."

"Yes, my friend … I'll go home soon. Back to the farmhouse. A nap, and then I'll be better."

At home, a royal messenger announced that King Jeng requested Marcus's appearance at court. Reluctantly, he obeyed. If Sari's heartsickness worsened, he'd send Dr. Wu.

CHAPTER 36

TAO (227 BC)

Morning light glittered through glossy, rain-washed leaves, chasing darkened hues. The pungent aromas of rotted leaves and refuse filled the air. As the market bustled, Tao hurried to the caravan depot. Part of him feared that the old beast would not be there.

The familiar musky scent pervaded the caravan quarter. Camels endured the off-loading of rugs, frankincense, and myrrh. A deep rumbling stirred Tao's heart, because the old bull had finally returned and sighted Tao, who walked deliberately as the camel's head descended. He clung to the thick, hairy neck. They held that position with closed eyes.

"He's been looking for you since dawn," the owner said. "Grumpy too. He bites and kicks all, but for you, he sighs like a lovesick puppy."

Tao paid no attention, drinking in the deep feelings. No one had loved him so. Old Juang cared in his own way, but this was different. Dao was his only love. Reluctantly, Tao released the camel's neck and pulled away. He would return in the next week. "How long will you be here?"

"Two weeks. I expect a silk delivery by the full moon and a load of mother-of-pearl shortly after. Then we're off to the west ... probably the far west this time. I don't know how many more trips the old one will stand. Pity you can't keep him here."

Death had claimed Tao's parents ... and now Dao, soon enough. If he were the king, he could take the old bull to the wild animal park to roam his days on trails and byways. Tao sat beside the beast. Its body heat gave him a snuggly feeling.

Finally Tao rose and set off for the Golden Cock. He saw the man in a merchant's robe (this time light blue) tailing him, but walking nonchalantly—one of Old Juang's men. Since the talk in Tao's safe house, Old Juang had had Tao followed, but had apparently failed to realize that Tao expected it. In fact, Tao would have been disappointed if there had not been a tail. Old Juang, undoubtedly shocked by Tao's revelations, surely wanted to see just how far his protégé had gone. A crime lord must always be certain about his successor. Tao smiled serenely as he picked up his pace. He knew that his own men formed a wider protective shield around him. His secrets were safe.

CHAPTER 37

KING JENG (227 BC)

The court debated where to attack. The Chin force in Jao awaited relief by a garrison force, and the change of units took months. Inaction frustrated King Jeng.

Forced by their king's prodding, the military command planned a late-summer campaign against Yen, the northernmost warring state. General Wang assumed personal charge. A veteran of numerous battles, he minimized losses, and his soldiers loved him.

King Jeng dispatched ever more urgent messages to attack, but his veiled threats angered the veteran general. Once, the general submitted his resignation, but the offer was ignored; as Chin's best general, he could not be replaced. At court, advocates of a swift strike included the illustrious Meng clan members, who had served ably for three generations. The father presently campaigned with General Wang and sent missives to his sons detailing the stalling tactics of the old veteran. One son, Jian, used his position as the king's paramour to slander General Wang. Meng Tian, the second son, had recently entered the Royal Guards. Yi, the youngest, studied law.

Marcus arrived as the debate on strategy concluded. Seeing the Roman, King Jeng relaxed. "Please approach and be recognized."

Marcus advanced with the proper number of deep bows and kneelings. He had ceased to regard the prostrations as silly. Still, he disliked knocking his head against the marble surface.

"Come closer," the king said. "You look well. How is the farm? Have you decided to be a full-time farmer or a physician? Must I call you a black-headed one? Your head is reddish brown with a scattering of gray. On second thought, take the medical examination. Dr. Wu is old and fat."

Marcus blushed, and courtiers who observed his discomfort welcomed the comic relief.

A young man rushed breathlessly into the courtroom and bounded up the steps to the throne. Any other would have been immediately executed. The protocol officer barely announced the arrival of Meng Jian, a royal favorite.

"Your Majesty, I have news … the best news."

King Jeng scrutinized his lover. "Collect yourself, or we'll never learn your news."

The slender fellow took a breath. "Your Highness. Two envoys from Yen plead for an audience. The head of the delegation, Jing Ko, just told me that he bears gifts from the Yen crown prince. One is the head of the traitor, General Fan, and the other is a map detailing territory that Yen offers you."

"The head of General Fan. For that alone, we welcome them. His evil clan perished when his treason became known. Let the diplomats approach the throne."

The envoys entered. According to security procedure, they'd been searched. Marcus retreated to the side of Dr. Wu. As the envoys mounted the stairs, bowing and prostrating themselves, the leader—a tall, erect man—turned back. Seeing his mate's fear, the tall man addressed the throne in a deep, sonorous voice. "Your Supreme Highness, I am Jing Ko, envoy of the great Yen state. My fellow, an ordinary mortal, has never been in the presence of a son of heaven. Would Your Highness grant him pardon to be excused?"

"So be it. Approach alone, and be recognized."

Jing Ko prostrated himself and reached the final set of throne stairs leading to King Jeng. After carefully placing the rolled map on the steps, he uncovered a metal container with the preserved head of the general. A murmur rose through the courtroom as he held aloft the trophy. After another bow, the envoy deposited the head in the container and retrieved the map. He presented it to the king, who unrolled it. At the end of the yellow silk brocade map was a dagger.

Before anyone could react, the assassin grabbed the royal robe and also seized the weapon. Jing Ko thrust. People in the room gasped, and the royal paramour fainted. The guards, unaware of the danger, stood passively far below; courtiers had no weapons.

As he pulled away, the king's robe sleeve tore off. "Assassin! Assassin! Save me!" King Jeng ran down the steps. He grabbed at his ceremonial sword, but could not unsheath it. "Save me!"

As Jing Ko circled his quarry, Dr. Wu and Marcus slipped from the crowd. The physician smashed the man's head with his heavy medicine bag, and the Roman tackled the assassin.

"'Ware, the dagger may be poisoned!" someone called out. Marcus clung to the assassin. With a powerful twist, the desperate man freed an arm and hurled the weapon toward the king. The force of the throw drove it into a pillar. King Jeng lunged with his drawn sword and mortally wounded Jing Ko.

The dying man roared, "I failed, because I had hoped to take you alive!"

The white-faced sovereign fainted. Dr. Wu hovered over him, looking anxiously for a wound. Poisons like the deadly Gu mix needed but a tiny opening to deliver their fatal sting. Officials and guards crowded the area. When revived, King Jeng babbled incoherently. After a few minutes, he shook his head and barked orders. "Minister Lee, I want a report in a day."

Minister Lee bowed. "Yes, Your Majesty."

"I want to interrogate the accomplice. Take him to a tightly guarded holding cell. Search him for a poison that he might swallow. All are dismissed, save for Marcus and Dr. Wu. Guards remain. I want a full detachment stationed at each entryway."

Marcus and the doctor helped their lord to his quarters. "You both saved my life—you, alien, for the second time." King Jeng bowed.

The shock of the event incapacitated King Jeng for three days. With recovery, he grew morose. Punishments mirrored the royal mood, and harsh sanctions were given for small infractions. The sovereign's bellows even emptied one minister's bladder.

On the third day, King Jeng requested that Marcus see him. "Let's go to the east garden to enjoy the chrysanthemums and pine trees." They strolled around the open courtyard—one of Marcus's favorite retreats. Miniaturized trees graced tiny mounds representing mountains.

After a dreadful silence, the king spoke. "I've been irritable lately, because I fainted in public! What must my officials think? Save for you, I trust no one. Not even the beautiful boy."

Marcus wiped his face with his sleeve. "As far as I can tell, Your Majesty, no official's laughed or thought you cowardly. In fact, I heard compliments about the way you slew him!"

Narrowed eyes bore into Marcus. "Don't try to cheer me. You have been truthful. Don't betray me." An ash gray dove flew into the yard and pecked at the ground.

"Twice, my lord, I've helped save you. Believe me, I'd rather die than lie to you," the Roman said.

"I believe you."

After idle chatter, they left the beautiful place and went to their rooms. King Jeng slept well.

Three days later, the investigation concluded. Marcus and Dr. Wu received citations and fifty gold bars each. Minister Lee got a commendation for summoning the guards. The guard captain forfeited his life for permitting the assassin to enter with a weapon. Because of his former service, he was allowed to commit suicide rather than forced to suffer strangulation. Each guard on duty paid a fine equivalent to a suit of armor for failing to respond. The royal favorite, who had fainted, was cleared of any complicity in the assassination plot.

The remaining assassin detailed the plot. Prince Tai, heir to the Yen throne, had hatched it along with the chief assassin, Jing Ko. Names went forward to the eastern command. People were to be taken alive. The assassin suffered execution by methodical dismemberment.

New orders reached General Wang in the east. He must attack immediately or be decapitated. The campaign resumed, and the Chin army routed the Yen army. The Panthers bagged two generals and a dozen other high officers. Two fell to Sister Chi, who received a promotion to the eastern command staff. After a brief pause, a general attack opened across the front with Yen. To fight late in the autumn seemed unusual, but the Chin force moved with the fury driven by a vengeful monarch.

With defeat, Yen's king and the prince of Tai surrendered and were sent to Chin by fast relays. The Yen king went to jail after a flogging. The prince of Tai suffered death by ten thousand cuts. A body part was sliced off; then he healed, and a new part was severed. The prince lingered for three months.

CHAPTER 38

OLD JUANG (227 BC)

The city map showed that the Blue Gang's territory had relentlessly shrunk, while that ruled by the Yellows remained the same. The Reds controlled the greatest swath of the Chin capital. Old Juang permitted himself a slight, hidden smile before turning to Tao.

"What do you see?" It remained their game. Old Juang monitored his apprentice's observation powers and self-control.

"Obviously, we are winning. It's only a matter of time until we control the city. The last report you shared told of the Yellow Gang's isolation. Their alliance with the Blues means nothing now; they have no political allies, and their income is shrinking."

"What else?"

Tao towered over the dwarf. "The Yellows will fall and need not be quickly destroyed."

"And why is that?" Old Juang could not contain his curiosity.

"Of course, we could end it all for the Yellows in a major strike, but that might be costly. More dangerous would be the reaction of the Metropolitan Police and the Public Security subministry. A major battle in and around the city would attract attention. Let the state do our work. Keep feeding tips."

Old Juang looked at the young man. Despite his relative youth, Tao wielded magnificent self-control. Old Juang had investigated Tao for months. The only discovery made was that Tao frequented the caravan unloading area to resume contact with the old camel.

"My own thoughts precisely," Old Juang finally said. "No use in the royal bigwigs feeling threatened. Crime under my control bothers no one; it's an occasional murder or robbery, but nothing alarming. Most business is quiet and sometimes removes troublesome people for the state. I do favors, and so do they. Yes, it's best to be quiet and invisible."

"Perhaps we might think about doing more with our money. It lies safe, but it does not grow."

Old Juang raised an eyebrow. "What are you saying? As long as I've been involved in crime, we've stashed our takings. I refuse to risk our reserves. How would we survive a catastrophe—a government crackdown, a fire, or a quake? Our money is readily available. No, we will follow the old ways."

Tao shrugged his shoulders. "Yes, you're right."

"It's time for you to move from the Golden Cock. The night master post is about to become vacant, and it's time for you to step into those sandals. Your time at the whorehouse has given you a spell at managing a business—a very successful one, I might add ... even though you skim more than a little. Don't deny it. It's all right. I'm relieved that you're not honest. What do you think?"

Tao turned back to Old Juang. Their gazes locked; neither turned away. Tao smiled. "Thank you. I used money for personal expenses and a songbird. Damned thing eats exotic insects."

"You should have asked me for a gift."

"Something I had to do on my own." Tao looked down.

Old Juang put a hand on Tao's shoulder. "I found out that the bird's a female. I'll see about getting you a male so that they can mate."

Tao smiled, but his eyes conveyed nothing. Old Juang's neck hairs raised. He would dig more deeply about the young one.

CHAPTER 39
MARCUS (227 BC)

The Roman returned to his farm after an additional two weeks attending to King Jeng. Dr. Wu had advised against a long trip for Sariputra before spring, and the Roman's spirits ebbed. When he arrived home, his fears were confirmed: the monk had hollow cheeks, emaciated arms, and a sallow complexion.

"I'm sorry, my beloved friend," Marcus said. "King Jeng suffered an assassination attempt. He's unharmed, but shaken."

"No matter ... king jealous of me. And of her, later. Fated to die here. There understood ... loved for self, not stared at. Worked out karma, so next time higher life stage like Sister Ming. Know I love you." As Sari's eyes closed, visions of his home beckoned.

"You can't leave, Sari. You can't say good-bye. Fight. Do you hear me? Fight!" Marcus shouted. "We'll go home, where there's peace and people who love you. I'll carry you!"

Friends and family gathered around Sari, who finally at peace and back home after all these years.

Marcus had tried to rekindle the flickering flame. Sariputra had died while Marcus chattered like a caged monkey: "I promise you, Sariputra: we will meet another time."

The mourning lasted five days, and his body was cremated in accordance with Buddhist custom. Ashes and charred bones were placed in a silver urn. One day, they would be returned to Sariputra's home and scattered in a sacred river.

Marcus returned to his duties. There would be times to remember and to forget.

CHAPTER 40

TAO (226 BC)

Tao smiled. Old Juang had sent spies through his house, clothes, and effects. He was tailed all of the time. He wondered why the old man worried. The Reds' boss was suspicious … and yet he trusted Tao at the deepest level. The smile widened.

Tao would assume the night master post in two weeks or so—a little more than twenty days. He needed to get ready. As the young man emerged from his thoughts, the cry of the fried-pork seller startled him. The wiry man's twin baskets were filled with cuts of pork and were covered with hemp cloth that kept off the flies but showed enough to tempt passersby. Tao loved fried pork rind and belly fat. It was his rebellion against a steady diet of meat and vegetables with grains. He had acquired a taste for rice, the delicious grain that was showing up in the capital.

Tao bought slices of fried belly fat wrapped in a thin hemp strap. It didn't look all that clean, but Tao didn't care. Once every two weeks, he permitted himself this treat. Tao reached into his robe sleeve and pulled out a tiny bag of salt. Reaching in with his elongated fingers, Tao retrieved a pinch and spread it over a pork strip, brushing away a fly. He strolled on, lost to street noises—though not to the peripheral vision of his shadow. Old Juang was getting careful, allowing two and sometimes three spies to tail him at a time.

Tao walked down the thoroughfare toward home; it was his own place, given by Old Juang when he reached sixteen. Of course, the old man knew all of its secret places. Tao had assumed that years ago, so he hid nothing there. Besides, Old Juang was a master thief—one who kept keenly honed his considerable skills.

Tao had operated in plain sight at the Golden Cock.

CHAPTER 41

KING JENG

In the late spring of the succeeding year (225 BC), a Chin army attacked the state of Wei in north central China. During the siege of the Wei capital, the local river, diverted from its channel by Chin's hydraulic engineers, flowed to and then under the capital's walls, collapsing them. The city surrendered, and Wei was annexed.

The next target was southern warring state of Chu. A Chu army numbering half a million fought a Chin army of comparable size. When the Chin force withdrew after heavy losses, King Jeng demoted his commanders and summoned the retired General Wang. The sixty-seven-year-old veteran approached his sovereign, who was alone save for one courtier.

"You've arrived at last," King Jeng said as he regarded the phoenix candleholder.

"Your Majesty." Wang prostrated himself, and a sunray caught his white hair, gilding it.

"You feign illness, but you remain my general. If you defeat Chu, I'll reward you. Fail, and you'll die." King Jeng looked away.

The general straightened, even though he suffered from severe back pain. Wang looked directly into the eyes of his sovereign. "I've heard that the enlightened ruler loves his state, and a faithful general his good name. An injured state cannot be made whole, nor can dead troops be brought back to life. Never again will tens of thousands of my soldiers die."

King Jeng's face showed a mix of contempt, fear, and anger. "Do you know the Son of Heaven's wrath? It can produce corpses by the hundreds of thousands and make blood like a sea. Perhaps you desire to see your clan, your friends, and their clans exterminated. We have had them arrested, but they will be treated generously, so long as you obey. Otherwise, say farewell to your children, grandchildren, and great-great-grandson."

"I will give you Chu!" the general roared.

The Chin army moved swiftly. General Wang drove a Chin army numbering one million across a wide battlefront. Within two weeks, the Chu capital fell; a month later, the king of Chu was taken and sent to the Chin capital (223 BC).

Later, the Yangtze River was crossed, and within weeks, the remaining enemy areas fell. News of the victory triggered festivities in Chin.

Late one afternoon, King Jeng and Marcus were idling in a garden when a uniformed woman entered and prostrated. King Jeng frowned as he untied the sealed thongs and scanned a report she brought. Curses erupted. Remembering himself, King Jeng informed General Chi, the former Black Panther leader, that there'd be no reply.

> To His Majesty, King of Chin
>
> I, General Bi, have the duty to inform you that the Chin army commander, General Wang, took his life. He left a letter saying that he'd fulfilled his promise and respectfully pleaded for the safety of his clan, friends, and their clans. He begs Your Majesty's understanding and compassion. None have read this letter. I will destroy it at your command. I have taken the liberty of reporting that the general died of a heart attack.
>
> Please advise me.
>
> Your obedient servant,
> Bi Po (Seal)

King Jeng's face looked like a Bactrian devil mask. "Filthy pig's asshole! Of course, I'll free them. Now he belongs to history, that son of a poxy whore. He'll be buried with honors. Why'd he have to spoil my celebrations?"

CHAPTER 42

OLD JUANG (221 BC)

The long table faithfully reflected the two diners' images. Two candles illuminated each end. Silver bowls of delicacies were placed at strategic spots. Fruits, including a white-skinned variety with slightly red rims from where the seed was extracted, lay in two ceramic bowls. Delicate aromas wafted around the diners.

Tao and Old Juang dressed splendidly. The young man wore a silk shirt with golden stags decorating a red base. He raised a hand to his throat; it was covered by a light yellow silk scarf, the tapered end of which draped over his left shoulder. Tao's red trousers bore silver threads bunched at regular intervals. These nodes whorled like beach shells. Red silk brocade slippers snuggled his feet.

Old Juang wore a simple but elegant black silk shirt fringed in red. He had chosen not to wear a scarf. The crime lord wore blood-red trousers decorated with black dragons—two in front and two more on the back. He wore black leather shoes with red straps. Old Juang's eyes reflected the candlelight, giving off gold flecks. The boss smiled. "What do you see?"

"Wealth and a radiant crime lord. It is unlike you to spend freely on a meal, and I'm puzzled by the occasion. The two mutes standing near the doors seem out of place. I wonder if they will keep people out or in," Tao replied as he slightly bent his head.

"Their presence will become clear. For now, let's concentrate on the meal before us. Relax and enjoy yourself. You have done well as night master. Our income has grown steadily, and I wish to reward you without being interrupted … except by the servers." Old Juang looked intently at the young man, now in his midtwenties. Tao, tall and self-assured, had mastered much of the Red Gang's asset management and inner workings.

"I am honored by this meal and occasion. I remember that night long ago when you rescued me from death. When you helped me begin my new life … this life," Tao said softly as he rolled up his left sleeve, revealing the red scorpion.

Old Juang gazed at the tattoo, a permanent reminder of the boy's obligation, needled into his flesh. "Yes, the scorpion. I remember when I took you to the parlor. You didn't cry when Bu began his work. I've admired your control—at times, seemingly inhuman. And the snake?" Tao rolled up his right sleeve, revealing the red snake tattoo, which writhed as Tao flexed his muscles.

Old Juang admired the muscle control needed to accomplish the feat. "At least I know what you've done in some of your spare time, Tao."

"Oh, I have learned many things, sire," Tao replied. The whisper forced Old Juang to cock his head. He frowned at the title, remembering the boy's first lesson about addressing him as sir. Old Juang let the use of the title pass.

"Please eat, my son," Old Juang said in a lowered tone. He too could use titles and speak softly. Both sampled the dishes. Both drank moderate amounts of alcohol. Both made appropriate jests. Old Juang raised his glass; both his and the boy's had been refilled by a servant who had been with Old Juang for years. "I toast sons and successors. Although you are not of my flesh, you have learned what I could teach and more. Yes, I know about your investments. It took a while, but I found the ledger where you kept your accounts, hiding the sums and investing them in a jewelry store. Before you answer, let's drink to sons and successors. Fear not—the liquid is not poisoned."

Tao obediently raised his glass. "Thank you, sire."

"Once I told you never to call me that. Why now?"

"The time has come to thank you for what you have done for me, have given me. With your permission, I would like to shed this shirt, so that you can remember my back." Tao's whisper held an undertone of command.

"Of course. I would like to see." All Old Juang had to do was raise his hand, and the mutes would strike.

Tao slowly took off his shirt and scarf, then turned, revealing the red flower and a whole garden of flowers and bushes.

"See, I have added to the work. It seemed a shame to have one puny flower. I wanted a garden. If you look carefully, you can even see a snake—a poisonous blue snake, in fact—hidden in the thorns," Tao added as he flexed his back muscles. A blue adder emerged from the garden. Old Juang wondered whether he had drunk too much alcohol. He seemed listless, and the snake grew larger.

"Yes, the drug's beginning to take hold," Tao said. "You see, I am about to become your successor, although I am not nor will I ever be your son. You had me followed and investigated, and you only found out about the money skimmed from the Golden Cock and the amount recently. What you—or, should I say, your men—missed was the fortune I created under your nose." Tao smiled sweetly. His eyes did not share the sweetness.

Old Juang could not raise his arms. How was this possible?

"It is very possible. Are you surprised that I can read your thoughts? Not all, of course, but enough. First, the money. I told you to invest, but you refused. At that time, I already had a small fortune. I worked with the merchant Liu Wan. Remember him? He passed in and out of the Golden Cock almost on a daily basis. Right in front of your spies. He and I have been allied ever since I was given charge of the Golden Cock. Liu and I formed a business alliance. I skimmed off tiny amounts at first, and Liu invested them. Soon we had tens of thousands … and eventually millions. You missed that, thinking him oversexed. He and I did business in one of the whore's abodes. Then I suspected that she might learn too much and told her about the hidden door.

"Yes, the hidden door. To survive, one must go down as well as up. A whole world awaits below in the sewers."

Tao paused and licked his lips. Old Juang's lips dried out. "That's an effect of the poison. It's working toward your heart, and that'll be the end. Yes, I know that you were going to kill me. I can see more than you think … thought." Tao smiled. "I knew about your plans for the dinner and that you'd order the mutes to kill me. What you didn't know was that they are in my pay. So, too, is the man who served us tonight. Shocked? I hope so."

Old Juang became numb from the words and the poison that wrenched his heart. How could he have missed all this?

"Simple: you trusted me too long. I built the fortune—learned the trade, so to speak—and waited for the right time. I slowly built a shadow system within the Reds. You were looking outside; I was inside all the time. Money is power. You wished to hoard it, when the thing was to invest it, watch it grow, and then spend to build one's own base."

Old Juang's eyelids drooped. He fought them open. *Please, let me live.*

"Just like you let Lefty Lu live. Oh, yes, I knew about that little trick. People talk. You used me, beat me—you and the others. Yes, I learned. Much was beaten into me. Each jab of the needle, each blow on my face etched your death in my heart. I asked for the slower poison so that I could tell you this before you died … so that your ghost would wander, knowing how you were hated and despised. Thank you for the meal. The sea slugs were a bit salty, but all is forgiven. Perhaps one day we will meet. I doubt it, but if we do, you can repay me as I am repaying you … only I am repaying with interest."

Old Juang saw the smile on Tao's lips and in his eyes …

CHAPTER 43

MARCUS (221 BC)

The campaign against Chi, the remaining warring state, began and ended in 221. Chancellor Hou of Chi, a Chin mole, counseled peace, winning over his sovereign, who waddled like a pregnant cow. The king refused to ready the Chi army.

As Chin's eastern army crossed the Chi frontier, scattered resistance met them. The Chi king committed suicide. Although the garrison force treated Chi people mildly, locals cursed their sovereign's cowardice.

News of Chi's collapse reached Chin by swift relays. The last rider broke protocol and ran in on the assembled ministers. "Your Majesty, Chi is yours!" he shouted. A prolonged cheer broke out. The land was united at last.

That night, Sariputra visited Marcus in a dream. "Peace at last, my friend. Life *is* suffering, and my homeland has war."

"When will it end, Sari?"

"Have hope; tomorrow's new. For a time, there will be peace."

King Jeng summoned Marcus to court, where red, green, black, and gold dragons gamboled across the ceiling's blue sky. A scarlet phoenix boldly pierced the clouds. The king spoke clearly.

"Insignificant as We are, We have punished the rebellious states. Unless We create a new title, how can We record Our achievements? Deliberate upon a title suitable for Us."

The officials pretended to discuss the matter. The senior chancellor approached the throne.

"In the past, the five great sovereigns ruled over one thousand miles of land, including the barbarian domains. Now Your Majesty has tamed all under heaven. Not even the ancient sovereigns could match this feat. Learning that in ancient times, there were the Earthly Sovereign, the Heavenly Sovereign, and the Supreme Sovereign, we suggest that Supreme Sovereign be Your Highness's title."

The king replied, "'Supreme' is unnecessary, and 'sovereign' should be modified. Let Our appellation be emperor. We will henceforth be known as the first emperor of Chin. Our successors will be the second emperor, the third emperor, and so on. Our empire will endure for ten thousand generations!"

The ministers roared, "Long life to Emperor Jeng! Long life to Emperor Jeng!"

New celebrations began. A newly titled ruler dominated the Chin empire, China; he was the emperor.

CHAPTER 44

SU MA (97 BC)

The grand historian of the Han dynasty twisted his sleeping robe's sleeve. Unnoticed, the rose-colored sky tones subtly reached into the dark study and caressed the Chin-style phoenix candleholder, the ancient Shang greenish bronze incense burner, and the warring-states-era lacquer tray.

Su Ma's thoughts wandered as his dark study gradually lightened.

Chin: A name befouling mouths of Confucian scholars. Loathed and reviled by decent men. Liao's agent, Chancellor Hou of Chi, befuddled his monarch into surrendering the last state. Perhaps Liao's brutal death atoned for the later suffering.

Oh, brave Jing Ko! His assassination plan thwarted by a physician's medicine bag. Fortune makes emperors and slays heroes. Su Ma's left hand mischievously landed atop a writing brush.

King Jeng had lived, and heaven had awarded him its mandate. The empire had been forged, and a new age had dawned. Chin changed with the times and triumphed through wars costing hundreds of thousands of lives. For a time, Chin halted warring, stored weapons, and invited scholars to court.

Su Ma's right hand traced the edge of a shadow thrown by the bronze lamp. It was shaped like a kneeling servant; one simply could not discern where the maid ended and the lamp began. *All of us serve, in how we write or in what we light.* Su Ma's crooked grin rippled across his wrinkled face like a stone tossed in a stilled pond.

Dr. Wu had mentioned a barbarian who saved the first emperor's life and who befriended him. How could a son of heaven befriend a barbarian? Tales warned of women serving Chin. *Lies! They are suited to birth and raise children only.*

Su Ma paced like a caged panther. Outdoors, oriole melodies teased him to throw wide the window and glide, like them, across the sleeping city. He sniffed the rain-washed odors like an old dog.

Sweet air soothed his lungs. Then a coughing fit convulsed him. Perhaps his lungs couldn't stand the fresh air. He laughed and choked, then spat out a yellow-green mass.

The twisted cypress glistened. What monarch gazed at trees and flowers? *All the power and little joy; simple things are best.*

Women in government, a barbarian as Emperor Jeng's trusted companion! Why would he encourage females when his mother's meddling nearly cost his life? Peace is an oasis in a desert of warfare. If only Jeng had left the north alone.

The golden age had been peaceful and prosperous for peasants. Su Ma had to be true to the facts, merely embellishing for dramatic effect. He had to begin a new section. He ground the ink slab; later, he dipped the brush and wrote.

PART 2

(221–215 BC): CHIN'S GOLDEN AGE

CHAPTER 45

MING TIAN (221 BC)

Creating a national structure taxed everyone. Emperor Jeng dipped deeply into one reliable talent pool: army officers. The obedient soldiers served with few complaints.

Another source of talent were those of lofty scholarship. Word of the widened talent search reached the Great Mother Temple. On the clearest day in weeks, when one would become lost looking up into the bluest sky, Sister Ming received a summons.

"Enter," Mother Lo said before Sister Ming knocked. Mother Lo's hair tumbled down her back like an ebony waterfall. Sister Ming's tresses coiled into a topknot dangling at the edge of disaster. Her almond-shaped eyes were haunting. Her prominent nose had offended her mother, and its comic quality contradicted the sober cast of Ming's perfect chin and delicate mouth.

"Yesterday … forgive me, please sit," Mother Lo began. "Yesterday, an imperial summons commanded me to send an outstanding scholar for the Imperial Academy of Scholars. Only seventy-two permanent positions will be filled. Since the Great Mother Temple has rendered services to Chin, our choice will be heard. There is but one—you."

"I can't. I've reached key self-revelations." Ming bowed.

"One may have spiritual bliss, but insights must be tested."

Ming's eyes rested on Nu Gua's stones. "But the conflicts."

"You're the finest scholar I've seen and possess spiritual depth to ground your learning. Go inward, then tell me your decision. Know that I love you, Sister Ming."

Ming shuffled out and nearly bumped into a wall.

CHAPTER 46

LEE SU (221 BC)

In the capital, courtiers debated a proposal by Junior Chancellor Jang that royal family members be allocated fiefs in newly conquered realms. The current practice was to annex the new territories as centrally administered commanderies. Law Minister Lee Su opposed it, arguing that ancient fiefdoms had grown into the warring states. The first emperor agreed and divided the empire into thirty-six commanderies—each with a civil official, a military official, and an inspector.

Junior Chancellor Jang submitted his resignation, opening the secondmost important administrative post. Then the emperor selected Wang Wan, a distinguished general, to fill it. Minister Lee hid his disappointment by rationalizing that unifying the empire's laws was vital. Law educated people on living correctly.

Marcus asked Minister Lee if the laws were infallible.

"We ensure that they are understandable and fairly enforced. Major legal decisions undergo review. Mistakes are corrected. Stern, but fair—that is our guide." The minister stroked his elegant beard.

Marcus leaned toward the white-haired, balding man. "What if an innocent person is jailed?"

A reflexive inhalation brought the remembered phrase. "Better an innocent punished than criminals roam free." Minister Lee poured tea without spilling. "Most important is to remove criminals from the streets. When we liberated Chi, we learned about its gangs. We jailed all. Now Chi people live peacefully."

The minister's hands worried an incense bottle artfully shaped like a woman. His desktop was clear of reports and memos. Marcus thought of how his own quarters were in permanent disarray. "Our Roman codes came from ancient lawgivers. We rely on our magistrates. By the way, I learned that private weapons must be surrendered."

The minister smiled. "We decided that a permanent peace would best be realized by extending the commandery system, unifying the codes, and disarming the people," the older man explained. "Bronze weapons will be melted into statues of giants. Preliminary estimates indicate that each one will weigh fifty tons and will stand nine paces tall."

"Monuments to peace. I like this."

Minister Lee caressed the alabaster incense bottle. "There is more. We razed city walls. The collapse of the Wei capital's walls a few years back gave us the idea. I suggested that all walls outside the Chin homeland be demolished and the moats filled. By the way, the program of curbing troublemakers continues."

"What's that?"

As soon as Marcus drained his cup, Minister Lee poured another. "We decided to tame local ruffians ... rather like gelding stallions. Around eight hundred years ago, the Duke of Jo forced similar groups to live at a secondary capital. Troublemakers from the liberated states are moved to our metropolitan region. Eventually, nearly one hundred thousand families will move."

"That means half a million people!"

"Yes. Aristocrats, wealthy magnates, military officers, high officials, local notables, and the like. The lazy work too. If they refuse, they'll be sent to convict labor sites. I also wrote a statute that peasants cannot be made to perform tasks that are unreasonable; nor may they be kept beyond their length of duty time. Specific food rations have been standardized, and laborers' housing units—tents mostly—are to be of uniform size."

"In my country, farmers aided our people. One man, Cin-ci-na-tu-su, answered a crisis call from the people and took charge during a crisis. He solved it and went back to the farm."

Minister Lee smiled politely. "Here, simple folk seldom govern." The smile broadened. "I know you're a friend to my youngest son. At six, he already knew simple poems. I secured him a sinecure in the capital, and he became a capable official."

"You must feel proud of him, sir," Marcus said.

The minister frowned. "My son troubles me, because he refuses to marry. Although my first and second boys have given me grandsons, the third should do his duty." Immaculately manicured fingernails drummed the tabletop. "I have implored him to marry. He has refused eleven women."

"Your Excellency, I'll say something to Bu."

Lee's smile—almost a shy mask—reappeared. "Excellent! I know he'll listen, because he speaks highly of you. Forgive me, but I must attend another boring ministerial conference. Would you like to go in my place? Ha, ha."

Both rose and left the room; one had a lighter step.

CHAPTER 47

TAO (220 BC)

The room clutched the fading sunlight, willing it to linger. A massive table shaped like the body of a stringed instrument dominated the room. Along the walls, chests congregated like groups of children. Some held vases with freshly cut roses.

Tao entered the room and paused. He loved the old table, which he had purchased from a secondhand store on Third Avenue, just below the West End Slaughterhouse. It radiated solidity and agelessness. Decades of polishing had left a mirrorlike sheen that reflected the ceiling or faces of people seated around it. He caressed the surface and looked at the flowers near the window—the fading sun backlit the arrangement, muting the bright colors into pastels.

With a sigh, Tao turned to his desk to examine the reports from last week regarding investments and takes from the various criminal operations. The two topics flowed together, but needed separation.

Before yielding to the writing desk's contents, Tao gazed at the city map artfully painted on the north wall. The Yellows had disappeared. Two of their houses had been purchased three moons ago, and the police had raided their remaining house yesterday. Crime was almost totally controlled by the Reds. China itself had been unified by Chin; crime in the capital had been unified by Tao and the Reds. Perhaps he should build a government of crime in the empire. He frowned. Crime gangs were too local.

Unity is pleasurable, Tao thought. Old Juang had been the first to see this, though he was spurred by the need for survival. Tao had buried the old man in the backyard of the old safe house. Old Juang had loved the garden, especially the flowers. Now he was planted, like the flowers—and the old pine tree that tilted toward disaster.

Tao's only worry was whether any given investment would yield appropriate returns. He wondered if peace would last. It might be boring.

A servant lit the room's candles. Tao preferred bear candleholders. Besides, the phoenix was a mythical bird. Bears were real. Tao had seen one pacing, ever angry. He wanted to own a bear—to watch it, to befriend it. He smiled ruefully.

Tao thought of the caged animals in the basement of his rural mansion, where he communicated with the *others*. Where had he learned about burning animal body parts to extend his powers? From the shaman, White Horse, who had lived in the north. Nearly every exposed body part of that sorcerer was tattooed, and the man moved like a king. Tao had invited him for a meal, and their unlikely connection had blossomed. Of course, it had been difficult communicating about the power rituals. And yet, both realized they needed the other, if only for a time.

White Horse had lived on the grassy plains and wandered the worlds. And now, Tao had begun his own journeys, which required the burning of animal body parts. Tao remembered the wail of the rat as he severed its left hind leg. The blood and life force gave Tao power to summon the creature who called to him through the smoke. Tao recalled the inhuman voice hissing like a snake. He had almost stopped the experiments, but the need to know propelled him. Besides, he could not admit weakness to White Horse. Eventually, the shaman had left Tao and continued his journey.

CHAPTER 48

MARCUS (220 BC)

On a day when the sky was smothered by a dust storm, the Roman visited Lee Bu. Marcus loathed the dust that seeped through windows and left a film on everything. He turned to see his tracks disappear. A carriage burst out of a cloud and barely missed him.

Marcus entered Bu's office. The roomier new office gave a sense of openness. Two clerks' desks were crammed into one side, and a young man bent diligently over his work after regarding the intruder. A woman conferred with her boss, and both looked up.

"Marcus? Welcome!" Bu's eyes brightened. The effect obscured his haggard appearance. He turned to his aide and the young man. "You both may take a break—one level of the water clock. Although ... with this storm from the west, I'm uncertain where you might rest." Turning to the Roman, Bu beamed. "You look healthy!"

"Thank you." Marcus appreciated that the clerks no longer stared. "I recently met your father. We chatted about the momentous changes taking place all over the land."

Bu frowned. "My father?" Bu's fists clenched just like his father's. "Is my fath ... the minister well? How are you?"

"Reasonably well, thank you. This prolonged dry spell even withers my crops ... and, of course, this cursed weather and storm try my patience. Do you notice how edgy people seem to be?"

Bu tugged his earlobe. Badly bitten nails drummed on the desktop, and a tic transformed his visage. "I'm fine too ... merely a problem sleeping. How's my father?"

"He appeared animated," Marcus said.

"Why? He's just lost the chancellor post to a general."

"We conversed about the programs that aim toward a lasting peace. His Majesty does not realize what a valuable servant he has."

"What?" Bu's concentration had apparently wandered. "My father works too hard. That's why his abdomen acted up last winter. Speaking of working too hard, I'm caught up in standardizing written characters. The Chin writing system is to be made the sole way of writing. Three other scripts had been forming; now there will be one. This will ensure that documents can be read by all." Bu spoke forcefully; yet, his hunched shoulders and forlorn face troubled Marcus.

Since Sari's death, only Bu and Dr. Wu had been close to Marcus. "That's quite an important policy. Was it your idea?"

Bu brightened. "If we are to govern effectively, we must communicate well. My father proposed the clerks' script."

"An excellent idea, my friend."

"Yes, standardization is vital for lasting change. Our government committed itself to a uniform system of weights and measures; peasants won't be cheated by merchants. We've fashioned standards and tolerances. They're checked annually."

"The government distrusts merchants?"

Bu wrinkled his nose. "They evade laws and taxes."

Marcus nodded. "Then they must be punished."

"Another measure is the standardization of axle lengths; our rutted roads, carved out by our carts, won't accept wagons from other states. Now we can move wagons anywhere."

"Your father spoke about you, too. That you haven't married. He believes that you haven't done your duty."

"Why do you trouble yourself with a family matter, Marcus?"

"I've been your friend for two decades. Remember the time I came to your cramped quarters in the old office building to ask about the Panthers? Also, despite his stuffy ways, there is much I admire about your father. I regret that I did not know my father."

An ominous silence troubled Marcus. "If you wish to tell me anything," Marcus continued, "please know that I would keep it to my breast. I have been silent about what the emperor confided to me."

Bu bent over. "I-I ... don't like women. I can be actually very good friends with them. That one in here a while ago is pretty, bright, and sociable, and possesses a sense of humor. There's a man, beautiful and sensitive, with whom I delight in sharing the scent of a flower or the pleasure of a horseback excursion. To share a life with him is improper. Why? I can't even take my life; my father would never make chancellor. Help me, my friend!"

"I'm not certain that I have answers for you, my friend."

Bu whispered, "And you don't despise me? I despise me!"

"I admire your courage in telling me."

"Death has been my companion for years."

"You might live a lie to please your family. He will not let you stay unmarried. You could end your life ... but why waste it?"

Bu brightened. "Yes, duty's important. You did not condemn me." Bu's head raised, and a sleeve dabbed the tears. The two men rose. Bu opened the door and led his friend out.

CHAPTER 49

TAO (220 BC)

The young crime lord slipped into the purple robe with a large eye embossed on the back. It had been made according to the shaman's specifications. White Horse called it the eye of the Nameless One.

Tao had waited two weeks to visit his rural retreat. The business of crime could do without him for a time. He would explore the other world—the one with voices promising power.

Tao's eyes glistened as he walked down the stairs into the basement. He lit a candle held in a panther's paws; the panther reared like a horse. Tao heard the rats in their cages.

The words slipped into his mind as White Horse had taught him. He chanted to the spirit of the dark. Shadows gathered on the walls, flickering and whirling. After sealing the room from unwanted forces and grounding it to the earth and the cosmos, Tao walked to the nearest cage. He donned gloves and reached for a rat. Fat with a sleek coat, it squealed when he cornered it, and the leather protected him from its bite.

Tao forced the rat, a young male, onto the dark-stained table. A brazier smoldered in the near corner. *Next time, I must ask for drier wood*, he thought to himself. Tao reached for the knife. Pinning the rat, Tao severed its legs.

Soon, body parts covered the table. Tao smiled grimly as he walked to the brazier and fanned the flames. The room brightened. Chanting loudly, Tao threw on the legs. *Some in the city love to eat roasted rat*, he thought. In other realms, beasts fed on the transformed energy. As the cooking odor filled the dingy room, Tao deepened his chant.

The smoke darkened, then cleared. "Who summons me?" a voice hissed. White Horse had warned Tao never to give his name to the dark forces. He'd been told that beings would try to trick him to reveal himself, but that he must remain shadowy.

"A friend," Tao replied. He shivered off the radiant energy of the demon.

"Hahahahaha, I have no friends. Say what you will, then let me go … or I will devour you."

"What is your name, master?" Tao asked. He felt a chill.

"A name for a name. You first."

"You may call me No Name." Thrills surged through him; he was alive as never before. He felt an erection.

"And I am Balzul. Tremble at my power!" the beast roared. Flames shot from his mouth, and the apparition began to fade, so Tao added another body part as the demon spoke. "Best have a beating heart … and next time, from a larger animal. Rats are insignificant." The smoke cleared.

"What will my fate be in the coming year?" Tao whispered more from fear than to get Balzul's attention. The rats smashed themselves against the bars of their cages.

"Greater power and understanding. If you make a circle of power—I will show you the way—I can come directly to you. If we work together, you will dominate your world. Feel your power and knowledge grow," the dark lord purred. An odor more pungent than a camel's pervaded the basement. Bile surged to Tao's throat.

Tao noted the beast's fiery eyes and cruel mouth—with teeth like medium-sized daggers. He could feel the power swelling within him, akin to the sexual rush of men bragging about their female conquests.

"It's better than sex, my little one. Now give me the rest of your tiny animal," the beast commanded. "I grow hungry.… Indeed, my little one, come closer, so that I might whisper in your lovely ear." The dark lord's voice coaxed and teased.

White Horse warned Tao never to touch the smoke. This would be a worthy challenge.

"Not tonight, great master. Let's talk," Tao replied as he lay the last bit of rat on the brazier. He would need better wood for the heat to burn the body parts of larger animals.

"More and drier wood will do nicely," the demon responded to his thoughts. "Next time, wash your hands in blood to cleanse you for clearer communication. You will read my thoughts as I read yours. Hold this burning and calling at the dark of the moon. Favorable forces will enable us to know each other better. Perhaps I will befriend you. I grow weary from the drain on my power. You have done well tonight, little master. Remember the dark of the moon and bigger animals. Remember, little master …" The dark lord's voice trailed off.

Tao reveled that he had established a clear link. *Should I use a cat … or perhaps a dog? Yes, a very large dog.*

CHAPTER 50
MARCUS (220 BC)

One day, the Roman flitted in and out of his room at the palace. After the noon meal, he practiced writing. A shadow crossed his desk. He turned, brush in hand, and smiled. Sister Ming was by the window; sunlight framed her head.

"Good afternoon, Ma-ku-su."

He stared. "You didn't write. Now here you are. At the temple, I spent the happiest days of my life! Then we were separated."

"Shall I leave?" Her face held a troubled tension ... and yet her eyes were dark pools. Her tone said that she didn't want to leave.

"No! My heart was torn to pieces because I didn't wish to leave you, but had no choice. This time I do. Stay! Please, stay!" Marcus implored as he reached out to her. She entered his embrace.

"My time is brief. In the last ten years, two months, and three days, I have prepared on all levels. You did not fit into my plans then. You may not like my words, but they are true. You need to hear, so that we be what we will."

Marcus's professed belief in hearing truth crumbled. "Didn't our last meeting mean much?"

"That reconnection transformed my life," Ming said as she coiled her hair around her finger.

"Do you care for me, Sister Ming?" he asked shyly.

"Yes!" Her lopsided smiles transformed her face.

"I knew it."

"I love you, Marcus. The first we met. To cut you off wrenched my heart. Women must never say these things openly."

"I love you, Ming. You fill my dreams." They blushed as they clasped one another tenderly. Marcus snuggled into her. As he pulled away, Ming stepped into him and fondled his beard. "Are you real?" he asked.

"We'll be together in the next days. I make no promises about the exact time. If you need me, go to the academy building," Ming replied. She smiled broadly and pirouetted to the door. Her beaded yellow robes swayed gracefully as she glided through the portal.

CHAPTER 51

OLD LIU (220 BC)

Peasant Liu of Wanshi Village believed that fortune ruled his life. When the simple peasant desired a good harvest and relief from the illnesses afflicting his sons, or when he longed for his wife to be struck mute, for more land, or for rain, he'd deposit a coin at the shrine. As the last three years had witnessed exceptionally bountiful harvests, Liu's debts had been settled, and he'd saved coins and stored five bushels of rice.

War had spared Liu's village: no raped women, stolen livestock, or trampled fields. Thrice, there'd been four-day celebrations. Peasant Liu loathed high taxes and was too old for military conscription. The new government had praised the black-headed ones. When he looked at himself in the purplish river waters, his hair seemed more gray than black. Yet, the sandals he'd recently purchased were made of rough-hewn leather instead of hemp, and his work clothes sported a better weave of hemp. He certainly wouldn't begrudge a celebration honoring the black-headed ones.

On the heels of the last festivities, the Chu prince's lands became state property; the hapless prince had been taken to the Chin homeland. The estate property had gone up for auction, and locals had traveled to the district capital to bid. Liu purchased two acres, a spade, and a hoe. Pooling his resources with his sons, he had bought an ox to shoulder the plow and to provide additional fertilizer and funds from breeding.

Peasants rejoiced, and in the spring, activity on their parcels grew frenzied—the busiest Old Liu could recall. To everyone's surprise, tax assessments dropped. Only three people from Wanshi Village would work that winter.

Liu might not go that year; he'd aged a bit, and the stroke last winter caused him to drag his right foot. The military-service obligation had been abolished. No longer did Chin—it was hard to get used to the name, Chin—need soldiers.

Liu couldn't really complain—or, rather, he could complain, but it wouldn't do any good. Chen never sided with him. Perhaps he'd bribe the conscript agents to take him; it usually happened the other way. No matter, it'd be worth the price to be free from her.

He dropped yet another coin onto the wooden structure.

CHAPTER 52

SHU WEI (220 BC)

Two thousand miles to the northeast, Shu Wei took stock. Despite the annexation of the Chi noble's beloved homeland by the Chin barbarians, they ruled efficiently. Princes, high nobles, large landowners, and wealthy magnates lost property and were deported. As Shu Wei scanned the horizon, he delighted in the fact that his place was insignificant. He had to remember to order the cook to pick winter melon, pale green and already ripe. A crow called from a distant maple. No one could imagine him wealthy or powerful; better a minnow than a succulent carp.

The harried manager, Bang, entered Wei's courtyard. Perspiration ringed his neck and armpits. Wei scorned the white-haired man, who was nearly seventy-two years old and who grew frustrated with a body that refused to respond to mental commands. That anger transferred to the hapless tenants. Bang limped to his master, then stood until recognized. He remembered protocol and tenaciously guarded the system that kept him subordinate.

"What is it?" Shu Wei didn't look at his foreman. He sniffed, knowing that some kind of manure had gotten onto his man's feet.

"Master, winter comes. We must harvest before a freeze. With your permission, I'll go to Linzu and hire six hands."

A cloud wisp caught Wei's eye. Perhaps it portended a squall. "Why so many? I see how you've slowed recently."

The man winced. The call of wild geese tugged at the manager. "Master, signs demand action. Hear the geese. Squirrels have more fur. We can't gamble on a friendly southern breeze. That cold spell four years back claimed half the millet crop. Normally I'd say seven men, but I'll rise before dawn and work by moonlight."

The aristocrat recalled that grim autumn nearly two decades earlier when a loan from the industrialist had saved him. Everyone had economized to enable Wei to repay it; he sighed at the memory of losing his mistress.

"We cannot risk another setback," Wei said out loud. "How much will this cost?"

"Since many look for work, we can pay less than last year. If I hire a woman, I'll get six at the price of four."

Chrysanthemums showed their golden heads in the garden. "Good. Leave for the capital. I will go to Linzu too," Wei said.

The diminutive man still stood like a withered oak.

"Yes?" Wei asked.

"Bandits are active, sir. I'd urge my lord to repair the outer wall and hire two former militiamen who come cheap."

Shu Wei scowled. "We'll discuss it next week. Leave!" The older man bowed stiffly. Wei contemplated his sojourn into Linzu. He'd sleep with the singer he had met the week before. She had fled the carnage in Chu and been a delightful bed partner. His breathing quickened. All he recalled were her endless legs.

Wei became aware of eyes on him. A glance revealed his son watching. Gangly, with a skin rash and overlarge teeth, the young man approached. "May I speak?"

"Can't you see I'm busy?" Shu Wei said. "If I'm late for town, I might not close an important deal. We'll speak tonight."

"But I ..." The lad's eyes seemed drawn in, and his hair stuck out in all directions.

"It can wait," Shu Wei said, and the teen dropped his head.

"Good. I'll bring you a little something from the city." Something shiny caught his eye. A second-story window held the boy's mother, whose stare forced the noble to scurry away.

When he reached the capital, Wei went straight to the tiled-roof dwelling. There he rushed into the arms of his beloved. She had the whitest skin and an exquisite nape. In bed, he loved to caress that part of her. He smiled as his hand left her nape and reached for the wine cup. He must remember to leave before the gate closed.

Wei awoke in the dark and touched supple curves. Smiling, he rolled off the bed. He hunched over the chamber pot and waited for the flow. He padded back to bed, and his hand groped again for her breasts. She moved as he played. As he stiffened, she yielded.

At midmorning, Shu Wei rode home, saddlebags stuffed with gifts. In the distance, a smoke column curled skyward. Shu Wei rode hard, racing through his gate.

Two servants lay crumpled lifelessly in the courtyard—including Bang, whose legs were twisted unnaturally. The miniature cypress had been torn from its terracotta bowl.

"My son!" Doors ajar ... tables overturned ... items strewn across the floor. Shu Wei stepped over a servant's broken body. He reached his bedroom.

"Heaven, let it not be!" The youthful shape looked like a doll tortured by a child. Gashes rent the silver, blood-drenched robe. Wei cradled his son's head. Clothes chests had been ripped open, their robes tossed everywhere. The jewelry box was missing. The boy's mother lay supine, throat torn open.

Wei caressed his son's dark hair. His nape had those skin bumps. Wei's fists hammered his cheeks. Through the bloody haze, a persistent noise alerted Wei, who saw Lotus's blood-streaked face. "Lotus, you're alive! My son?"

She winced. "He fought like a young tiger. Defended her." Each word condemned him.

"How'd you survive?"

"Fought a bandit who threw me ... and head hit something ..."

Wei wept.

"Wei, you must be strong!"

His head rose just in time to see her fall. Tearful convulsions wracked her. "What happened? We expected you last night. At least you avoided this ..." Lotus's outstretched arm swept over the cluttered room.

"I was delayed, and when the gates closed, I couldn't leave."

"Don't blame yourself," Lotus replied.

They formed a plan. As the morning waned, farmhands who had fled drifted in and were immediately put to work.

Bodies were hoisted to tables in the kitchen and shrouded for burial. Fires were doused, and clutter was removed. Wei hired seven men and plunged into the battle against the wreckage. At night, he'd collapse into bed with blistered hands and broken nails. Sometimes, Wei and Lotus huddled to survive the nights. Wei learned that Lotus had memorized many of his favorite literary passages; he felt like a man who had discovered a gem lying in a pile of common stones.

Income from the harvest cleared three small debts, and Wei congratulated himself that the bandits had missed the buried gold. A new set of servants returned the manor to a familiar routine. One morning, a cavalry detachment circled the front part of the manor, and an official drove into the courtyard. Wei expected news about the bandits, but received a wooden tablet with this inscription:

> In the twenty-sixth year of His Imperial Majesty, The First Chin Emperor, be it known that these subjects of the former Chi bandit kingdom must settle their affairs in three weeks. Their properties, except for that moved by two bullock carts, will be confiscated. Each family will be permitted two servants. Assemble in the Linzu Western Market in three weeks. Failure to do so will bring severe punishment.
>
> Respect this.
>
> Ju Bo, senior civil official
> Linzu Commandery

Wei tugged on his sleeves. "I'm a poor farmer who was robbed."

"The law is the law. Though the metropolitan region has harsh winters, you're lucky not to be going to the disease-ridden south."

Wei's outstretched arms beseeched heaven.

Lotus appeared from the side of the house, carrying a load of squash. She smiled until she saw Wei's face. He slumped to the ground and banged his head on the hardened surface in a plea for mercy. She dropped her vegetables and ran to him.

"They came to say that we have three weeks to pack and leave."

"Tell them that they made a mistake ... we're poor."

"There is no appeal."

Wei purchased two large carts and loaded them; the task had been simplified by the bandits. Farming tools and the remaining valuables were passed to Wei's younger brother, Pi, to whom Wei had seldom spoken. The cause for that rift was Wei's sole inheritance of the family property after their mother's death.

Wei's generosity dissolved the animosity. Pi appreciated the pigs and chickens, and the young ox. Pi had little property and thus avoided the exile. Tung, son of the younger brother, had planned for a governmental career as a ritual specialist, but the conquest by Chin terminated that. When the first load reached Pi's house, the sight of his nephew, Tung, recalled his own son to Wei's mind.

Pi promised to tend their parents' graves.

Two weeks later, the final trip came. The primary item left behind—gold—caused great anguish for Wei. When the assembly day arrived, Pi's family gathered. Wei'd gained dignity through his travails and generosity.

Lotus packed heavy clothes and blankets. They slept in military tents and arrived at their exile destination in the dark after a long travel day. An official directed them to a row of simple, earthen buildings.

CHAPTER 53

OLD LIU (220 BC)

As the summer months dragged into autumn, Wanshi villagers happily faced another good harvest. The government rested lightly on them. The emperor had issued a decree read by the local magistrate. It announced that peace and demobilization of the armies permitted the government to lower tax rates again. Never had so many been so favorably inclined to government.

The next winter, Chu nobles who'd fled deportation tried to organize a rebellion. The villagers turned them in.

Mistress Chen readied the kitchen, dicing leftover pork roast, mixing it with duck eggs and a garlic infusion. When steamed and topped with a sauce of vinegar, chilies, and leeks, it tasted like a banquet dish.

Old Liu trudged through the doorway with slumped shoulders and an ashen complexion. Chen barely noticed him at first, then finally turned. "Well, what are you doing back so soon?"

He gripped his belly. "Don't feel well."

Chen frowned. "Your leg or your back?"

"Neither. I have the body fire."

She bowed her arms. "You don't look sick. How will we eat if you're always abed?"

He shrugged and shifted his feet. "I'm sick. Leave me alone."

Her shrill voice sent knives of pain into him. "Leave you alone! If I didn't care for you, who would? No one cares!"

Fever licked his eyeballs. "I do."

"Yes, I know! What about Widow Fang? I know you slipped her some cash. Is she pretty? I know how men think."

Tomorrow he'd lay a whole string of cash on the altar. "Of course not. How can you accuse me of that? She was ill."

Chen's pointing, fat finger resembled an obscene baby mouse. "I know you well. You secretly admire her."

"I felt sorry. No one else cares."

"I've seen you look at her. Leave me and marry her. You'd fall for any pretty face. See if I care!" she shrieked.

Old Liu summoned his remaining energy to rise to full height. "May the green goddess take me if I lie."

She maintained her pout. Their cat, a gold-striped tabby, bolted through the door and nearly caused him to fall. "I don't believe you," she said.

"I only care for you, my dear. Please don't fight. Tired." Bile gushed out of his mouth.

Seeing that he was ill, she tenderly put him to bed, brought him water, and massaged his arms and legs. That evening, she fixed his favorite soup—pork with vegetables—and coaxed down several mouthfuls. He slept, and next morning, she encouraged him to take the day off. All day, she mothered him.

That night, they made love; the moon was full, and everyone slept. She let him on top, and they clung desperately during the climax. The next morning, they slept late and made love again. Within a week, however, their familiar pattern reasserted itself: she nagged, and he fled to the peaceful fields.

CHAPTER 54

EMPEROR JENG
(220 BC)

Officials worked hard, with Emperor Jeng setting a hectic pace. Audiences commenced before dawn, lasted until the morning food break, then resumed until dusk. Most days, the first emperor read one hundred twenty pounds of wood and bamboo documents. An official from the Bureau of Standards weighed each day's load.

The imperial secretary, Feng Jie, exhorted officials to emulate the royal example. During the first imperial winter, conscripted laborers within 350 miles of the capital were ordered to the metropolitan region. A third worked on dwellings for displaced rich and powerful families. The remaining workers built palaces and offices. After the defeat of a warring state, architects and engineers were sent to sketch that state's palaces and famous buildings. Following their return, scaled replicas were built, dotting the landscape.

Emperor Jeng also collected rare instruments and beautiful women. His favorite retreat, the Willow Palace, duplicated a Chu palace. Willows undulated in any breeze, and an elevated palace balcony afforded a panoramic view of the Wei River.

Ensconced in the Willow Palace was Beauty Shi, the legendary concubine upon whom the Chu king had lavished a fortune. One summer, the king had had snow and ice carted from distant peaks to mimic a snow scene for her. After Chu fell, a special detachment had brought Beauty Shi to the Willow Palace.

The emperor's breath had stopped when he first beheld her. Shimmering hair reminded him of a mysterious waterfall vibrating against a deep blue-green kingfisher feather robe. Green eyes highlighted the effect. Prominent cheekbones hinted at a barbarian ancestry, but ample flesh moderated her facial structure, and three dimples added a sense of playfulness. Willowy arms harmonized with her slim torso.

Shi danced gaily or sulked moodily. They strolled in gardens where twilight spirits hovered. "Shi, I'll never let you go," Emperor Jeng said. "I've never been happier ... yet, when I peer into your eyes, I cannot fathom your thoughts. You seem melancholy. Anything—clothes, serving women, gold—is yours. Promise that you'll never be sad."

As they left a willow canopy, trailing branches teased their exposed flesh. "My lord, I'm wonderfully happy. Some evenings, I gaze at the moon and wonder if you think about me."

"I'm busy, my little dove. I have to share time with others."

Somewhere in the shadows, a cuckoo called.

"Your words, please, my lord." Shi bowed to hide a tear. Brushing it aside, Shi gasped as she beheld a massive golden moon, edged with a reddish hue, above the horizon. "Look, my liege! Lovers' moon, as we say in Chu. Let's go in, and I'll warm you with something new—a technique to increase your penetration and our pleasure."

CHAPTER 55

TAO (220 BC)

The crime lord jerked awake and twisted in his coverlet. He had been stirred by that recurring nightmare.

In the dream, he saw a dark, dreary room with three doors on the near wall, with something sinister behind each. Tao's heart constricted and breathing became difficult as he heard the rasping sound: nails or claws, scraping along the corridor.

He had to leave, but only the doors were outlets. He cleared his mind and went to each door to sense its threat. The scraping sound neared. Tao inhaled deeply, opened a door, and went through.

The room was brightly lit and filled with the sickly sweet aroma of burning meat. "Welcome, little master!" The voice boomed in Tao's head as he turned to his left. A hideous creature grinned. "Yes, little master, it's your teacher. Let's explore a world that will give you an erection to celebrate!"

The beast extended a taloned hand. Its mouth widened into a lascivious grin. Tao sensed that the creature would enjoy devouring him, but it held back. Why?

"Why do you think, little master?"

How could he get away? It knew everything.

"Yes, little master, I do." The grin grew more lascivious and cold as the hand reached out ...

His dream had seemed real. The sessions with the demon lord were destroying him. Yet ... the power! The feelings! The knowledge! He could read people's minds and sense their desires. It was simple to manipulate them for his own purposes.

Tao lit a candle and inhaled its jasmine aroma. Chests and tables, each polished to a mirror sheen, reflected golden light. This was a room fit for the emperor, with rarities purchased from wholesalers in the former kingdoms—castoffs of the rich and powerful ones who had been forced to relocate.

He rose and shrugged into a robe. Although Tao enjoyed sleeping naked, lately he felt vulnerable without clothing. He jumped at house noises; he, the greatest crime lord in history, was increasingly fearful.

What time was it? Just before the dawn. Perhaps he'd go for a walk before the meeting with the syndicate: a stroll in the marketplace to witness the unfolding day, to savor the aromas, to watch the vendors. Tao moved to the dresser and opened a drawer. He would wear nondescript clothing and use the secret exit. Perhaps he'd go to the caravan terminus. *Who knows what will be in today?* The old bull was most certainly dead. Perhaps Tao would meet another beast.

The dream faded before the prospect of a sojourn amid people—to be among them … to look, to see, to dream without specters of demons or monsters.

CHAPTER 56

MARCUS (220 BC)

Marcus and Ming savored the same moon as Emperor Jeng and the Willow Lady. It had reached a quarter of its sky transit when they spied it, and the golden, reddish cast had yielded to chalk white. They chatted in Marcus's quarters while jasmine-scented liquor jugs waited; one was warmed, the other chilled.

"What's the academy of scholars, my love?" Marcus asked.

"It's modeled on ancient academies that housed the world's most famous intellects. Our academy follows them, though we advise, interpret royal dreams, and compose his majesty's decrees."

Marcus reveled in her musical voice; the crisply pronounced tones flowed like a merry mountain stream. "This academy reminds me of the Athenian Academy … or perhaps the Lyceum … or even the Library of Alexandria. Plato's school is the most famous, having the great Aristotle and others in attendance. I recall its inscription: 'Let no one ignorant of mathematics enter.' But none, save for the library, had connections with a government."

Ming nodded. "We have private students."

Marcus was dressed in a dark blue silk robe with a brocade weave for warmth. "What will happen to them, my love?"

"Most become officials. Presently, there are seventy-two academicians and thirty-two apprentice academics."

Marcus stared at the fully mature woman. The moonlight dancing on her black mane cast a silvery sheen. "How does one become a member? Are you the only female?" He watched her supple flesh quiver, then settle.

"There's Lin Dai of the Way of Lao Tzu, and we hope to increase the number of women. I was nominated by Mother Lo."

Marcus smiled. "A remarkable lady! I met her ten years back, and you said she was eighty."

The academician corrected him. "Marcus, it was just over seven years ago. Abbess Lo is most remarkable. Females rarely serve in governments. Chin permitted us to fight and to work. Its victory is our victory." The musical quality of her voice sang with a harder edge. She went on. "Yet, one must help oneself before assisting others. I have cured many, but I couldn't have done a thing for them if I hadn't studied medicine."

The night chill caused Marcus to shiver. "I disagree. We first help others. Certainly, I've seen here that the individual sacrifices the self for the family or the clan."

"You told me that you'd left a wife and son because you'd fled a battlefield and couldn't stay in your homeland. Weren't these actions self-centered?"

"Yes, but ..."

"Please let me finish. You acted to save yourself ... but in doing so, you stopped killing others. Your actions led to the abandonment of your family, stemming from a personal choice."

Marcus looked away. His head drooped.

Ming's cheeks tightened as she followed the skein of her argument. "You had a choice: to stay and kill, or leave and save a life. Would you have remained under any condition?"

Marcus regarded his sandals. "No. I'd have died first."

"Then you chose neither as a coward nor as a deserter."

The blackness deepened. "Ming. There's something else.... In a Gaul village, a young woman lay with a doll beside her. Ming, she'd been raped ... her throat slit. I can never save her—"

"Marcus, it's all right ..." She started to reach for him.

"Ming, you interrupted me. In Bactra, a city north of Sari's home place, once we passed an alley. I heard sobbing and moaning. I ran into a dark alley, but I could see perfectly. I took my staff and smashed the rapist. A knife was on the ground. I hammered his head, shoulder, and side. His victim fled. I grabbed the knife and cut him. I'm cursed by my father's temper."

She cradled him and rocked him gently. An owl hooted three times, and Ming shivered slightly. "My beautiful, wonderful love. Your fury saved her from a terrible death. How I love thee."

CHAPTER 57

JIN MI (220 BC)

The thief cased the house for the third day. He'd seen four servants. The master, a wealthy merchant who entertained frequently, left the home every other day. Jin Mi followed him to his main liquor warehouse … and then to his mistress. The man was worth millions, but where did he hide the gold and the jewels?

Jin Mi worked for the Red Gang. No one worked alone if they valued their heads. The Reds took a dim view of solo contractors; when discovered, they usually lost a limb. Jim Mi loved life—and his limbs. He had joined the Reds as a teenager twelve years ago. Now the Reds were led by a new man: Old Juang's adopted son. Tao ruled with less violence and more subtlety, that was fine with Jin Mi.

Jin Mi considered the house's defenses: broken glass along its wall and a dog that barked during the day. Jin Mi suspected that it was kept indoors at night. Getting past the dog would be his greatest challenge—but of course, he was the master thief, a title conferred by Old Juang and reconfirmed by Tao. Both knew that Jin Mi brought in more than all other thieves. They also knew that he kept little back. Jin Mi liked to live comfortably, but he also liked to live. Since Tao had taken charge, Jin Mi received significant annual bonuses. Old Juang had given a trinket now and then, but never anything worthwhile. The old fart had used threats to keep the men in line. Tao gave all an interest in the Reds' success.

The master thief left his observation spot, strolled by the house one last time, and inclined his head. *Tonight's the night.*

CHAPTER 58

MARCUS (220 BC)

As Marc us wrote characters, a familiar tread turned his head. Ming was a radiant contrast to the dreary afternoon. A thunderstorm had drenched the garden, intensifying the color of the chrysanthemums. She toted a bundle. "I've brought something for you to read, my love."

"Are you certain I should be trusted with it?" asked Marcus.

"You will handle it with care." Ming smiled at Marcus.

Marcus slowly read the strips.

The Golden Era dawned, and the myriad creatures harmonized with the universe. Actions, decisions, decrees lovingly synchronized with the natural way. Pretense and deceit were unknown. People did not divine for the propitious times to begin. Scheming and prudent calculations did not occur.

The body naturally connected with heaven and earth. Complete in themselves, at one with nature, people were attuned with the four seasons. They paired as male and female to complement creative forces. Heaven formed a covering above, and earth formed a base below. Seasons succeeded one another naturally, and winds or rains came without harm. Favorable omens heralded a golden time: the phoenix flew, the unicorn pranced, and honeydew appeared abundantly. Hearts were free.

Time passed, and the golden time waned. Tunnels were probed for treasure; gold and jewels were mined. Oysters were torn apart for pearls. Humans smelted ores; creatures became stunted. Animal wombs were ripped open to bare the unborn as a delicacy. Unicorns fled. Nests were torn asunder, eggs smashed; the phoenix left. Forests were burned for pasture and farming; lakes were drained. Nature revolted. The sun seared crops; rains deluged homes; quakes shattered buildings. Humans robbed, and governments appeared. War and death stalked the land. Mothers and daughters wept. Contests left winners and losers. A shadow time descended—illuminated by a flash, then darkness.

Marcus frowned. "A grim vision. The Greeks had another: Pandora was given a box by the gods and was warned to keep it closed. She opened it, and woes came out. Only hope was left."

"Your tale blames a woman. In this tale, it is men who mine and kill ... who war and enslave."

"Yet, the Black Panthers killed," he said. "Female officials serve government. It's not fair to blame us for everything. Emperor Jeng's government regulates in harmony with nature. Timber should not be cut during certain months, nor should water courses be blocked. Only in summer are young animals taken."

"A few women have done bad things. I contemplated joining the Panthers. Now we have a unique chance to change things. We didn't create the state; we can create a new golden time."

"You must work with men to change that which you despise," Marcus said. "Cooperation and harmony are better than hatred and working alone. Blaming men for all the troubles creates hostility."

Ming looked at Marcus and smiled.

CHAPTER 59

TAO (220 BC)

The Reds' leaders sat in a semicircle. On the far left was Bai, the night master. Bai had come onto the team after the death of Old Juang. Being able to read and write, Bai was excellent with accounts, and he was honest—or should it be said that he feared reprisals if he held anything back?

One-Eye Lee sat next to Bai. He was the illiterate but trustworthy day master. Lee had come to the board shortly before Old Juang's death and pledged support to Tao as soon as the former leader's death had been announced. The one-eyed man favored a white patch, though he would remove it at meetings. Although Lee's actions unnerved some, Tao found the eccentricity amusing.

Ju sat next to Lee. He was burly and presented a tough exterior. Ju was the house supervisor and kept books for the whorehouses of the capital. Ju scowled a lot—but orphans, widows, and cripples could count on him for money.

Mao sat on the far right. He was the enforcer—the one Tao trusted to do the quiet things, like intimidate officials who wanted to go straight. Mao kept his mouth shut and obeyed Tao. Others had tried to outbid Tao for Mao's services, but the young man always took the offers to his boss. Mao had been one of Tao's bodyguards and knew the secretive crime lord better than anyone. Mao preferred to live than cross one who possessed superhuman powers.

"Well, what do we have today?" Tao asked. "You first, One-Eye."

"Boss, things look good. The wild-animal fights have attracted betting. More people pay to watch the bears and tigers."

"What are the receipts for the last month, One-Eye?"

Tao looked to Mao, who nodded, then looked back to the day master.

"For the month, 3,224 gold pieces, 4,235 silver, and 70,000 bronze coins. The new standardization policy helps. I recommend that we turn in at least half of the old coins each month for the new ones. According to our money lenders—I asked three separately—the new coins equal the old, except for the silver, where the content of the new is better."

"Better?" Tao repeated. "If you are certain, then exchange as much as you can for the new silvers. We might as well make that little extra before the government learns of its mistake. Can't say as I wish to be the one who made the mistake when it's discovered. What about information?"

One-Eye scratched his chin. He had had a beard, but it had caught fire in an accident. One-Eye's chin scar could not grow new hair—and besides, the day master refused a new beard. "There's a big gathering at the palace. The big one's entertaining some group or the other. It might be good for our catering service. A senior officer naps in his office. New caravan shipment next week ... rare incenses and perfumes."

"In the old days, the Reds would rob the caravan or the merchants. Now we see that our agent gets there first and makes the best deals. Is Old Ba ready to bargain?"

"Yes, boss. He's ready ... though the merchant from the Black Oasis will likely remember him. The merchant could have made more from the government. We might do better if another handled this."

"Good idea. Night master, what do you have?"

"Plenty, Excellency. The master thief struck again. He found a cache of rare jade probably seven hundred years old. Bought in the east from a power gent who had to come here. But the big find was this slip of bamboo. Since the master can read, he provided a translation. Seems there's a plot on the big 'un's life. Soon, seems like."

Tao took the bamboo and the silk piece. He would check it. Tao entered Bai's mind easier after each visit to the demon lord. *He's loyal and believes the master thief to be loyal. I'll check that.* Tao shook his head as he left Bai's thoughts; some were decidedly unpleasant.

The gang leaders had become used to Tao's glazed eyes and his brief mental absences. One look from Mao early on warned them about trying to take advantage. Bai shook his head.

"Any ideas about what to do about the plot?" Tao asked.

"I say let the politicos deal with their own," Bai blurted out. The others nodded. Most criminals wanted little to do with officials. They couldn't be trusted; often they'd turn in informers or break deals when their bosses got involved.

"By the way, that break in at the subprefect's house ... another job by the master thief last month, boss," Bai interjected. "He looked at a report saying that crime was down in the capital for the third year in a row." They all laughed. Tao joined the merriment but marked Bai's undertone of arrogance and the fact that he had waited to divulge the information. *Time for other means.*

CHAPTER 60

MARCUS (220 BC)

The Roman returned to his farm, summoned the overseer, and checked his accounts. The new barley strain promised a doubled yield. While rummaging in his toolshed, Marcus heard horses; six riders and horses trotted toward the farm. He squinted, as his sight had worsened. Marcus's acute hearing distinguished a hawk's cry over the din of the pounding hooves.

The emperor looked tanned, healthy, and energetic. "Marcus, I haven't seen you and thought I'd stay the night."

Another hawk shrilled. "Cook Chai will prepare delicacies," Marcus said.

"Actually, some simple fare would suffice."

Dinner included roast duck with plum sauce, steamed carp, chicken with mushrooms, and pork with vegetable soup. When the soup appeared, Emperor Jeng began sneezing. Mercifully, the attack ebbed. Fortified by liquor, they went out.

"Marcus, I love the most beautiful, wonderful woman, who has conquered me like an invincible army. She's my finest possession."

"Possession?"

"I brought her from Chu and built the Willow Palace for her."

"Why don't you bring her to court?"

"I was thinking of that. Then I wouldn't neglect my duties. Perhaps she'd be my empress. The ministers would object, but I can overrule them." Jeng wore an informal robe crested with a phoenix. The deep purple color shimmered in the half moonlight.

Marcus's simple robe, cut in the fashion of a toga, gathered at a waist still slim. "You must be in love, sire."

"Beauty Shi is her name. I hear that you've finally taken a lover ... an academician, if I'm not mistaken."

Marcus's ears reddened, and he appreciated the dark. He hadn't realized his private activities had become common knowledge. "Yes, I love another, although it hasn't yet been physical."

"What?" Jeng exclaimed. "I thought foreigners were oversexed."

"I'm not oversexed. In fact, I wonder if I'm undersexed." Emperor Jeng chortled as Marcus began anew. "Academician Ming works hard to set an example for other women. Several times when I went to see her, she was busy."

"Perhaps she has another romantic interest. Your remark brings to mind another issue. Women really shouldn't be in government. Their place is at home," the emperor opined.

"Haven't they done well in office?" Marcus asked. Frogs were croaking; the night air was still.

"Yes, but if your woman no longer had a job, she'd be tending you instead. When my mother left her quarters, trouble began."

The Roman's nape tingled. "Your Majesty, I deplore your mother's actions, but you shouldn't blame all women for her misdeeds. If you force women into the home, you'll cripple farming families that depend on their wives toiling in the fields."

The ardor surprised Emperor Jeng, who considered this as the moon went behind a cloud. The darkened environment urged night insects and frogs to intensify their nocturnal emissions. "Production might drop," Jeng mused. "The black-headed ones must be kept contented."

"And the women I've seen in offices seem to be hardworking. If what Academician Ming says has validity, they are highly intelligent. Why would you penalize them for helping you govern?"

The emperor's eyebrows knitted as the moon escaped the cloud's clutches. "You're blinded by love, my friend. I agree that some women perform well. Their ratings confirm that. Independent women chill me. My mother nearly caused me to lose my life. Yes, my friend, women are better when controlled."

Marcus scowled. "Controlled?"

"All my experience with them—and I have plenty—convinces me that they long to be ruled. Even history says so." The discussion forced Jeng to think.

"Near my home place, women defeated men many times," Marcus replied. "One writer argued that women should rule."

The darkening imperial face could be clearly seen. "He was a fool and a traitor. If he lived here, I'd have him punished."

"I believe that women can rule as effectively. Would you have me arrested and punished?" Marcus stepped into a puddle.

The ruler's eyes narrowed. "Twice, you have saved my life. No, I'll never have you arrested. But you must hold your tongue in public. Women who presently hold government positions deny them to men who've served their emperor and who must support their families. Yet, I'll wait. See, the moon has again sought refuge behind those clouds; perhaps it doesn't wish to see old friends quarreling."

The moon again escaped its cloudy shackles and smiled brilliantly white.

CHAPTER 61
TAO (220 BC)

When Tao walked through the red door, the crime lords awaited him. It had been a week since the last meeting. Bai was absent, and the master thief sat far away from the others. He picked at his fingernails with a tiny knife.

Tao looked drawn, with blue-black rings under his eyes. Yet he wore a slight smile. "Gentlemen, I apologize for keeping you waiting. Urgent business came up a short while ago," Tao said as he brushed back an unruly lock of hair. "Gentlemen, you notice that the night master's chair is vacant. That is for a reason, gentlemen: Bai is a traitor. He played a dangerous game by keeping his thoughts clear. But he failed to realize that I had other means. Bai tried a foolish thing—one where he skimmed off sums from his accounts and bribed the cross-checker, Old Fu. If Old Fu had a chair at this table, it too would be empty.

"My predecessor, Old Juang, had a dramatic flair. He used an attention-getting act to kill Lefty Lu for betraying the Red Gang. Lefty was stung by a scorpion, dying right there." Tao pointed at another chair, also empty. "My way is different. I dislike theatrics, preferring the silent approach. The results are equally permanent, if less messy. Bai and Old Fu are no longer with us. They have served other purposes. This means that the night master's position is vacant. I propose that the master thief be the new night master. What say you?" Tao had delivered one of the longest speeches at the board meeting.

The day master nodded. Tao knew that he was secretly pleased to have a rival gone. The new man would take time to learn the routine and to build a faction. Mao also nodded; he would support whatever Tao wished. He looked disappointed that he had not been in on the crushing of Old Fu and Bai.

The master thief, who had been staring at the floor, raised his eyes and regarded Tao. "Master, I am honored by your choice, though it is not one I myself would have asked for. I prefer streets and solitary times to an office and companions, however worthy they might be … and these men are most excellent." The master thief's arm swept wide, indicating all his colleagues. "Having said this, I accept the appointment. I would only ask that I continue my trade on a part-time basis to maintain my skills."

"Granted. You will find your new duties not overly time-consuming or difficult," Tao said. "Others will report their figures to you, and you will verify them. Now there will be an extra verification by another party. Please do not feel insulted; after what happened with Bai and Fu, one cannot be too careful. All will be subject to this process ... even you, Mao." Tao spoke softly and evenly. He wanted all of them to know they were subject to the same rules.

After the meeting, Tao lingered, greeting each of the crime lords for a private chat to reassure them of his support. The master thief kept his eyes on the floor, but his ears remained cocked as Tao explained the rules for being a crime lord.

"I extend my personal thanks for the information you have provided about the caravan and about the possible attempt on the emperor's life," Tao said. "It is best that we avoid politics, at least for the present." He looked at the thief. The young man finally raised his eyes—green eyes with gold flecks dancing in them. Each held the other's gaze until the thief looked away and left with a slight nod to Tao.

Tao idly snuffed out the candles and sighed languidly, contemplating how he would use his two new human sacrifices to the demon lord. Vast powers awaited.

CHAPTER 62

MING TIAN (220 BC)

On the eve of the autumn equinox in the second year of the Chin empire, a gala party and dinner graced the Ganchuan Palace. Seven hundred guests came, including Marcus and Ming. In keeping with the season, the invitees wore gold, brown, and light purple robes. Marcus and Ming sat at the emperor's enormous mat, along with high officials and royal family members—including a princess and her fiancé, Lee Bu. Marcus smiled at the couple.

After the banquet of thirty-five courses, an enchanted spell settled when a young dancer mimicked a giant yellow crane soaring through the clouds and descending to a marsh. Standing contentedly on one leg, head tucked while frogs croaked and fish jumped, she awoke and dove. Later, she flew back and alighted on the marble floor. As echoes of the music reverberated through the assembly hall, the spell lifted.

An elderly harpist directed by a young girl took up a place near the imperial party. Like most harpists, he'd blinded himself to highlight his musical sensitivities. He had a long, white beard, and his breath smelled of cloves—the spice used to kill certain parasites. While the harpist tuned his gilded instrument, the audience members chatted amiably. Emperor Jeng complimented Ming on her hair, which had been artfully coiled in two side loops, each fastened by a simple clasp.

The harpist listened intently, then strummed a haunting melody. Ming flew to a mountain summit alive with deer and goats. A beaming goddess wearing a green robe that sported a unicorn crest landed atop the summit. She dismounted from her green dragon. Ming recognized the queen mother of the west and pleaded, "Your Majesty, will you create an opportunity for me, a lowly academician, to catch the emperor's attention? I want persuade him to welcome more women to serve our empire."

"Do you really desire to win your emperor's interest?"

"Oh yes, Your Majesty! If I could speak with him, I believe that more women will be permitted to serve. Please help me, Mother." As Ming bowed, the goddess communicated an image showing the harpist readying to assassinate Emperor

150

Jeng. Ming saw the grimly determined face and watched as he edged nearer. She entered his mind and learned of his desire to avenge the assassin Jing Ko. The harp bottom, filled with lead, was a weapon to crush the emperor's head. Ming had to warn her sovereign. The harpist plucked a string as he lifted the harp. Ming screamed and flung herself at the emperor. The blind man missed.

Before anyone could react, the harp shot through the air again. A sickening thud told the musician that his effort had been rewarded, and he crowed. "Vengeance is sweet! The tyrant's dead! Jing Ko's deed will be remembered. Long live Yen, and may its heroic crown prince be laid to rest in his homeland!"

Palace guards overpowered the harpist. Emperor Jeng struggled against the body that covered his own. He saw the harpist carried away. One guard seized Ming, but the emperor interceded. "Unhand her. She's the one who saved us!"

When Ming arose with her hair in chaos and the gold clasps askew, he smiled. "Academician Ming, we must keep you and the Roman nearby as my lucky charms. Without you two, we'd have been dead many times. We'll determine if that son of a swine acted alone. Then we'll reward you."

The emperor looked at Dr. Wu, who bent over a prostrate official whose head had been crushed like an eggshell. "Bury him as if he'd died a battle hero," Jeng directed. "I decree that his survivors will be generously compensated." The first emperor spoke to Marcus. "You were correct about having women in government."

The investigation concluded that Gao Jian, the harpist from Yen, had acted alone. He had been a companion and admirer of the failed assassin Jing Ko. After detailing the plot, the blind man suffered the slicing death.

Academician Ming, summoned before the investigating tribunal, satisfied the inquisitors that she had acted properly. Promoted to the highest rank and rewarded with ten thousand gold pieces, Ming was uneasy about the admiring gaze of Jeng.

At the end of the ceremony, she asked permission to address the throne. Her request was approved, and she pleaded eloquently with the emperor to employ more women.

"We grant your wish," the emperor said. "You have spoken well."

Ming retreated to Marcus's side.

The following day, the two of them went to Marcus's farm. The next day, they idled at the brook. Flocks of geese honked throughout the day. After lunch, the couple walked across the plain to the great canal.

Dusk came earlier now, and narcissus buds pushed up through the garden soil. Ming admired the lovely flowers—especially the red-rimmed, cream-colored ones.

They undressed in the candlelight and made love tenderly. His eager fingers explored and probed her secret places. Ming chased away the nightmare scene of her father from so long ago. Her hand hesitantly pushed down to his groin and stroked his penis, remembering a different feeling with her father. Marcus motioned for her, and a thrust brought a gasp and a tightened grip on his shoulders. Blood oozed from her loins, and her nails scratched his back. He pushed in and pulled out, then began a natural thrusting rhythm. The involuntary ejaculation gave release and completion.

They awakened before dawn. Marcus grew hard. "Please hurry," she whispered as she spread to receive him. They slept late.

As they awoke the second time, Marcus asked, "Ming, will you marry me? I'll do anything to make you happy. Please say yes."

She gazed at a green vase from the Western Zhou era. It had to be at least seven hundred years old. "Marcus, I cannot ..."

"Why not? Is it because I have a wife?"

Ming struggled for the words. "No. I must stay in government, given the emperor's well-known views. To have a husband and a career ... not to say a family ... would be impossible. I love you, and I pledge my fidelity. But I will not marry."

That afternoon, they rode silently to the capital.

CHAPTER 63

EMPEROR JENG

Just before the winter solstice, the emperor selected a replacement for the murdered academician. Three months later, a scholar known as Hu Zi (Venerable Hu) arrived with thirty-seven students. Their number caused a logistical nightmare.

In the second year, the emperor ordered that a system of linked roads be built to carry messages, soldiers, and supplies swiftly to the capital. When completed, the network would span seven thousand miles, with highways eight paces wide, and with trees planted at ten-pace intervals. Roads near cities were surfaced.

Construction began on a special road linking Shu to the capital. Since mountains blocked the most direct route, engineers designed a suspended roadway. Wooden planks, secured by ropes and chains embedded in the rock or fastened to trees, formed the roadbed. Wary travelers gingerly trod the elevated span.

At the end of the second year, Emperor Jeng inspected the western frontier—his ancestral homeland. At Mount Jito, he sacrificed a bull to a warrior king of the Sha dynasty. Later, the monarch commanded his ministers to plan for a trip to the eastern realms. The journey also provided an excuse to see sacred places, like Mount Tai.

The imperial academy researched the appropriate rituals for sacrifices at the holy places and gathered ceremonial artifacts. Roadways had to be blazed on each sacred mountain.

Just before the departure, officials decided an important local sacrifice had to be performed. General Tian, head of the metropolitan garrison, argued that Chin should maintain the martial spirit. To that end, he commanded that an aide research the ancient spirit warrior Jur Yu.

Emperor Jeng appreciated Jur Yu, who'd fashioned the first sword, spear, arrow, and crossbow. In the northeast, Jur Yu had often shapeshifted into a bear. Two weeks later, in a secret ceremony, battle-attired Chin officers exercised the whole day. When the combat drills ceased, Emperor Jeng ardently addressed the throng. The last exercise ended with a human sacrifice. The ancient way had been honored, and the ancient spirits had been appeased. Even though peace covered the land, Chin's elite soldiers would always be ready to fight and to die.

CHAPTER 64
TAO (219 BC)

"Little master!" The demon lord's voice pierced Tao's dream. Would he never have peace or time alone? "Less and less as our connection solidifies," the demon answered. "Yet only I can satisfy you—much better than a woman or man or ... hahahahaha."

Tao awoke with the coverlet bunched up around his neck again. He threw it off and inhaled. He had learned of another shaman, Black Bear. Tao had asked to meet with the medicine man, who agreed.

His residence was northeast of the capital in a stand of cedars. Made of wood and stone, it had been lovingly crafted in a northern barbarian style. A set of deer antlers was affixed to the front of the house, just over the doorway. Tao had come alone.

The door opened on a tiny, thin man whose face was grooved with wrinkles. What held Tao's interest were the man's deep, silvery eyes. A kind of sweet sadness permeated the little one.

"Welcome. You are?" the shaman asked.

"I am Tao, and I seek your help," the crime lord replied. In this setting, Tao felt like a nature spirit. He inhaled deeply of the clear, energy-suffused air. Its sweetness warmed his being.

"Then enter, after removing your shoes," said the shaman, adding, "I am Black Bear. Would you like water?"

"Yes. The way has been dusty and dry." Tao regarded the simple, naturally decorated room. Dried flowers were arranged in a ceramic vase, and animal bones decorated the walls—at least, Tao thought they were animal bones. A cat peeked furtively from behind a doorway, then ducked back inside a room.

"Don't mind Calico. She doesn't trust anyone," Black Bear said. He wore his long, black hair in a ponytail reaching to his tailbone.

After Tao had refreshed himself, Black Bear spoke. "What brings you to me?"

"I have trouble sleeping; nightmares haunt me. Sometimes there's something in my mind. It's coming more frequently, and I can't get it out." Even though it was cool in the house, Tao pulled a cloth out of his sleeve and mopped his brow.

Black Bear looked closely at Tao, and then his eyes focused beyond the young man. "There's darkness around you, and your eyes are tinted yellow. You are possessed. I must ask you a question if we are to be successful. May I?"

Tao clenched his jaw and nodded affirmatively.

"Do you want to be rid of this being? I sense it strong within you. I can rid you of it, but if you invite it back, it will grow in you, devouring until only a shell remains."

"I want it gone. I called it up and have worked with it. I have done things to animals and human beings to strengthen my connection to it. But it leaves me no peace."

"Yes, I know these things. You may not be able to leave the power and knowledge alone. They hold you more than the dark one. You must put yourself in my care and follow my directions. Will you?"

Tao mopped his forehead. "Yes, I will."

"Good, then let's go to a room at the back." Skulls and strange scents filled the room, though Tao discerned the scent of sage. Black Bear lit some leaves and chanted; the cry ululated to a high pitch and then dropped to a guttural chant. Black Bear went into a trance, then finally opened his eyes. "The room is cleared and sealed to forces of the dark. The ancient ones are present to watch over us." The medicine man chanted and placed his palm over Tao's forehead.

Later, Black Bear escorted Tao to the door of the house. "That one will try to reassert itself over you. I have made medicine for you and a bone necklace to wear at night. That's the time of the dark one's power. I sense energy in you from the beings you offered to the dark one. I suggest that you cleanse yourself. It may take weeks. Here are powders to burn while you cleanse yourself. I have done all that I can. The rest is your responsibility. I wish you well on your path."

"Master, how do I cleanse myself?"

"You must lie in a quiet place and clear your mind. Then imagine your feet flowing into the ground like the roots of a tree. Imagine your hands extending out to the sun and stars. Pick a star and attach to it. Imagine the dark energy flowing away through your roots and branches. The earth and sky will receive your offerings, but you must remember to be thankful."

"Thank you, master!" Tao bowed low and held the posture. He smiled with his eyes when he looked at Black Bear. Tao felt lighter than in a long time; he also felt empty.

CHAPTER 65

MARCUS (219 BC)

Before the imperial party would set out, the most auspicious day for departure had to be determined. Since the Roman had never seen a divination, he visited the Diviners' Bureau.

A dwarf greeted the Roman. The headquarters, a white, cubical building roofed in purple tile, sat in the exact center of a circular compound. The precise location had been determined by feng shui, the art of ascertaining lucky building sites. The setting displayed the perfect combination of topographical elements: water, a shallow depression, and a stately cypress grove. Marcus relaxed.

The dwarf, who waddled with dignity, nodded. "Welcome to my cosmic domain. I'm the supervisor of the diviners and am master of the tortoise-shell method." The little man had dressed in a gaudy red robe girthed with a brilliant orange sash. His head seemed fused with his black conical cap.

Marcus smiled. "It's pleasurable to be here. I long to see your techniques. In my homeland, seers read the future by consulting oracles and by examining bird and animal entrails."

The dwarf scrutinized the alien. "Our method—the shell way—reaches back seventy-two generations. The milfoil way's more recent: only forty-two generations. I'm not going to discuss the milfoil today. Perhaps you might speak with those experts later."

They negotiated a maze inside. Marcus saw bloodshot eyes, sinister smiles, jagged teeth, and a host of unfamiliar patterns on the walls. An inward quickening frightened him. A vision of a two-legged monster roared, and the fetid stench of swamp decay clogged Marcus's nostrils. With supreme concentration, Marcus forced the beast away.

Sensing the inward struggle, the dwarf turned to the Roman. "You are powerful. Only two in ten make it." Marcus nodded weakly.

Three men dressed in jade green robes hovered over a giant tortoise shell. The guide addressed his colleagues: "Don't let us interrupt." Turning to Marcus, the dwarf continued. "They are making final checks. The shell has been aged for thirty years to dry it out completely. We locate a suitable spot and scrape off the outer casing until it is as thin as an eggshell. The question is asked and written down on the shell, and a white-hot metal rod is applied. The result is a series of cracks, which I'll interpret."

The dwarf's flamboyant manner disappeared as the process commenced. He donned purple robes bordered in white and embellished in front with a centered yellow spot. Now, he wore a wide-brimmed crimson hat, which fit snugly on his bald head. He carefully washed his hands in a silver-inlaid, red-lacquered bowl, then dried them.

The assistants positioned the shell, over which the high priest bowed. Then, the white-hot rod was given to him. One end had a wooden handle. The metal seared the sere, ultrathin surface. Acrid fumes caused Marcus to sneeze. Meanwhile, the rod was gingerly handed back to the youngest assistant. When the smoke lifted, the diviner peered at the cracks. He retreated to a dark part of the chamber, lighted a taper, and consulted thong-laced strips. Calling for an inked brush, the dwarf expertly wrote strange characters on the shell, prostrated himself, and then marched from the chamber.

When the diviner returned, Marcus asked him about the process.

"I cannot say much. This way reaches into a dim past, and I wander among powerful spirits. Any slip means disaster. That's why we live a simple existence. Divining chooses us. To lead exemplary lives and be truthful is our way. One must be perfectly clear about what one asks a deity."

The first Chin emperor announced that the mou-yin day would be propitious for the departure. He commanded Marcus and Ming to accompany him. Emperor Jeng stunned the court by announcing that the new empress would travel with him. The cortege, which included carriages and carts as well as mounted soldiers, moved leisurely eastward.

The journey went smoothly. Often, the ruler rode on a horse when they were far from cities and towns. At Mount So-yi, the emperor ascended and had a stone monument erected. As the procession moved to the sacred Mount Tai, the empire's most holy spot, scholars—mostly black-hatted followers of Confucius and Mencius—had gathered. Minister Lee met some former classmates.

Seventy scholars prostrated themselves before their sovereign, who commanded them to determine the rites for the imperial sacrifices to heaven and earth. Since the last ceremony had occurred fifteen generations ago, they argued over which ceremony would be best. After a second debate failed, the sovereign dismissed them. Twelve academicians recommended a rite based on that of the four sovereigns at Yung.

Early the next morning, a party rode off. The support wagons carrying tents, food, and other supplies had departed earlier. Soon, the royal party reached a stand of pine trees, where Ming and Marcus detached themselves. After tethering their mounts and finding a peaceful spot under the trees, they sat, closed their eyes, and breathed with the heart of the grotto.

Marcus awoke to sunbeam motes dancing among whispering, needled trees. Liquid sounds smiled in his ears, liquid colors soothed his eyes, and liquid pine scents cleared his nose. Ming's eyes slowly opened, and she smiled at Marcus. He responded with a caressing touch. Fingers silently communicated a powerful desire.

Under a green canopy, caressed skin folds opened like flower petals. The lotus opened to the sun. Tender cries echoed through the grotto.

By the time Marcus and Ming reached the peak of the mountain, the sacrifice had ended. After dinner, some sat on an outcropping to watch the sunset of pastel clouds and sky.

The next morning, Ming emerged from her warm tent into frosty air. Anxious to see the sunrise, she located Marcus's tent and shook it. Marcus scrambled out, and they walked to an overlook. The sky lightened, and pinkish purple hues colored the horizon, giving way to pinkish yellow with a hint of orange. Ming exclaimed, "There! Did you see it? A green flash."

"No, my love. Did you say green?"

"Yes, a pinpoint of light just as the sun's edge appeared."

"That's a favorable omen," Marcus said. The emperor arrived and commanded silence as the earth birthed the sun. A distant river snaked across a plain, flashing sunlight.

The party returned for a simple morning meal. His Majesty, appearing in excellent spirits, led the procession down a narrow trail, hoping to reach bottom before the western thunderheads unleashed their fury. Less than halfway down, the air stilled, and the sky darkened. A fierce gale arose, tossing tree branches. Under a massive, protective oak, the emperor remained dry; when the tempest abated, he rewarded the giant tree:

> All hear this. We wish to thank our leafy servant. For an effort beyond duty's call in granting us shelter and comfort, we proclaim you minister of the fifth rank and command that a bronze plaque commemorating this be erected at your base. Respect this.

At Mount Tai's base, the royal party joined the rest of the procession. Following a noon snack, all moved to Liangfu, a foothill, where the emperor sacrificed a goat and asked for that deity's blessing. The party turned southeast toward the legendary Langya, where the emperor dallied for two months.

CHAPTER 66

MARCUS (219 BC)

Langya's idyllic setting captivated the emperor, but Marcus and Ming had become bored. Early one morning, Marcus left his tent to find the academician grinning at him. Her back faced the morning sun; shadows enveloped her head and eyes.

"Well, my love, what gives you that Pan-like expression?"

"Pan? What is that?" Ming replied. Seagulls chased a kingfisher that had nabbed a fish. The gulls always wanted others to do their hunting.

"He is a nature spirit who loves pranks. What are you about to spring on me?"

Ming turned to the source of the squawking. The fish dropped, and a large hawk watching the chase dove to grab the fish. "I've no tricks, but rather a treat," she answered. "I've learned about a retreat dedicated to Master Lao less than a day's ride into the mountains."

Marcus smiled. "A Daoist retreat? I should like to break this routine. I guess I'll put up with the journey."

She looked at him with mock disgust. "Suffer if you will … or stay here. If you go, eat breakfast. We leave within a water segment."

By dusk, they reached the retreat, which was snuggled in a pine grove. Marcus realized this was his childhood memory place. A miniature waterfall and gurgling brook stirred ancient echoes. The retreat's entrance was a green door that blended with the prevailing pine green. The wood-shingle roof was covered in green moss. Two knocks brought a green-robed man, who greeted them with a toothless grin. They trailed him to the abbot's quarters.

CHAPTER 67

MING TIAN (219 BC)

Before them was an ancient man. An emaciated face stared briefly; then his eyes opened wide. "Where have you been? I've been languishing here for decades. You promised to come long ago. Really, you might have been considerate!"

"Uh, I don't seem to ..." Marcus muttered.

The abbot dismissed the confusion with a sweeping gesture. "Don't apologize. I know your tricks. Probably spent two or three lifetimes dawdling. You left me here, covered with cobwebs. Why'd you save his life? I needed you more than he did!"

Marcus shrugged. "My name is Ma-ku-su, and I come from the western lands. My companion, Sister Ming, studied at the Great Mother Temple and is presently His Majesty's academician."

"Yes, yes, I know about all that ... so serious. We'll fix that. Academician Ming, it's a pleasure to meet you. Your friend and lover, Macu ... or whatever's his name, was a follower of Master Lao. Pu was his temple name. He was my teacher and friend."

"Knowing Marcus, I'm certain he's bewildered. Please forgive his eccentric manner," Ming said as she regarded the wizened man. How small, hunched, and unsteady he looked.

"I'm tiny, but the correct size to do what I have to do. Unsteady I'm not. If you'd like to try some martial attacks?"

Ming cleared her mind.

The abbot continued. "Was the trip pleasant? Will you stay an hour or a lifetime? Our accommodations are spartan. Marcus, explain that to her later. It's in the same category as Pan. You'll sleep separately and have to abstain from lovemaking within these walls. The forest is another matter ... and probably not unlike that grove on Mount Tai. Sorry I peeked, but you were so noisy.

"We serve two meals a day and encourage twice-daily meditations. Other than that, your time's your own. Please send the escort to Anshi. I'll alert them when they're needed. By the way, inform the guide his horse's left hoof needs attention.

If untreated, he'll have a lame animal … and a good-souled one at that." The abbot scratched himself. "Oh, I'm Bo Lo of the Green Dragon Lodge. Marcus, of course, already knows, but probably forgot in some lifetime or other."

As they were leaving, Bo Lo called, "Please see me tomorrow after the dawn meditation."

After the escort left, Ming and Marcus talked. They heard the cry of a large bird—some kind of hawk, or perhaps an eagle. "Bo Lo's strange, yet I have seen him," Marcus said. "Something's been whispering to me since I entered this forest. I heard the water when I reached the courtyard. I've come home, just like Odysseus when he returned to Ithaca after twenty years. I didn't remember Bo Lo."

Ming ignored the mosquito buzzing her earlobe. "Who's Ody?"

"Sorry, I forgot again. He was a legendary Greek traveling warrior. That's unimportant. What do you think of Bo Lo?"

"Reminds me of Mother Lo. It's unnerving to have one's thoughts read. Yet it happens; sometimes I hear yours, my love." Ming smiled. The mosquito drank its fill and flew off; she scratched the bump. "Ease your mind. We're supposed to be here."

"You're correct as usual, Ming. I'll be myself … whoever that is. Should we stay five days?" A sweet, boyish smile spread to his ears.

"Difficult to say, but we can't …" Ming frowned.

"The forest's a possible site. I wish Bo Lo wouldn't spy. I'll speak to him," Marcus said.

"And the horse's hoof," Ming said as she moistened her finger to place saliva atop the bite spot.

CHAPTER 68

MARCUS (219 BC)

That night, Marcus dreamed of a dimly lit hall and came to a huddled man. When the man lifted his head, the skin on his face vanished, revealing a laughing skull. Soon it mutated to his own face … then a woman … a black-faced man with green eyes … a Chinese woman … a white-faced man with black hair and a thin mustache … then another Chinese. At that point, Marcus levitated. The thing reached for him, and he fell.

Marcus shook awake. *What a dream! Where? A starved tiger stalked me as I meditated. My spirit left, but my body remained. Back to the body. Hurry.* He went into a dreamless sleep.

At dawn, a knock signaled meditation. Marcus dressed, found a water vase, and splashed his face. He met Ming, and they walked to the meditation hall. The session began, and Marcus left his body, rushing beyond the moon, sun, and stars to a place blacker than the darkest night. He sped through a tunnel ended by a rainbow. He entered the Green Dragon Lodge, went to his cell, lay down, and died. The lodge members happily surrounded his bed.

After breakfast, Marcus visited Bo Lo.

"Did the dream and meditation clarify?"

"I'm beginning to see, but much confuses me."

"That's to be expected," Bo Lo answered. "We're tied to our present bodies, and past lives seem erased. Then you have that feeling … the one that says you've been in a particular place before."

"I felt that, somehow, I was home … the pines, the brook, the waterfall. All seemed delighted to see me." Waves of energy pulsed through Marcus, beating in time with the universe.

"This retreat was your home. You were my teacher, and now I'll repay the debt. Will you stay until then?"

"When I was a child back in Rome, I saw this place many times. Yes, of course … now I remember! I saw your face; you smiled each time."

A serene, knowing face regarded the Roman. "Yes, I remember. A few times—once, in a brief crisis—you called, and I came. More to reassure that all was well."

"This place is home," Marcus said. "This lodge, the pine forest ... all is friendly. I'd like to come here when I die."

"You evade the question. Will you stay?"

Marcus scratched a louse's bite. "I've many things to do. I love her, and hope to marry her. I've a farm, and ..."

Bo Lo's face darkened, but his eyes twinkled. "But she won't marry ... don't you know that? What if I told you that your life will be filled with tragedy if you leave, but peaceful if you stay?"

Marcus rubbed another bite site. "I will stay with Ming and the emperor, whatever that brings. Someday I'll return."

"Sometimes we choose unconsciously, and sometimes we would not select a way if we knew how difficult it would be," Bo Lo said. "We choose our paths, though we blame others. Even not choosing is a choice. At least you know that the choice is yours alone."

Marcus looked at the wall hanging—a calligraphic representation of the written character "peace."

"Bo Lo, please tell me about myself. Who was I?"

"You came to the Green Dragon Lodge sixty years ago. You were a Chu prince ousted in a court intrigue, and then you wandered the countryside, lamenting your fate and writing poetry that is avidly read today. You left clues that you drowned in a river, then came here. Within ten years, you became a sage, and I was your disciple ... then you transitioned. Before that, you explained things and promised to return." Bo Lo looked young.

"I'm happy we met again—especially if I ... he ... *whomever* promised."

He left Bo Lo's study and sought the soothing waterfall. Later, he found Ming in a flowered courtyard. The sweet jasmine scent intoxicated. She nodded as he touched her fingers and left. This time, he wandered on a needle carpet and sat in a meditative posture. He heard ants marching up and down a nearby tree, and he noted a beetle relentlessly moving a clod of dung. His eyes roamed up into a sea of the richest shades of green. A breeze cleansed the needles. Marcus allowed sounds to transport him through the trees and the wispy, cool, damp clouds. Casting off the chill, he gamboled toward the sun, recalling the exuberance of Daedalus. Marcus blinked like a fish at the bottom of a clear stream. Sounds, sights, and smells were liquid. He stood and somehow walked to the lodge. Fortunately, his feet remembered the way.

Ming and Marcus devoted themselves to their spirits, bodies, feelings, and thoughts. They sat in grottoes, lounged by streams, savored falls of hissing, gurgling sounds. Twice, they loved with fewer than a score of words passing between them. As the departure time neared, the Roman knew he must leave.

On the departure morn, they rested in a special place: at the base of two meshed pines taller than the rest. Neither tree felt stifled; they flowed as one—deeply rooted, proud, and wonderfully ancient. Ming and Marcus sat and began a single yet separate spiritual journey. At Mount Tai, they had witnessed their lovemaking; and after they had parted, a being remained.

Near the horizon, a black dot mushroomed until it enveloped the grotto and the sacred mountain itself. When the dark retreated, the tiny one tugged at him. He tugged back, feeling joyous love. Ming and Marcus awoke, bodies sweat-drenched, a salty tang hanging diaphanously on the edge of knowing. They stretched slowly. Ming arose and walked to each forest giant and stroked a trunk; then she left to finish packing. Marcus went to see the new friend who was also an old friend.

"Saw your futures?"

"Yes."

"Still wish to leave?"

Blackness crushed his spirit. Marcus finally answered. "Yes."

"There are many futures, but that one seems likely."

"I was alone. It's hard to fathom, but I was certainly alone."

"Your lessons will come at proper times. Permit the world to unfold like a rose. Alone, you say ... but forget not the small being."

"Master, how may I be as serene as you?"

Bo Lo's calm mask dissolved. "I appear serene but face my fears. If I had all answers ... let me put it this way: you never get it wrong, and you never get it done. Some ancient friends of mine said that. Besides, who'd spy on you other than your emperor? I enjoy playing the sage. I love giving advice; that's the best way to learn. Trust your feelings ... the inner wrenchings and chills."

"Will we meet again, old friend?"

"Sooner than you imagine, my brother. I may travel to the capital. I trust you wouldn't mind a visit from an ancient fool."

Marcus smiled lopsidedly. "Certainly not. We've much to discuss ... and unsay too. Always welcome you'll be. Of course, you already know that."

Bo Lo grimaced. "Brother, know this: should you feel in the darkest hole, call my name, and I'll arrive."

"Thank you, brother, for the help and probing."

After he left the abbot's room, Marcus found Ming. After the escort arrived, they returned to the imperial encampment. Bo Lo did not see them off.

CHAPTER 69

EMPEROR JENG (219 BC)

The tour wandered south, then west. At each sacred peak, Emperor Jeng sacrificed to the local deity. When they reached the Long River, Emperor Jeng couldn't believe its width.

Courtiers boarded specially constructed ships, with two decks and four masts affording river worthiness. They sailed to Mount Shang to visit a temple. A squall forestalled landing. Soon, another gale blew in. Emperor Jeng assembled his academicians.

"Why am I being opposed?" he asked.

Academician Jo, the former leader of the White Panthers (a special detachment created during the unification wars then disbanded) and now head of the academy, replied, "A goddess is angry. Since she has an unruly temper and a high sense of herself, she is jealous."

The emperor smiled, knowing he must teach women a lesson. An imperial decree spelled out the circumstances:

> Hear this! An evil princess opposes our visit here, because she's jealous of powerful men. She must be punished. Three thousand convicts will cut down her trees, pull down her temple, and paint rock outcroppings red—the color of convicts. Know that we immediately return home. Local officials will send dispatches every ten days to keep us abreast of the punishments. Respect this!

The party retraced its route. Reaching Mount Jurfu, the emperor fell in love with its rugged beauty: the crags, wild waterfalls, and shrouding mists. He commanded Minister Lee to compose a eulogy to be carved on stone:

In the twenty-eighth year in midsummer
His Majesty, the first emperor,
inspected his realm.
He ascended this mount

and saw wondrous beauty.
His subjects followed in his train
and admired his illustrious virtue.
Laws were set down, and principles clarified.
He chastised and taught the rebel states
and spread his light abroad
to illumine the correct path.
His just penalties and true actions
carried his name afar.
All submitted to His Awesome Majesty.
He rescued the black-headed ones
and brought peace to the world's four corners.
The universe obeys his will;
his subjects praise him, asking that
his fame be made known to all by these timeless stones.

Blustery winds and rains announced autumn. The day dawned cold and damp. Gloom locked the caravan in a slimy grip as the travelers snaked through narrow passes on the imperial road. Lumbering vehicles hugged the narrow mountain way.

Rumbling shook the imperial carriage; crashes and screams pierced the shrouding mist, then ended. Emperor Jeng spied broken carriages and gaps where vehicles had been. "Guards!"

After what seemed an eternity, one man rode up.

"Find the Willow Empress!"

The report took one water level to compile. "Seventeen carriages are missing, and their occupants are presumed dead. The senior chancellor is gone. The junior empress ..." The officer turned from the emperor's pain. "We're investigating the cause. If I may give a personal view, Your Highness?"

"Speak your mind!"

"It appears an assassination attempt, sire. I saw logs cut by human hands. More were still atop that cliff and ready to be rolled off. There may be another attempt on you, sire."

"Inform Commander Lu that we'll depart at once."

"He is missing, my lord."

"Then you're the acting commander. Your name?"

"Han, sire. Han Lin." He stood up slightly in his stirrups.

"Commander Han, order people to their vehicles. We'll move immediately!"

After three harried water levels, they reached the Lu encampment. Minister Lee and his son had escaped unharmed. Three academicians had died, but Ming and Marcus reached the fortress.

The Willow Empress had perished. Twenty-seven other bodies had been recovered. It was decided to bury all, save the empress, in a single grave. Her broken body, wrapped in a golden shroud, would be rushed to the capital.

Commander Han came and reported. "We have learned that the landslide was begun by assassins. Boulders and logs, placed atop the ridge, were pushed as the caravan passed through that section of the gorge. We don't know who planned this evil deed, but we're scouring the countryside."

"Well done. You saved our life. Find the evil ones, and we'll make them regret the day they were born." When the commander left, all save Marcus and Ming were dismissed. Emperor Jeng collapsed on his bed. "Three times ... and now the Willow Empress. Why? Why?"

The next morning, the emperor summoned a cavalry detachment. He joined it, and within six days of hard riding, he reached the capital, where he donned mourning robes. Two weeks later, the caravan arrived. Han Lin was promoted to head of the guards and received ten thousand gold pieces. The senior chancellor's post, along with several others, needed to be filled.

CHAPTER 70
TAO (219 BC)

Crisp autumn weather invigorated Tao. He savored the musty scents mixed with the acrid odor of burning leaves and logs. The morning fog lifted, and a slight chill underlaid the sunny day, portending colder days.

The master thief walked with Tao. (The young man had been the night master for months, but the title "master thief" fit better.) The thief wore black in the broad daylight.

"Why do you wear black all the time?"

There was a hesitation. "The night is my element," said Jin Mi. "I am comfortable with the black sun, the dark moon; stars soothe my soul. I cherish the world of shadow, the world of possibilities. This sun's too bright; my eyes seek the dark. I am a creature of the dark time." He frowned as he spoke. He clearly knew of Tao's formidable powers and did not choose to match the crime lord.

"I too enjoy the night, though both day and night have their individual treasures. I relish the dawn and twilight times, when the multiworlds mesh; I also enjoy shadow times, when spirits walk and trees are backlighted. If I were an artist, my drawings would be of those times."

"And yet, we are walking when the sun's high," Jin Mi remarked with a twinkle in his eye.

Tao chortled, because he delighted in being with another sage—another adventurer—to match wits, to weave words, and to taste them with the mind and the tongue. "I wish to learn more of you, Jin Mi. Should I call you master thief or night master?"

"Call me as you will, master. I feel uncomfortable in this day's glare; too much energy of the yang. I am a yin creature. What do you wish to know?" Tao knew Jin Mi had been surprised by the promotion and verbal appreciation of his skills. Tao also knew he and Jin Mi trod kindred paths for the time being.

"I seek to know you not because I distrust you, but rather because I admire you. Because of what happened to your predecessor, my motives must seem nefarious ... and yet I spread my hands and arms before you. Truly I bow my head before you. I seek company—perhaps companionship—not your death or weakening. Harken to my words, and my deeds over the months will bear them true."

Jin Mi slightly bowed his head and stepped into the abyss. "Please call me Jin Mi; it's not my birth name, but it's my name. My mother was a whore, and my father is but a dream … perhaps a nightmare. Mother claimed that he was some high official, but she had so many clients, how could she know? I grew up on the streets … but also in the house with tender whores who read to me, fed me well, and showered me with gifts. Yes, master, I come from the yin world—from the world of moon cycles and the dark. I learned to read while young and have continued my passion for books and ideas and words. Sometimes I steal rare editions rather than jewels."

Tao nodded. "I love books; to converse with the ancients is pleasurable, especially after a day with sums and reports. I share your passion. Being raised by Old Juang, my world was yang. I have vague memories of my mother. One of my favorite ancients is Master Mo. His writings are tedious and his arguments clumsy, but I like his idea of universal love and his passionate concern for people's welfare. And, like him, I believe in ghosts."

Jin Mi opened his eyes. "Ah, Master Mo. Would that he were running things instead of our emperor, a little boy who plays with armies as if they are toys. Does he not imagine all those who die, all those who are bereft, all those who weep? Defensive war as Master Mo would have it. War is too ravening to leave to rulers. I spit on their glory!"

Tao smiled, savoring the fruitful connection—especially enjoyable after breaking from that other master of the dark. The sun dipped behind a cloud, and Tao pulled his light brown cloak around his shoulders.

CHAPTER 71

MING TIAN (219 BC)

As the wintry day dawned, a dust-laden wind howled out of the west. Ming's troubled sleep produced a sweat bath that matted her hair, leaving one unruly clump sticking straight out. A heartrending sigh suffused her quarters. Her waist had expanded in this, the fifth month since her period had failed to arrive.

At midmorning, the lanky academician shyly entered Hu's office. A potted palm languished beside the desk over which Ming's colleague worried at two bamboo strips. Hu's silver hair flashed in the lamplight. The taper holder wasn't a phoenix; rather, it replicated the giant black and white bear found in the Shu and Ba commanderies. The friendly looking animal gripped a candle in each upraised paw. Ming smiled.

Hu's tresses were barely held in place by clasps shaped like shaman staffs. She peered up from her work and smiled. "Academician Ming, you've returned … and I've come back from a visit in the south. How are you?"

"The assassination attempt stunned us. The survivors are fortunate," Ming replied, grateful for the warm greeting.

The older woman looked serious. "It must have been terrible. This is the second attempt you've survived. Someone mentioned that you were instrumental in getting me appointed to the academy."

Ming smiled wanly. "I wanted more women in service."

"Too bad the junior empress died. His Majesty's sorely grieved, I hear," Hu noted absently.

The conversation sapped Ming. "He doted on her," Ming said.

Hu's mouth tightened. "Peace can be grim. If only the attempts would cease, because they strengthen the military."

Ming nodded sympathetically. "What are you reading?"

"Something by Mencius, who prates about women obeying their fathers, husbands, and sons. He uses words like 'duty,' 'obedience,' and 'propriety' to bind us. In my homeland, women own property. Property is vital to one's independence." Hu got up and paced. Her light brown rug was decorated with an unfamiliar pattern. "I'm glad that I never married," Hu added as one hair clasp fell to the floor.

"I won't be chained!" Ming interjected, then sighed.

"Ming, I've been researching ancient texts passed from mother to daughter, speaking of a time when children knew only their mothers," Hu spoke quietly.

Ming's pupils dilated. "If people didn't know their fathers, then it must have been believed that women were sole life-givers."

Hu's silver tresses tumbled down. "The man who learned of the male role in producing a baby ..."

"... must have given his mates invaluable knowledge for their subjugation of women." Ming finished Hu's thought. "But how could they defeat us?" she asked as something moved within her.

Hu's chin jutted out. "One text mentions metallurgy and weapons."

The younger woman nodded as she lifted an incense vase. Incense reminded Ming of the times when her father dressed in ceremonial robes and bowed reverently to the ancestral tablets. "Of course. They forged weapons and mastered us." Ming emphatically jabbed the text with a finger. She loved the passion of discussion—and the sometimes fiery nature of a debate.

"Precisely. Swords and spears targeted us first," Hu added. "Writers like Mencius seek to complete the subjugation by forging mental bindings more powerful than those of iron or bronze." Academician Hu hurled the work against the wall. The passionate action seemed to both startle and soothe her. "If one can dictate the meaning of words and the scope of an argument, they win; weapons are not needed. My book said that marriage was invented to limit women. If men fought away from home, they needed to ensure that they alone had impregnated their women." Hu, lost in thought, muttered the last few words.

Ming grew somber. "Then mother and child became his property. In fact, if the child—if a male child—was desired, the wife only served to relieve the sexual urge and breed the children. I'll not be another's property!" Ming shouted. "I decided to remain single because of my position. Our words resolve me not to be bound to him."

"The barbarian? I thought you and he ..."

A frown creased the expectant mother's forehead. "He's not a barbarian. In fact, he's the most cultured, gentle man I have met. If I did marry, he would be the one."

Hu smiled wistfully.

"Sometimes I love him so much that I can't do a thing. It's good I came, sister. I'm confused, because I'm pregnant ..."

"You're too pale. Come. Sit here."

Ming sobbed. "I ... I don't know what to do. I can't—won't—marry him, and I must keep this position."

"What about the fetus?"

"I could have it cut out, but I want to birth it." Ming broke down again; she hated losing control. "Oh, Hu. I just don't know what to do ... I feel trapped."

Hu calmed herself. "What would happen if you carried it to birthing? Would you stay here or have it elsewhere?"

Ming's breath came in short gasps. "I can't give it up."

Hu enfolded Ming. "Where would you go?"

"Home? It would be natural for me to be with my mother ... but an unwed, pregnant daughter would give our town enough gossip fodder to last long. I must go to the Great Mother Temple."

"What would you do with the child?" Hu queried gently.

Ming straightened. The black and white bear smiled. "I could leave it there. I'm certain it would be treated well ... but I don't know if I could abandon it like that."

"You could bring it here."

"No. There wouldn't be time to mother it, and that wouldn't be good for my baby ... or me." Ming sighed. "I must see this through. I'm due a leave, and I can say Mama's ill. Surely the emperor would permit me to go home and tend her."

"You'll be gone for months—perhaps a year."

"I'll be back by autumn. How hard it will be, sister! Well, I must prepare a petition of leave." Guilt overcame Ming, and she felt a rush of nausea. She despised lies, yet would have to spin a web of them.

She drafted the petition and three days later received an imperial summons. Apprehensively, she dressed in a formal black robe and the wide, black cloth scholar's cap. Ming's credentials had suffered minute inspection. Each section had its own seal. All served as passports. Most types of people had something in common with a species of animal; academicians often resembled tortoises. Some said that academicians were slow, stubborn, and long-lived.

Escorts accompanied her to the audience hall, where Emperor Jeng conferred with an aide. "Academician Ming, come and be recognized. It's not necessary to crawl and bang your beautiful head. We've learned that you've requested a leave ... something about tending a sick parent. We can't permit this."

The center of her heart felt like a deep, black hole. "Your Majesty, my mother is ill and may die, sire."

Jeng's eyes sparkled. "I cannot let you both leave me."

"He will not accompany me and does not yet know."

"He does not know? Was it wise for you to tell your sovereign first? What would he think? Why haven't you married?"

Ming flushed. "I ... we ..."

"Never mind. You have not yet married. It's unusual; being single means that another might steal you away." Emperor Jeng leered. "Very well. We permit your leave on condition that you return to us immediately once your mother recovers. Your sovereign should not be too long alone."

Ming lowered her head. "May you have a long, long life."

"We appreciate your thoughtful words and sentiment. You saved our life, something we'll not forget. You please us much." Ming backed out. Now, she had to tell another lie to Marcus.

The Roman was out. There were the writing brushes she gave at New Year's and the black stone she found on the seashore ... treasure and memories of wonder-filled times. She dashed off a poem.

Empty, your room
Empty, my heart
The winter bird, forlorn
Softly I call thy name.

She left a note asking that he come to her. She'd decided they would spend time at his farm. In the afternoon, Ming returned and found light yellow chrysanthemums in a terra-cotta vase atop her desk. A poem lay beside it.

Hands with beautiful stems
Entered your silent abode
Mums endure the wintry blasts
I survive your absence, alone.

The lovers agreed to leave for the farm. She told him on their second day there about her journey and refused his offer to accompany her. Ming planned to leave alone, but nearly yielded to his suasion. On the departure day, they clung desperately to one another. Marcus watched until wetted eyes and poor eyesight blotted her out. Cold rain forced him home.

CHAPTER 72

TAO (218 BC)

Fat snowflakes swirled, gently blanketing the city. Tao tasted them: cold, yet deliciously soft. He retracted his tongue and looked around. No one saw. In fact, he could hear or see nothing.

Tao lifted the collar of his fur coat and trudged onward. He must keep mindful, or it would be easy to lose his way. Thoughts of the dark lord snared him.

Tao had been faithful to himself, but the power and the knowledge called. He shrugged as he recalled his nightmares and the dark lord's smothering hold. At the time, the crime lord had craved raw meat with blood dripping from it and the energy still radiating. Fresh kills were best—large animals or humans. His dreams had been filled with ravenous beasts devouring him, sucking out his brains and bone marrow.

The snowfall swirled, covering his hair and coat. The cold penetrated his boots. His toes grew numb.

Tao read minds, knew people's innermost thoughts and secrets, knew the future, heard voices whispering knowledge, held secrets of power and immortality. Moisture collected on the head of his penis. Tao's hand fumbled at his trousers; then he jerked it away, cursing his weakness. Perhaps once more with the dark lord … to have the release and then sever the connection. Black Bear had warned that going back meant strengthening the dark lord's hold. Tao recalled looking in the mirror just before the exorcism. His face had been emaciated, his eyes hollow; normal food had been tasteless. He'd not follow that path again.

CHAPTER 73

EMPEROR JENG (218 BC)

On a bright winter morning just after a dusting of snow had brightened the capital, Emperor Jeng summoned his two favorite sons, Fu Su and Hu Hai.

Fu Su, the eldest, arrived first. Dressed in a formal black robe with a blue snake crested on it, he seemed ill at ease.

"Fu Su, you've grown tall. Soon, if I remember, you'll be twenty-one years old. Someday, you'll sit on the Dragon Throne," the emperor said. The solitary official in the informal chamber room gasped. No crown prince had been selected, despite memos from ministers and dignitaries pleading for a designation.

"I ... uh ..."

The emperor laughed at his son's discomfort. The bewilderment assured him that the lad had not yet planned to rise to the top. "Never mind. How are your studies?"

"I completed Han Fei's brilliant writings. Did he die here?"

The memory brought an imperial facial tic. "Yes, as a part of a power struggle against the minister of the law. Han Fei was a piece on a larger strategy board. His death was a great loss."

The prince's face brightened. "I train with General Tian. I shoot the crossbow, handle the battle-ax and the heavy sword. Sire, may I accompany a hunt? General Tian said it would give strategic perspective. Although at peace, we should be prepared."

The emperor was pleased. "Yes, my son. Peace must never dull the skills. General Tian comes from an illustrious family. Heed his words."

The prince blurted out, "Sire ... Father? May I be so bold as to ask whether you have selected a senior minister? I asked General Tian, who refused to speak until I commanded him. He said that General Wang Ben would be an excellent choice. Was I wrong to ask?"

Fu Su desperately needed facial hair to produce a full mustache, unlike the scraggly one sprouting under his long nose.

"No. In fact, I'm pleased by your initiative. You were astute to sound out the general. What he said is correct."

A short time later, Hu Hai, a pimply youth, sauntered in. He respectfully waited for his father to speak. Jeng gaped at a boy who'd grown a full hand since last they'd met. Like his elder brother, Hu Hai walked with dignity.

"And how are you, little one? I can no longer say that, because you've grown so in the last months." The emperor smiled.

Hu Hai regarded his father. "I'm fine, sire. This last year, I've worked extra hard. Please ask the imperial tutor about my progress with the writings of Lord Shang. Yesterday, I truly felt the rhythmic power of his words as they hammered into my poor head."

The precocious understanding of Hu Hai delighted father and teachers; that was why the imperial tutor had already begun his education. Perhaps one day Hu Hai might become an academician—a signal honor. The boy's feet, unusually large for someone so average in stature, always seemed in motion.

"Excellent," the emperor responded. "Before long, you should begin with the texts of Han Fei, one of the great minds. By the way, how's your mama?"

Hu Hai frowned. "She's unwell ... eats like a mouse. I believe she misses you, Papa. She won't admit it. Will you see her, please? I worry."

"The exorcism ceremony's in two days; after that, the three of us can enjoy a nice dinner. What do you say?" the emperor asked.

"Yes! Yes! Yes!" Hu Hai exclaimed and twirled. Even the first emperor laughed aloud. "Just we three ... wonderful! Mama will be thrilled." The boy crowed at the ceiling mural, then rushed into his father's arms. A look of horror overcame him as he realized the breach of protocol. "Forgive me, Your Majesty. Didn't mean ..."

"There's nothing to forgive, my little monkey. When we're alone, you need not feel constrained. Look at the aide's face. Shock, wouldn't you agree? Hahaha-hahahaha!" Mirth bubbled up as they pointed and howled at the obvious discomfiture of the staid, old man across the room.

"Yes, sire!" Hu Hai prostrated himself and bounded from the chamber. The emperor's body felt warm where the boy's hands had touched him. Who would be the new senior chancellor? Minister Lee seemed the logical choice, but General Tian's observation was sound. *Yes*, he decided. *Wang Ben, my old warhorse, it is.*

Gloomy thoughts forced Emperor Jeng back to the silver throne. *Easier to sit there for hours than on that blasted sandalwood seat in the Great Hall. Custom! I am a slave to it.* The fierce itching in his bowels grew unbearable after long, formal audiences there.

CHAPTER 74

MARCUS (218 BC)

The Roman was struggling with writing the complex character for "tortoise" when an imperial messenger announced that Emperor Jeng wished to visit the farm. After the man departed, Marcus bolted from the palace and raced to the Western Market to order peacock breasts and catfish steaks. Then he rushed to the Heavenly Wine Shop, which stocked the best plum vintages. The frenzied pace banished the bottomless bog swallowing him.

Upon arrival at his manor, Marcus ordered a quick cleaning. Narcissi stood proudly in the chipped pink and green terra-cotta vase given him by the emperor. Imperial guards soon ringed the estate.

Within a water level, Emperor Jeng arrived. "Greetings, my friend. Now you too are alone. Tonight, we'll jointly mourn our losses." A hawk cried out nearby.

"I'm truly sorry about the loss of the Willow Empress."

"And Academician Ming grows more lovely. Marcus. I warn you, marry." A sardonic laugh brought bumps to the Roman's arms. "Come now, it's only a jest. Learn to enjoy a laugh. I just saw little Hu Hai ... actually, not so little anymore. His impish ways delight me. Since your lady's gone for a while, I'll visit often."

"I miss her already, sire. I didn't realize how much I depended on her 'til yesterday ... and today, of course."

They scoffed at the chill and trod the road to the stream. A majestic elm thrust heavenward. The day was darkened by massive clouds that hurled winds, but no rain. With a fox coat and down-padded leggings, the ruler could endure extreme cold. Marcus wore a padded jacket dyed black to absorb the sun's rays.

"As I said, Hu Hai came to see me; so did Fu Su. Both are good boys, and I plan to spend more time with them."

"Yes, sire, children need the firm hand of the father. Alas, my eldest son is over twenty years, and I haven't seen him."

The monarch smiled. "Sons are treasures, daughters nuisances. Before they're married, girls must be watched. That daughter of mine who married Minister Lee's third son ... you know ..."

"Bu, sire."

"Bu. Now, her husband ... there's a strange man. Kept leading her on. How could anyone not want a princess? Now they seem happy with my grandson."

The Roman hadn't paid a call on his old friend since he'd returned. He wondered how the marriage worked.

"Will you select another junior empress, sire?"

"None could fill her place, my friend. She was rare, with the most delicious thighs and a wicked tongue." They turned for home.

"Ming's ticklish, especially her feet." Marcus immediately regretted talking about Ming, quickly changing the subject. "Will you name a crown prince?"

Emperor Jeng's brow knitted. "No! Doing that implies that I expect to die. If the magicians find the elixirs ..."

Marcus persisted. "No one lives for an eternity, Your Highness. Wouldn't it be better to name a successor?"

"Fu Su's too young."

"He's twenty-one, if I recall. You were capped and girded at that age, sire."

Emperor Jeng scowled. His eyelid shook, and his teeth clenched. "Have you spoken to anyone about this? The old farts are pressing me. Perhaps I'll not name anyone. Let them fight after my death. Are you in league with them?"

"I have talked with no one. You should know that I would never be a vehicle for others. I merely thought ..."

"Enough! You've been outstanding in service to me, but no more of this!" Jeng's finger nearly poked Marcus's eye.

They reached the mulberry grove; trees denuded of their foliage stood huddled, awaiting the siren call of spring. Outside the farmhouse, the emperor admired the freshly painted walls and asked about the particular kind of whitewash used, as it gave a better result than that used at the palace. Finally, they burst through the crimson door, fleeing the icy wind. Marcus preferred a brilliant red on the portal to give him a warm, happy feeling; it helped him endure the frigid winter months.

After many cups of heated, scented liquor, the tension evaporated. They ate dinner and drank even more. Around the following midday, the emperor roused Marcus, who felt as if he would die. Later, Marcus began to hope that he would die. Relief from the foul taste and the pounding behind his eyes was his top priority.

CHAPTER 75
LEE SU (218 BC)

As Minister Lee finished office tasks, his son Bu burst into the office. "Father! Father! Have you heard?" Bu asked.

"What, Bu? Please remember to be dignified."

"Father, Wang Ben is to be the new senior chancellor."

Lee Su dropped the bamboo strips and jumped up. "Wang Ben! Chancellor! How can that addled old bastard be made the most senior official? He's a general!" Lee's jaw froze like the taut cheek on the bronze warrior in the market.

"It's true, Papa. I checked carefully. The imperial seal's on the announcement. The general is to be sworn in in two days."

"That military bunch must have gained his ear. Why are we tied to whims of a mercurial monarch?" Shock swept over the elder man at what he had just uttered. "Close the door, so none will hear my foolish ramblings."

Bu closed off the sole access to their conversation.

"That military claque should be purged before they really cause harm," Lee said. "Soldier boys playing at government. How can he have permitted such stupidity, just because the Willow Lady perished? Has he completely lost his sanity?"

Bu flushed. "What about you, Papa?"

A dismissive wave attempted to bring calm. "Me? I'll be fine, my son. If this is His Majesty's will, so be it. There's work to be completed. Thank you for this news. Better to have come from you than a rival. Now I must get back to work. Deadlines, you know ... even if they're my own. Remember, not a word of my sentiments to anyone else—especially to your wife."

Bu nodded and left. Minister Lee felt betrayed. He'd been thrown a life rope as he fought against the overwhelming river current, and suddenly it had been pulled away. He scratched his bearded cheek.

From that moment, Minister Lee planned a campaign to gain the top post. Lee decided the ruler's pining for the Willow Lady presented an opportunity. His intelligence agents fanned out in search of a new consort.

After two months, Beauty Hai was located. Thin and fair, she had wavy hair that reached to the ground, and she radiated a dynamic effervescence. A southern beauty like the Willow Empress, she spoke with a slight accent that highlighted her charms. Beauty Hai was brought before a delighted sovereign, who rewarded Minister Lee with a noble rank and a doubled income.

Along with the search for a royal plaything, the justice minister submitted a memorandum outlining a program to reduce the number of women in government. Only men were to fill vacancies, and women were to be retired with generous benefits. Soon, their total numbers shrank by one third. Minister Lee recommended that unmarried females be taxed at four times the rate of other adults. Five female officials who protested this order were dismissed.

Helping the black-headed ones became the cornerstone of Lee's effort. He proposed opening some imperial lands to private ownership. Farmers could stake out their claims.

The final jewel in the program was a general tax refund. Because of bountiful harvests, the emperor would refund each village fifteen bushels of grain and two animals, such as sheep or pigs, in the early winter. Most villages used the bonuses to celebrate imperial generosity, and peasant delegations streamed to the capital to wish Emperor Jeng a long life.

In former times, Minister Lee would not have claimed credit, but now the Ministry of Law tracked the achievements. Jokes surfaced about the next day's great feat, but Lee Su didn't mind—as long as he received the next promotion.

CHAPTER 76

MING TIAN (218 BC)

The last weeks had been a torment of swollen legs, distended belly, and the constant need to pee. Ming Tian refused to look at herself in a mirror. She also missed Marcus, whose stillness calmed her nervousness. *Marcus, our baby is about to arrive; will you hate me for hiding all this?* Ming looked around the spotless room, where the few pieces of furniture had been cleared away for the birthing. She inhaled the scent of the cleaning agent and gagged. Why had she decided to carry her baby to term?

The contractions grew closer and more intense. Mother Lo had summoned the midwife, who hovered nearby, saying, "Breathe deeply, child ... ever more deeply ... good, good. Breathe through the pain. Welcome it as a deliverance from your travail. Now pant." Ming's water broke.

"Oooh, Mother! Why did I leave him? He doesn't suspect a thing. Why, Mother? The pain, Mother, the pain ..."

Mother Lo grasped Ming's sweaty palm and dabbed her forehead with the damp cloth in her other hand. It would be a difficult delivery. That she knew from the midwife's face and Ming's gasps.

"Mother!" Ming screamed. "When will it stop! Please make it stop!" She felt her insides tearing, shredding, rending in a never-ceasing flood of searing pain.

"Breathe deeply ... ever more deeply. Good, good. Now pant like a dog. Keep that image before you, child. You can do this. I must push on your belly, my dear. I need to turn the little one, so that she can come out headfirst. Breathe deeply ... ever more deeply. You can do it. I have not lost a baby, and I don't plan to now. Pant like a dog, little one. See, I have begun to turn your little one. See, it's working. She'll arrive in her own time. Breathe, little one, ever more deeply ..."

The room began to spin until Ming rhythmically inhaled, then exhaled. Gradually the room calmed down, centering itself.

"Mother, Mother, MOTHER!"

Later, she heard the squall through her pain-seared fog, and the bloody little one was held up for Ming to see. Ming could smell the cloying aroma of birthing. "Mother, Mother ... she's so tiny, so beautiful, so pure ..."

After a day, Ming sobbed into Mother Lo's shoulder. Her baby wouldn't nurse; Ming felt a failure. She couldn't even feed her own daughter. *Failure, failure, failure.* Mother Lo held Ming firmly and waited.

Weeks later, on an early summer day, Ming toted her daughter in a bag looped around her neck, with the baby's tiny legs dangling below. Heart to heart, they made their way to a rocky tor overlooking the vast plain beneath. Ming sat and smiled at her little one, listening to the hawks' keening cries. "I cannot leave you here, beloved, and I cannot take you there either. What must I do? I've already failed you in nursing. Will I fail you in not being here to see you walk, to watch you run, to behold your explorations, to hear your first words? How can I leave you behind? What kind of mother am I? Perhaps I should leap from this stone and fly to a distant land, where we could be just ourselves, away from life's relentless snares. I'll stay, beloved, and let other women carry the flame. Let others mark the trail."

The tot looked up at her and seemed to smile. Ming sniffed the light brown hair and nuzzled against her daughter's cheek. The sweetness of the wet nurse's milk filled her nose.

Later, amid a summer torrent, Ming carefully picked her way down the mountain. More than once, she slipped, but righted herself. Head downcast, she sobbed and sobbed, wondering if she had done the right thing to leave her daughter on Mount Hua. The simple farming couple had been delighted to take the infant. Mother Lo had recommended them to Ming. *Failure ... always a failure.* Ming deliberately placed one foot in front of the other, hiking downward in the rainy stillness of the forest. She was going home ... or was she?

CHAPTER 77

MARCUS (218 BC)

The Roman attended the great exorcism ceremony at the Ganchuan Palace. As he entered the gaping audience hall, Marcus spied Academician Hu, who wore a glossy, black robe; her silver tresses elegantly set off its red trim. As she smiled, he noticed a small mole on her cheek. Its color duplicated the color of her robe and also proudly displayed two facial hairs, "You look especially beautiful, Academician Hu. The robe highlights your flawless complexion."

Hu beamed. "Thank you, Ma-ku-su. You too look handsome. The silver of your robe crest matches the silver of my hair."

"What is that creature on your robe? Is it the phoenix? Sometimes I have difficulty distinguishing it from the other birds." Marcus squinted.

"Yes. This bird's especially lucky for me, as it cried out when I was birthed. Judging from the candleholders in the palaces, it's a special bird for His Majesty too," Hu added.

"During our sovereign's youth," Marcus said, "illnesses wasted him and caused some to plot against him. By about the age of twenty-one, when I first met him, he'd recovered completely from his childhood afflictions. Emperor Jeng uses the phoenix as his totem."

Hu's eyes widened as the Roman casually discussed the emperor's life. "What brings you to this ceremony?" she asked.

"His Majesty learned that I hadn't seen one like this in over thirty years. I'm curious to see it," answered Marcus.

"His Majesty personally invited you?"

"When he visited my farm a few days ago, we compared Chinese and Roman customs. That's when I mentioned the exorcism rites. Later, I received the invitation," Marcus added.

Hu gaped. At that moment, drums announced the emperor and main empress. Dressed in black, they were trailed by princes and princesses. Marcus squinted and sighed. One princess wore her hair in a style favored by Ming. Spectators roared, "Long life!" Drummers picked up a beat, and within moments, the great hall vibrated triumphantly.

The master of ceremonies—a dignified man with a long, white beard—came in, trailed by a fantastically attired group. At the head was a black bear with four large eyes: two in front and two in back. The bearman carried a shield and spear.

Hu whispered that this was the exorcist. When the party reached the imperial platform, the bear began thrusting its spear in all directions. The four eyes were to watch out for demons, while the dance and thrustings scared them off. The drum sounds also scared away the demons and diseases. At the next pause, Hu added that the ceremony came in the winter, because evil forces drew their strength from the yin force.

"That's how Chinese men control women," Marcus noted. "They cause them to think that females are responsible for bad things. Male control is in the very air we breathe … not to say in the thoughts we think."

Hu's mouth gaped as if she were a waterless fish. She recovered. "Men have learned how to control our minds and bodies."

"Indeed. Sometimes, Academician Hu, I get depressed and wonder if they'll ever change." Eight fierce-looking creatures raced into the hall, chasing twelve monsters. Mock battles broke out all over, and to the audience's delight, the eight vanquished the twelve. Hu said that the eight had names like Virile One, Trusty Lad, and Male Elder. They smashed The Baneful One, The Nightmare Critter, The Drought Demon, The Fever Spirit, and The Flying Corpse.

The eight dragged out the evil ones to be buried in a huge pit. Hu shivered. "Certainly, Marcus, we would never be so barbaric to bury alive creatures or humans."

After the ceremony, Marcus escorted Academician Hu to her quarters, where they chatted pleasantly. When he reached his own quarters, he found Bo Lo, who said, "It's about time you returned. Why go see old men jumping around? A primitive display."

"How do you know, and just what are you doing here?" Marcus asked his friend from many lives.

Two unblinking blue eyes bore in. "I'm here for many reasons—not the least of which is keep you company while Sister Ming solves her family matters. I travel in my own fashion, young man: quickly, conveniently, and more safely than your ill-fated monarch. Too bad about his favorite, although she'll be happier across the eastern water expanse."

Words, questions, ideas—all sorts of things dawned on Marcus. A vigorous headshake quieted his chattering brain. "How long have women been tied to men?" Marcus asked.

"In China, for thousands of years. Once, females gained influence because of their association with birthing and creation. Some say it was a time of harmony, though others have asserted that all eras have shortcomings. Our own peace is a pause between two terrible wars ... and already people plan for a northern conflagration. Peace begins in the heart; that's the difficult terrain to conquer."

Marcus could see that his teacher had become troubled. Once again, the broken young Gallic woman floated in Marcus's inner vision.

"Is the answer for women to rule?" Marcus asked.

"Too late. Besides, successful women often must become like men to prevail. Bloodlust is human—not a sex thing," Bo Lo said.

"Will women be better off under His Majesty?"

Bo Lo's twinkle faded. "Depends on what you mean by better off. Plans are being formulated to chase them from government and to force them into marriage. Many get security from marriage."

The dusty sky began to boil. Dust arms swept over the city. "There's security in bondage," Bo Lo mused. "Meals, housing, clothes ... all are supplied. Most prefer bondage to solitude. We fear ourselves. Yet, marriage helps powerful ones who are needed and wanted. Sometimes the weak control the strong. Life's a morass, yet is also an absolutely beautiful spider's web. It's a bird's song. We choose lives, futures, pasts. Listen, hear, find your own path. Better yet, let your path rise to meet you."

Marcus gently touched the wizard's back. "Stay, friend. Your riddles refresh me like a bath in a mountain stream."

"Until Ming comes back, or you tire of me," Bo Lo assented. "I have no special truth. Yours is within."

They shared times, minds, spaces. One crisp day, when the maples and other trees had donned their autumn hats and robes, Bo Lo said good-bye: "The lodge calls. Remember, if you need me, call. Go deep within, and call."

"Thank you, my brother. When will I go home?"

"Two will come, one overfilled with great sadness."

Other questions formed, but disappeared before the outstretched, gentle hand of the wizard, who said, "No more now. Until we see each other again."

They stood on the dusty road that passed the farm. Bo Lo lifted his bag and began walking. Willows lined the road, their limbs swaying and twisting in the breeze. Leaves blew everywhere. Marcus sneezed and turned home, but stopped when he remembered the horse. He'd give it to the old man for his long journey. Turning back, he saw that the green-clad traveler had vanished.

CHAPTER 78
TAO (218 BC)

Autumn's chill brought bare trees in blacks and browns, and gray skies. A cold rain doused Tao's uncovered hair and blighted his spirit. He looked at Jin Mi, who seemed braced by the cold, damp weather. They were returning from an inspection trip to check on one of the houses.

"Miserable day," Tao commented.

"And yet, I love the changing patterns and the rising cold. Duty calls, and we answer. At least, you did … why drag me out into this wondrous weather?" Jin Mi looked at Tao's face; it was clear, without the black rings about the eyes. More than a year ago, Tao had born a much stronger resemblance to a raccoon.

Tao smiled in reply. "It's such a pleasure to look on your sour face. No, really, I love your stimulating conversation. You've said perhaps four sentences in the last water mark."

A solitary oak leaf was detached by a gust. Tao watched it plummet to the earth—not the usual floating-in-the-breeze sight. Tao's spirits sank. The air blurred, and he felt a malevolence all around him.

"Yiiiie ahhhh!" The air opened, and a slender being attacked Tao, who felt an icy blade slice through his little finger and bite into his hand, which had been thrown up defensively. The assassin wore a white mask; the eyes behind it bored into Tao.

"Yiiiie ahhhhh!" The figure pirouetted, and the blade screamed for his throat. Tao threw up his good hand to block the killing thrust, knowing he was too late. All of a sudden, the blade fell from the assassin's grip, and the figure flew to the side. The master thief tackled the assailant. He had drawn a thin but deadly blade and clutched the dark figure's clothing. As the assassin struggled, Tao closed in. Having lost the advantage, the slender figure twisted away and fled, with Jin Mi on its heels.

"Stop!" Tao shouted at the master thief. "Let him go." Jin Mi slid and almost lost his footing on the wet leaves, then gingerly pivoted. Tao removed a rag from his sleeve and wrapped his bloody hand. He nodded at Jin Mi, who had returned to his side. "Please retrieve my finger. I'll want it as a souvenir," he said as he felt a distancing settling in—an otherworldliness. Let's leave before there's another attack."

As Jin Mi located the finger, he asked, "What was that?"

"I don't know. I saw a shimmering in the air and felt an evil presence. Then it appeared and tried to kill me. Thank you for your aid. I would have died if you hadn't reacted so quickly."

Jin Mi shrugged. "I was surprised to see him just appear out of the air. How can someone do that?"

"Some have a power which allows this kind of coming and going. By the way, it felt like a she rather than a he. It also felt as if she were toying with us. Let's go to my place, but not in a direct way. Following a straight path may have been what left us vulnerable. Who would want me killed?" Tao asked.

Both men strode rapidly away.

CHAPTER 79

MARCUS (217 BC)

The Roman returned to the capital. Back in his study, he spied the familiar shape. Ming! He ran and swept her up. After a joyous twirling, he held her away for scrutiny.

"Thin! Have you been ill? How's your mother? You look so sad, Ming ... yet you also give me strength. I'm alive again!"

Marcus laughed, and Ming smiled. "And I too, Marcus, my love. It gives strength seeing you. Just hold me for now, my love. Please hold me." Ming snuggled into him and breathed softly. Marcus beamed happily, though he was concerned about her physical appearance.

CHAPTER 80

FENG PING (217 BC)

Feng Ping was radiant. Cotton-ball clouds lazed in the sea blue sky as a gentle breeze caressed his cheeks. Soon, it tousled his sparse hair tufts and mussed his heavy, black beard.

Feng Ping smiled. Two soldier escorts marched erect and breathed a dignified air into the small traveling party. In the front of the wagon sat An, a plain woman of average height and an enormously generous heart. At thirty (one year younger than her husband) she exuded serenity—a needed quality when her husband's infamous temper flared. Her family, prominent in Chin politics, had arranged their marriage.

Ping and An had met at the joint family gathering announcing their betrothal. An fell in love with the short, pudgy soldier, whose face flashed scintillating energy. At the moment she saw him, An had vowed to be the best possible wife and mother. Ever cheerful, she'd intently listened to her husband's work reports. She read his mind and bolstered his low self-confidence.

At the wagon's rear, opened because of the balmy day, two boys tumbled in play: the elder, a shy lad of ten, and a brash, confident eight-year-old. The nanny, a twenty-three-year-old cousin of An, watched them like a hungry hawk.

The boys explored the baggage-laden vehicle. They hadn't begun to scrap, because the trip had only just gotten under way. Their mother could leash them, but they feared their father.

Officer Feng was traveling to a new post as civilian head of the Ba commandery. He should have arrived already, but a delay had been caused by the death of Shi Lu, chief inspector of the Nan commandery. Because Feng Ping had been a prefect in the Nan commandery capital, he had filled the vacancy caused by the sudden death. The extended stay permitted Feng to supervise the funeral of his boss and friend. An outstanding officer in this place where his family originated, Inspector Shi merited the great affection of the people he served.

The practice of appointing people to posts in their home areas was undesirable; it smacked of nepotism and power building. Even though Inspector Shi had not wielded his power inappropriately, Feng Ping planned to write a memorandum on the subject. Ba, his new post, seemed a notorious place; the remote post attracted people of questionable character. Feng Ping's charge as the civilian head of Ba was to uproot a nest of corruption. Inspector Shi, a taskmaster, had monitored Feng's career and admired his subordinate's organizational skills and hard-working habits. In evaluations, Feng scored the highest marks. Only his unruly temper and blunt manner kept him from a career at the imperial capital.

Inspector Shi had counseled Feng to memorize and apply maxims that he had recently published:

> The mouth is the tongue's crossbow trigger guard,
> the tongue's the trigger mechanism.
> Once a wrong word's loosened,
> four horses cannot retrieve it.
> The mouth's the control station,
> The tongue's the sealed letter.
> If the seal's unopened,
> one will not bring oneself grief.

In addition, Shi Lu had admonished his subordinate to

> Act as if preparing for a sacrifice,
> be solemn, serene, dignified.
> Speak as if making a covenant.
> When outside, be reverent.
> Keep to the constant middle way
> and you'll shine resplendent.

Feng mastered his character defects and isolated his decisions from his moods. By subjecting himself to a thorough self-examination, arresting his desires, and softening his manner, Feng Ping had risen to chief prefect—and, most recently, to the Ba posting. Inspector Shi knew that Feng could be chancellor one day.

Feng Ping supervised his mentor's burial at Yun-Meng, famed for its idyllic lakes nestled in majestic mountains. Both men loved the Rainbow Falls. On summer afternoons, they had feasted on spectra of colorful panoramas. Often, they'd play at poetizing. Feng smiled in remembrance of simple lines:

> In the mountain's shadowed fastness

a monkey's mournful cry.
Might it miss the colored spray
or pine a love gone far away?

Feng Ping's reply flitted by:

The solitary pine, erect
braves winter storms
waiting summer's warmth
and the rainbow's radiant forms.

Happy, happy times. Buried deep and protected by thick timbers, Inspector Shi's coffin would withstand water and pests. His wish to be surrounded by favorite sayings and official writings had been respected.

The government took good care of families of officials who died in office. Feng Ping thanked Shi Lu's outstanding tutoring that had tamed his temper. The tiny pine stood tall.

The party finally arrived in Ba, and Feng reported to Wang Li, the Ba military commander, who said, "Feng Ping, you served in the Jao wars. I was there. You have an impressive record."

The casual military chatter relaxed the new man, who noticed an exceptional Shang-dynasty wine vase on Wang Li's desk. "I was fortunate to bring back three enemy officers' heads. How the Jao people hated us," Feng Ping said as he looked about the well-appointed room.

The other man looked wistful. "Yes, yes."

"Some said the Jao campaign was Old Wang Jian's greatest." Feng scrutinized the old veteran, whose skin sagged from his chin and partially hid a jagged battle scar. "The best I served. Wang knew the enemy's weaknesses and hammered through them."

Wang Li's jowls shook like jellied fat cakes. "I served on the old man's staff in Chu. By that time, he was bent by age. His mind was still razor keen."

Feng Ping's curiosity was piqued. "Died at the end of it?"

"Some say he took his own life, sickened by the slaughter."

A disgusted look crossed the diminutive new man's face. He'd almost been too short to fight, but pressure from family supporters caused the recruiter to add another inch on the bamboo tablet.

"Warfare's not for the meek," Feng Ping said. Feeling the former officer's rising temper, Feng changed the subject. "I hear that Ba suffers from bad morale."

The older man's face smoothed. "We're in barbarian-cursed land, far from the capital. Duty here's not unlike a death sentence. Ba's where people finish undistinguished careers. That's why your posting surprised us ... er, me. Your record's outstanding, save for brushes with colleagues."

"I have a bad temper and foolish tongue."

"Well, it won't take long to learn the ways here." The bald man with a well-trimmed beard and squinting eyes assumed a coy manner. "You know ... slow living, wink here, oversight there, funds find the way to your door. Local food's spicy; so are the women. I'm too old for either. Local dialect's impossible, and we let the locals handle preliminary investigations. For their aid, we give a tax break—legal, of course. One old bitch, Widow Jing, is always moaning 'bout this and that. Someone ought to marry her and take a whip to that tired flesh. Bet it stinks."

An incisorless grin accompanied the description. Galled by the man's coarse manner, Feng longed to throttle the man, whose jowls resembled a hog's ass. Feng Ping's orders said to submit secret reports to the imperial secretary.

CHAPTER 81

JING LING (217 BC)

A week later, Jing Ling, the widow who had been cursed by the military commandant, saw the new civilian head walking to her home. Tall, with a lion's mane of hair that frustrated hairpins, she had recently celebrated her fiftieth birthday.

Her family, prominent in Ba for three generations, included a grandfather who'd been a Chin army commander; a father who'd developed cinnabar mines; and herself, who'd inherited her husband's mines and fortune. Widow Jing's marriage had come with three mines as a dowry. Her husband permitted his wife to operate them, while he had been content to raise horses and farm. In his last years, jealous of Jing's business acumen, he had drowned his sorrows in liquor and sought comfort in town whores. One day, a stroke stopped the carousing.

Five men who courted Jing were unsuccessful, because she wanted to safeguard a legacy for her two children. Although Jing preached fairness in their treatment, she favored her son, who wasted his years in liquor and gambling. The daughter, Pu, inherited her mother's business knack.

The mines thrived, despite the efforts of three competitors to force her out of business. Jing suffered from special tax levies and fought each assessment. After five years, she contemplated selling out, but stopped in order to thwart inheritance laws favoring males.

In this frame of mind, she opened her house to Feng Ping, who had to look up to her. "Please enter my humble dwelling. I'm Jing Ling, a worthless person who stands before you," the widow said.

CHAPTER 82

FENG PING (217 BC)

"My pleasure. I'm Feng Ping, the new civilian head of Ba."

Feng Ping's neck was severely pained from looking up, and he asked if they might sit.

Jing guided him to a seat. The household furnishings reflected her elegant tastes. "Forgive my frankness, but you seem young to be in such a post. Forgive this foolish mouth, but I hope you clean up our mess. It's disgraceful how top officials favor friends and hurt others."

The diminutive man smiled inwardly. Three intricately fashioned bronze lamps quietly awaited night duty. One resembled a kneeling male servant. Feng, who took a modest interest in antiquarian artifacts, had not seen such fine work. "I've learned about your honesty and courage and came to pay my respects—and to seek advice and aid."

"Me? Assist you? Whatever might I do?"

"I need a pledge of absolute silence," Feng Ping said.

Widow Jing edged closer. "You have my word. I'll send my servants out, although that'll cause comment."

After the house emptied, the two conspirators huddled. "I'm here on a special mission," Feng explained. "His Majesty learned about the corruption here and commissioned me to eradicate it."

"Your words warm me like the sun on a winter-chilled blossom." Jing seemed to grow younger as they sipped on cups of orange juice with a hint of cinnamon flavoring.

"I need names and activities, as best you can recall. Any other trustworthies need to be interviewed. I must have evidence that will stand up in court ... and in the post-sentence reviews."

The widow's face grew strained. "Please forgive. I follow your words with difficulty. My right ear is poor, and the left little better. Also ... your accent."

Later, on the way home, Feng hummed a childhood tune about goblins.

Over a period of four months, Civilian Head Feng meticulously compiled the evidence. He tried to keep it secret, but his investigative activity triggered suspicions. The dialect differences slowed him as he double-checked things.

All senior officials, save for the chief inspector, had been involved in graft. Two prefects and magistrates had avoided the rotten taint. Many landowners, merchants, and industrialists participated too.

While on his way to a secret meeting with an informant, Feng was attacked by two thugs. He drove them off with his walking staff and small sword. One assailant suffered a broken jaw; the other, a badly bruised rib cage. Feng lost three teeth, but he bore his wounds like battle decorations.

When the net was pulled in, outside forces came from Shu. A team of legal experts, along with temporary replacements, arrived too. Most confessed, and their property was seized. Some of it passed to people wronged by the officials. Upper-grade officers suffered facial branding and convict labor. Those who confessed under torture lost a foot; their families were enslaved, and their property was passed to the state. All were sent to camps.

Merchants' property was confiscated, and their families were sent to sites like the imperial retreat at Langya. Although ruined, the merchants were thankful they'd remained whole. Landowners who could prove peasant origins were either fined or beaten with bamboo rods. Although such punishment was painful, the body usually healed from the beatings. Wealthy landowners who could not prove peasant origins suffered property confiscation.

Civil Head Feng Ping received a cash award and a promotion. As a singular honor of appreciation and trust, he became the civil head and the chief inspector, with the current inspector being demoted to Feng's assistant for failing to report the corruption.

After the trials, the new officials began to arrive, and each was met by Feng, who gave them documents for memorization. The first set concerned laws and their implementation; another set discussed the respective duties. Soon, Ba became the best-governed commandery in the empire.

Feng's methods and documents were passed to other administrators. One innovation was the creation of a traveling inspectorate—including a financial expert, a legal expert, and a security expert. The teams visited subunits and local governments. Feng Ping authorized a brief biography of Widow Jing and added a supplement about her role in the case. The biography and supplement were forwarded to the central government.

CHAPTER 83

OLD LIU (217 BC)

In the springtime, the families of Wanshi Village celebrated the equinox festival, honoring the earth goddess. Although blessed with successive, bountiful harvests, seasoned farmers warned of lean years to come.

Old Liu's fortunes increased beyond his fondest hopes. Both sons had purchased land and bought a brace of pigs. Only Lily remained unwed. Last fall, Wanshi had been given rice and extra pigs by the government. The elders suggested a communal fund, but that fell before stiff opposition; thus, they had divided the rice and slaughtered the pigs. Liu lamented this fate, because a hog and sow could have given many litters.

Since the state had abolished labor conscription, Liu would be paid for laboring that fall, and in two years, he'd have saved enough to retire. Of course, *she*'d never let him idle. Besides, he'd have to be home with her. The next day, he'd go to the imperial warehouse and rent a steel-tipped plow. Also, he'd take a hoe, rake, and sickle. The new granary even afforded the peasants a supply of seed grain.

That afternoon, Old Liu fished with his boys. Fragrant peach blossoms meant another good crop. As they started to leave, the old peasant noticed an object floating on the surface of the jade green, powerfully moving river. "Jang, the hemp bag there ... see it? Pull it in."

"Can't get a hold on it, Papa. Current's too strong."

"Here, I'll get it." Old Liu gingerly stepped into the water; he hated leeches.

"You'll get soaked, Papa, and Mama will scold you good."

Liu growled, "Never mind her. Let's see what's inside." They dragged in the hemp bag, untied the binding cord, pulled open the flap, and retrieved a shriveled fetus with a full head of dark hair, closed eyes, and the stub of a severed umbilical cord.

"A baby girl, Papa. I'm gonna be sick."

"Throw it back. We'll only have trouble if we keep it."

Peasant Liu glared at his eldest. "Shut up! We've a duty to report this to the magistrate."

"We shouldn't get involved, Papa. Remember what happened to the Jins. No one will believe that we didn't kill her."

A glare cowed the boy. Old Liu would obey the law. "I don't care; this is our problem ... or, if you wish, my problem." Old Liu scowled like a tattered tiger trying to subdue younger males. "I'll obey the law." Old Liu gently cradled the corpse and walked home, boys in tow.

Chen quietly prepared five meals, laid out a waterproof covering, and went to her money stash.

Night travel was uncommon. Despite the low crime rate, few braved the roads after dark, but Old Liu wanted the dead baby off his hands. Ba, the younger son, accompanied his dad, and they arrived at the magistrate's house just as the moon passed overhead. Mosquitoes worried them, but generous applications of animal fat helped. Old Liu tenderly carried the dead child, though his arms had long passed the weary time.

They rang the summoning bell. When the door opened, a sleepy female face poked out. Her hair was disheveled, and she had no eyebrows. Guards, half dressed and angry at being disturbed, rounded the house and were preparing to thrash the impudent peasants when they spied their boss, Han Yu. She dismissed them, smiled at the peasants, and stifled a yawn. "What can I do for you at this late hour?"

Old Liu thrust the bag forward. "We found it ... her, in the river."

"What is it?"

"Baby girl, Your Excellency. Found her this afternoon."

CHAPTER 84

HAN YU (217 BC)

Han Yu unfolded the cover and gently pulled out the infant. The corpse was difficult to see in the torchlight ... besides, it wasn't her responsibility to examine it. Yet, she was fascinated at seeing a stilled life. She'd summon the forensic expert after dawn. Han Yu turned to them. "My thanks to you. When did you discover it?"

Old Liu proudly recounted the day's adventure. After he finished, she asked, "Do you know the parents?" Both men shook their heads negatively. "I'm afraid you'll spend the night here. We'll ask for your statements in the morning."

"We always do our duty, Your Highness."

Old Liu looked at his son. When the father opened his mouth, his words were directed to the official. "We won't trouble you, Excellency. We'll sleep on the roadside and return at dawn."

"Nonsense! You'll remain here as my guests. Breakfast will be one water level after sunrise. After you give your evidence, you will be free to go."

Han Yu tossed sleeplessly. Although previously a subprefect in Pi to the east, she'd never investigated a death. Being a woman, she'd not have been promoted because of the new policies, but there was no mention of her gender. The male cast to her name reflected the fact that her father, disappointed that his child was not a boy, gave her a name honoring his teacher, Yu. The daughter's outstanding record had qualified her for a transfer.

Han Yu would dispatch an investigative team to villages and estates upstream. Both sides of the river would be covered, as well as inland for at least fifteen miles.

Han Yu recalled her decision not to marry. The decision had been forced on her after her mother died—and after her family had lost their property in last year's fire. Her father depended on her. At least, with the salary increases, she'd been able to afford a servant for him. She'd planned to bring him with her to her new post, but his pride would not permit him to be visibly dependent on her. Han Yu planned to save enough to marry after this term in office.

A candle dimly silhouetted the bookcase as Han Yu plucked out the manual on criminal procedure.

Indictment
1. Initial accusation or denunciation
2. A detailed description of the crime and circumstances of its discovery
3. Names, residence, and occupation of the accused
4. Ranks, if any, of those involved
5. Verification records

She needed to check the criminal records and carefully read the interrogation reports, as well as the reinterrogation reports. Han Yu tripped and banged into the bookcase. Her heavy flow and cramps discomfited. Nausea came in waves. It was only the third day, and she was drained.

The manual cautioned her to listen to everything the accused said. She needed to allow the statement to unfold, recording it. If she suspected a lie, she should still let them continue. She could use documents and other evidence to track down the truth.

Immersion in the procedural manual banished the abdominal pain.

The investigator, she read, should avoid intimidation, because the suspect might say anything. Truth was the investigator's primary obligation. Only if lies persisted might a beating be initiated, and the interrogator "must" record it in writing.

After the peasants' statements were taken, they had been released. The next day, the culprits—the Jia family, wealthy peasants—had been located. Officials sealed the property. The household head, his principal wife, and chief concubine were brought in for questioning. Han Yu scanned the report.

1 Compound including a house of seven rooms, each with a door, one cooking area. All covered by a tiled roof.

1 large outhouse above a pigsty.

1 large livestock building with four pens holding 1 horse, 2 cows, 2 buffalo, 7 sheep (6 pigs were in the pigsty).

25 mature mulberry trees.

13 house occupants.

2 adult males, 6 adult females, 1 nonadult male.

2 adult male servants.

2 adult female servants (1 absent adult female servant, see appendix).

1 dog (male).

2 cats (male).
Appendix

After the report was completed, the adult female—a concubine—returned to the compound in the company of a woman who was identified as a midwife.

Han Yu had sent a runner to locate the midwife and bring her for questioning. Then she ordered a bondwoman who'd birthed five times to examine the female.

Testimony was received, and the forensic report stated that the fetus had died by drowning. Examination revealed that its legs differed in length. Han Yu considered the evidence. The statutes were clear; she needn't exercise discretionary power. Yet, her emotional state delayed her. She drafted the judgment:

> The concubine, Dai Lao, had been pregnant and delivered her child in the morning of the ping-lu day—the spring equinox. Subsequently, the household head, Jia Bu, with the concurrence of the family, ordered that Dai Lao drown the deformed infant. The mother, assisted by a midwife, performed the duty.

> Han Yu imagined the mother sobbing by the water's edge.

> Since Jia Bu's actions are supported by the criminal statutes of Chin (Section 15–7, an incomplete child may be destroyed at birth), no crime occurred. Therefore, they should be released, with their property unsealed and returned. The case is closed.

Han Yu imagined the infant's cries choked silent by the chilled river water. Her jaw ached. She'd add an appendix.

> Wang Liu, fifty-three years old, of Wanshi Village in the Changsha District, Shiang commandery, and his son, Ba, nineteen years old, are to be commended for their exemplary service in promptly reporting a possible crime. A reward of four gold pieces will be given. A proclamation commending them will be read in Wanshi Village.

Han Yu knew the reward would inspire others. The two peasants might have dumped the bag in the river. She sent the corrected draft to the chief clerk. Two copies would be made, with one sent to the commandery capital. The other would be sealed, then forwarded to the records department.

Han Yu retired to her quarters, where she reflected on a time that her mother had argued with her father. Rarely would the woman have opposed him. On that occasion, her will prevailed.

Han Yu limped to the bed. She had been born with different-sized legs. Because she was an only child—and especially because of her stubborn, loving mother—Han Yu had not been drowned or smothered, though "incomplete."

Han Yu faced herself in her first legal case. Head bowed, cheeks wet, Han Yu collapsed on her bed. Thoughts of marriage evaporated. She wanted to be alone.

CHAPTER 85

SHU WEI (217 BC)

Shu Wei inspected his tiny garden plot. After a morning meal of millet porridge and dried plums, he strolled along the gardening area—a field of two acres neatly sectioned and marked according to the housing-unit number. Nearly two hundred fifty gardens had been plowed in the second year after Wei's arrival, because the residents petitioned that vegetables from the plots would supplement their government rations.

As Shu Wei walked down the dusty road, an aching hip reminded him that he neared sixty. A few years earlier, manual labor would have horrified him. Now, the plot offered a retreat. Cutting his long nails had been painful, but necessary, because the garden supplemented their meager fare. Working the soil salved his soul.

Each year, Wei weeded and counted new vegetable blossoms or measured plant heights with a practiced eye. He chatted amiably to discern others' gardening secrets. A thriving market allowed residents to trade for what they lacked, or to earn sleeve money.

As the old man waddled home, the sun shone on his head. In the past year, Wei had worn the ugly black clothes and head wraps of the peasants, because he had learned that dark colors absorbed the rays. In fact, he'd learned many things. If only he'd brought more books.

Chicken flesh rose on his arms and legs at the memory of his confession to Lotus about that last night with his mistress. Initially, she scolded him for it, but after discussion, they decided the past should not be used to punish. They'd apologized and enjoyed wonderful lovemaking that night.

Lotus yielded to his urgings … except for last winter, when she'd taken ill. Out of desperation, Wei had told her about "playing the flute." He recalled how she had flushed, then covered her face. With effort and determination, she'd grown proficient.

An official carriage and driver waited near his building. In their home, Wei found Lotus talking with an official—an academician, by his looks. When the man turned, Wei recognized his nephew Tung.

"Greetings, nephew! I am delighted to see you!"

"Uncle Wei, you've grown thin!"

"Look, Wei," Lotus said. "He's brought pickled daikon, dried mushrooms, and preserved meats … including the salt fish you love." Lotus smiled—as she often did, despite their meager circumstances.

"These come from Papa and Mama. Only now have I had the time to bring them."

Wei knew that his nephew must have postponed the visiting day, but said nothing. It was good to see him and to have the food. Wei sat upon the faded Chi mat. "Never mind. You are here in official robes with a carriage and driver. I thought the Chin barbarians hated the followers of Confucius."

"No, uncle. Followers of Confucius, Mencius, and Master Shun serve," Shu Tung said. "Last year, I was selected as an apprentice academician. Now there are thirty-six like me, along with seventy-two full academicians."

"Congratulations! This honor merits a celebration. Your father must be proud, and I know your grandfather would have been elated … even though you serve Chin."

The young man blanched. "We have no choice if we wish to direct the administration toward proper ends. Perhaps one day, you'll return to Chi."

Sadness wrinkled the older man's face. "Not soon enough. Could you loan me books? The few I brought are worn out."

Tung seemed surprised. "I'll do my best. Uncle, the government is well intentioned. The laws are mild, the taxes low; peasants have been encouraged to farm their own plots. Bronze weapons have been recast into statues of giants; one is a scholar. I don't know how the artisans managed to get the faces so lifelike. Even the nails are long."

Wei contemplated his own fingers. His sole treasure, a lacquer chest, sat firmly by the bedroom door, maintaining dignity despite their troubles. His anger rose.

"Statues! They took our arms to control us. Artisans live off the peasants' labor, don't forget. Look at us here. We've lost everything."

Tung redirected the conversation. "Father sends you this and apologizes for the delay … but no one could be trusted."

Wei opened the leather packet and counted the substantial sum. "We could have used this when our funds ran out. Lotus took ill last winter. Forgive my manners; how are your parents?"

"Papa nearly died last year from some chest problem caused by a severe yin imbalance. He's better. Mama's in good health and spirits. Still, I worry because they're getting old," Tung replied.

Wei felt comfortable with family matters. Having Tung there afforded a chance to hear news. "He's fifty-six. Tell him to take care. As a child, he often took sick."

"Uncle, Papa says that you'll be sixty this fall. I'll send a carriage for you both around the autumn equinox. We'll celebrate. Few are virtuous enough to reach sixty years."

"It's nice to see such a filial young man come to see us. Isn't that right, Lotus?" She answered in a muffled affirmative from the cooking area. Wei heard the boiling of water for tea and the opening of other jars. Ants were a problem in Chin; their complex seemed to rest on a large hill of ants. At least the native peasants had taught Lotus to keep everything in containers.

"You're too thin," Tung said. "I'll send some blood tonic from the capital apothecary."

"The rations aren't sufficient. With the garden, we barely survive. Many nights, we go to bed hungry," Wei said. Of course, he exaggerated, but he was entitled to a bit of stretching the truth.

Tung blushed. "Really, the state must treat you better. I'll come regularly and bring things. It's a disgrace!"

As his belly growled, Wei shouted. "Lotus, I'm starved! Tung, you must stay for the noon meal."

"I should be leaving."

"Nonsense! Our meager fare is the best we can manage in the springtime. Having you here and hearing about your parents are worth celebrating."

"How does the state treat you here?"

"I'm fortunate to be old. All men between sixteen and fifty-two work four months every year for the emperor," Wei answered.

"Four months! The peasants worked less with their labor duty before unification ... and now even that's abolished! The refugees have replaced peasants. Disgusting!" Tung's thin arms flailed. He favored the extended sleeves now fashionable in the capital.

Talking about misery excited Wei. "Refugees plant trees and repair roads, bridges, or buildings. Many had not labored before. I saw their bloodied hands and heard their tales of brutal guards and bad weather."

Shu Wei would have made a splendid actor; his leathery, sunbaked face exuded dignity.

"How do the local officers treat you?" Tung asked.

"The first two years were bad, with makeshift housing, inadequate heating, and cruel officials. The current crop is good ... more civilians. Two years ago, we even had a female official! I was scandalized, but when she left, most were sad."

"I'm pleased to learn that things are improved. Minister Lee, a student of Master Shun, was behind the move to oust the women."

Lotus, who followed the gist of the conversation in the kitchen, added, "Women don't belong in government. If they work, who'll mind the house and the children? They never should have been let in." The men smiled.

"How did you come to the imperial academy?" Shu Wei asked.

"Apparently, my reputation as a ritual expert impressed someone at the academy. I feel unworthy, although some must have seen something in my foolishness." Shu Tung's feigned modesty was, of course, perfectly appropriate.

Wei unbound his hemp sandals and massaged his feet. Blood rushed into his toes and appeased the gathering storm in his head. "You always excelled as a student, Tung. I admire your calligraphy. Your bamboo painting there is a treasured possession. You honor us all. Let's hope that the Chin beast may be tamed. Lotus, some food!" Wei exclaimed.

Lotus called them to the eating mats (tightly woven in the Chi style). Terracotta bowls steaming with fish and bamboo shoots, stir-fry cabbage, and boiled sweet millet lay before them. The room darkened when thunderheads blotted the sun. Swallows twittered in the skies.

CHAPTER 86

LEE SU (216 BC)

On a lazy midsummer's morning, Chin's senior officials listened to reports about population estimates, building projects, military campaigns, and the state of internal security. Later, the senior chancellor ate a huge lunch; as the speakers resumed, his snoring disgusted Emperor Jeng. When the meeting adjourned, the courtiers departed, leaving the hapless man. Wang Ben awoke to an empty chamber and, realizing his gaffe, marched to the emperor's quarters. After guards refused entrance, Wang Ben resigned.

Court gossip favored Minister Lee as the replacement. Cynics cautioned that he'd been twice passed over. The next two days were difficult for Lee.

In the afternoon of the second day, Bu burst into his father's office.

"What ... is it?" Minister Lee's hands trembled.

"Mr. Senior Chancellor, Official Lee Bu at your service. Father, if anyone deserves this position, it's you."

"Officials never display emotion!"

"Yes, Your Excellency!" An infectious smile ringed the younger man's face. The old man looked away.

"I must get busy. That old general left things in a shambles. Thank you. You're a good son ... well, almost always." The mild rebuke angered Bu, who stormed out.

Lee Su sagged in his seat. The formal robe was replaced by a worn hemp robe—Lee's first in Chin. He'd begun as a member of the Second Father's entourage, an innocent in court affairs. Minister Lee fingered a frayed sleeve and left the building.

A longing came over Lee Su, who wandered the streets. In the artisan quarter, he located a simple restaurant; for hours, he stared at a cup of half-swallowed cheap liquor. Alcoholic conversations buzzed. Staggering outside, he fell into a ditch. Lee retched violently, then crawled to the roadside and lay in a fetal position. A passing security patrol stopped to escort the drunk to a holding cell.

Searching his sleeve pockets, they were surprised to find a minister's seal. The drunk was escorted home.

The next afternoon, Lee awoke with a murderous hangover, a terrible taste in his mouth, and a lingering stench in his bed. Emptiness welled up, and the face of Han Fei, bloated and purple, haunted him. The next morning, the worn-out old man stared blankly into his wife's worried face.

CHAPTER 87

TAO (216 BC)

The crime lord inspected his deformed hand. He still felt his finger; he tried to scratch with it, to retrieve objects. Tao reached to his neck and touched the pouch containing the severed finger. He had decided to wear it for luck and to remind him of that wintry day. Because that day's weather was balmy, he considered whether he should walk in the garden or go to his rural retreat.

Tao looked at Jin Mi, who sat patiently by his bedside. In fact, the young thief had been with him nearly all of the time.

"Night master, shouldn't you attend to your duties or visit one of your women?"

Jin Mi smiled broadly. "No, I'd rather sit by you—a musing, absentminded fool ..."

Tao smiled. "What is the state of the Reds? I should have recovered more quickly."

"Fortunately, Ping discovered the poison and its antidote, or you never would have attended another meeting. The Reds are fine, though there have been police raids on two of our gambling dens ... that's six in the last three months. I've put out feelers. I hope I haven't offended, but I wanted to learn something concrete while you were abed." Jin Mi looked at the medicine chest. It was around four generations old, carved of teak, and polished to a sheen.

"Thank you for your efforts. Truly, I wouldn't be alive if it had not been for your quick thinking and acting." Tao clutched his neck pouch and looked into the master thief's eyes. Then he bowed to Jin Mi, exposing his neck.

"I have no leads on our assassin. To appear and disappear like that is terrifying," the thief said. His heart fluttered at this singular honor from the crime lord.

"I know the assassin was a woman. I read her mind just as she struck. Malignity like the ..." Tao halted at the abyss.

Jin Mi followed his own thread. "I didn't have a clue; really, I assumed a man had struck. What does it mean?"

"I ... the Reds ... are under attack. There's another group in the capital. I feel them, underground like moles or rats in sewers. That's it: they're using sewers rather than streets. We need to get hold of old city maps from the Bureau of Records. A subprefect owes me a favor. Would you come along?"

"Yes, master. I'd like to learn about our rivals," Jin Mi said. "I confess that I have seen or heard nothing of another gang. How did they develop without our being aware?"

"No need to use the honorific with me; I see us as friends. Your knife ... hand it to me," Tao commanded. The night master drew his knife and presented it handle first, with a bowed head.

Tao wiped the blade and cut his thumb. "Now, you."

Jin Mi cut his thumb, and blood trickled down his hand.

"Give me your thumb," Tao said. They pressed thumbs, with Tao intoning, "With this mixing of our blood, I, Tao, swear eternal friendship: to guard your back, to share my heart, to soothe your weariness. We are brothers from now and beyond death."

"I, Jin Mi, pledge you my life, my truth, and my strength: to guard your back, to share my heart, to soothe your weariness. We are brothers from now and beyond death."

Each smiled and released their thumbs. Jin Mi pulled out a cloth and offered it to Tao, who spoke as he wiped the blood. "Now is the time to find out what this bitch and her gang are up to. She's so arrogant as to toy with us. Let's show her the error of her arrogance ..."

CHAPTER 88

EMPEROR JENG (216 BC)

The same night as Minister Lee's escapade, the emperor planned some fun. Although he preferred a hunt, he donned a disguise and saw a commoner gazing back at him from a bronze wall mirror. He'd conscript expert fighters, eat at a simple restaurant, and travel the metropolitan region.

The restaurant was in a large building and commanded the bottom floor. Bustling with customers, its speciality was deep-fried catfish. After the meal, the party rode out the southern gate, heading southeast. That evening, they stayed in a local inn; at dawn, they set off for the nearby mountains.

When the party reached a narrow gorge, bandits cut them off. A burly man attired in a garish yellow and purple cotton cloak and patched black trousers shouted, "Give us your money and other valuables, dogs, or we'll open your gizzards and feast on them. Come to think of it, I haven't dined on human innards for a long while."

Laughter echoed in the sunbaked hills. The guards quietly formed a protective shield, and each fingered his weapon.

"Drop your bows, rich scum. Bastards like you make me spit." The leader grew uneasy at the precise way his victims moved.

Captain Tso feigned cowardice. "Please hurt us not, kind sirs. We'll give you everything. See, I raise my hands." With that signal, two guards yelled and whirled their horses. The bowmen unleashed darts in the blink of an eye ... then a second volley. Three bandits screamed. The guards shouldered short lances and heaved. One shattered a horse's leg, and another pierced a bandit's chest. One bounced off a boulder. Swords drawn, the guards charged.

When the guards returned, they found the emperor tending their captain, who'd taken a crossbow dart. An expertly tied bandage staunched the blood flow. The captain barked out orders: "Form a protective ring about His Majesty. We must leave."

"I don't think they want another fight, sir," one man panted.

"Silence! Check the fallen bandits for identification. Finish off the wounded scum; we want no witnesses," the captain commanded. Emperor Jeng remained silent as they remounted and returned to the inn. There they ordered local troops to escort them back. Captain Tso went in a litter.

The metropolitan garrison was mobilized to hunt bandits. A twenty-day search netted three hundred twenty-seven men—seventy-one of whom were wanted for murder.

Emperor Jeng ordered a new inspection tour of the east, but before leaving, he rewarded the guardsmen who had saved his life. Dr. Wu operated on Captain Tso but could not repair the shattered limb. Emperor Jeng departed a week later, with five thousand elite troops and one hundred officials. All rode to the coast.

One morning, just before sunrise at Langya, His Majesty climbed a ridge overlooking the oceanic expanse. The sea fused with the sky and was wrinkled like a well-used cloth. As the sky lightened, a dark horizon line divided water from air.

Nearing the beach, the undulations swelled into waves and heaped upon themselves until they crashed and became a whitewater veil skipping along the beach. The dark horizon bar cleared, like sediment in an old wine bottle that settled to the bottom. Flat bars of white, green, and yellow striped the firmament. The sea surface slowly grew glassy until the stripes vanished. A fiery arc burned the horizon's rim, and all about, the sea blazed gold.

Later, Emperor Jeng commanded three local magicians to seek immortality elixirs. On the return journey, the imperial party halted at a city of 300,000 people. Surprised to find its wall unrazed, the emperor ordered its leveling and its moat filled. A description was carved on a city gate. In the briefest time, the riders returned to the capital.

Four days later, a comet appeared in the northern sky, portending heaven's anger. Emperor Jeng summoned the private invocator. This ancient post had been created to deflect heaven's wrath. When summoned, the man occupying the post donned a set of imperial robes. He was the only person who could wear them, save the emperor. At over six feet, eight inches tall, he made a highly visible target. After sacrificing at the temples of heaven, earth, and the sovereigns, the invocator went to a remote imperial residence to await heaven's punishment.

CHAPTER 89

TAO (216 BC)

Jin Mi sat cross-legged on the mat, casually looking around the restaurant. He had finished his plate of fried catfish and licked his lips like a sated cat. Tao caught his eye and nodded slightly. "See the group of six that just came in?"

Jin Mi smiled and inhaled the thick, acrid scent of cooking fat. He would have his clothes washed the morrow. "Seems we have an unusual clientele tonight."

"Indeed … a group trying to look like ordinary folk. What do you think?" Tao asked, his curiosity piqued.

"It's a government group—perhaps a special investigative team with clumsy disguises … or possibly a prince who's out for a lark with his guards. See how five of them focus on the one with the beard and the laborer's hat. He's the royal."

Tao nodded almost sleepily. "You're close. Notice the burly man with the star tattoo on the back of his neck. He's the guards' leader. See how he scans the room, looking for trouble. Except for the poor disguises, they're an elite team with that tensed state of professionals. Wait, that's not a mere prince. I'll bet that's the old man himself."

Jin Mi's eyes widened as he sipped his plum wine. It was cheap but cut through the greasiness in his gullet. "You're right. Look at him … a coiled tiger waiting to pounce. On what? See his eyes flash as he surveys this room. He's having an adventure … a game. But what game?"

Tao smiled. "Brother, he's bored and seeks adventure. Imagine having that power and responsibility and being bored! Oops—he's looking this way." Tao looked at his hands and quested for the other's thoughts. In the crowded, chattering place, it was difficult to discern a single person's thoughts. In the emperor's mind, Tao sensed a general giddiness at being free, at being away from it all—at having a chance for adventure, a little danger, and some fun.

Tao returned the stare. What an ordinary-looking man with a false beard and tattered clothing! The captain of the guards picked up Tao's stare and frowned. He started to rise, but the royal lay his hand on the man's forearm and whispered. The captain nodded, then dropped his head.

"What do you see?" Jin Mi's query brought a shiver to Tao, who heard a ghost from the past.

Tao reported, "I see a little boy playing a game. Tired of bureaucratic routine and the imperial life, he craves danger. He seeks the extraordinary with risks and a kind of gambling. I see an older man who is wholly alone. I see that apart from us, no one recognizes who or what he represents. Perhaps that's for the best. The royal has an eye tic and wrings his hands. He's nervous and needs stimuli like this on a regular basis. I pity him."

Jin Mi smiled. "And yet, in your field, you are a kindred man with power and position. You sigh in idle moments and grow bored with responsibility. Can you really be free of the Reds?"

Tao looked at his hands, which had been clenching and unclenching. "Yes, brother, I have wearying tasks. And yet, I prefer the criminal life. He's had several assassins try to kill him." Tao grimaced. "And so have I, I guess. How are we different?"

Jin Mi smiled. "You have me. I'll wager that he has no friend. He must be on guard with all of the plots and intrigues at the court. Who might he trust?"

Tao shrugged. "Only you know my secrets ... or at least the simple ones. My trust perished with my parents. I learned quickly in Old Juang's care to trust no one, to hide my feelings, to nurture my hates and fears. And when I struck at Old Juang, he was unprepared, for he thought himself safe; he trusted me. Just now, you asked what I see. Old Juang asked me that regularly. It was part of our game. I could discern more in a situation than he ever could. I told him what he wanted to hear—and a thing or two that he didn't know, to keep him off balance. I hated him all of the time, though I felt kindly for his teaching me and keeping me safe ... as far as he knew." Tao stared and gasped for breath.

Jin Mi looked at his friend. "Are you all right?"

Tao smiled ruefully. "I was reminded of my faults. Something broke through and mirrored my own failings. The royal leaves. We will wait until they've gone. No need to borrow trouble. It's disappointing to see how ordinary our illustrious emperor really is. No wonder he needs to play these games. Child, indeed."

CHAPTER 90

SU MA (96 BC)

The study door burst open, and Su Ma stomped to the window to let in the twilight sounds. The sultry conditions couldn't decide whether to unleash a thunderstorm or simply scatter the threatening clouds. Sweat stung his eyes.

Su Ma rued his appointment as the martial emperor's secretary, because he had become immersed in the intimate life of the inner court. He regretted watching an aging monarch play the virile warrior. The emperor strung a crossbow to hit the black bearskin target, and ten shots missed before the first hit—and the emperor reeked with the effort afterward.

Restlessness permeated court life, and today the sovereign had met with his generals to formulate a new western campaign. How many bodies would litter distant battlefields?

In the outer court, Su Ma had watched a splendidly arrayed sovereign strutting in dragon robes. The historian had succumbed to the playful feeling and praised his sweaty lord. He pictured the toothless, hairless, honorless Magician Lu who had walked the inner court but two water levels back. Su Ma knew that the charlatan hatched plots to ensnare a gullible monarch seeking elixirs, potions, or herbs to revitalize his broken life. Who wouldn't like to live forever?

Su Ma suspected that the first emperor of Chin had proved equally gullible. Emperor Jeng had had an excellent chance for a lasting peace when Lee Su became senior chancellor.

The northern campaign … had Emperor Jeng craved the excitement of warring? He continued the southern campaign even in the golden years and foolishly courted danger in the incognito excursion immediately before the second eastern trip.

Thunder startled Su Ma; shutters flapped back and forth as rain burst into the room. Su Ma grabbed one errant window and secured it. He lunged for the second and slipped. Righting himself, he snared the offending shutter.

Su Ma changed to his tattered brown robe with padded elbows. The historian poured himself cold tea.

Emperor Jeng had summoned magicians. The last Chin years saw warring, book burnings, and the executions of scholars. Searing pain stabbed the historian's heart, but he ignored it.

Emperor Jeng had linked the walls in the north and built the Straight Road. Laborers leveled hills and filled in depressions. To have cut the earth so deeply, severing its veins!

Emperor Jeng had exhausted the black-headed ones, shifting them to the borders and to Langya. It had been madness to increase taxes, revive the corvée, and cast wider the legal net. Su Ma sleeved his eyes. A thunderclap jolted him. An acrid odor assailed his nostrils as the rain drummed a staccato rhythm. The eunuch sipped from his teacup. Rising, he looked at the mindless phoenix holding the candle as he lit it.

He savored the cool. Why had the Chin regime changed so radically? Even Chancellor Lee couldn't check the maelstrom. *It must have been the magicians who had charmed Emperor Jeng. Now they enslave my own emperor. I'll create a Magician Lu who will warn Emperor Jeng that the Chin government will be toppled by Hu, and the monarch will imagine that Hu referred to a northern barbarian tribe.* Su Ma purred like a milk-sated kitten. Two other magicians would revile the Chin emperor and flee, igniting Emperor Jeng's hatred, and hundreds would perish. A charlatan would convince the Chin monarch that the isle of immortals couldn't be reached, because a giant fish prevented it. He would go the seashore, shoot a large fish, and ...!

Emperor Jeng had craved immortality after the assassination attempts. *Imagine bringing peace, yet being hunted like a beast. Everyone dies. Why couldn't a son of heaven see that? The Son of Heaven heeds a magician and loses an empire.*

The storm abated, and Su Ma reopened the shutters. Sweet, dust-free air filled his lungs. Doves cooed, and sunrays warmed the receiving earth. Su Ma fondled the inkstone. Characters darted down the bamboo strip; the last section of the first emperor's annals marched to muted cadence of bird cries.

PART 3
(215–210 BC)

CHAPTER 91

LEE SU (215 BC)

The announcement of a northern imperial tour surprised Chancellor Lee, who had not been invited. This fact, as well as the presence of many elite warriors, unsettled the high official.

Chancellor Lee learned that Marcus would accompany Emperor Jeng; he sent for the Roman. This visit was Marcus's first to the chancellor's quarters. Chancellor Lee stayed in an inner office, the centerpiece of which was a teak desk. Two phoenix candleholders framed the desk.

When Marcus entered, Chancellor Lee stood. "Greetings. Please make yourself comfortable. Would you prefer some juice?"

"Your Excellency! These quarters suit you better than the cramped box you previously occupied. Congratulations on your appointment. I do not wish anything, thank you."

"Your words are too kind. Permit me to congratulate you on being made an honorary academician. It's a worthy position."

"Thank you. It surprised me, especially being a barbarian."

Chancellor Lee poured for himself. The bronze pot looked ancient and expensive. "Well spoken. If I'm not mistaken, you now can speak about public matters."

"That's correct, and I will not shirk my duty."

"Did you know that His Majesty plans a northern expedition?" The pot seemed to be of late Spring and Autumn vintage—perhaps fifteen or twenty generations old. The slight crack along the base gave it an air of fragility and character.

"All I know is that it seems to be an inspection trip, like those to the east," Marcus admitted.

Chancellor Lee smiled. "And nothing else?"

"Not that I know. Why do you ask?"

A familiarity crept into the chancellor's manner as he brushed his robe of heavy silk brocade, dark in the Chin colors, with a snarling tiger on its front. "Once you helped me in a ... er ... delicate matter," he murmured.

"How might I help?" Marcus asked. His robe had been sashed at the waist in a modified toga style that was imitated by a few junior officials—the barbarian sash, some called it.

"What are your views of war and peace?"

"Years ago, I entered the army, and we fought an enemy whom we branded barbarians. Did you know that the Chinese written characters for 'barbarians' use the 'dog' signifier?" Marcus paused. "Anyway, we learned the locations of their towns and fortifications, then surprised them. The slaughter appalled me. Even now, I hear screams in my dreams. Ours is a beastly time."

Lee smiled sympathetically. "What if war resumed?"

"I would do anything to stop it! Your words dismay me."

The chancellor cooed. "I believe that this northern tour will be the prelude to a campaign against the northern bar ... peoples. I desire a permanent peace. General Tian heads a militarist clique and will use the upcoming expedition to sway His Majesty."

"We must stop them."

Chancellor Lee smiled. "For the present, watch and inform me about General Tian's conversations with the first emperor. The warfare clique blocked my attendance, knowing I oppose them. See how the trip develops and whether my suspicions are accurate."

Marcus frowned. "Your Excellency, I will stand by your side to sustain peace, but I will never act against His Majesty."

Chancellor Lee's raised hand reminded Marcus of a Bactran Buddha. "I would never ask you to betray His Majesty."

"I'll oppose war, but I'll not be a spy."

"We'll talk when you return. You can tell me anything you feel I might want to know." Warmth lit up the older man's face.

Marcus rose and departed. Chancellor Lee looked pleased.

CHAPTER 92
TAO (215 BC)

Tao and Jin Mi sat in the subprefect's office, poring over the schematics of the capital's sewer systems. "Look how these intersect under the central market … and then the line going to the zoological garden," Tao said.

"Yes, and the one running from the Ministry of Law to the river." Jin Mi wiped his brow.

Tao regarded the subprefect—a thin, middle-aged man with a wisp of a mustache. The man's eyes darted from one criminal to the other—and occasionally at the door, although it was late in the evening. The other officials had left the Ministry of Records.

"Are these all of the schematics? It seems some sewer and water lines are missing," Tao said quietly and raised an eyebrow.

"Older charts in the imperial library are difficult to get," the subprefect said.

"But, of course, you will bring them."

The man shivered. "Yes, I will see that they're here by next week. When may I have the honor of another visit?"

"You will be informed in the usual way. For tonight's effort, one-tenth of your debt is canceled. If other charts are useful, then another tenth will be taken off the books," Tao added softly. The official bowed.

When Tao and Jin Mi returned to Tao's place, both were disguised with false beards and merchants' attire. Tao spoke to his friend. "What do you think?"

"It's good our government keeps construction records; otherwise, we'd have to check out all sewers. Ugh, the stench."

"What do you think?"

"I'm guessing that the older maps will show abandoned sewers. The one under the eastern market seems promising," Jin Mi said.

"Yes. The one going to the gardens runs by an abandoned warehouse. We need to check it, too."

"I'll go out tonight. She may be invisible, but the night and its shadows are mine. This time, I'll see from the heart, as you said. Your ideas have been useful

225

in honing my skills," Jin Mi added as he looked up at the moon sliver. The next six nights would be perfect for spying.

"Take care, brother; she has power. I'll pay a visit to Black Bear, who should be able to enlighten me. Her magic can be countered. I'll bet on that," Tao noted as he regarded the moon and felt the dark lord's tug. As the men walked along, the air shimmered slightly behind them, and then grew still.

CHAPTER 93

MARCUS (215 BC)

Marcus and Ming dined on steamed fish, pork and vegetable soup, and stir-fry cabbage. The food didn't matter, because they feasted on each other. Although they'd been intimate for six years, their feelings continued to deepen. Marcus resented parting from her, but the emperor had commanded him.

After the meal, they communed in silence. Then Marcus recounted his meeting with Chancellor Lee.

Ming voiced agreement with Marcus's refusal. "How could he ask such a thing? And yet ... a new war is troubling."

"It can't happen, Ming. I get furious when I think about the generals plotting. I'd like to ..."

"To what? Kill them? Would you kill for peace?"

"But to launch another campaign! I'm appalled by ... alas, you're correct. We must employ peaceful means. If it all really did begin again, I don't know whether I'd want to stay."

"Where would you go, my love?"

Marcus was oblivious to the impact of his musing. "Perhaps to Sari's home," Marcus replied. "But then, I remember that Sari appeared in a dream, saying wars had resumed there. Is any place free of conflict? Everywhere I go, there'll be killing and maiming. Best stay here. Besides, I'd never leave thee."

The next morning, as they parted, their fingers released last.

In the evening, as he unrolled his bedding, Marcus found secreted wooden strips:

Stars, moon, sun smile
on you, us forever.
Joined in this life
we'll touch endlessly,
no matter the weather.
This brief journey,

not the last,
separated by time or death;
rejoined anew,
problems resolved,
joys shared,
birth, life, rebirth.

Marcus's reply revealed how his own simple views had altered.

Bitter northern breezes
wither my tender-shoot heart.
Brief sojourn, much to ponder;
if only I knew it one
of many
I'd not grieve the orchid's death.
Alone, no strength, no hope.
Tender words warm
'til we reconnect,
time after time.

If only he could compose better.

The northern tour reached the pounded barrier walls. Marcus gawked at the earthen snake wandering hills and valleys. Chin's wall measured two paces tall, with watchtowers at regular intervals. A concerted attack would not be stopped, but the slowing would permit defenders time to mobilize.

The imperial party halted for a three-day hunt. The evening meal featured rabbit, deer, quail, and antelope. War chants echoed across the hills. If he hadn't known better, Marcus would have believed this to be a war party.

The force passed through the Great Wall, heading into a land with tents and herds of sheep and horses. These peoples differed from the Chinese. Most stared, and only boys and men could be seen.

At a central encampment, the emperor hosted chiefs—men attired in skins and sporting necklaces of wild-animal teeth. All complained about Chinese encroachment and raids by northern tribes. Emperor Jeng promised that if they'd submit, he would protect them. They agreed, on the condition that the Chinese stay south of the Wall. The sovereign promised to heed their wishes.

The party turned southeast until it reached the Great River. Marcus had heard of the legendary Great Yu who tamed the river two millennia ago. Yu had been the perfect official, because he never once went home in twelve years.

They hunted and fished. Marcus preferred roasted fish steaks.

At dawn on the last day by the river, the Roman was roused from his tent. He rubbed the sleep from his eyes and saw the assembled elite force in full battle dress. Many wore red sashes. Campfires gave the scene an eerie glow not unlike the one in the Gaul village so many years ago. The emperor, attired in crimson, stood before a man securely tied to a post. The captive fearfully looked around. A crimson-robed official handed Emperor Jeng a gleaming knife. Just as the sun crested the distant rolling hills, the monarch slit the captive's throat, then gutted him. Entrails spilled forth.

As the soldiers roared approval, Marcus choked back a cry of horror Tears welled up and rolled down his cheeks. Emperor Jeng smiled, tossed away the knife, and showed his blood-smeared hands to the cheering throng. Marcus turned away and vomited.

The next day, the imperial party turned southwest and headed home.

Riding hard, the force reached the capital in less than two days. Marcus cloistered himself with Ming.

The Garrison Commander, Meng Tian, submitted a memorandum calling for a northern campaign. Emperor Jeng called for a general debate. Several academicians signed a memo drafted by Ming and Hu Meng arguing that war undermined the peaceful era. The memo also urged the construction of more schools and libraries.

Chancellor Lee crafted his own memorandum:

> In spite of Your Majesty's boundless virtue and immortal military triumphs, I fear that attacking the northern barbarians will bring danger. Warriors would have to negotiate treacherous lands with dangers unknown and conditions unlike those of the liberation wars. The barbarians have no forts, no cities, no supply areas. They fly over the land like flocks of birds and can swarm like a horde of beasts, then quickly disperse. Alas, they would be difficult to snare. If we send lightly armed forces far north, our warriors will soon lack even the basic supplies, and if we heavily provision them, the baggage trains would bog down.
>
> Even if we could seize the barren lands, we could never completely control them. If we massacred them, this would hardly befit the son of heaven, the people's father-mother lord. With all due respect, General Tian's plan shows serious flaws.

A great military exercise commenced. The Chulu sacrifice and the grand military review, which coincided for the first time in sixty years, were celebrated. Twenty thousand crimson-attired soldiers assembled at Yung, and Emperor Jeng mounted a scarlet war chariot drawn by four red-maned white horses. The army headed to the imperial hunting preserve and formed four columns. A crimson sea flooded the game reserve, slaughtering hundreds of deer, foxes, bears, and other animals. Later, waves of cheers proclaimed a long, long life to the first Chin emperor.

CHAPTER 94
TAO (215 BC)

Black Bear opened his door and smiled. "Your field is clear. It's been long since you called on the dark one. I salute you."

"Thank you. The dark one teases and tempts, and then I long for the power, the rush of energy through my loins, the sweetness of his lore. But the dreams tore my soul. I will remain free of the lure of the dark one."

"Please enter. What brings you here? By the way, there's a being in the trees. Don't turn; just act natural."

To Tao, the cozy room looked as it had when Tao last visited. No, he corrected himself, there was a clear quartz crystal on the table with the rat skull. "The being's why I'm here. Some woman can appear and disappear at will. She tried to scare or kill me, but she was thwarted. She trails me to learn my secrets. See what she did?"

Black Bear examined Tao's ravaged hand and the pouch on his neck. "You were wise to keep the finger. As long as you are bound with it, she cannot destroy you. Her first effort was to remove the finger to weaken your defenses; then she could kill you at her leisure. Tell me as we sit: what did you feel during the attack?"

Tao told the shaman. Suddenly he remembered the sheen of blue from the shimmering. "Blue … there was blue … a kind of slate blue, like the sky near the horizon at dusk."

"Slate blue and a malevolence that caused your hair to tingle. She's a gray lord and likely got her training in the far north. She's moving in on you. First, I must bind you energetically to your finger, so that if it's lost, you'll be protected. I'll give you a powder to throw her way when she's near. You don't have to reach her with it. I have a staff for you, and I'll bind this crystal to it." Black Bear indicated the quartz piece on the table. "When you leave, if she's still here, you'll know. I'll also give you a spell to negate her magic."

"Why do you help me?"

"Young man, you have special gifts ... treasures, in fact. Most have been used for power and gain, but you have shifted to a different purpose, though you crave gold. That's for another life, when you will abandon all wealth. I ask that you give a tenth of your wealth to needy ones ... especially those from the north. You have exceptional talents, and if you avoid the dark lord, you will use them wisely. You sought me over him in your struggle. I see you have found your soul brother. You will need to share the spell with him. I have another crystal for him. He must carry it, particularly in the day. The night is less of a concern for him. Bring him here to let me see you both. She has left because she knows who I am. Let us begin."

CHAPTER 95

MARCUS (215 BC)

Marcus hesitated to write down his opinions; yet, the longer the debate dragged, the more Marcus felt compelled to do something. The horror of witnessing the human sacrifice lingered, causing despair. More than once, Marcus wished to leave China and never look back. Instead, he asked for a private imperial audience and was received in the chrysanthemum garden. Emperor Jeng slumped with a bent head topped by a crimson turban.

"Marcus, too bad you missed yesterday's ceremonies. I haven't had such a grand time in years. I'm in the shade, because my eyes are warring with the sun and losing badly. What can I do for you, my friend?"

Marcus grew uneasy. "If I'd known, I'd have come later."

"Nonsense. I have time for you." Two doves flew into the garden; one courted the other bird, who'd have none of his ways.

"It's about the northern campaign, sire."

"Not you too! I should have closed the debate."

The Roman continued, "It should not take place."

"Why?"

"Before I came to China, sire, I joined the Roman army and participated in a campaign where thousands were massacred."

"Yes, I recall."

"We killed women and children," Marcus said.

"We will not slaughter children and women of the Huns, even though they massacre Chinese. We are not barbarians."

Marcus's heart sank. "Why fight? Try diplomacy. You've built a peaceful era ... melting the weapons and all. War wastes all."

"Barbarians know nothing about diplomacy. There's no other way than to smash them once and for all. Weakness invites attack."

"No group can threaten China," Marcus said.

"Academician Ming and her group said the same ... lecturing me! If she hadn't saved my life, I would have punished her insolence."

Marcus saw a dark pit yawning. "You've made up your mind."

Bloodshot eyes regarded him. "Yes. I insisted on the joint exercises and planned the northern tour."

"But why the debate? Having it fooled everyone."

"I knew that the campaign would be controversial and held a discussion to build support for it. Many, including Chancellor Lee, oppose it. He at least did not lecture me."

Marcus spoke softly, "But why war?"

The imperial chin thrust up. "War strengthens the state and its people. Without it, we grow lazy and weak."

"Large numbers of people will die," Marcus moaned. A chill wind blew. Gusts swirled into the garden. The coldness invigorated the flowers and the miniature pines. The doves had flown away.

"Weak plants must be weeded out so that the strong will get their share. Only three hundred thousand will be sent. I was sickly ... then rode hard, fought with swords, wrestled. Look at me: healthy and vigorous, save for this too-big head. The campaign will be a tonic!" Jeng straightened.

"I thought ..."

"People think too much. It's useful to know the opposition. They should be wary," Jeng said.

"But you called for a debate," Marcus said. "You need many views. To offer those views, officials must be fearless in their words. Even Han Fei believed that."

"Fei stuttered his way to jail and suicide. Yet ... I need advice. Still, I won't be lectured," Jeng said.

"Then you won't change your mind?"

"The campaign begins."

"I apologize for bothering you," Marcus said.

Jeng smiled. "Nonsense! Won't you stay for dinner?"

"I must go, Your Majesty."

"I'll visit your farm on the full-moon day. We'll talk."

Marcus wandered the city and stood before the bronze warrior who faced north, sword upraised. After solemnly regarding the colossus, he retired to his quarters to be alone.

The following day, the first chin emperor ordered the garrison commander, General Tian, to lead three hundred thousand warriors against the Huns. The general mobilized the unit, which had been readied for the recently completed war games. Others would be drawn from guards units and other forces in the region.

CHAPTER 96

TAO (215 BC)

Tao and Jin Mi paced in the large garden. Chrysanthemums bloomed, creating a golden carpet on each side of the path. Both men wore fur coats.

They needed to talk. In the last month, three Reds had been slain.

"The bitch is a deadly foe who will do her best to wipe us out or turn us into a fearing, sniveling band," Tao muttered. He was sleeping less those days, but not because of nightmares of old. His nightmares now focused on a deadly opponent … one who commanded the forces of nature.

"Yes, she creates chaos," Jin Mi said. "We Reds are fat and careless. It's time we renewed the training of new ones and extended the training of the regulars." The morning rain darkened the oak's trunk, highlighting its shape and essence.

Tao looked at his friend. It felt good to think about all of the details and angles with another. "Let's plan orientation sessions with groups of ten to fifteen. It will give us a chance to talk with each and boost morale. I got several things from Black Bear. I'm amazed that he is willing to help me … er, us. Here, this crystal is for you," Tao said as he revealed a smoky quartz to Jin Mi. It was warm to the touch.

"It will protect you in daylight. Black Bear knew of your night abilities. I'll give you a spell to ward off attacks. Do you think we should change residences?" Tao rooted out a ball of earwax and flicked it among the flowers.

"It might be prudent until we can destroy the invisible one. She knows where we live, and I assume she knows of our hideouts." Jin Mi looked at Tao, reading the vulnerability in the young crime lord's face. "Perhaps we might find places that have multiple and secret entrances. As well as taking precautions, brother, I think we must take the offensive. Return to our notes about the sewer systems and aqueducts and locate their dwellings. We need to bring in perhaps three to five others."

"Good point. I'm pleased that we've found each other. Black Bear said we are soul brothers. He was happy we'd met. We need to see him together," Tao said. The wind had picked up, and there was a faint scratching nearby. He turned at the sound. Tao relaxed when he saw the branch scraping the side of the house. "Old Juang's safe place has two secret entrances—places he'd dug in case of attack. I haven't been there for a long time. Perhaps I'll sleep there once in a while," Tao added as his eyes swept the garden and its walls.

"We might do more tunneling. As a warlord once said, 'Know yourself and know your enemy ...' Let's meet them at their level, but let's gather information about them. I'll move into a new dwelling, but in a way that won't attract attention. I'll move at night. Let's go in. Night comes, and the wind chills."

CHAPTER 97

EMPEROR JENG (215 BC)

Autumn turned unseasonably cold. As General Tian prepared to march north, trees donned their colorful coats earlier than anyone could remember. Birds massed for southern flights shortly after the initial troop mobilization concluded. Farmers harvested their crops and prepared for a long, bitter winter. Squirrels scurried for nuts and fallen seeds.

Emperor Jeng ordered celebratory send-offs. Vibrant blue, green, and red banners of the first, fourth, and sixth columns vied with the brilliant autumnal hues. His Majesty presented General Tian with the seal of command, and they rode past gaily decorated buildings and cheering people to the ancestral hall. Attired in ebony robes, Emperor Jeng drove a black chariot with a team of black horses.

Within the month, the first battles were fought. Victories! Emperor Jeng pressed General Tian, and casualties mounted. When the commander pleaded for a halt, Emperor Jeng petulantly agreed.

During winter, new conscripts were mustered to fight the Vietnamese in the south—launching a two-front war. On advice from the naval command, Emperor Jeng commissioned a fleet of triple-decked ships, each capable of transporting one hundred armed men. By late spring, the navy had landed two thousand veterans behind Vietnamese lines, where the Chinese captured or destroyed seventeen fortifications. Two weeks later, the force drove inland to link up with Chinese land forces.

By spring, General Tian had assembled his complete force. Because of the unusually dry winter, granary stockpiles were tapped.

Five months later, General Tian proclaimed the pacification of barbarians south of the Great River. Sparse rain and withering plants failed to dampen the imperial celebrations.

By late summer, imperial armies swelled to half a million men. Emperor Jeng ordered the conscription of those who had previously escaped the draft: husbands living with their in-laws and sons of merchants. Southern duty was detested because of tropical diseases—and because rice rather than millet was eaten there. A battalion of northern regulars rioted over food.

A year after the northern campaign commenced, a scandal rocked the court. The imperial secretary accused the equipage officer, Jao Gao (who served as an imperial tutor to Prince Hu Hai), of accepting bribes and abusing his office. The emperor asked a brother of General Tian to be imperial prosecutor. After investigative reports were studied, Prosecutor Tian recommended that the bribery charges be dismissed, with the accuser tried for slander.

Concerning the second charge, abuse of office, a pattern of irregularities had emerged. Prosecutor Tian suggested torture to exact a confession and dismissal of all posts. The report saddened Emperor Jeng, who respected Jao Gao's service and the excellent job he'd done in teaching Hu Hai.

One day, as the monarch paced in the rose garden, a haggard Hu Hai entered and prostrated himself.

"My son, what brings you here?"

"Father! I must speak to you on a vital matter."

"Have you taken ill? What troubles you?" Emperor Jeng asked.

"My tutor, Jao Gao," Hu Hai answered.

"The case is not good," Jeng said.

Hu Hai sobbed and coughed violently. "Oh no! Papa, Paaaa. I *know* that he's innocent! He's not guilty. Please!"

"I find it difficult to believe him guilty. He might have exercised better judgment, but the record's unclear. That's why torture seemed appropriate. Given the lack of hard evidence, though, the prosecutor's decision surprises me."

"You … can dismiss … the case," stammered Hu Hai. "You are emperor. Oh, Papa. I could not live if something happened to him."

"I haven't made up my mind. Run along, and let me consider."

The young man's eyes cleared. "Please save him, Papa. He is innocent. I would speak the same for you!"

Hu Hai's ardor pleased the emperor. "Run along, young man. I hope that you will defend me as energetically. Don't fret; nothing serious will happen." Hu Hai rose, composed himself, and marched away, smiling like a cat that had eaten a sparrow.

The following day, the first Chin emperor issued a decree absolving Jao Gao of wrongdoing. Prosecutor Tian was commended for his investigation, and other principals in the case received relatively light reprimands. Chancellor Lee was delighted, interpreting the decision as a slap at the prosecutor and his family—one of whom was General Tian.

CHAPTER 98

TAO (214 BC)

Information accumulated. Tao created a war room in the building where the business of the Reds was now conducted. It was formerly a storage cellar, but Tao had it refurbished and extended. A new tunnel ran from the war room to the outside.

Tao inspected a massive map spread across the oak table. It had to be taken in sections into the underground room. On it, Tao had drawn a composite map, combining old and new versions.

Tao mustered a special team of the Reds: the moles who would explore the sewers, with orders to avoid conflict. If there was no choice, they were to fight, but capture one enemy alive.

The Reds had lost another five men—twenty-seven for the year. Tao fretted about the growing unease among the Reds. Meetings with new recruits buttressed feelings of solidarity, but continued losses sapped morale. Tao feared infiltrators and personally interviewed newcomers. But he worried that some masked their true thoughts. Tao looked at the bear lamps lining the walls. They gave the room a lively glow.

Tao touched the pouch containing his finger bone, then examined the map. If he only knew what to look for; the leads they had gathered turned up nothing. The nest was somewhere ... but where?

Jin Mi entered the room, unwrapping his scarf and folding it neatly. "Boss, we have a solid lead. There was a watcher at the Golden Cock last night. I followed him when he went off duty. After wandering the streets beyond the Central Market for a water level—he was good, by the way, kept doubling back and checking and rechecking—he ducked into a hole-in-the-wall place, the Fighting Badger. Just as I entered, he exited out the back. Because of my mission, I couldn't follow. I ordered liquor and sat for three water levels. Found a place in the shadows."

Tao watched Jin Mi, observing the animated cast to the master thief's face. "It sounds hopeful, night master," Tao said. "The Fighting Badger? The one on

Sixth and Eternal Harmony? The new map arrived last night, through the secret way." They had agreed to keep a formality between them when others were present.

Jin Mi pointed as he spoke. "It should be there. If they use sewers and aqueducts, then they'd go through that aqueduct and possibly on to the sewer system … there. Perhaps it's as simple as a room beneath the Fighting Badger. I should nose around." Jin Mi smiled ruefully and wrinkled his nose.

"Do you think that wise? After all, she has probably gotten a few good looks at you," Tao said. He knew the determined look in the master thief's eyes.

"It's time to learn about the enemy," Jin Mi replied decisively. "Perhaps some of the special detachment might come with me." He scratched his chin and tugged on his earlobe.

CHAPTER 99

MING TIAN (214 BC)

As the administrative year began, Emperor Jeng forbade sacrifices to the morning star. Academicians Ming and Hu puzzled over the curious prohibition.

Hu said, "Wait! Wasn't Si Ho, mother of the ten suns, associated with the morning star?"

Ming started. "In the far south, there was an ancient tradition about Si Ho. Let's check." The academicians hurried to the imperial library—a calm eye in a storm of bustling activity and political intrigue. When the women reached the stacks, they beelined to the southern section, finding a faded, termite-ravaged wooden tablet: "Ancient Legends." They deciphered the part about Si Ho and the morning star.

Si Ho
Mother of the ten suns
Who birthed the heavenly bodies
Who created the calendar of
the ten-day week.
Who puts all into motion
by her celestial design.
Each morn we peer
into the Valley of Light
watching her bathe a sun.
The one she chooses
lies in the sweet gulf waters.
We see her place the orb
in the branches of the Fusang Tree
where it sits among
the tiny leaves.
Raised one hundred miles
into the sky

until it starts the trek
across the celestial arc.
Finally it rests
upon the western peaks
only to return to her again
as each of us does
after our earthly sojourn.

"Ming, such exquisite words. Let's make copies. No wonder His Majesty forbade the sacrifice."

"Besides, another Si Ho legend speaks about peace and harmony, when our sovereign demands war, war, war." She sneezed violently.

"May you live to be a hundred! This must be preserved. Too many books have already gone to dust," Hu replied. They made three copies to share with students and trusted colleagues.

At the winter-solstice ceremony, the royal academicians received imperial invitations to a special banquet in their honor at the Ganchuan Palace. The date was Lunar New Year's Day (213 BC).

CHAPTER 100

MARCUS (213 BC)

Ming and the Roman were to attend the banquet, along with officials of the fifth rank or higher and field-grade army officers. Preparations for the august occasion occupied Emperor Jeng, who desired to bridge a gap between his military officers and the scholars who were critical of each other.

Marcus selected a yellow-bordered brown robe; for some reason, his clothes tended toward dark colors. His shoes—sandals really—had leather embedded with jade, in the traditional Chin style. Ming selected a sky blue silk robe laced with silver threads and accented by a shimmering silver border. Her hair, arranged in the ancient Shang style, coiled at the top, with a forearm's-length, thick tress running down from the topknot below her left ear. Silver unicorn hairpins romped in her hair, and her slippers were heavy black silk, with silver pieces sewn in.

Marcus beheld her. "Ming, you are the world's most beautiful woman!" They touched, content in themselves and each other.

"I've heated some scented Chu liquor, my love."

"Tonight, Ming, I've fallen in love anew."

Ming giggled, and mirth-filled notes danced gaily in the room. She glided to the flask. Marcus blinked again; she personified beauty better than the marvelous Greek statues.

His face had softened, and his belly bulged. Time flowed better in loving smiles and sighs than in years when one's heart ached with love. The evening stretched like a diaphanous web to the twinkling stars.

"A toast to the ever-lengthening night," Ming said. Cups were hoisted, saluted, then tipped. "Another to the magic. Long will it tarry in my breast."

"Whatever should happen, my love, I'll treasure thee. Partners we are: unique in ourselves, complete in the other. The sum larger than the parts." Marcus's words moved Ming.

They savored the moment. Silence is of different kinds and breathes different meanings.

CHAPTER 101

JIN MI (213 BC)

The master thief held his breath as the turgid water flowed sluggishly around him. Bits and pieces of ... things ... bobbed in the river of sewage. Jin Mi did not look closely. His tiny lantern, with three sides and top covered, shed light to the front. All was cold—as well as foul-smelling.

Two men waded ahead five or so paces apart from each other. No one spoke. If Jin Mi's memory served, they were near the abandoned warehouse identified as a likely meeting place and nest. He saw the man's hand close into a fist—the signal to halt. Jin Mi repeated it to the trailing man. Jin Mi wished he could see ahead; he disliked being at the mercy of another.

The night master heard a muffled commotion. After Jin Mi waited for what seemed like a water level, the team leader emerged from the dark, carrying something.

"Lookout," the short, stock man explained in a whisper. "I throttled him before he could sound the alarm."

Jin Mi would never face this man anywhere. "Give him to Cha for questioning. We'll go ahead." Jin Mi kept his voice low, though he could feel the energy rush through him. The leader nodded and carried the unconscious body back to the ledge where they'd entered the water. After a few minutes, he slipped by the night master.

The team stopped before stairs leading up to the Fighting Badger. Splintered boards lay everywhere. Some stuck out like hairs on a street urchin's head. The team communicated through hand signals and whispered commands. The leader crept up the stairs. After a time, he returned and signaled that another watcher lurked above. They'd agreed beforehand that two missing watchers would give away the scouting mission, so they left the second alone. The enemy gang would be difficult to surprise.

Later, after washing and applying ample amounts of flower scents, Jin Mi reported to Tao, who was alone in Old Juang's former residence. "You were correct. Our enemy is well led and careful. This will not be like the old days, when we swept up our opponents."

Tao shrugged his shoulders to relieve the tension stored there. He had slept little in the last two nights. "Perhaps we can force them to make a mistake. We can storm the Fighting Badger or burn it down and simultaneously hit the warehouse. It would be our opening gambit—a frontal assault and a morale booster."

Jin Mi regarded Tao. It was past midnight, and the master thief felt alive despite his ordeal. His face lay partly in the shadow. "Some kind of attack should bring a response. A fire along with a sewer assault might be the thing. If the attack fails, we can start a fire from below."

"That might be difficult because of the damp, but whale oil burns hot and consumes damp wood quickly. I'd like to experiment with the best way to start a blaze before we begin. This will take a lot of Reds. Can we trust them?" Tao paused, listened, and looked. Jin Mi moved to the window. Their crystals had begun glowing, just as Black Bear had said they would. They knew she was not in the house; the glow was too faint. They signaled to one another and left by opposite doors.

The garden was dimly lit by a moon smile. Tao uttered his spell under his breath. The air shimmered and briefly materialized into a caped form. Tao threw his knife and heard a thud as well as a muffled grunt. He saw the form race toward the garden gate. Jin Mi burst from the shadows and knocked the figure off balance. It righted itself, shimmered into nothingness, and slipped away. Jin Mi and Tao reached the gate at the same time.

"Damn! At least I did some damage with my knife," Tao said as he closed the gate. It was unlikely that she would circle back for another attack, but he took no chances.

As they searched the garden, Jin Mi spotted a foreign object. He stooped and retrieved a clasp, holding it to the light. "A crystal skull … ruby chips for the eyes. A scrying device."

"Look for blood. We should get a candle." Tao trembled. Jin Mi went into the house and came out with a candle. Tao stayed at the spot where the skull had been discovered. On careful inspection, they found a tiny blot of blood.

"Let's go to Black Bear's house tomorrow." Tao added.

"Brother, we have the leadership meeting. Let's wait. Let me scoop the blood and some dirt into this cup."

"Brother, if the bitch bleeds, we can kill her."

CHAPTER 102
MARCUS (213 BC)

Ming and the Roman strolled into the banquet hall: Chinese and barbarian, man and woman, brown and blue. They prostrated themselves before the first emperor of Chin, then moved to their seating places.

A five-piece orchestra's harmonies encouraged civility. Seating arrangements wove scholars with officials and military personnel. Guests sat in circles to facilitate servants' dispensation of liquor and snacks. Flavored, regular, regional, warmed, and chilled spirits were urged. Marcus sipped on a peppered variety. His nose dilated to the spices, and he focused on the mat's members, watching rather than joining conversations. Ming sat beside a much-decorated general and adeptly drew him out. They laughed, and their heads nearly touched. The silver-headed man was her kind of man: Chinese, elite, and handsome. Marcus suddenly felt helpless, vulnerable, and alone.

Baked suckling pig arrived. The flesh fell easily from the bones, and as Marcus chewed, juice filled his mouth. The alcohol diluted the heavy feeling. Among the trays of roast fowl, he recognized duck and chicken. He looked at Ming and watched the liquid words tumble from her mouth: "Vulture and curlew. The small one's more succulent."

Succulent: what an appropriate word. Marcus tried the two birds. The vulture surprised … or was it the curlew?

Two meat dishes arrived. Ming used her fingers, and Marcus took her cue. Ginger with pork, leeks and garlic with puppy—savory. Someone asked him to try the badger's paw and monkey brains, but he declined. They dined on red carp steamed with greens, mullet with a peony sauce, and then turtle meat flavored with smartweed.

Time to relieve himself. Winding hazily through the servants, Marcus remembered to prostrate himself. Emperor Jeng smiled. Marcus reached the bathroom and lifted his robes. Someone approached.

"Your Majesty," Marcus said.

"Finish your business. How's the meal?"

246

Marcus emptied his bladder. "Delicious ... especially the piglet, carp ... and curlew or vulture. I'm not sure which."

The emperor smiled. "Try the monkey meat and badger's paws."

"Everything's splendid ... even the music, sire." Dribbles landed on his feet.

"Did you know that all the musicians are blind? I selected them and the music. I want to harmonize my servants—all of them." Jeng beamed. "Any quarrels? My officers can be barbaric. Haha. Get it?"

"All's quiet, sire."

"Excellent! A couple of surprises will come."

By the time of Marcus's return, the grains had arrived. Two intrigued him: brown and white rice, he learned. He savored the brown. A sudden longing for the foods of Rome overwhelmed Marcus.

Dried fruit and three soups completed the banquet. Marcus felt like the piglet. The foulest fart stench swirled around him. When the orchestra halted, acrobats tumbled in. Five men performed energetic balancing feats. They yielded to a stout man and two young boys. The man managed a pole about one person tall, with two extensions looped at the top. Each child grasped an extension loop as the man lifted. They twirled energetically. Marcus feared a crash. When the spinning halted, the tykes threaded their feet through the leather circles. The pole reached the man's forehead. As they twirled furiously, Marcus started to rise to their aid, but the performance came to a successful end.

A young woman dressed in bright colors entered. Marcus had heard that she lived where the Wall ended in the east. The girl artfully prostrated herself, then awaited the placing of nine suspended drums: three to a side, with the open side facing the audience.

The girl regally grasped the drumsticks and struck. A liquid rumbling echoed through the hall, sound chasing sound. The tempo accelerated; her green, blue, and purple robe flashed. Cadences built to a crescendo. A musical tidal wave swept over the room. Lightning flashed, thunder boomed, and electricity crackled.

Marcus flew to the edge of an abyss where cold winds howled, and a crash chased him home. The audience members rose and bowed first to the emperor, then to the youthful performer. Emperor Jeng nodded to her; following a wave of shock at that singular honor, approval filled the hall, along with a chorus of "Long life, long life, long, long life."

A figure rose from the emperor's entourage. Head Academician Jo prostrated himself, stood erect, and spoke. "A toast to His Imperial Majesty: Formerly, Chin covered but a thousand miles. Now the lands within the four seas are one. The barbarian tribes have been driven far. All under heaven acknowledge your sovereignty, my lord. States have been transformed into commanderies and districts. Your subjects enjoy tranquil lives. So shall it last for ten thousand generations. From ancient days, there has been no equal to Your Majesty's might and virtue. I wish Your Excellency a long, long life."

"Long life!" chants reverberated. One hunched man walked to the front. Heads followed his deliberate march. Academician Chun, an old-fashioned scholar, was alternately ridiculed and admired. Chun solemnly turned to Emperor Jeng, prostrated himself, and stood. "Your Majesty. I have heard that the Shang and Jo dynasties lasted more than one thousand years because fiefs were parceled out to younger members of the royal house. Now Your Majesty holds all of the land within the four seas ... yet your blood relations are still commoners. Should disloyal subjects arise, how can the dynasty be saved without the aid of your loyal kin? I have yet to hear of any enduring government that was not based on ancient precedents. Academician Jo's flattery will lead you into error."

The white-bearded man prostrated himself again and walked out the main door. Emperor and guests sat hushed. What had he said? Was Jo Jing-Jen disloyal? Angry shouts chased the eccentric speaker.

The mediating skills of the emperor's men could not cope with the rising fury. Emperor Jeng walked to a drum and banged it. "Quarreling is forbidden. Good night." The crowd again rose as cries of "Long life!" swept him out the door.

At home, Marcus looked at the liquor flask that had been chilled to await their return. Now it seemed out of place, because his heart had been saddened by the strange and angry turn of events caused by the academicians' speeches.

CHAPTER 103

EMPEROR JENG (213 BC)

Emperor Jeng summoned his senior officials to discuss Chun's speech. Already, he'd received petitions calling for the man's dismissal, trial, and punishment. A few requested the abolition of the imperial academy. Although angry about the evening, His Majesty knew that punishing the scholar was unwarranted. Instead, the debate focused on the substance of the brief speech.

Chancellor Lee waited. Horrified by the Academician's challenge to his original memo about the establishment of a centralized polity, he took the words as a personal assault. Doubt might be cast on those like him—those who followed Master Shun.

His memo began,

> The five sovereigns did not emulate each other, nor did the three dynasties adopt each other's ways, yet all enjoyed good governments. This fact is no paradox, because the times changed. This great empire will last for ages. All of this befuddles a foolish pedant who praised the early dynasties as if they were models that might be followed for eternity. In times long past, the barons fought among themselves and gathered wandering scholars. All was chaos. Today, the land's pacific, and all laws and orders come from a single source. The people support themselves with farming and crafts, while students study the laws and prohibitions. Scholars wish us to learn only from old ways rather than from the new. They use learning to oppose government and confuse simple folk.
>
> As senior chancellor, I'm compelled to speak on pain of death. In former days, when the world was torn by chaos and disorder, different states arose and argued from the past against the present. Now, Your Majesty has conquered the world, distinguished between black and white, and set unified standards. Yet, these opinionated pedants slander the laws and judge each new decree according to their school, opposing it secretly in their hearts while openly discussing it in the streets. They brag to the sovereign to gain fame, propose strange arguments to gain distinction, and incite mob actions. If this is not prohibited, Your Majesty's prestige will suffer, and factions will be formed among the people.

I humbly propose that historical records, save for those of Chin, be gathered and burned. Any non-academician or nonofficial who keeps ancient songs, historical records, or writings of the hundred schools should be severely punished.

All of these works must be confiscated and burned in the commanderies. Those who quote old songs and records must be publicly executed; those who use ancient precedents to challenge the new order should be exterminated along with their families. Officials who know of such cases but fail to report them should be punished.

If, in thirty days from the issuing of this order, the owners of these works still possess them, their faces should be tattooed, and they should labor on the Wall. Books on divination, medicine, and agriculture will be spared. Those who wish to study can learn from the officials.

Emperor Jeng read the memo, which reaffirmed the new ways and linked the critic to other subversives. The recommended actions would stop external criticism and chill inner posturings. Destroying the histories would be a masterstroke. The memo was published as an officially endorsed decree.

CHAPTER 104

LEE BU (213 BC)

Lee Bu, the son of Chancellor Lee, believed that his father had gone mad. Books' ideas flavored conversations! Who would wish to live in world without books? Bu reverted to his gloom-filled days, side by side with easeful death.

After composing a letter to Marcus and a terse note to his father, the middle-aged man went to the inner offices. Lee Bu calmed himself and centered a knife just above his left wrist. A deep gash opened along his inner forearm. Reddish purple fluid flowed down his arms. Blood-wetted fingers transferred the blade, and a second gash opened along the inner right forearm. Bu's life poured out and down to the mat.

CHAPTER 105

FENG PING (213 BC)

Feng Ping peered at the irrigation system that stretched to the gloomy horizon, where workers toiled in the drained channel. Some hauled dirt. The log stockades that held back the muddy river water would soon be removed. Feng felt the solidity of the barrier they formed. One log was lashed atop another, mortared with earth and braced by half-split beams pounded into the ground.

As a chill wind blew, an aide—a thin man of twenty-seven with a beard that looked moth-eaten—interrupted.

"Your Excellency, we must return to the carriage. The morning grows late."

"In a moment. Did you know this project came from the vision of a father-son team?" Feng Ping asked.

The aide stamped his foot to warm himself. "Wasn't it Lee Bing and his son, Erh?" he queried. Everyone knew the tale of the Lees.

Feng Ping ignored the impatience. His aide was an accomplished administrator, even if he had no poetic bent. "More than two generations ago, Bing wrestled with the problem of the flooding Min River. Over there! One can barely make out that rock and log formation—the Diamond Dyke. Bing was a visionary." Feng Ping admired the genius.

Logs floated on the dammed river. Cut far upstream, they waited for spring—when they'd be released, then sorted by workers with iron-tipped poles.

"People seem like ants carrying dirt specks and twigs."

Feng Ping whirled. "They are humans! Each has a father and mother, wife, children, brothers, or sisters; just like you, just like me. They have fears and joys; they dream, just like us." The startled aide contemplated his feet. "Never regard another as a beast, bird, or insect. I fought in the liberation wars. Officers called our enemies snakes and rats. I killed more than a dozen. Then I had a dream where each man I killed came to me and talked about his life. We must go down there to pay respects."

The wind picked up. Feng Ping tripped over a tree root. His cheek was gouged, and his arm twisted. The horrified aide assisted Feng. They reached the wooden shrine—a monument to a father by a filial son. A scroll with characters meaning "service," "dedication," and "fidelity" had been posted. The script showed strength; each stroke was a knife cut. An engineer's square and sighting rod rested by the statue.

"Your Excellency?" the aide asked.

"Yes?"

"One day, there'll be a shrine to you. Last year, your foresight prevented disaster. The drought reduced the harvest, but your granaries supplied the needy. And the irrigation project on the Pi River brings water to new farmlands. One day, my lord, you will be the imperial secretary, and I will erect a temple to you."

"I'm content to serve in Ba." A roiling thunderhead loomed.

"With due respect, Excellency, you'll live out your days in the capital."

Feng appraised the man. The cold made wet mucus drip from his nose. Reddened cheeks highlighted the admiring eyes.

"A tempest comes. We must outrun it."

CHAPTER 106

TAO (213 BC)

Two men rode to the rural retreat, arriving just as dawn broke. Icy air invigorated them. There was no way that the northern bitch would be following, unless she had mastered the art of turning horses or carriages invisible. They dismounted and strode purposefully into the small mansion. The cellar burned with a brilliant illumination. Jin Mi sniffed the air.

Tao spoke. "What do you think, night master? Did you take any wounds?" Tao's cheeks were ruddy, and his eyes burned brightly.

"I think we gave them a powerful blow, brother. You were correct to just burn the warehouse from below and await the fleeing enemy above. Many died like the animals that are slaughtered during the emperor's hunt. Blood everywhere."

"A strong but not fatal blow," Tao said.

"I agree, brother. But we gave them something to think about, and we know about another headquarters from the captured lookout." Jin Mi picked up a liquor tripod and drank.

"This room has a feel," Tao said. "I thought it could be cleaned away. Servants have been at it for days." He signaled for the servants to leave. "Brother, in this room, I summoned a dark lord. I cannot say his name …" Tao broke off. "Brother, I poisoned Old Juang at a banquet before he killed me. Part of me celebrated his death, even though he had treated me like a son. Yet, he had me educated by hard men—one of whom used me as his sex slave, threatening to kill me if I ever told. I kept the secret, and then I became an expert in poisons." Tao could not bear to look at Jin Mi.

"I had such a life," Jin Mi said. "But the one who used me was my mother. She did things when I was young. She had men, but used me too. Perhaps it made her powerful. I'll never know, because one day I strangled her with a silk cord … twisting and twisting," Jin Mi whispered.

"The dark lord gave me powers. My ability to read minds was expanded. I could see the future's strong possibilities and could move things with my mind. I could even see through walls. But to gain and expand these powers, I fed the lord with sacrificed animals … then humans. Remember, before you were made night master, I took the lives of your predecessor and his accomplice." Tao looked at the master thief, who never flinched.

"The dark lord flattered me as he extended his control," Tao continued. "I ate raw meat. I thought of suicide but loved life. I turned to Black Bear, and he led me out of the blackness. I love that old man. I have been free for years. Then you came into my life. I thank you for your trust and your faith," Tao said and raised his thumb. Jin Mi raised his; they joined thumbs again.

"We have a second campaign phase. The bitch is wroth. If we can hit her again, we can pull her out of hiding."

CHAPTER 107

FENG PING (213 BC)

Feng Ping and his aide arrived at Laibu village, a little over five miles from the district capital. Local prefects waited. Laibu had been selected to implement an idea that Feng Ping had developed. Laibu counted 45 families, with 226 people in all.

Feng summoned the village heads. "We've come to help your village. Every village has tensions, feuds, and hostilities. We need the names of men who will speak about problems," Feng said, looking at the subdued faces. "I need you to promise that if no one speaks, you will. Tensions must be released. No one likes to hear bad things, but we must help Laibu." The clear, blue sky held a wintry sheen, and the stench of pig manure lingered.

Feng spoke slowly. "We need someone to record the session. We must help people see their mistakes and know that they will not be punished. The goal is to help. When we finish, we'll have a feast. I'll provide the food and drink. We want all to feel good."

One toothless man spoke. "Let me understand this. I or we will speak out against those who cause problems. That will start the criticizing. What if people resist or lie?"

"Others should support you. If someone resists, treat them in a friendly manner. If things get out of hand, I will act. Tomorrow will be a better day." Two elders looked skeptical, but others seemed willing—likely thinking about the roasting pigs.

After a simple meal, Deng Lao, the eldest, complained of tormentors who teased him about his slow pace and head tic. Tears wet the ground as he imitated their taunts of "Old man, old man, can't walk, can't hold your old head still. Old man, old man, funny walk, funny talk!" Deng Lao continued, "I've helped others all my life. It's bad enough to feel useless without being taunted by the little monsters. Sometimes I just want to die."

When Deng Lao sat, Old Shu struggled to his feet. "When I was a boy, our village was a family. People helped each other. Now, no one has time. The only

ones who notice are ruffians who curse me! If we don't stop it, the next genera-
tion'll be worse."

Voices urged the two to name their tormentors' fathers. Five were finally
pushed to the middle. Four bowed, but the fifth, Jang Pu, stood defiantly. Deng
Lao shouted, "You should be ashamed!"

Four heads went lower, but Jang stiffened. Someone called for the five men to
apologize. One asked people to tell him when his son did bad things. Another
slapped himself and said, "I'll correct my son, and myself. I swear on the Soil
Lady's altar. I'm sorry, Deng Lao, Old Shu. I'm sorry he cursed you."

Each repented, save for the defiant one.

"Don't stand there, Jang Pu! Your boy beats my little one and kicks dogs.
Speak!"

"Why don't you say something, Jang Pu? Too good for us?"

The man's eyes flashed. "Who said that? Stand up!"

"I said it!" A husky man with a barrel chest rose. "Your boy kicked a dog 'til it
couldn't walk. You saw it but said nothing."

"Lies, all lies! My son's not bad."

"He's the worst! Many don't let their sons play with him."

"Admit he's bad!"

"I'm not a bad father," Jang Pu protested. "I beat the boy."

A dogfight erupted at the edge of the crowd.

Deng Lao pushed forward. "One day, this bad boy will commit a crime for
which we'll all pay. Your boy's a demon. He fools you, because you choose to be
blind."

Jang Pu bent. "I've been wrong," he said in a low tone. His face was wrought,
and veins in his temple stood out like ropes.

Deng Lao said, "Go on, go on."

"My wife spoils him. I'll … beat her when I return."

Deng Lao waved his hand. "No! It's you! Admit!"

Jang Pu mumbled.

"We can't hear. Lift your head and tell us."

"I'm sorry," Jang Pu wailed. "He is bad … cruel. I spoil him, my only son. I
saw the dog but did nothing. I love my son!"

A voice called out. "Go on, more!"

"Hush, let him speak."

The father saw that at least one had a kind word. "He bullies. He hurts animals, and I know he hurt the men who spoke. I have been a terrible father, but I

vow to train him. Our village is a family. Watch him and beat him. I'm sorry, Deng Lao. I'm sorry, Old Shu." Jang Pu banged his head on the ground.

Deng Lao wobbled as he addressed the father. "You confessed; that's good. Most children are spoiled. Help each other."

"Deng Lao's right. Train them before they break the law." Others confessed to arrogance, rudeness, and quarreling loudly.

Feng finally spoke up. "I praise your honesty, candor, and sincerity. Congratulate yourselves. Of course, some apologies hurt. Who likes to lose face? Think how to help. I have spoiled my own sons. I'll correct them. Tonight we'll celebrate. Jang Pu will be the honored guest." The subprefects reeled before their superior's self-criticism. Some thought him eccentric, but most gained new respect for the diminutive man.

At the feast, people ate and drank heartily. When Feng reached home, he was buoyed by the day. An waited with a bowl of hot soup and washcloths. In a short while, he was refreshed, and they chatted. His animated manner warned her that he was too charged to sleep. It was best to let him talk.

The next day, a wave of polar air—rare for Ba—gripped the land. The slate blue sky was the same color of people who had frozen to death during the night. Farmers found dead animals and birds. Feng Ping shivered in his carriage. Although he was heavily bundled, the frigid air clawed his bones like a hawk's talons.

The carriage ride unsettled Feng, and an intake of the arctic air seared his chest. He arrived late at the newly constructed office complex—functional in design and simple in decoration. The most prominent decorative items were the phoenix taper holders. As one wag moaned, "Ba must be the refuge of cast-off phoenix lamps."

The chief aide presented Feng with salutations from the staff and offered the book-burning decree. Feng read, then reread the document.

"Madness!" Feng exclaimed. "This stupid order is madness! I won't do it." Feng recognized his blunder. In his mind's eye, he saw the four horses failing to retrieve careless words. "Thank you for greeting me. You are dismissed," he said abruptly. A clerk posted the decree.

Four months later, an imperial investigative team arrived, commandeered two offices, and took testimony. The team members included two vice-ministers (war and internal security) and two army commanders; the team head was Head Academician Jo Jing-Jeng.

After weeks of gathering evidence, an arrest warrant charged Feng Ping, who surrendered as officials sealed his house. An, sons, and servants had to live with Widow Jing's daughter.

A public trial was held in a huge courtyard, and citizens massed to hear the proceedings. The investigating team constituted the jury. Five members sat according to rank at five tables before the central office building, each wearing the insignia of their units. Academician Jo presided; he was dressed in white.

Feng Ping, in chains, sat at the left side of the panel. He impassively faced his accuser, Pi Bi, who sat on the panel's right. Jo Jing-Jeng began. "You first reported the treason."

"I cannot know if my charge was the first," Pi Bi said. "I did submit one, however. When the accused arrived that morning, he cursed the imperial decree and asserted that he wouldn't enforce it." Pi Bi's hands worried an embroidered, white silk scarf. Beady eyes shifted from face to face.

Jo continued, "Besides that statement, what evidence have you that the accused plotted against the state?"

"He hid fugitives from the book-burning decree officers."

"And how do you know of this?" asked Jo.

"One of the accused's aides remarked that a few released convicts had passed through our town and stayed with the accused. I knew from the records we received they were released convicts."

"And what other evidence have you?"

"The accused failed to thoroughly check the houses of suspected scholars. He, in effect, ignored the decree."

Loud murmurs rippled through the crowd. The panel members adjourned the trial and continued the testimony in secret. After Pi Bi was dismissed, Feng denied harboring fugitives and insisted that he believed Ba's citizens were obeying the decree.

"And were your words on the day of your receipt of the book-burning decree, 'Madness. This stupid order is madness. I won't do it!'"

"Yes, Your Excellency. Those were my exact words, except for the emotional inflections of the time. I had returned from an exhausting trip, and it was the coldest day in memory. My patience was frazzled, and my judgment was impaired."

"Are you saying that you would have replied differently otherwise?"

Feng realized the panel had to make an example of him. "I believe that it is an unfortunate decree and will defend that conclusion if given an opportunity. But I believe that my actions demonstrate that I did, in fact, enforce it."

"Please tell this panel why this decree, authored by Chancellor Lee, one of the empire's most brilliant minds and approved by the first Chin emperor is, in fact, stupid."

"Esteemed officials and generals, the issue of the debate at the imperial capital centered on the Chin polity. The matter had been settled, and because one cranky scholar presented his views, a national issue erupted. Why not ignore the man's antiquated views? Did they merit a full-scale debate?

"Let's assume that they merited debate," Feng went on. "Why suppress external discussions? Why drag commanderies into a court matter? Why not charge the eccentric scholar with treason, execute him, and be done with it? Why focus on works in private hands? Why spare books on divination? To divine is treason. In the interest of saving the panel time, I will conclude: I am innocent. I am guilty of uttering foolish remarks. My career here has been exemplary, as has my military record. My main accuser, Pi Bi, is a man caught up in the corruption case three years ago. He strikes back now."

The panel deliberated for two days, and Feng learned that only extreme pressure put on three panelists won a conviction. One general, who admired Feng's service record, would not be budged from a not-guilty vote. The panel found Feng guilty of treason and dereliction of duty. Because of his record, execution was commuted to labor at the Wall. Feng Ping would be tattooed, but his property would not be forfeit, nor would his family be punished.

The verdict and sentence were published in the central square. Feng Ping informed An, who sobbed as the boys ran to her. After feeding the children and sending them to bed, they talked quietly.

"Papa, we must pack for the northern journey," she began. Her silver-streaked hair glistened in the candlelight.

"No, Mama. I will be in convict-labor areas. No civilians will be permitted nearby. This is something I must do alone."

"How long will your sentence be?" A gnawing sound buzzed just on the edge of consciousness. A rat had removed an obstacle to a storage container.

"Seven years ... perhaps three. My primary effort will be to return to you." Feng reverted to his official monotone. His eyes were alight, but with a different fire. "You and the boys must stay with your family. What do you think?"

"That's good, Papa. We can take our things. Lucky we kept the wagon. Remember when we set off for this isolated land?"

A deep sadness swept over Ping. "Such high hopes. Old Shi knew that my temper might get us in trouble."

Fire blazed in her eyes. "You have done splendidly! I married you because of our parents, but also because you are the finest man I'd ever seen. You stay alive!"

Feng Ping wiped his eyes. "How blessed I am, Mama. The day I first saw you, I knew that I'd found my lifetime mate."

In the next months, Feng walked and fished with his sons. He'd gently waken them, quietly talking their eyes open. At night, he'd tell stories or snuggle with them.

The sentence was confirmed. The total sentence was reduced to five years, with a two-year reduction possible for good conduct.

Feng Ping marched to the squalid, brown building where tattooing occurred. He sat still when the foul-breathed man stabbed the black-tipped needle into his cheek. When the needle pulled out for the last time, Feng Ping examined his face in a mirror. He went home, his shame in the stares of the townsfolk.

CHAPTER 108
TAO (213 BC)

Green was everywhere. Despite sparse rainfall, leaves burst forth. Flowers blossomed in variegated hues, bobbing in the breeze.

Tao strolled in the garden of his rural retreat. Bees flitted from flower to flower, dancing for pollen; the crime lord feared nothing. He'd bared his breast to his brother and found compassion. Tao shielded the sun with his hand.

The book decree was a blunder. Even locals were furious about having their collections ablaze. How could a state be so inept?

Tao cared little for politics and statecraft. Only when affairs affected the Reds did he interest himself. Tao picked a yellow flower that wanted to come into his hand and share its scent.

The Reds owned five bookstores, because Tao loved books—a legacy from his parents, he guessed. And he possessed an exceptional collection. The bookstores were shuttered, their contents surrendered to officials.

Even after culling his favorite treasures, Tao still hauled thirteen carts to the collection center. Tao and Jin Mi were present at each burning. Their red-rimmed eyes silently regarded the pyres. Tao secretly relocated his valued books to the rural retreat. Only Tao or Jin Mi had access to that library.

He shook off the dreary thoughts and contemplated the green scene spread vast before him. Best to look without thinking—to shift one's eyes from place to place, object to object, with full attention, keeping the chattering mind at bay.

An oriole flew into the oak tree, and its melody soothed his heart. How blessed to be alive … to be here … to be!

"Would you like to learn to disappear and appear?"

"Who are you?"

"It matters not."

"Ah, but it does. Are you a being of light?"

"Yes."

"Are you a being of light?"

"Yes."

"Are you a being of light?"

"Yes.

Black Bear had taught him the test for determining the authenticity of the being channeled.

"I'd love to learn. But why me?"

"Do you wish to learn, or to chatter like a magpie?"

"Let's begin."

"Precisely. Clear your mind. Set your intent to learn. Relax. First, imagine a fox, then imagine yourself as a fox, then ..."

CHAPTER 109
FENG PING (213 BC)

The convict had hoped to slip away. A small escort of five men would accompany Feng and his family; save for the tattoo, he might be a traveling official.

The tiny procession arrived at the office complex in the capital. Hundreds, including officials who usually did nothing to mar their records, milled there. Many touched Feng and gave flowers or fruit, or asked him to touch their babies.

He'd donned his tattered green robe. The boys were smartly dressed in matching blue shirts and trousers. Hung An selected a white mourning gown. The escort members sensed the crowd's mood and feared a riot if the departure dragged on. Feng and his family climbed into their old covered wagon. This time, Feng and his eldest son rode in front. The crowd reluctantly parted as the procession drove to the imperial road. Women keened, and babies squalled. Curses erupted. A drizzle changed into a regular downpour.

As the caravan reached the outskirts, people lined the roadside. On rural paths, farmers held up children for a glimpse or doffed turbans. When they reached Laibu village, people blocked the road. Feng Ping thanked them and then gently admonished them to obey the law. Jang Pu strode up to the wagon, pulling his son by the hand. "Excellency! My boy works beside me in the fields. All make him respect others." Two elders informed Feng that Laibu had become like in the olden days.

As they left, Ba local prefects asked the convict to tarry, because his reputation as one of the empire's best administrators had preceded him. Officials had consulted him about intractable problems. Feng might have refused their pleas, but the problems whetted his appetite.

Two months passed before the separation point. Long before, husband and wife had decided to part on the road. When the time came, the father hoisted high each son, although the strain taxed his arms. "Obey your mother while I'm gone."

An smiled through tears. "Take care, Ping. Dress warm in that winter cold. No one will look after you. Eat well and rest too."

"Yes, Mama. I'll be fine. Take care of the boys. Don't spoil them. Remember to have them watch their tongues."

"Return to us!" An chased the boys into the wagon, and a single soldier rode beside them. The cart rumbled down the lane to her parents' estate; three figures waved at Ping. Head drooping like a dying flower, the convict pulled himself onto the white horse. As they trekked north, a dust storm caught them, limiting visibility. A future lay ahead … only he couldn't see.

CHAPTER 110

MARCUS (213 BC)

The Roman poured his heart into farming. Although working with earth eased him, his disquiet deepened. In the morning, his jaw ached.

Especially disconcerting was the death of Lee Bu. Although they'd not spoken recently, Marcus knew that his friend had been depressed. Lee Bu's death had been reported as a heart attack, but Marcus learned from Dr. Wu that Bu had committed suicide.

The Roman grieved for the destroyed books. He admired the measured cadences of Master Shun's essays; the elliptic, epigrammatical lines of *The Classic of the Way and Its Power*; and the haunting lyrics of *The Songs of Chu*. His modest library of a hundred bundles had been spared because he was an academician.

Drought withered crops. Only thrice did the metropolitan region receive rain. That moisture staved off a complete disaster.

There was a quick response to one of the Roman's memos calling for an increase in irrigation works and for the construction of new storage facilities. Seven water systems were built, and fifty-six new storage facilities dotted the metro area. A new granary design that elevated the storehouses a pace above ground inhibited pest infestations. Thousands of cats also prowled the storage facilities.

Marcus experimented with drought-resistant wheat varieties grown in the western deserts and dabbled with soil rotation. In his research, he discovered a treatise about mixing soils to produce the best characteristics of each. The concept derived from spreading river mud on farmlands. Since the author described land far east of the Chin homeland, Marcus could not rely on its data. Through a careful study of plant growth on his farm, he concluded that the northern part had poor soil. He searched for deposits of the brownish-black loam described in the text. In the foothills to the southwest, Marcus located a similar soil. A preponderance of poplar and ash trees added to his conviction that the soil was close to that described in the work.

Marcus had three wagonloads delivered to his farm. Transfer of the soils to test sites was aided by a wheeled dirt hauler. Marcus had seen one in the capital and commissioned two for his farm. His soil mixings pushed him to further experiments.

CHAPTER 111
EMPEROR JENG
(212 BC)

To the Lunar New Year's audience, His Majesty announced the building of a new capital. When work commenced, the corvée was resumed. Never had farmers worked so close to planting time. Resettled families had to mobilize all able men between fourteen and sixty-five years. Three palaces were to be raised near the Shanglin Gardens. The largest would be the Afang Palace. Five hundred paces wide and six hundred long, the palace would dwarf other buildings. Its upper terrace alone would accommodate nearly ten thousand people. Magnetite was worked into the imperial entrances to discover would-be assassins who secreted iron weapons. They would be tugged to one side or another when walking through an entrance.

Under normal weather conditions, the conscriptions might have been less disastrous, but drought continued into a third summer. When the corvée summer draft occurred, Magician Lu, who'd promised to find life-prolonging herbs, returned empty-handed.

A cowering, scruffy man was hauled into a private audience chamber. "Magician Lu! Explain your failure!"

The mage's quaking limbs flailed in the air. "Your Exalted Highness, the search for the magic fungi, rare herbs, and immortals stalled. Some force acts against us."

"What is its nature? Speak!"

"We don't know, Excellency. It's our humble opinion that you should regularly move to avoid baneful mists and influences."

The emperor's curiosity took over. "Why?"

"Subjects must not know your whereabouts, because that knowledge weakens Your Majesty's vitality and divinity."

"Continue!"

"A pure being can neither be wet by water nor singed by fire. He rides clouds and lives eternally. Since Your Majesty cannot be expected to lead a simple life, you must, sire, with all due respect, not let it be known where you stay. Secrecy will be realized, the evil ones will be confounded, and the pure one will descend," the magician said.

"Continue."

"When these conditions are met, sire, you'll find eternal life."

Emperor Jeng stroked the bronze phoenix. "Are you certain?"

"We agree that secrecy is imperative," Lu clucked.

The ruler announced, "We, henceforth, wish to be a pure one and hereafter shall be known as 'I' rather than 'We.' Lu, be gone. I'm sending a cavalry detachment to accompany you, so you won't be harmed—and so that you will find the items."

At the autumnal equinox, two comets appeared. Less than a week later, an imperial messenger arrived at the court. "Your Majesty, I come from Liyang, a prefectural capital in the Min commandery. Locals are chatty, but honest … and friendly to strangers."

"Yes, yes, go on."

The man's eyes swept over the four men. "Because of the town's excellent location, it attracted a thriving business clientele, as well as poets who sang of its excellent cuisine, hospitality, and scenic delights. Nestled in low hills, the views charmed all. The climate is moderate."

"Yes, yes?"

"Forgive me, sire." The messenger took a deep breath. "Two weeks ago, a blood-red moon appeared."

He began the account: He had ridden home after a reconnaissance tour. His cavalry detachment spurred their horses to arrive before dark. Then they saw the moon. When they reached a scenic overlook, they dismounted and looked down at the city. The earth rolled toward them like giant waves upon the ocean. Liyang's buildings rocked like children's toys.

Cracks yawned around the city. Structures collapsed. The city slowly slid into a ravenous maw. He raised his hands to screams, then silence. Earth tremors continued. He fainted and awoke to find a black hole where Liyang had been.

The man came back to himself in the chamber.

The emperor exclaimed, "The whole city, gone?"

"Yes, sire. Tens of thousands, including my wife and daughters. The next morning, the rumblings lessened, and water filled the hole, creating a huge lake."

The emperor excused the man and ordered that the troop of survivors be quartered in the guards' barracks. As the man stumbled away, courtiers debated the report. The invocator received a new summons. With all of the portents, heavenly and earthly, he'd been exceptionally busy.

CHAPTER 112

MING TIAN (212 BC)

Prior to Liyang's disappearance, Ming, Academician Hu, and others had discussed discriminatory policies, military campaigns, book burnings, and the abuse of farmers. As one meeting commenced in Hu's apartment, the discussion turned to ways of influencing policy. A couple of men had been included, and one spoke. "We should consider a private audience with His Majesty."

Ming replied, "If a large group met with him, he might feel threatened. This would not be helpful."

"Three or perhaps four might present things without publicly placing His Majesty in a defensive stance," he said.

Ming pressed, "Wouldn't it be more effective to write an extended memo? The advantage is that we could develop our points, and everything would be clearly delineated without rebuttal."

"Yes, but in a meeting, after we presented our case and a rebuttal began, we might be able to better defend our positions." Seeing little agreement, he effected a compromise position. "Why not submit a joint memorandum and then ask for a private audience? The memo could be an eyes-only document, and the private meeting would permit us to answer questions. His Majesty is not publicly challenged, we present our points, and we can later defend them."

"What issues might we raise?" Hu asked as she rose to get another drink of water. Her cup had a panda painted on it.

"Restoration of the corvée, the campaign drains on resources, the heavenly and earthly portents, the labor resources used on the multiple construction sites ..." Sister Fei began. Normally a quiet person, she expressed her upset with recent events.

Ming added, "We might state that instead of trying to build the Wall, the Direct Road, the palaces, and the new capital, the government should postpone some."

An older man with a perpetual smile, Academician Jai, spoke. "Our actions might rebound. We might be arrested and sent north."

Sister Hu replied, "People perish, and old folks are worked like young people. If we fail to speak out, who will?"

A Daoist expert in portents ventured an opinion. "In the last three years, the number and intensity of the signs is startling. The extended drought, earthquakes … if we don't change, a catastrophic event will occur. Given His Majesty's 'interest' in magicians, he might be influenced."

Ming added, "We must help our sovereign see that he needs our loyal support. I'll draft a memo. The final copy, with our signatures, could reach His Majesty within a week. Since I once saved his life, I'll deliver it."

Universal consensus emerged, and the meeting concluded. Ming entered her rooms and tossed off her wraps. She went to the window and stared out at the heavens. A smiling moon beamed down.

Ming began writing. Occasionally she rolled her head to ease her neck. At dawn, she slept fitfully. She rose, ate peaches and pine nuts, then marched to the library to do more research. Near dusk, Ming returned with books and renewed spirits. She worked through a second night.

Bird cries and a scorching sun forced open her eyelids. Ming stumbled to the wash basin, filled it, dropped in a light blue cloth, and wiped her face. As she picked up the first wooden writing tablet, a sparrow lighted on the windowsill and sang. Ming smiled and wrote,

> Pure One,
>   We, your loyal subjects, prostrate ourselves before Your Awesome Majesty to present these humble words.

She decided to quote Master Lao's words about "truthful words not being beautiful and beautiful words not being truthful." Ming pleaded for an end to the warring and added Master Lao's notion that weapons were instruments of ill omen. She also included the passage, "in the wake of a mighty army, bad harvests follow." She included an idea about converting the barbarians by righteousness rather than might, and appended words by Han Fei about "popular support." The view that peasants should plant and harvest in the proper seasons seemed apt. Ming concluded:

> Nine years past, the mighty Chin united the empire and brought forth a peaceful era. People rejoiced and rested; heaven and earth were quiescent. Let us return to these tranquil times. We, your faithful and loyal servants, tremble before the Awesome Imperial Majesty. Unleash us, and we'll usher in an immortal golden age.

A long, long life.

Respectfully submitted,
Academician Ming, Imperial Academy of Scholars

Later, after a cup of pear juice and a handful of pine nuts, Ming returned to the text. She arranged the tablets and carried them to Hu. Only the thought of seeing Marcus buoyed her.

CHAPTER 113

FENG PING (212 BC)

Icy winds pierced the desert waste. Even the best-wrapped traveler winced from the bone-numbing whip of the wind. Feng Ping examined his calloused hands and flexed his muscle-sculpted arms. That first workday, he had toted rocks to the Wall's base. Soon, his left arm had cramped; then a cramp hobbled his right arm. The thin, wiry overseer had bawled out that rest time would be soon. Blisters broke, and Feng Ping worked on.

That night, he devoured the millet porridge and boiled cabbage. He gulped down water and moistened a cloth for his eyes. As soon as he lay down, he fell into a dreamless sleep.

The next day, Feng wound a turban of dark cloth around his head and covered his neck. Every pain competed for attention and relief. Food seemed tasteless, and he craved sleep. One night, Feng awoke, feeling darkness clutching his chest.

He worked on the monster Wall—seemingly a dragon-devouring land—and was surprised that convicts were treated well. Officers went calmly about their business. Tents covered the landscape, like mushrooms in Ba; six slept in a tent. Feng Ping's tentmates included two commoners and three officials swept up in the book-burning laws.

Two weeks after Ping's arrival, three tentmates were chatting. The youngest sported a full beard, and the other had been a subprefect in the Min commandery. He slowly enunciated his words, as if savoring their individual tastes. Feng recounted his story, then asked the older man, Zhang, about his misfortune.

"I was an officer who worked to see that the state was respected by the people. When the book-burning decree arrived, I implemented it and accompanied a detachment to a follower of Confucius." The man looked gentle; nothing haughty.

"The library was in the first room," the man said. "A set of three candles about a scholar's mat was all he had for night reading. He had an enormous library that we carted outside. He begged us to burn them in front of his house. The scholar lighted the pile, which smoldered all night. He lay beside the ashes, wrapped in a tattered hemp blanket, and died of a broken heart a month later. I called off my officers after that. Someone ratted, and here I am."

Feng Ping frowned. "We're trained to enforce the laws, not to judge them. It was a stupid law. You did your best."

The older one nodded politely; he knew the real truth. Dust eddies swirled about the tent.

The younger one spoke. "I hail from Lu, Confucius's homeplace. In fact, my best friend is the fourteenth direct descendent of the great sage. Like the famous one, he's tall. I don't follow that way, because all schools and thinkers have good and bad points.

"When the order to burn arrived, all despaired. The great one's descendent hid his ancestor's writings; his house walls had nooks for valuables. I hid my hoard. One day—I can remember it clearly—the soldiers came and went straight for the cache. Smashed the cabinets into splinters and threw all the writings into the privy."

Feng Ping spoke. "That must have torn out your heart."

Hate-filled eyes blinked. "I imagined hideous tortures. I dared not resist—that would have been fatal for me and my girls. My wife passed away four years ago."

"Then they must be with your father."

The young man's blazing eyes turned to Feng Ping. "Never! He's the one who turned in his son. Always disliked me. At seven, on my naming day, he refused a celebration. My brothers got gifts. When I married, he wanted a grandson. How my wife and I tried! Three girls. He wouldn't even see the youngest two, and then my lovely woman died in labor, the boy stillborn. My girls live with their aunt on their mother's side." They sat long in the silence.

Feng Ping soon preferred fruit to the meat rations, which he traded for nuts or wheat buns. His tentmates shared. Overseers flogged people only if a tool broke or a man malingered. Feng Ping thought that former officials merited the lenient treatment, but fairness was common to all. Each flogging had to be witnessed.

Spring brightened their spirits. One hour every other day was alloted for gardening. The water shortage ended when the convicts dug a well. Feng Ping felt like a plant hungering for the sun's life-giving rays. In unguarded moments, memories of Hung An and the boys would crash over him, leaving him gasping.

Each could write and receive one letter per month. Ping treasured his brief missives. Although some officers grumbled at the coddling, General Tian knew morale would be high. After the summer solstice, Feng Ping's camp transferred to the Direct Road. The convicts packed, feeling great curiosity. They would head south ... but what was a straight road?

CHAPTER 114

SHU WEI (212 BC)

The Chi aristocrat tottered home after visiting a pal who had forced a cup of wine on Wei to salute the past. One drink had led to another. Lotus would scold him, but he didn't mind a caring fuss. Shu Wei opened the door.

"Lotus? Lotus! I'm back." Wei changed his robe and wandered to the cooking area. His mouth tasted too sweet; time for a sour, preserved seed. He saw her lying on the floor. "Lotus ... what's the matter? What's happened?" He rushed to her. In a haze, he recalled other supine forms of an earlier time.

"Lotus! Lotus! Not you too! Don't leave me!" Her eyes stared blankly. He carried her to the bedroom. Laying her on the bed, he sobbed. He composed himself, properly arranged the corpse, then summoned the neighbors.

Two days later, Wei's nephew Tung arrived, and the two buried Lotus in the project's cemetery near a cypress that received the afternoon sun and was shaded in the morning.

Wei missed her. Of course, he could feed and care for himself. When Widow Lee hinted that she'd tend to his needs, Shu Wei declined. Sex had become a sharing. To his surprise, Lotus had been a passionate woman when he courted her.

At the spring equinox, the project head posted the conscription notice. Men between sixty-one and sixty-five years had to work for six months. Wei was caught up in the net. He wrote to his nephew.

When the young man arrived, the news was uniformly bad. "Uncle, I cannot change the order. I have no influence."

Wei used his sorrowful-eyes ploy. "Surely, Tung, you can do something. I'm your father's brother, and Lotus is dead."

"Uncle, I tried the minister in charge of internal security, but he refused me. Here's money to bribe overseers."

Wei poured another cup of tea. "Try the emperor himself. As an academician, you have the right to an audience. My wife died, and I'm sick. Tung, I'll take my life."

"Yes, uncle. I'll see His Majesty and tell your story." Shu Tung rose, bowed, and left.

Preparations for the northward journey continued. Shu Wei arranged his clothes, prepared extra food, and retrieved his money from the stash in the garden.

The sojourn took two weeks, and the party members shared a modest tent. Shu Wei found the camp food inedible. He worked six hours daily, hauling dirt or stones.

The overseer tormented the helpless ones. He verbally terrorized them, knowing none would tell the inspectors. Each night, Shu Wei collapsed on his bed. The end of his home supplies meant reliance on camp fare. At times, he would miss the noon snack as well as dinner. A tentmate took Wei to the doctor, who diagnosed malnutrition and exhaustion. After a week of rest and some meat, the old aristocrat's appetite and energy improved.

The old pattern resumed. One summer evening, the emaciated old man, who had been taking a night walk, tripped and fell hard.

CHAPTER 115

FENG PING (212 BC)

Where was he? Feng Ping's bladder complained; if he didn't piss soon, he'd do it in bed. Cursing quietly, Feng Ping crept outside. Stars glittered as he groped to the latrine and opened the door. He lowered his pants. When he wanted to go, the stream took too long. When it came, the hissing lulled him, and he lurched and tottered over the waste pit. Feng Ping gasped, and the gulp brought in ammonia-laden gases. His stream stopped, and he cursed. Finally the stream rushed out anew, but he wet his feet. Bile swarmed up his esophagus. Ping rushed out, stepping in something soft. Deep breaths tamed the vomit surges, yet the stench clung.

He wiped his sandals. A lump blocked his way. Bending, he saw a body. Feng Ping ran for the nearest torch, then returned.

A thin man, bald and ancient, breathed in shallow gasps. "Wher ... where am I?"

"In camp twelve. Convict laborers on the Direct Road."

The scraggly beard moved along with the parched lips. "My dear one, is it you? That night ... never came home ... all these years regretted ... thank you for helping your papa."

"Yes, we'll talk soon. Rest." He cradled the old man.

"Auntie Lotus died ... miss her ... why did I come north, don't want to live ... Let's go ..."

"We'll go soon. You're almost home, Papa."

"You did come ... sorry ... Forgiv ..."

"Yes, Papa. I forgive you. Be at peace, Papa." As the withered man walked the path of death, he gave Feng Ping a tender smile, squeezed his hand, and relaxed. Shadows flickered across both men, with one holding the dead father who'd found peace.

In the morning, the pair were discovered, and Feng Ping earned a day to bury the old man. Refusing the common burial site, he took a shovel and carried the body to a hilltop.

Ping cut through rock-hard earth, and by late afternoon, he'd dug a narrow trench. He lowered the man and gently threw in the dirt. He sat until dark. After talking with the man and the stars, Feng Ping returned to his tent. Another hate tattoo had been etched in his heart.

At summer's end, Ping left for the capital. With the old man's death, the facial tattoo had transmuted into a badge of honor.

CHAPTER 116

TAO (212 BC)

He stood before the mirror, completed the spell, and vanished without shimmering. That had taken the longest: to move without vibrating the air.

Tao still did not know who or what was helping. He felt confident that it was not the dark lord or any being of that kind. He practiced moving silently. Of course, Tao had told Jin Mi, and the two played a game where the crime lord would sneak up on his friend, trying to get close without detection. It worked better in the day than the night, when Jin Mi became a creature of the shadows. Besides, the master thief used the crystal.

Tao recalled their joint meeting with Black Bear. They had brought the blood and a piece of torn clothing, and Black Bear cast a spell on the blood, so that the northern bitch could no longer get within twenty paces without alerting them. The shaman refused to use the blood residue for dark purposes. Tao was pleased with their progress in limiting her harm.

Black Bear had regarded Jin Mi and nodded approvingly. "Your blood oath was heard and received, as was the recent reaffirmation. It is good that you share burdens, that you were vulnerable each to each. You agreed in an earlier life that you would meet in this life and continue your journeys side by side. The blood pact strengthens your bond." Black Bear looked as if he were in another world, with eyes glazed and mouth agape.

Black Bear had given a staff to Jin Mi, cautioning him to use the staff to focus energy, but to be clear in his mind when it was unleashed. "Don't release in anger, only to defend—to shift energies or throw them back at the user."

Jin Mi had vowed to follow the shaman's instructions, and the two departed. Black Bear's place shimmered with green and energy, despite the prolonged drought. Wildflowers, such as the milkweed thistle, grew in a riot of blues, reds, and yellows. Tao spied a lizard skittering up a tree. It stopped, regarded him, and rhythmically raised and lowered. Black Bear had said that lizards were guides into dreamtime. Tao swayed in time with the lizard ...

The crime lord came back to himself. The vision had been realistic. He had to remember to call on the little lizard before sleep.

He smiled at the emptiness in the mirror. It was time to catch Jin Mi—hopefully in a mental fog, though that seemed less likely these days. Damned staff—if only he could separate it from the night master. Soon it would be time to strike anew at the northern bitch.

Tao left through the back door and lazily wandered through the tunnel maze beneath his new house. He inhaled the musty scent of earth and stepped into the bright sunlight. Yes, it would be a fine and successful day.

CHAPTER 117
MING TIAN (212 BC)

Ming rushed to the farm. She had intended to stay two days, but added another. Clear days opened with cool, crisp mornings and ended with chilled, sparkling nights. Trees boasted vibrant, cold-kissed golds, scarlets, and crimsons.

As Ming and Marcus wandered the hills, Ming saw the world with childlike wonder, as if a bronze giant had crafted the landscape. They strayed to a mountain freshet, where fish shadows played tag. They chatted more than usual, reliving the past and planning idyllic futures.

Ming blossomed like a golden chrysanthemum. With her, Marcus explored breathtaking worlds; the flower unfolded, petal by petal. He touched the diaphanous butterfly.

Ming admired his distinguished, silvering beard; its touch tickled as he rubbed it along her thighs. He delighted in her skin: the bumps on her forearms, the tingling nape hair. Oh, the slightly trembling fingers and caressing lips. She inhaled his musky scent—the full-bodied aroma of a mature man. Once, she discovered a ticklish patch and massaged it to open him.

Hearing Ming's shy request to have her feet rubbed, Marcus hastened to obey. When he kissed the insoles, her toes thrust like dancing sea anemones in a watery current. He'd nip at and run his teeth on her soles and heels, propelling her on waves of pleasure.

In sleep, a tactile knowing drew them, iron to magnetite. Arms entwined legs; feet caressed. On the fourth morning, while they were abed, Ming announced her return to court.

"Stay, please," Marcus pleaded.

"I wish that I could, my love. I couldn't love you more."

"Please stay."

Ming raised her knees and reached for her robe. "I must complete this project."

"Duty! My father used it like a binding thong."

Ming's heart contracted; she was already late.

"Tarry another day ... just one."

"I've lingered too long. Marcus, I've come to a decision. I'll resign this month. We're too much apart. There's something I must tell you. When I finish the project, I'll resign. If you wish, we can marry."

The Roman's face glowed like a torch in a dark pit. They parted happily.

CHAPTER 118
TAO (212 BC)

The fire-scarred building looked like a wreck out of a nightmare, with bodies strewn everywhere; women outnumbered men. The Golden Cock had been burned again, and assassins awaited the fleeing women and their clients. The scent of ash mingled with the sweetish odor of charred flesh. Stains saturated the ground and the street. Throats slit, necks broken, bellies eviscerated, bodies in unnatural poses … it was as if some monster had harvested a human crop.

Tao murmured to Jin Mi. "I worked here, making friends with many women. Although most I knew have retired, it still feels as if my family's here."

"Brother, they have launched their campaign in a reply to ours. We face all-out war. When do we strike?"

Tao bent and gently traced with his fingers the cheekbones of an older whore. He recalled the first time they had met; her gap-toothed smile had utterly charmed him. "As soon as these dead are remembered. I want all families compensated as if they were military veterans' families—or, from what I have learned about our soldiers, compensated better than how veterans are treated these days," Tao said quietly as his rage smoldered. The reek of blood drew flies, which paid attentive court to the victims.

"We must capture more of the enemy and plant agents among them," the master thief said as he watched Tao.

"I must wait until I've released this fevered hatred," Tao whispered. "I refuse to strike foolishly. I need to reconnoiter. I caught you last night. I must be improving, but I've really only been playing childishly, rather than using this gift properly. Part of this carnage comes from my frivolous behavior." He clenched his hands, then forced himself to relax. Finally he touched the pouch.

"Don't blame yourself, brother. You have needed to hone your skill. I was caught unawares last night, in my native element. You have perfected this talent. Gather information about their lairs, their command centers. Where does she reside? How many do they have? These things all aid our war. Despite this setback, I know we will win." Jin Mi spoke softly as he lightly touched Tao's fist. It relaxed. Crows gathered. Officials would soon flock too.

"Come, brother," Tao said. "We must help our comrades. Dawn comes. Too many watch already." Tao looked at his glowing crystal. He walked to the nearest body and, with Jin Mi's assistance, gently lifted it.

CHAPTER 119
MING TIAN (212 BC)

Within a water-glass measure after Ming's return, Academician Hu entered Ming's quarters. The radiance of the woman before her testified to a marvelous time at the Roman's estate. "Amazing that a visit with a barbarian can rejuvenate you like a visit to a masseur."

"One of life's delights is sharing female things. Thank you for your sage advice, your enduring support, and your humor-filled views," Ming said as she twisted an unruly strand behind her ear.

Both flushed. "I've passed your draft to the others," Hu reported. "One man—the tiny, prim one—added lines from Master Mo, and I added a few more from our foresisters. Sixty might sign." Hu sniffed the scent of burning sage and watched thin smoke curl from Ming's incense burner.

The news animated Ming as she saw her vision take shape. "Make a list of possibles," Ming said. "Time is no longer a friend. We must push this through with no further emendations. I'll have a final draft by dusk tomorrow," she added.

"Splendid! We will have it to His Majesty within three days. Omens wax potent; an earth tremor struck in Chi. Buildings suffered damage, but few died. Thank you, Ming, for your words of appreciation. They come hard for me, but believe that I have never known another in all my years with whom I have felt so akin."

Darkness clouded Ming's face. "I've … decided to resign."

"You can't. You're the perfect model for our sisters."

"My career has stunted me. I want time for myself, for Marcus, and for my baby. Hu, I've not seen her in years. I missed her first words and her first bout of mischief."

"Will you marry?" Hu asked as she lightly ran her fingers along an edge of a ceramic piece shaped like a crescent moon.

"That's unimportant … no, it is to him. I'll leave it open for now, but I want to see my baby … his baby … our baby."

"I hope you stay, but I feel your determination. Just be happy, sister." Hu sighed. "Let's go to the library."

As the sun set over the autumnal peaks, Ming sat at her writing desk. She gazed at the scroll painting of a panda mother tending her little cub in the bamboo grove. A knock interrupted her, and she frowned as she walked to the door. Marcus, toting some wilted flowers, walked in past her. "I stopped earlier this afternoon," he complained.

"Not now, my love. I'm working on something important." Marcus's wary look warned her that something was awry.

"Let me stay."

"Marcus, I need my creative faculties. You'd be a distraction," Ming said.

"Is this more important than us?" Marcus countered. He looked slightly offended.

"That's unfair, my love. You should know how vital you are to me. I need to be alone to finish this memo." Ming lighted a taper.

"Where were you this afternoon? Are you ... have you been seeing another man?"

"Another! How could that be? I love you, Marcus. No other. Please believe me. I'll marry you. Can't you see?"

"I'm sorry, Ming, but there's something you won't tell me, and that causes troubling thoughts!" The cloying sage smell irritated him.

"There's no one else, my dearest, most handsome love. I have a heart only for you!" His face relaxed, telling her he was somewhat reassured, though disappointed. She snagged his beard in her fingers and gently twisted.

"Do you love me, still?" Marcus whined.

"Of course, from every corner of my being. Now, always." As Ming released her fingers, they clasped tightly. Marcus went out, head down, shoulders slumped.

Ming returned to her task, but her attention wandered to her daughter. She had failed the little one ... but if she told Marcus, perhaps something might be redeemed. Perhaps Marcus would come back; she'd like that. A knock startled her, but answered her wish; she disliked quarrels. She opened the door. "Your Majesty!"

The emperor pushed past. His face was flushed, and his thinning hair was tied into a disheveled knot. A wine stain marred his white silk brocade robe, embroidered with a snarling dragon.

"What can I do for you?"

He chortled. "Something special for your emperor. Just a little. I've been patient. Come here!"

"I … I don't understand."

Narrowed eyes and panting foulness warned her. It was a feral scent that promised violence. "Of course you do. I've wanted you since the day … night … you saved … Tonight, you can do it again."

"You've been drinking," she stalled. The panda mother got in front of her cub. She bared her teeth and growled.

"S'what. Mine. You never married him." He pawed at her breasts. Ming pushed him away.

"Hard to get! I like spirited women. I grow hard."

"Your Majesty, I can't. I …"

"You can't? I can give you more women in government … anything." He ripped her gown and pursed his lips.

Ming knew enough martial arts to break his arm, but something inside her burst as her father's face rose before her. This time, running was impossible. "Please stop, sire … for a moment, at least. Permit me to shed these clothes. You won't regret it."

"Knew it. Few minutes won't matter!"

"In a moment, sire, you'll soar like an immortal." Before Ming left the room, she covered the wooden tablets. She went to the secret compartment and unstoppered the bottle, pushed it to her lips, and drank. As Ming shuddered off the acrid taste, she unsheathed her knife and calmly calculated the cut site. She grabbed the inlaid-pearl handle. A hawk's talon unleashed.

"Hurry!" the emperor shouted. Ming looked at the treasured mural: Marcus's farm with the little brook, her favorite spot. The talon moved to the pulsing throat. As she drew hard across her creamy, white neck in a semicircle, delicate flesh parted in a hideous leer, and blood spurted. The talon drew aloft for the killing strike. Above the heart, guided by the mind's eye, it plunged down and thrust deep.

"Love you, Marcus, little moon. Love you!" Her brain exploded. Not hearing the silent scream, the drunken monarch bumped into and jarred Ming's writing table, uncovering the memo. His interest, however, was with another matter. Finally, he stumbled into her bedroom. He saw the prostrate body and did not comprehend. "No need to fear; it'll be … nice to serve your emperor."

He bent closer and lifted the body. Blood stained the floor, and her head sagged to her chest. He dropped the corpse, but blood stained his hands and robes. He stumbled to his quarters in the academicians' building, where he summoned a guard.

"A crime has been committed. I want guards posted outside the room with the scarlet door. A special assignment team must be constituted. Search the room. A woman's body will be found in the bedroom. I want it immediately transported to the vagrants' cemetery for burial."

"Yes, Your Majesty." The guards officer, a man of thirty who stood six feet, two inches tall, took the news impassively, bowed, and raced to find the guards' head. After the tall man left, the emperor remembered the barbarian.

CHAPTER 120

TAO (212 BC)

The ancient building topped by a lovely, sloping roof was a moderate-sized structure near the western outskirts of the capital—built, perhaps, by a merchant. Dawn's purplish blue yielded to a brilliant orange. Tao shivered and shifted his weight. He released the gas that had been building in his bowel. Invisible, he had been observing the place for at least two water marks. A side door opened, then closed, but no one appeared. Tao's heart raced. The northern bitch had entered the world. She had felt no need to disguise her exit. That was a fatal mistake.

Tao saw shimmering imperceptible to most eyes. It moved down the street, staying to the right side but not fully in the shadow of buildings. He followed, hoping he could stay within sighting range. The shimmering moved slowly—sometimes shifting right, then left. Tao lagged back. Near the Central Market, the shimmering entered a liquor store. The day warmed, and Tao grew uncomfortable in his heavy cloak. He dared not remove it, because that might trigger visibility. A man ambled by, hawking roast pork. Tao's stomach growled, and he quietly released more gas.

A man in a hooded coat left the building. Tao followed, using less caution than earlier. As far as he knew, people had no way of discerning his presence. Tao dodged pedestrians, as he did not wish to cause a disturbance. He needed to practice slipping through crowds like the wind. Tao grinned. He was the wind … a breeze that could become a typhoon.

When the setting sun was an orange ball just above the horizon, Tao finished his tailing exercise and headed to Jin Mi's residence. He would arrive just before the master thief departed for his night duties. Tao entered through the back door and was grabbed.

"I've got you, brother. Say 'yield' before I crush you."

"Yield." Tao cleared his mind and materialized. He smelled fresh-cut tuber roses. Tao tasted their heavy and musky scent.

"My crystal lit up about two minutes ago, and when the door opened, I knew that you were mine. First time in two weeks." Jin Mi grinned triumphantly, and he lightly tapped Tao's shoulder.

"I've had a productive day and am famished. Stay and feed this poor traveler." Tao grinned.

Jin Mi headed for the kitchen. "I have dried fruits and nuts, or a quarter of a duck I ate around five water levels ago."

"I want all of it," Tao said as he regarded a hanging scroll of a mountain scene with a tumbling waterfall framed in a snowscape. Old Mu must have painted it.

Jin Mi chortled. "All of it? You seldom eat more than does a waif. Why the appetite and the eagerness?"

"I located a residence of the northern bitch, who does not hide her going and coming. I found three other lairs; one's a possible headquarters. It was worth battling my hunger and fatigue!" Tao exclaimed. He felt giddy and safe.

"We are going to win this war," Jin Mi predicted. "You have been hesitant, brother, in proclaiming this. I know we will win." Jin Mi became caught up in the crime lord's joy. *This will be another late evening*, the night master mused.

CHAPTER 121

MARCUS (212 BC)

Marcus slept fitfully. A large pitcher of wine lulled him into a series of troubling dreams. Then he heard a scream. "Ming!" She appeared in a shimmering blue robe. "Your cry scared me!"

Ming smiled as a white light blazed around her.

"Ming, I'm sorry about today. I didn't mean it."

"Don't worry, love. I've come to say good-bye."

"Where are you going? I can't bear being apart from you."

"You have things to do. Remember that you've been my only love."

Marcus awoke, pleased that it had only been a dream. Someone pounded on his door. Three guards confronted him.

"You're under arrest," the officer announced.

Marcus stepped back. "Why am I under arrest? I demand to see His Majesty."

"We're here at the emperor's command," the officer replied. The guards gathered clothes, writing materials, and personal effects, then placed them in hemp bags. More guards patrolled the entrances. Horses waited. The party exited an auxiliary city gate. Once, Marcus looked up into the starry sky and saw a comet.

As he gained his bearings, Marcus realized that they headed toward Yung. They changed mounts along the way and arrived at the Yung Palace. At the darkened front gate, guards were hailed. During a brief but intense conference among the guards and caretakers, they stared at him. At least he was alive.

CHAPTER 122

EMPEROR JENG (212 BC)

When the emperor awoke, a guard officer brought him materials from Ming's residence. He read the draft memorial, cursed, and hurled the tablets to the floor. Upon reflection, he relaxed. The conspiracy meant that he need not feel remorse. He gazed at his favorite ceiling mural, the destruction of the Jao army at Changping that had taken place a year prior to his birth.

"Guard!"

"Your Majesty!"

"Arrest all academicians, save for Jo Jing-Jen. Send the imperial secretary to me at once."

The next day, Feng Jie, the imperial secretary, began the interrogation of the academicians. During the inquisition, in which torture was either threatened or applied, five scholars implicated three score others in a variety of plots and conspiracies. As their stories were checked, others were arrested. After two weeks, four hundred sixty academicians had been condemned to death. Nearly five hundred more were tattooed and sent north. Others, including Shu Tung, escaped punishment.

The monarch reviewed the cases and affirmed most. That night, he slept without massive amounts of alcohol.

After the final sentences had been confirmed, Prince Fu Su requested an imperial audience. On this occasion, his father selected the Orchid Retreat. The tense young man prostrated himself. Sweat dripped from his nose.

"Rise. What do you wish, my son?"

The boy's face resembled his mother's: a stubby nose and a weak chin. The eyes burned. "Your Majesty, I've learned about the sentences concerning the academicians. Forgive me, but the imperial secretary's verdict is too harsh."

"You dare question my officials!"

"Please allow me to finish, sire. I know many of the academicians. They are honorable, loyal subjects who desire an end to people's sufferings. I have perused the weekly security reports. The black-headed ones grow restive. I was wrong to recommend the northern expedition. I've idolized General Tian. He's wrong. Halt the building projects; let the people recover. I will accept death if that is Your Majesty's command."

The emperor wanted to hit Fu Su, but restrained the impulse. "You infuriate me! It's well we speak alone. For these terrible thoughts, you will be sent north. General Tian, your former teacher, will put sense back into your head."

The young man stiffened. "Please, Father. Heed my words."

"Leave me!"

The powerfully built prince prostrated himself and backed out.

Despite his anger, Emperor Jeng relished the fact that his son had risked death. After a year or two in the north, he mused, Fu Su would be ready for important assignments.

CHAPTER 123

FENG PING (212 BC)

The convict received a summons to see his overseer at the Apang Palace work site. The northern command skillfully deployed its human and material resources, but there, work camps showed sloppy construction methods and haphazard management. The state deemed it unnecessary to monitor overseers. Feng Ping hated Lu Chi, a fat man of average height and build. Overseer Lu humiliated people. Feng Ping longed to serve in the capital, but not in this capacity.

When he arrived in the overseer's tent, the coarse man bellowed, "Convict Feng Ping, you scum! Report to the north gate's execution grounds. You will be gone three days. Soon you'll be back in the range of my lash."

After an hour, Feng Ping joined about two hundred others digging a massive trench pit, two paces wide and two and a half paces deep. It stretched along the execution ground for about two hundred paces, like a scar on a bandit's face. Feng Ping noted the symmetry: northern part of the city, northern part of the execution grounds. The yin force must be appeased. The pit-trench took another day.

As the sun neared its zenith on the third day, Feng and the other diggers spied a long line of people plodding toward them. Soldiers herded them toward the trench. Townspeople crowded the site. Just at noon, an imperial war chariot drawn by four black stallions pulled up. Feng could barely discern a flock of ravens—or were they vultures?—roosting on a giant, leafless elm at a distance. A smaller chariot stopped by the trench. Down stepped the imperial secretary, a man whom Ping had met briefly years ago. The imperial secretary unrolled the imperial proclamation. Because of the wind, Ping heard few words: "a plot," "the law," and "death by burial," "alive."

Hands bound, the scholars stumbled to the pit. Because of the crush and confusion, half a dozen immediately tumbled in. At the trench lip, the first line waited for what seemed an eternity. Soldiers walked behind them and shoved.

CHAPTER 124

HU MENG (212 BC)

Academician Hu filed toward the pit. Death was not so bad ... but being buried alive! Her heart heaved as she thought back to the dark room where she'd been locked by her brothers. She had felt the walls closing in and passed out. If they untied her hands, she could swallow the poison.

Hu looked at her students—some fearful, most calm. She heard cawing. Her bonds were severed, and she looked ahead. A tattooed convict caught her attention. Then she heard his words in her mind: "Don't fear. I'll avenge you! You will be remembered!"

Hu felt better. As a hand shoved, she tumbled down on top of people and heard a sickening crack. She lifted the death vial, but then caught sight of a frightened student. She passed her the poison. Closeness stifled.

Dirt clods rained on them. Hu Meng looked up and saw the convict. He shoveled fast, then faster. A clod hit her face and she looked again. The dirt reached her mouth. She inhaled deeply.

CHAPTER 125

FENG PING (212 BC)

Feng Ping watched Hu before their eyes locked. She looked frightened. The overseer bellowed for them to shovel. Feng Ping's arms became a blur. The maw
filled. He drove his arms brutally. Guards and thrill seekers loitered. The convicts
returned to their camps. He forgot food until he returned to his base camp. He
forced in the food to combat dizziness. He'd see her face beside the old man's:
two burdens burned in his heart.

CHAPTER 126

MARCUS (212 BC)

Marcus paced. Cloudy, cool days brought little relief, and no one offered more than a few guarded words. Marcus began a routine—a habitual pattern of exercise and activity.

Less than two weeks after his arrival, Emperor Jeng came to him in a miniature pine garden. Seeing royal visitor, Marcus prostrated himself.

"How are your living arrangements?" A miniature cypress tree flat to the ground with a long, curving branch was at least four generations old. It rested atop a miniature hill; nearby was a tiny streamlet in which a miniature fisherman had cast a line.

"With respect, Your Majesty, I find them stifling. The food's adequate, but the company's terrible. Why am I being held?"

"Because you conspired to overthrow me!" The outburst shocked the Roman. Sudden movement caught his eye. He saw a long-legged white bird flying overhead.

"Never, sire! Twice I saved your life! I've been your friend for three decades. I would do nothing to harm you!"

The ardor undermined the monarch's anger, and he averted his face. "I knew that you wouldn't betray me, but you were intimately associated with the conspirators."

"Who was involved, sire?"

The emperor looked down. "Most of the academicians ... traitors!"

"Nooooo! Ming wouldn't betray you! She saved your life."

"She was a ringleader and wrote a document attacking me!" The emperor's tone grew uneasy. Bamboo wind chimes tinkled.

Marcus looked up at a darkening thunderhead. "Never!"

Imperial anger faded. "The handwriting on the treacherous document matched hers. She was a leader."

Marcus sank to his knees. Now he had a glimmer about Ming's secrecy. "What happened?"

The emperor turned away. "Arrested. She was arrested."

"I want to see her, sire. She's loyal to you."

"But, treason ... she had to die."

Marcus gasped. "Die! But you could pardon her." The royal expression of sadness, fear, and fading anger told him. Marcus collapsed and crawled to the emperor's robe.

"She's dead, Marcus."

"Nooooo!"

"She left this."

After some minutes, Marcus accepted the bamboo strips.

> My love,
>
> If you are reading this, I have gone ahead. I am writing this in case I do so. I'm sorry to precede you, but few of us know precisely when our time's over. There is much to say. Most of all, know that I've loved you ever since that time in the Great Mother Temple. You did come for me as well as for yourself. We found each other to complete our business this lifetime. Marcus, I have never been happier than when I've been with you. I go before, but know, my love, we shall meet again.
>
> I kept something from you. The time I took leave, I did not nurse my mother back to health. I was pregnant and went off to birth our child. She was healthy and is beautiful. For the briefest time, I was with her. Then I returned to the capital and to you. It was the most difficult thing that I have done, and I know now that it was wrong to keep this from you. How you must despise me for doing this.
>
> Our daughter, Bright Moon or Little Moon (Ming Yueh), lives near the Great Mother Temple. I beg you to claim her—for you, for me, for her, for us. Our blood flows in her. Raise her to know her mother and her heritage. Beloved, you are given a second chance to raise a child; she was the third entity in our meditation. Remember how she clutched your hand. Little Moon needs her father. MARCUS, I LOVE YOU. NOW, ALWAYS.

He blinked away anger, sadness, dismay, fear, love, joy, and unbearable pain. He frowned at his sovereign.

"Yes, I know; you are to claim a child. Strange she never told you," said the emperor, who averted his gaze. "I'll make it easy. I absolve you of blame concerning the conspiracy on the condition that you leave immediately for that place. Find your little girl and settle someplace. I'll provide all you need."

"May I see Ming's grave?"

"No. She rests in an unmarked place." Marcus looked at the tiny fisherman, who had no hook at the end of his fishing line.

"May I bring a companion?" he asked.

Emperor Jeng regarded Marcus. "No one from the capital area."

"He comes from outside," Marcus said.

A sly smirk came over the imperial lips. "If he can be here by tomorrow. I must leave. Many times you've helped me. That's why I help you." As the monarch departed, Marcus clutched the strips.

After a water level, Marcus called. "Bo Lo! I need you!"

"What took you so long?" asked the materializing mouth in the center of the wizened face.

"We go to the Great Mother Temple. It seems I am the father of a girl. Brother mine, I'm going home," Marcus sighed.

CHAPTER 127

EMPEROR JENG (212 BC)

After his return, Emperor Jeng summoned Academician Jo to a private garden. The bald official was attired in white.

"Reactivate the White Panthers, veterans, and trusted guards who are sworn to secrecy. Train them and visit the Great Mother Temple on Mount Hua. Destroy it and similar ones in the empire. Check with the Bureau of Records for locations," the emperor ordered.

"Yes, sire. It will take four or five weeks to get ready."

"I'll have the necessary warrants and monies ready. You will have a special account and may use the central armory's weapons and armor." Emperor Jeng smiled.

"My lord! And the women at the temples?"

"Do what you will with them. Leave none alive!"

CHAPTER 128

TAO (212 BC)

Dogs barked furiously, and sooty scents of burning fires hung thick in the air. Flies buzzed excitedly. Hawkers cried their wares. Tao walked the streets, inhaling the bustling city life. Watching people pleased him.

He navigated the crowds. Being able to read people's thoughts helped, once he relaxed while invisible. He wondered if he should be going over accounts or refining battle plans. He questioned whether he was lazy or unfocused. Tao smiled ruefully and meandered through the streets.

A man wearing a green turban weaved toward Tao. Danger! Tao saw the glint of sunlight from the stiletto emerging from the man's sleeve. Tao shifted into visibility, watching the man's eyes widen. Twisting to the side and striking with his leg, Tao heard the crack of the assassin's ribs and a muffled cry as his knife fell. The enemy rolled away from the blow and lunged. Tao whirled like a dancer and kicked with his other leg. The assassin grunted and fell. Tao looked for other assassins but could see none.

He knelt before the man, who had no tongue. Tao searched the unconscious man's robe, finding a heavy pouch. A hired man ... one of the Voiceless Ones. Then he spied the crystal and retrieved it. The gathering crowd meant trouble. "See the knife?" Tao said to them. "He tried to kill me. The police must arrest this assassin."

Tao pulled away the hood, revealing the man's face. He could not place it. As a crowd formed, Tao rose and slipped through. Reaching an alley, he shifted to invisibility.

Tao reached Jin Mi's place. In the shadows, he shifted to visibility and entered the low-level dwelling. The night master was in the basement, poring over records and accounts.

"At least one of us is working hard," Tao remarked.

The night master turned and smiled, then turned sober upon seeing Tao's face. "What?"

"I have grown careless. Our own detecting methods have been discovered and used by the enemy. Only the inner voice and a quick reaction disabled the assassin. He came at me as if I were visible. I found this." Tao proffered the crystal.

"Black Bear?"

"No. Before I knew the shaman, I had befriended another, White Horse," Tao said. "There must be others. Black Bear said that he had faced the northern bitch's brother. I must be careful."

"I was just checking. There have been no assassinations in the last three months. Just the disaster at the Golden Cock."

"That was enough. I have decided to rebuild the Golden Cock to show her that we are not afraid. What do you think?" Tao asked. He looked at a scroll depicting a tiger hiding among bamboo. Only the deadly eyes and stripes could be seen. Tao admired the bamboo more than the haunting effect of the animal.

"Brother, I think this is a splendid thing. She will be thinking about our resources, and it will be a morale boost for the Reds. Finding women for the new house might be difficult, considering the fear of ghosts and the like," Jin Mi mused. He gazed at the scroll, which had been in one of his wealthy victim's homes. *A work by a master—just like me*, he mused.

"Yes, you are a masterwork. And I'll have the Golden Cock exorcised by someone Black Bear recommends. We can offer double for the women and station guards inside and out … perhaps develop an alarm system, along with a firefighting system. The capital needs one. It might be that we could contract out firefighting and security services. Hahahaha!" Tao chortled.

Jin Mi laughed with the crime lord. When they finished, Tao remembered his purpose in coming. "We need to execute our new plan. The time for refining has passed. I must learn about the Voiceless Ones. My assassin had no tongue."

"I know little of them, except for the usual rumors and romantic claptrap. We must attack. I like the idea of involving the imperial government. That's one asset we haven't used." Jim Mi walked to the cabinet and opened to door to retrieve some dried fruit and pine nuts—roasted and salted, of course.

CHAPTER 129

MARCUS (212 BC)

While traveling to Mount Hua, Marcus endured waves of emotion. During the day, he enjoyed charming talks with Bo Lo, but in unguarded moments, dark forces dominated him.

They scaled a mountain muted with the autumn's last breath. Rain unleashed odors of decay. Marcus bore his heart's heaviness. As they went higher, familiar pine sights, scents, and sounds greeted. Liquid sounds of the breeze caressed the pine needles and salved his soul.

The Great Mother Temple relaxed in the invigorating mountain sunlight. Marcus admired its rough-hewn wood shingles, stone walls, and sunbathed courtyard. Mother Lo herself answered their knock.

"How long do we have the honor of your company?" She directed the query at Marcus. Even at ninety or one hundred, the woman brought a weary smile.

"I'm uncertain. At least until we—I—finish my task."

"Which is?" Her eyes held him.

"Here's a letter," Marcus replied. "Please meet Bo Lo."

"You two may stay, but the soldiers must go elsewhere."

Marcus directed the men to the nearby monastery. A sudden thought of Sariputra opened another wound. In Mother Lo's study, still simply furnished, Marcus and Bo Lo quietly sipped peach nectar.

The venerable lady's mien announced the time for sober words. "Gone. I feared this possible future when she was called."

"She's dead, and I've come to claim my ... our daughter."

"Why do you wish the child?"

"I don't know. I've thought that I might travel easier without her. But Ming charged me with claiming our little girl. I worry about being a good father. I'm ancient. At least I'd like to meet her, Mother Lo."

The abbess relaxed. "You speak openly. She's living with mountain people chosen by her mother. Obviously, she's attached to them. If she agrees to travel your path, I believe they should accompany you. Would you take three?"

Marcus looked at the altar. That pine scent ... fresh yet. "Yes, I wish her to be secure. Does she know?"

"She's been told that the people she lives with are not her real parents. I believe she understands as much as a child can. She'll be here tomorrow. The two of you should get acquainted. A final decision, in which she participates, will be made. If she refuses, she will stay. You may return when she reaches puberty. I hope she decides to go, but I have no control."

The prospect of leaving without Little Ming troubled Marcus. In the background, he heard squirrels playing tree tag. "I'm nervous. What if she doesn't like ..." Marcus sighed.

Mother Lo and Bo Lo shared a smile. "Just be Marcus. Relax and enjoy your daughter." The words and good wishes settled him. The abbess summoned a nun who led him to a cell.

After depositing his belongings, Marcus went to the garden where he and Ming had often sat. He watched the mountain sparrows chasing the last bugs of the day. The scent of narcissus salved his heart. Marcus closed his eyes: insects buzzing, birds chattering, pines sighing. He walked to an ancient pine, and his fingers traced its bark ridges while he listened to the ageless song. Ants went about their business, oblivious of sorrows or joys. The tree enfolded his shattered heart.

On a rocky outcropping, Marcus squinted at the dying sun. He remembered the sunrise on the sacred Mount Tai. Was that the time when Little Ming had been conceived? Assuredly, she came from passionate loving. Mountains, trees, vistas reduced and clarified. Thoughts ceased before a slate blue canopy. He wept.

The next morning, a middle-aged couple appeared on the trail. A gray, bushy-tailed squirrel sprawled atop a thick branch of a pine and cried in staccato bursts. They had come from the north-face side. The woman wore black peasant trousers and a short, loose-fitting jacket. A stocky man was dressed in simple garb, and his face bore the leathery, weathered look of a lifetime outdoors. Behind them hopped a little child. Marcus peered at longish, wavy hair flashing brownish black in the sunlight shafts. Little Ming gamboled like a spirited colt, sniffing autumn flowers, examining stones, and watching birds wheel above.

Mother Lo raised her left hand, palm earthward. The couple smiled. The man's face crumbled into a mass of wrinkles, and he yawned, showing darkly stained teeth. The little girl peeked out from behind the woman's oft-mended trouser leg.

"Come here, Little Ming. Auntie wants you to meet someone."

The girl advanced like a skittish animal.

"Little Ming, please greet your father."

She looked at the man and smiled. Marcus glimpsed Ming Tian's smile and wept. The tyke went to him. "Don't cry, don't cry."

"I'm not sad, Little Ming. I'm happy. You remind me of your mother." The little one looked at her foster mother and frowned.

"May I touch your face, Little Ming?" She nodded, though her parents had warned her about trusting strangers. He seemed like her invisible friends. His stubby fingers traced her eyebrows. "Will you walk with me?"

Little Ming looked to her parents. Her papa's head nodded assent. "Yes. Can we go to the big trees? I like to talk with them." Marcus chuckled. The tyke marched like a little adult. "Uncle, may I run ahead? I'll stay close." Her eyes glowed like dark embers.

"Yes, little one. Be careful." Her hair swirled like tempest of tossed wheat, and he focused on her spindly, coltish legs.

In the next week, Marcus and Little Ming tromped all over. Rabbits, quail, and mice ran, flew, or scurried away. Father and daughter danced among sere autumn grasses; he chased her through pine groves. Hurt and anger with Ming mellowed. Memories of her mirrored in the child: the way she held her head, the shy smile, the chin tilt when spying a thrush soaring aloft.

Since she had few playmates, Little Ming easily interacted with adults. She questioned everything. A leaf zigzagged downward, and she bounded to retrieve it. "It's pretty, uncle. May I keep it?" Little Ming smiled.

"Yes. I've not seen one so red."

"Why do leaves fall, uncle?"

"They appear in spring when the snow melts and the sun warms the branches. In summer, they grow green and big. Next summer, we'll see different leaves. In autumn, the cold puts trees asleep; the leaves die and fall off, so that new leaves can grow."

Ming's sun-darkened cheeks tightened. "What's death?"

"I'm not certain that I can say, my love. Everything has life: trees, flowers, animals, people. Then they die. They stop, turn cold, and don't move. For people, an inner life leaves the body and goes somewhere. Like with the tree, the leaf dies and falls, but a new leaf comes out the next year."

She looked uncertain. "Will I die, uncle?" The musically spoken words poured forth life force.

"One day, I will die. You will ... so too your parents."

"When I die, will my inner life leave and go somewhere else?"

Marcus felt the tree's calm. "Yes," he answered.

Her feet, covered by straw sandals, worried a stone. Then she bent, retrieved it, and awkwardly tossed it out in a clearing. The tiny head turned his way. "When will I die?"

The unbearable thought tore through him. "I don't know, little one. I hope you stay around a long, long while. Your real mother died a few weeks ago." Marcus hung his head.

Little Ming looked puzzled. "My mother is dead?"

"Yes." Marcus answered with tears rolling down his cheeks.

"Don't cry. Don't cry."

"Little one, it's because I loved your mother so much. I can't believe that I'll never see her."

"Was she nice?"

"You would have liked her," Marcus said as a squirrel peeked at them from behind a pine branch.

"Was she pretty?"

He caressed the pine. "The most beautiful woman I have seen."

Gentle hands brushed his tearstained cheek. "Don't be sad."

"It hurts here." As he replied, he pointed to his chest and stomach. She snuggled in. As they walked back, Little Ming skipped down the dusty mountain path. A stone tripped her, and she smacked the hard surface. Marcus swept up his daughter and ran to the temple door. Blood from her mouth stained his robe, and her sobs wracked his heart. Little Ming's foster mother came out, and the little one cried out, "Mama, Mama! I ... I tripped and hurt my ..."

"She fell and hurt her mouth. Please do something."

The woman looked upset, then relaxed as she went to the girl, who wriggled out of her father's arms to the safety of the familiar woman. "She'll be all right. If you'll excuse me, I'll tend the cut. It's not serious." The woman turned. As she reached the entrance, a little head and blue eyes looked back. His daughter smiled through her pain.

After another week of exploring and talking with the peasant couple to reassure them, all met in Mother Lo's study. The little one sat primly with her foster parents, but she smiled at her uncle. Outside, a gentle rain released the pungent odors of leaf and needle decay. Marcus sniffed the air. A sober look from the abbess brought him back.

"Do you wish to claim your daughter? Will you bind your life with hers?"

"Yes! I'll do my best to see that she's happy and secure."

"Little Ming, you heard your father's words. Will you go with him?" The tyke looked at her foster parents.

"If you agree to go, they'll accompany you."

"Then"—a merry twinkle gave away her decision—"I'll go."

Marcus sagged. "Thank you, thank you! Little Ming ... Bright Moon. You'll not be sorry," Marcus said.

His daughter frowned. "When do we go?"

"In four days, my love. We have far to go."

On the leaving day, the escort returned. As the party rode away, Marcus looked back. The sunlit retreat glowed. The descent was rapid, and his daughter eagerly soaked in the sights and sounds.

As they reached the imperial highway and started east, the girl looked back. "There, Papa, in the distance. A group of men, dressed in white. They're riding up the trail."

He couldn't see, but noticed Bo Lo frowning. "Brother, shouldn't you warn Mother Lo?"

"Don't worry, Marcus. She knows."

CHAPTER 130

MOTHER LO (212 BC)

After Marcus and the others departed, Mother Lo called a meeting. The sisters gathered in the sun-drenched courtyard. A few hardy sparrows busied themselves with seeds.

The abbess addressed them. "Last night, I had a vision. A group of white-clad soldiers—some call them the White Tigers and others the White Panthers—comes to destroy the temple and harm us. All of you except these four sisters will leave tonight. You must go down the path by the north face."

Protests erupted. Mother Lo raised her hand. "No. You have been trained to preserve our heritage. Each will return home and organize women to guard a single text. Cut your hair and dress like men. Leave in twos or threes. I have the necessary passports. The five of us can handle anything. May the Great Mother guard you." By nightfall, all had left, and those remaining prepared the temple.

The White Tigers rode to the temple. Twenty-three white-robed, armored, heavily weaponed soldiers surrounded the temple. Four warriors crept to the entrance, opened the door, and burst inside. A water level later, no one had come out. Commander Jo ordered five more inside with the same result. Then five tan-robed, ancient females walked out and assembled in a line facing the White Tigers, who loaded their crossbows.

Commander Jo called out, "Where are my men?"

Mother Lo's eyes did not twinkle. "Resting comfortably. What may I do for you?" Crows landed on a tree.

"His Majesty commands the destruction of this evil place. All nuns are to be taken. Resistance will be met by death."

"We're the only ones here. Why are we to be punished?" The crows cawed raucously, bobbing their heads.

"You are connected with a treasonous plot against His Majesty!" Jo shouted, unnerved by the fearless crones facing him.

"I know about that. We have done nothing wrong."

"Obey or die!" Jo called out.

"We'll not obey your false orders."

As Jo's voice grew louder, the crows became silent. "Then die, bitches! Fire!" The crossbows loosed their darts.

Mother Lo raised her arms. "We forgive you."

Bolts passed through the women. Jo's eyes bugged as the shafts smashed into the temple walls. A new salvo achieved the same result.

"Draw your swords. Kill at your leisure." Two fell with wounds from others' weapons. The nuns passed through them and vanished. Mother Lo briefly merged with Jo.

CHAPTER 131

JO JING-JENG

A search of the temple revealed nine sleeping men. As the force finally departed, Commander Jo warned them never to divulge what had occurred. He would say that the nuns had been killed.

Back at the capital, the report was accepted, and the White Panthers were disbanded. An imperial search turned up no nuns anywhere. After a year, all had been forgotten, except at Jo Jing-Jeng's farm, where the commander and former academician, terrified by nightmares, took his life.

CHAPTER 132

TAO (211 BC)

Towering thunderheads marched purposefully across the heavens. One mass seemed a god's lair of grays, blues, and blacks—all swirling, whirling. Lightning pierced the skies. Seconds later, a blast stunned the crime lord. Another, then another struck; the explosions closed in, rattling doors and shutters.

Tao stood under a roof overhang and sniffed the peculiar tang of ozone. Elemental natural forces drew him like a lodestone. He wanted to be part of that fury; he opened wide his arms. *O Father, Mother, all elements be with me, or permit me to be with you. Let us create together, forge a world where all have a place, dark lord and lord of light, male and female, old and young, wise and dumb. Masters of the darkened sky, let's dance this elemental curse and blessing. Let spring shoots burst forth in love to the healing, energizing, loving light. I am your son; let me share in this cleansing, in this healing, in this growth.*

"We are here, little one who calls. We offer knowledge, pain, and joy. What will you give?"

"My head."

"Let us begin ..."

Later, Tao came in from the storm. He was drenched. His arms ached from their continued spread, and his wet hair was plastered around his head. Clothes clung, showing the muscled contours of his arms and legs. His eyes burned with a new brightness, a knowing sheen. He moved purposefully, each step a meditation. He knew that he must dry out, but nothing seemed important on that deeper level.

Being invisible's a child's game, playing with power and revenge. Killing harms the killer as well as the one killed. And yet we all kill; we are all killed.

The door opened, and Jin Mi paused, wearing a waterproof cloak of blue-black material and a deep green scholar's hat. He looked at his friend, saw the shift, and slowly shook his head in silence. Tao looked back; their gazes fused.

CHAPTER 133

FENG PING (211 BC)

Spring arrived early. Although dry, the weather had not been bitterly cold. At the plowing ceremony, Emperor Jeng announced an amnesty. Work on imperial projects slowed, and officials were forbidden to use the corvée during the coming year.

Free! The short man danced when he learned about the pardon. Feng Ping received a retirement salary, along with all monies and things seized during his arrest. This largesse would help purchase a modest farm. He and An would decide where it would be located.

On his departure day, the former convict called on the overseer, whose quarters—a whole tent—had taken on the trappings of a wealthy man. Five bronze phoenixes provided ample light, and dense incense smoke clogged the air. The overseer was wearing silk robes when the convict entered.

"So you're free. What can a former convict do these days? That ugly mark on your face bars you from the company of decent people."

"I want to remember you, because someday, I'll make you regret the day you became an overseer. You think you'll be here forever. People like you make mistakes. From the looks of this tent, you already have!" Feng Ping spat and stomped out.

The convict went straight to his wife and sons. He walked the road to his father-in-law's mansion—a wooden structure in the traditional Chin style of supporting roof posts spaced at seven-pace intervals, buttressed by extended cedar roof beams. The massive central building supported a graceful, sloping black-tiled roof. Hung An's family had served Chin for five generations. The estate covered seven hundred acres of prime farmland.

The reunion was chaotic. Ping was amazed by how much his sons had grown. An's family considered the whole affair in Ba a disgrace. Her father, a stiff-backed pensioner, would have been pleased if Feng Ping had suffered a fatal mishap. Yet, the grandfather had provided his grandsons excellent educations.

The chilly reception prompted Feng Ping to hasten their departure. An agreed. Ba flavored their conversations, and they agreed with that destination: mild climate, sparse population, and friendly people.

The day after they settled on Ba, a Chin official arrived in a black carriage with the inevitable team of black mares. Feng Ping mused that all black horses in the empire must live in the metropolitan area. The carriage and military escort impressed the in-laws, especially when the official asked for Feng Ping. The two men met in a receiving room tastefully decorated with silk hangings depicting places where the Hung family members had served.

"I'm Feng Ping, and I understand that you wish to see me."

The other man wore a fashionable robe with brocade silk of blue trimmed with black. "I'm Jang Di, chief aide to His Excellency, Feng Jie, imperial secretary."

"Why would a lofty official seek me? See my badge?" Ping indicated his tattoo.

The other man winced. "The imperial secretary offers you a position in the imperial secretariat. You can begin immediately and have the title, salary, and benefits of assistant imperial secretary. You would have important duties, and your salary would be double what you last earned."

Feng Ping stared at a silver taper holder shaped in the style of a unicorn—the Hung clan totem. Even in his fantasy, the former convict would not have imagined this.

"Forgive my poor manners," Feng said. "Please have juice." The messenger's elevated hand forestalled drinks. "Because I'm overcome by this, I cannot reply today," Feng continued.

The official smiled reassuringly. "His Excellency asked me to invite you to his private office in the Ganchuan Palace in three days, midmorning reception time. I would like to add a personal note. I have admired you for years, sir. It would be an honor to serve with you."

Ping looked at the unicorn. "Please inform His Excellency that I shall meet him at the designated time. Thank you." Feng Ping showed the official out and went off to seek An.

On the meeting day, Feng Ping hired a carriage. Within a water level, he entered into a private receiving room of a simple, almost severe style. A single white silk scroll hung on the wall opposite the entrance. It featured a single written character: "Loyalty." A silver taper holder shaped into a panther artfully held a candle in its jaws.

After several minutes, the imperial secretary rushed in. He wore expensive clothes and footwear fashioned with heavy silk. Feng Jie looked about sixty, with a magnificent white mane and beard. He had been the presiding official at the scholars' burial.

"It's good to see you after all of these years, Feng Ping. Thin, but healthy," the imperial secretary said.

"The fat melted in my work details. Now I'm tanned."

"Definitely. How are your wife and sons? I believe that your sons have been taught by some of our best minds. When they are ready to join the government, let me know."

Feng Ping bowed before the personal tone. "Sire, I'm flattered. I would like to complain about an overseer for camp fifteen of the Apang Palace detachment. Last winter, he caused three men to lose fingers, and I believe that he's accepting bribes."

The imperial secretary nodded. "I shall act on your words."

"I will sleep better when he cannot terrorize his charges."

The older man smiled as he poured clouded liquor into two cups. The cobalt blue drinking vessels affected the southern style, with the familiar flat-cloud pattern. "I'll tell you frankly that I've worked hard for your release ... the back pay ... and retirement monies. You fuse exceptional organizational skills with exemplary integrity and had been marked for a top management post; then there was that unfortunate speech. I sympathized but could do nothing. Chancellor Lee aimed to destroy you and won His Majesty's ear. Of course, your departure had been carefully watched, lest you lead a rebellion. Certainly, you eschewed narrow political gain. Recently, the senior chancellor has been embarrassed, and I acted. The best way to reward me and yourself would be to accept."

Feng Ping looked anew at the elegant calligraphy on the scroll. "I have been in a quandary about your unprecedented offer."

"That's a comment on your singular talents," the imperial secretary said as he precisely poured two more cups.

Feng Ping sniffed a jasmine aroma—the man's body perfume. "Your Excellency, I have seen much and suffered more ... stark images of poignancy and horror. I helped bury alive the scholars. I cradled a delirious man who imagined me to be his son—a man older than you, sire, working on the Direct Road. I would need the power to affect a transformation. In the early years, we achieved great things; since, we've lost our moorings.

"At some point, I would have to face His Majesty. When you offer this generous package, you say that I am worthy of it, and if I accept, I am saying that I condone the actions of these last years. That I cannot do. Were I an official, perhaps I would follow another course ... but because of my tongue, I have an outsider's perspective. I must therefore respectfully decline."

The older man slumped, then elevated himself. He seemed larger than life. "But if you work with me, we can change things."

The smaller man straightened. "I'm branded for life. I cannot forget the old man nor the female scholar who breathed dirt at the last. I must decline. Possibly we will reach some sort of agreement after I spend a year or two in Ba."

The secretary looked at the scroll given by His Majesty's father to the official's father. "Take time ... months or a year. You are too valuable outside. You will miss the bustle of administrative work. Together, we will change the world."

The smaller man's face showed conflicting emotions. "I regret declining this opportunity. I also appreciate the honor of unburdening myself. We leave for Ba ... remote yet friendly, backward yet civilized." The two men bowed formally.

CHAPTER 134

HAN YU (211 BC)

Han Yu received three messages that would transform her life. The first announced her father's death. When she planned her leave to bury him, she learned that she would be relieved of her post. The government had finally discerned that she was a female. That news offset an official citation recognizing her multiple accomplishments, such as her direction of nineteen local irrigation projects and the establishment of residences for orphans and widows. Han Yu had formed mediation teams to resolve matters such as water-rights disputes. She received a commendation and a retirement bonus.

The third item pertained to the transfer of eight local villages south. To improve the security of its borders, the state shifted one hundred thousand families to various locations. The lot that included Han Yu's villagers numbered thirty thousand families. They would settle in the Guilin commandery, and Han Yu knew she must inform and assist the eight village heads.

Three days later, the men sat in the orchid garden, arrayed about her in a tight semicircle. Orchids swayed: pinks, reds, blues, and whites, wafting their delicate scents.

As Han Yu outlined the order, a voice interrupted. "How can this be? We've lived here ... and our fathers ... and their fathers before us. What will happen to their graves?" Cai Ro's silver hair had been bound in a ponytail. He sat fully erect, shoulders squared.

"But each village and family will not have to pay taxes for ten years. I'll see that you don't leave until after the fall harvest, which may be taken," Han Yu replied. The headmen became silent as they contemplated having an entire harvest at their disposal. Complaints about the long journey and the uncertainties paled against a decade of tax exemptions.

One lone voice whined, "Who will protect us against the barbarians?" Old Chi was completely bald, and he had but two teeth left. Sometimes air whistled out when he spoke.

"Old Chi, I will forward your concern and will get official reports. The more you know, the better you can prepare. You should know that I have been relieved as prefect."

Complaints and curses, although barely audible, indicated wholehearted support of her. A consensus developed for a delegation to the commandery capital. "We should tell those bigwigs that you must stay, little lady." Cai Lo smiled, showing that his teeth—most of them, at least—were still in his mouth.

Several men whispered, and Old Chi whined at her. "Little lady, you must leave us." Han Yu departed.

CHAPTER 135

OLD CHI

Old Chi sipped his citrus juice and began. "Old Jao has an excellent plan. Tell us."

"Let's have her as our head. She won't have a post, and she has the skills and contacts to give us the best start."

Old Chi broke into a smile and added, "Yes, contacts. She can get us things … even soldiers. We should pay her … but not too much, because she's a woman." All nodded, and Old Chi brought her back.

CHAPTER 136

HAN YU

"Why are you happy?" Han Yu asked. A long tress of her unruly hair fell across her eyes. She primly tucked it behind her ear.

Old Jao spoke. "We've solved our problem, little lady. We want you to join us. Please lead us to Guilin. Because of your skills, experience, and honesty, you would be perfect."

Han Yu's tress popped out and lay untended. "Thank you. That you trust me with this is an honor. I've worked hard, but I relied on you." She rearranged the errant lock. Kingfishers called out; it was the mating season. Han Yu took another breath. "I accept, but with the condition that you all support me. Agreed?" They nodded. "Also, you must pay me a subprefect's salary and pool our labor to build an official's quarters—half size, of course." Han Yu knew that if they paid her a respectable salary, they would consider her an investment. "You must leave for the capital. The civilian head must approve everything. Ask him to give me a title and a seal. That will make it easier in Guilin."

While lounging on her bed, Han Yu recalled some cases. Then she inhaled the ginger scent—her favorite. She looked at the double, oval-shaped white orchid. Around the edges, pink delicate veins crisscrossed the petals.

Han Yu closed her eyes again and dreamed of a warm pool, with orchids blooming, and irises—purple and regal—poking up their heads. Her hands dove into the water and hit a bag. Loosening the tying thong, she cradled the wrinkled feet. *Mama, don't let them drown me too.*

CHAPTER 137

TAO (211 BC)

The Reds hit seven buildings: two lenders' shops, three liquor stores, and two warehouses. Scores died. "We did it, brother. We've won!" Jin Mi exclaimed in his study.

Tao noticed the gray streak in his friend's hair. A new scroll showed a horse gamboling on a grassy plain—running free, without a rider.

"Yes, we have won. The bitch of the north has not been found, but her gang is destroyed. Our informant has been invaluable. Keep her in place another month, and make her a subordinate if she checks out," Tao said. He no longer spoke in a whisper and kept looking at the horse.

Jin Mi looked intently at Tao. "What is wrong, brother? You've been different for the last few weeks."

"My brother, I have given thought to my future and to my past since the time when the gods spoke to me. This way is no longer mine. No … let me speak." Tao raised his hand. "I need another path. I experimented with the dark lord and almost perished. I found you, and life has been a delight. The invisibility games are child's play—important for the Reds, you, and me, but still something to play with. I am bored. I would have left earlier if it were not for you and the enemy.

"Jin Mi, I want you to be the new crime lord—to take my place and to bring the Reds to new plateaus. I must journey alone. That is difficult, especially since it means leaving you. The Reds are your future. You are a natural crime lord.

"I am a seeker. I was taken from my dead parents. My lineage is scholarly. And yet that is not where my gifts lie. I can be like Black Bear … perhaps more powerful. That's not what I mean. I have abilities coming into focus. They would have emerged, but the experience with the storm accelerated things.

"I must find my own way outside crime. You must stay and maintain the Reds. You have enough weapons and tools to combat the bitch; with time, you can learn invisibility. We'll call a meeting of the leaders, and the leadership change will be announced."

Jin Mi looked back at the horse to avoid showing his tears. He wanted to go off with Tao, show his back to the city and all of its allure, but he knew that Tao was correct. At least for now, he was still the master thief, with ideas about the Reds and their future. "Brother, your words wrench my heart. How will I be without you? Our sharings have been natural, like breathing."

"Brother, you are the love of my life. I am not one for words, but I must say simple things. We have not loved physically, and yet we have been lovers. Someday, I will return ... or perhaps you will join me. I have a feeling we will meet again."

Jin Mi wept. "Brother, where will you go?" he asked.

Tao brushed away his own tears. "I will see Black Bear and seek his advice. I will see what he has to say." Tao went over to the scroll and examined it minutely, not looking at it as a piece of art, but rather as a place in the heart. He smiled at Jin Mi. "Brother, we have to plan if I am to leave before winter. Finish off the bitch and assure a smooth succession."

CHAPTER 138

HAN YU (211 BC)

The peasant delegation crowded Han Yu's office as a humid heat smothered the town. The civilian head had been reluctant, but after three hours, he drafted a document making Han Yu the acting head of Guilin subdistrict, northeast sector. She would direct the transfer and serve as liaison with the local prefect.

A month later, Han Yu received the documents with the powers of a regular subprefect, including an annual salary—two-thirds of which would be government subsidized (the rest came from the villages). She summoned the delighted village heads.

They would send an advance party of thirty men to construct temporary quarters and hire local laborers. Han Yu arranged for an escort and the loan of ten grain wagons.

CHAPTER 139

OLD LIU (211 BC)

The harvest exceeded expectations. A simple ceremony was held before the drought demonness's shrine in Wan-Li village. Old Liu would go south. Because of his arthritis, he traveled by a cart drawn by a water buffalo. Before they left, Old Liu went to the huge brownish-black animal. A nose ring and rope hung loosely. Liu brushed away the flies and stroked its silky coat. The massive head looked back. Old Liu loved the smell of water buffalo. Despite its size, the animal was reliable and even-tempered.

He returned to the open cart. A youngster helped him up, and he sagged on the wooden railing. Six people filled this cart, along with cooking oil and salt blocks. Chen had died two years ago, and though he denied it, he sorely missed her.

Now he stayed with his eldest son, but felt a burden. If only he'd the privacy of his own place. Old Liu looked wistfully about the cart. How would he be able to belch and fart? At least old folks would understand if something accidentally slipped out.

Drizzle wet his forehead. "Hard to see," he muttered and tried to suppress tears as the rain scents recalled days in the fields. He looked for the peach tree and stone marker. A local scholar had written out Chen's name characters, and the stonecutter had carved the lines and curves.

Old Liu saw Han Yu walking beside her horse. Was she limping? Perhaps they'd compare infirmities. Old Liu looked sadly at his useless hand. He turned one last time as the rain poured harder and blotted smells, sounds, and sights. Would Chen grumble if he talked with Han Yu?

CHAPTER 140

MARCUS (211 BC)

Marcus and his fellow travelers arrived at the Green Dragon Lodge. A north wind had given them ruddy cheeks; temperatures dipped below freezing for days. The night of their arrival, a snowstorm blanketed the forest, and Marcus awakened to a pristine white land. Cold rushed into his room when he opened a window.

A month later, an ice storm locked the mountain world in glittering crystals. Rainbows sparkled from bejeweled trees, causing Marcus to shade his eyes. Late that morning, while strolling, he slipped on the icy trail. Fortunately, he landed on amply-padded buttocks. Laughter became his distraction from the pain of repeated falls.

Marcus located cozy living quarters for Little Ming and her foster parents in a nearby village. During the year, Marcus tried different visiting times. One month, he tried every third day; another, three times every two weeks. He and his daughter agreed that a three-day stay suited them. By early spring, four days was common, with an occasional five-day visit. When the last snow fell, Little Ming pestered her father for a walk, and they plodded along until she scooped up snow and threw it at him. They chased each other around the grove. Later, Marcus tucked in a rosy-cheeked cherub who smiled so that her forehead seemed one large dimple. Marcus loved the scent of her washed hair and its glossy sheen.

After one tearful parting, Marcus bought a kitten for his daughter. Little Ming solemnly promised to care for it when her father warned that its life depended on her.

CHAPTER 141

LITTLE MING (211 BC)

Bo Lo took her for walks. Little Ming learned the names, shapes, and colors of safe and poisonous plants. As they strolled, Little Ming picked a leaf of grass. Bo Lo stopped. "Little Ming, why did you do that?"

"Uncle, I wanted to taste the green."

"My child, the grass was singing, and you cut off part of the chorus." Bo Lo laid his hand gently on her shoulder.

"I'm sorry! I won't do it again," the urchin said tearfully.

"Don't worry. Everything lives, even rocks and clods of dirt," Bo Lo said. "Sometimes we pick fruit or vegetables; some hunt animals for food. As long as you are aware of what you do and respect life, you will live in harmony with the forest."

Little Ming bent to the grass. "I'm sorry. Please sing again." As she picked her way along the path, Bo Lo growled like a bear and chased her. Since the little one took after her natural mother, she already reached his shoulder.

CHAPTER 142

MARCUS

Marcus resumed his spiritual journey. One discipline was the reduced dependency on animal products. He fasted a half day weekly. Fish and eggs were permitted once a week.

Frustration with uneventful meditations galled Marcus, who wished for dazzling insights with booming drums and lightning flashes. He sought out Master Bo Lo.

"Yes?" asked Bo Lo, who was regarding a miniature cypress.

"Sorry for disturbing you," Marcus apologized.

"Nonsense. What is it?" Bo Lo promised the cypress that he would have a gentle talk with it to discern its problem.

"I'm discouraged, master. Nothing works."

"If you believe that you can't do a thing, you can't. Negative thoughts are the strongest chains. You are precisely where you should be. Perhaps one lesson is patience."

Marcus teased his graying beard. "Help me get there."

Bo Lo replied, "I can't eat for you, shit for you, or attain understanding for you. I can give tips, but you must find your way." They rose from the plain, thin rush mats and walked to a remote part of the building complex. The stuffy room brought a sneezing attack to Marcus. Bo Lo called to the shadows, and a cat padded over and jumped into the abbot's cradling arms. She had green eyes, yellowish-orange fur with dark stripes, and a brick-colored nose. "We call her Teacher."

"What an odd name," Marcus remarked.

"Not at all, my friend. She can teach far better than I. When she sleeps, her tail curls about her body to conserve heat. Watch her breathe—only the abdomen moves. Children breathe thus. When Teacher awakes, she's instantly alert. She stretches to tone her muscles and adjust her spine. She eats herbs to cleanse her system. She can watch a mouse hole for hours."

Marcus smiled at Teacher. Her eyes narrowed into a semisleep. He knew of her reputation.

Marcus tamed his senses by imitating the temple's tortoise. His practice of silence for three days brought a new concentration. Once, after an extended silence, he heard the brook laughing and felt its merry bubbling through his pores. A breeze sang through pine needles and resonated in his abdomen.

Two months later, while he was in a meditative trance, a blow to his midspine opened him to an awesome brilliance. Bo Lo had delivered the unexpected strike. Now Marcus smiled at simple things.

A month later, Marcus came out of a mediation to find himself floating. Soon he'd raise objects and ignite candles. All he needed was to create an image, set his intent, and feel the result. Teacher gave him a clue when he watched her jump atop a high wall: she focused and made it. Once Marcus teleported into his master's study.

"At your service, master."

"So you've done it," said Bo Lo, who had nearly wet himself. Marcus moved a sacred stone into Bo Lo's hand. The older man smiled. "Well done, but don't get stuck in childish tricks."

Marcus teleported back to his cell, where he pondered the words. He also began to spirit travel to Rome, visiting his farmhouse. He saw two children: one blond, the other brown haired—a girl. *The grandmother with silver hair ... Julia, can it be?* A one-armed man entered the home. *Quintus! My son!*

Another time, Marcus arrived at Ming's quarters with her sitting at a desk. There was a knock—His Majesty! He tore her gown; she resisted, then retired to her sleeping area and retrieved a dagger. The blade rose, then dove into her. "MARCUS, I LOVE YOU!" Later, the emperor stumbled in. His leer transmuted to horror, and he fled to his quarters. Marcus saw himself taken to Yung.

Afterward, Marcus walked in the pine grotto and screamed and screamed and screamed. The next day, he visited Little Ming.

"Remember, Papa? Last year, we saw the Mount Hua leaves."

His hand closed on hers. "Yes, little one. I'd forgotten. You've got an excellent memory, Ming."

"I'm not Ming, Papa. I'm Little Ming."

Marcus mumbled, "I'm sorry, love. Ming was your mama's name too. Perhaps it was because I saw her die in a dream."

Little Ming examined her father's ashen face. "She had to die, Papa. Like the leaves, remember? She had to fall."

Marcus looked at her through tear-glazed eyes.

Back at the temple, Marcus warily resumed his travels. Earnest talks with Bo Lo settled him. After one satisfying trip, Marcus was idly practicing characters when he noticed unusual words flowing down the board.

Troubled,
I gaze within
and learn where
the primal spirit issues.
In emptiness and silence
I find serenity,
in tranquil inaction
I gain satisfaction.
Honor pure ones,
admire immortals.
The world's hazy
viewed from a height.
I leave the dust,
shed impurities,
and enter the realm
of the Great Beginning.

Marcus stared; the poem stared back. He took it to the master, who asked him to wait. Upon his return, he gave Marcus a poem.

"You wrote these same lines eighty years ago."

"Then I was ... am that poet, Chu Yuan?"

"Yes, my friend. Welcome." They planned for the future. At the same time, he found excuses to be with Little Ming. Six, seven, and then the full week—ten days—were spent with her.

CHAPTER 143

EMPEROR JENG
(211–210 BC)

The emperor's thirty-sixth year in power (211 BC) began ominously. Following an exhausting court debate, a group of astronomers dressed in characteristic turquoise robes approached the throne.

"Speak! My patience is spent."

"Great Pure One, we tremble to report that the red planet is approaching the Scorpion's Heart constellation. This inauspicious event has but once occurred since ancient times. On that occasion, a great uprising challenged your illustrious ancestor, Duke Mu. The historical records also mention a prolonged famine."

The sovereign's eyes approximated those of a ravenous wolf. "Do you criticize me like those despicable traitors I smashed last year?"

"We did not wish to come, but we are bound to inform you."

Emperor Jeng contemplated the signs. "You're certain about the drought and rebellion?"

Astronomer Pi relaxed as the emperor's demeanor eased. Earlier, he'd said his good-bye to his wife and children and had made funeral preparations. "Yes, Pure One. We compared four records."

"What do you suggest?"

"Have the invocator sacrifice to earth and heaven."

Emperor Jeng leaned back on the throne. Hour after hour of sitting there had wrenched his back so that he couldn't stand erect for ten paces. "Your words make sense. If the drought breaks, I'll reward you."

The groveling men backed away, then scurried out of the hall. A few days later, an imperial messenger from Dung commandery reported a meteor crash. Authorities found a message inscribed on it: "After the first emperor dies, the land will be divided." The report contained the written characters in the style of the former warring state Chi—forbidden for a decade.

The imperial secretary traveled to the Dung commandery and later submitted a secret report that he had interrogated everyone within two miles of the meteor site. Since none confessed, he executed all literate people as a precaution.

Nightmares and insomnia plagued the ruler, and sexual orgies could not satisfy him. Food and drink brought bloat and stomach upset. Following one vomiting episode, he abstained from alcohol.

The monarch loved Prince Hu Hai. A tall, fun-loving man of twenty, the prince joined his father's binges. When father and son walked the grounds, taking the covered walkways, they told anecdotes, bawdy stories, and dirty jokes. One day, Hu Hai proudly presented his father with a grandson—the young man's first male child. Once, the infant prince wetted the emperor's robes, and Jeng laughed jovially.

Heavy snows portended a year of significant rainfall. They also confined the sovereign to his palaces. With the completion of the plowing ceremony, a southeastern tour was announced. The tour party included Chancellor Lee, Prince Hu Hai, Dr. Wu, and Jao Gao—the imperial tutor—among others. The imperial secretary remained in charge at the capital. The party moved through an eastern pass and turned southeast, stopping at Yunmeng. Then they made for the Long River.

Along with the famous Yangtze River carp on which the party feasted, they were served rice. The emperor had developed a taste for "black rice," the origin of which was obscure. When it was properly cooked, one could count the separate grains.

South of the Long River, they followed an overland route. When the entourage reached the impassable Che River, they turned west and then south, coming on fields of orchids and mellifluous flowers. Emperor Jeng received a delegation of captive Vietnamese chieftains and half-clad barbarians with blackened teeth. The barbarians' malevolent looks turned pleasant when the emperor ordered their release. Phan Lo, the main chief, promised there would be peace when the Chinese left the Vietnamese homeland. His tone pleasantly conveyed the offer, but his eyes argued that resistance would prevail.

When they reached Langya, Emperor Jeng made off for the Green Dragon Temple. Arrival brought a face-to-face meeting with his old friend.

"Marcus. How good to see you."

CHAPTER 144

MARCUS (210 BC)

The sight of Ming's would-be rapist triggered rage. In meditations, intense discussions, and arguments with Bo Lo, Marcus had confronted his hatred. Yet, upon seeing the villain, he gritted his teeth.

"Your Majesty, I didn't know that you had come." He prostrated himself on the shiny pine boards. Outside, squirrels scolded Teacher, who whipped her tail.

Emperor Jeng composed himself. "How do I appear, my friend?"

Marcus sighed. "You look older, sire. More gray in your beard and on your head. The facial lines deepen."

Emperor Jeng gazed about the bare room, which was only furnished with essential things: the desk, three ragged mats, a simple altar. "We've been companions for three decades," the emperor said. "Each day, life grows more precious. At times, I wander in memories, yet cannot recapture the Willow Lady or the planning sessions during the liberation wars. 'Trust no one,' my father said. You have been faithful, and I need you."

Marcus looked out the window to see the cat scaling a tree.

"I owe no man anything, but I wish to tell you the truth," the emperor said. "The night Academician Ming died, I was drunk and desired her. I don't know why, but since the time when she saved my life, I have fancied her. I knew that she was yours but couldn't help myself. Ming was proper." The royal brow knitted, and the emperor bowed his head. Outside, Teacher got herself stuck up in a tree and mewed plaintively.

"I determined to have her … went to her room and forced myself on her. She went into the bedroom. At the time, I thought she was going to change clothes, but she took her life. I faked her death, then removed you. I taste, smell, and see her death every night."

The trembling voice shattered Marcus's defenses. "Thank you, sire. I saw a vision of Ming's death. Sire, your words give a different view. I hated you, but meditations and my daughter have helped me heal."

Emperor Jeng looked out the window and saw the lush, green trees. "Come, Marcus. Come, my friend. Come home."

"I'm uncertain about leaving, because I am responsible for my daughter. Each day is a gift."

"The two of you can stay at the palace or at your farm."

"I must speak with the abbot. Then I'll answer."

The royal face cleared. "Let me know in a day or two." Marcus started as he saw a yellowish-red streak drop from the tree.

That night, he met with Bo Lo.

"Marcus, you've attained a life's spiritual goals. Perhaps it's time to practice in the world of the senses."

"That way disgusts me, master. The monarch looked hollowed out by dissipated living. I might lose what I have gained."

"Meditate on your question. It's a divining of the future."

In the inward journey filled with forest sounds, the cuckoo's plaintive cries, the crickets' incessant chattering, and the cicada's buzz, the answer came: "Your Highness, I'll reenter the world. Permit me to collect Little Ming and her guardians."

Emperor Jeng smiled. "Thank you. I'll return to Langya."

As Marcus turned, a different trek loomed.

CHAPTER 145

JIN MI (210 BC)

The Reds' new leader looked around the table with his group in place. Former leaders had been promoted or retired, and Tao played a significant role in pruning the old guard. The old teak table had been replaced by an oak table, and the lamps were phoenixes—imperial favorites. A subtle scent of lavender pervaded the room to soothe everyone. Jin Mi smiled.

Big Lu, the new day master, had risen through the ranks and knew intimately the activities under the day master's purview. He had joined the Reds as a beggar four decades ago. In that sense, Big Lu was a bridge to the past. And yet, he was not mired in the old ways; he could change. He had had no choice when Tao led.

Tao had left two weeks ago, and it seemed like months. It was the correct decision ... yet it hurt Jin Mi. This was his life; this was all he knew; this was his past and his future too.

Dao Ji was the new night master and a risk, though skilled with a blade. It would be intriguing to see if he could grow into the job and its responsibilities. He would be mentored and left alone. Sweating profusely, with a strong body odor, Dao Ji sat ramrod straight, trying to look important.

Pi Li was the merchant liaison; he had worked with Tao for two decades. He was the investor of the Reds' funds and the liaison for the growing number of merchants who linked themselves with the Reds. Pi Li commanded attention and was dressed in a black vest over a white shirt with black trousers. His shoes were fashioned out of leather and dyed ebony. Somehow, they appeared glossy.

Subprefect Wang was a daring addition. Jin Mi felt that the Reds' government liaison needed to attend meetings. His perspective would be invaluable, and if something confidential to the Reds needed to be aired, the table members could meet a water level before the subprefect attended.

Lin Dai sat demurely despite the stares from her male cohorts. She wore an emerald green robe that offset her green eyes. An embossed white dove graced her robe front. Jin Mi had invited her as an experiment. She was the spy against the enemy, and Jin Mi watched the men glancing her way.

"Welcome to the Leadership Council. We have made some significant changes. Our former leader, Tao, has left the area and won't return. He chose me as his successor, and I am honored to lead the Reds." Jin Mi caught each member's eye and held it. "I am Jin Mi, the master thief—and under Tao, I served as night master. Tonight I'll begin the reports. We have fought a years long war against the Ghosts. We have taken losses, but we have given them serious blows. I intend for the Reds to finish them. Later, I will outline the general thrust of the campaign, but I'd like your suggestions. To help us, I invited Lin Dai, who spied for us these last three years. She got to know the Ghosts' leader, the infamous bitch from the north. Lin Dai, please tell us what you know about the Ghosts ..."

CHAPTER 146

MARCUS (210 BC)

Emperor Jeng welcomed Marcus, Little Ming, and her foster parents to the imperial encampment. One cloudy afternoon, His Majesty, Prince Hu Hai, Marcus, Little Ming, and some guards rode up the coast. They reached a beach of light brown sand where breakers swelled to the rhythm of an approaching storm. Little Ming built a sand house and scooped a moat using her hands. She would pause periodically to sniff the salt breeze and dreamily gaze at the rising waves. Marcus cautioned her to beware of the surf.

"Your Majesty, I speak as one who's seen war's suffering," Marcus said. "It's the people's bane. Bring home the armies."

The emperor listened as they walked. Marcus shed his sandals and wriggled his toes in the sand. His Majesty took off his footwear, and Marcus watched their prints wash away.

"A few months back, I might have punished you," the emperor said, "but now I'm more persuaded. Perhaps it's the wild beauty here; perhaps I'm tired. Peace bores me, yet the war against the northern ones drags on. My generals can give me no ending dates, only dead young men and wailing parents."

"Armies march off to cheers, but return in silence. Children grow up not knowing their fathers," Marcus replied.

The imperial shoulders bent. The thunder grew insistent as a breeze picked up. "I must triumph; otherwise I begin to wither like a squash on a drought-stricken vine. Yet I recently released some Vietnamese chieftains; although prisoners, their hearts were already free. Will peace bring me fame?"

Marcus regarded a tiger ready for his final hunt, with teeth dulled and claws broken. A wave crash jolted them. "Your name will endure, sire. Show that mighty Chin can forge a lasting peace."

"Your words sing like the siren call of the fox lady. Perhaps warring hindered the search for immortals. I know my ministers think me foolish for listening to magicians! Longevity potions may exist, and I suffer fakes for the possibility of eternal life. That's not such a bad bargain."

The sand's heat drove them to the water's edge, and the ocean's storm abated. They lifted their robes. "Your Majesty, I hope you can spurn death," Marcus said. "I know that my spirit endures through lifetimes. I have learned that in one life, I was a Chinese man; now I'm a Roman who lives like a Chinese."

A crafty smile crept over the royal mouth. "I knew that you must have been Chinese. You are Chinese now." Both laughed, and when they reached their children, they marveled at the elaborate sand dwelling with moats, trenches, and walls. Hu Hai wearied of the dig and commanded four guards to assist them.

"Your Highness, devote yourself and the government to peaceful matters. Whether you live or die—and I hope that you have as many years as grains of sand on this beach—with peace your fame, will endure forever."

The sovereign savored the cool water splashing against his feet and looked to where seagulls circled lazily. "Roman! Chinese! You speak guile-filled, honeyed words."

Marcus squinted at the roiling sea and saw a multicolored spectrum. "Little Ming! Look at the rainbow!"

CHAPTER 147

EMPEROR JENG (210 BC)

The following day, Magician Shu Fu and the other magicians bowed before their lord. "Pure One, life-prolonging herbs abound on Penglai, whose peaks we glimpsed … but a sea monster blocked us. Expert bowmen must slaughter it. Then we will retrieve the herbs."

"We agree with you, but for different reasons. Archers and soldiers will accompany you, and if monsters interfere, they will be killed. However, if you fail, then you will feed the fishes. Find the elixirs!"

The magicians scuttled away like frightened crabs.

That night, the sovereign dreamed that he fought a sea spirit who'd taken a human form. In his terror, Emperor Jeng awakened Marcus, who slept in an adjoining tent. Dr. Wu was aroused and prescribed a foul-tasting but effective sleeping potion.

Next morning, an academician was summoned. "Oh Great Pure One, sea gods are normally invisible, but they may take on human guises. This spirit must be defeated. Go to the Sea King's shrine in Jufu. Sacrifice to him."

Emperor Jeng commanded his sailors to prepare grappling hooks and nets and turned the party north for the Sea King's shrine. At the altar, His Majesty sacrificed a giant sea heron and a sea turtle. A whale-oil lamp shaped like a seahorse burned night and day. Locals said that it hadn't been extinguished for the last four generations, when a giant wave swept away half of the town.

Two days later, a school of dolphins cruised near shore. Boarding a skiff powered by four rowers, the emperor wrapped his head with a purple turban, tied back his beard, and prepared a repeating crossbow. A water level later, a triumphant sovereign shouted to Hu Hai that he'd slain two monsters. Flesh from them was presented to the Sea King.

The next evening, Marcus and the emperor walked to a sea cliff. Breezes chilled them, and a courtier retrieved a bearskin covering. Alternating patterns of silver and dark swam the sea surface as the silvery moon shone through clouds. Patches of iridescent silver relentlessly moved shoreward over the water's surface.

CHAPTER 148

MARCUS (210 BC)

Marcus mused about Ming's flesh reflecting the moonbeams while Emperor Jeng slumbered under the thick brown bearskin cover. Marcus soon beheld a singular silver circle floating atop the water. The orb touched the shore and crept up the cliff. Marcus peered up through the radiant cloud gap, and the moon's brilliance blinded him as he breathed silver, tasted silver, heard silver, thought silver, and vibrated a timeless silvery dance.

A cough alerted Marcus to guards huddled about a flickering torch. After they returned to the encampment, rain fell through the night. Morning dawned cold. At a tent conference, the courtiers decided to return to the capital. Camp broke in the mud.

When the party reached the district town Pingyuan, the emperor fell ill. Dr. Wu treated the affliction, and the sojourn resumed, but the emperor's raging fever would not abate. After days of delirium and convulsions, Marcus feared the worst.

One sunny afternoon, when orioles sang merrily from bright green treetops, Marcus was summoned to the imperial tent and heard labored breathing; sweet camphor scent clogged his nostrils.

"Your Majesty." Marcus kneeled.

Fevered eyes opened. "Marcus, you've come. Magician's too late. Who succeed? Fu Su's best, but Hu Hai here, trouble …" The dying man's eyes closed. "Arranged for you … safe … Little Ming … pretty … like mother … not you." Wheezing coughing turned to a laugh. "Still able joke. Officials know … Hu Hai too. Go, friend. Only one … trust."

"Thank you, sire. May you find peace." The fevered eyes widened, and a smile flickered.

"Peace? Call Lee!"

CHAPTER 149

CHANCELLOR LEE
(210 BC)

Marcus ran to Chancellor Lee. "His Majesty wishes you."

The chancellor scurried off to the familiar black tent where Dr. Wu paced. Chancellor Lee nodded and passed through the flap.

"Been through much, you, I," the emperor said laboriously.

"Yes, my lord, but you'll live for …"

"Must say things. No successor, trouble … should have been Fu Su, Hu Hai as emperor … spoiled, watch tutor."

"I'll see Hu Hai on the throne and will guide him. Your legacy will last—on that I pledge my life, Your Majesty."

The dying man smiled. "Good … see Hai."

The senior chancellor left.

Hu Hai burst into the tent as the imperial physician bent over the bed. "My father sent for me!"

"He's dead."

Hu Hai wailed, "Dead! He can't be!"

Dr. Wu took Hu Hai's shoulders. "His Majesty's dead." Hu Hai bawled. Chancellor Lee summoned Hu Hai, the imperial tutor, Dr. Wu, and the emperor's trusted servants to his tent.

"Gentlemen, the first emperor's dead. Before he passed away, he wished me to announce that Prince Hu Hai would succeed him. Our situation's grave until we reach the capital; ambitious men may take advantage of the confusion to foment trouble. We must pretend that His Majesty lives and deliver food to the tent and later to the carriage. Bring reports to the tent as well. Our task is made easier by the emperor's passion for secrecy. We'll take a direct route back."

Jao Gao's face resembled a fully round spring Chu melon pitted by the blackest eyes. Now he patted a crimson brocade scarf against his forehead. When he spoke, words rasped out spasmodically. "What about the barbarian?"

The chancellor's hand reached out in a calming manner. "His Majesty commanded that he be safeguarded."

Jao Gao's eyes and stubby snout reminded some of a weasel. "Excellency, can we fool people?"

"We have no choice." As people left, the imperial tutor motioned to the senior chancellor. "Yes?"

"Did His Majesty truly name Hu Hai?"

"Of course." Chancellor Lee sniffed.

"What about Fu Su and his bunch?" Inwardly, Chancellor Lee smirked at the buffoon, who clearly wished to avenge himself for that fact that he'd been accused of crimes by General Tian's brother. He watched passively as the obese man licked his lips. "We'll deal with that later. If we make it home, the advantage of surprise is with us," Chancellor Lee said. The fat man's pupils dilated.

"You realize that Fu Su must die," Chancellor Lee added.

"Yes, and General Tian," Jao Gao replied. His tongue kept swiping over his lips.

"Excellency, exterminating the Meng clan would forestall revenge."

"When Hu Hai ascends the throne, I hope that he'll end warring, the massive building projects, and so forth. We skirted on the edge of calamity last year. A time of repose and relaxation might be beneficial, don't you agree?'

"I'm certain that he'll be a fine and conscientious ruler." The senior chancellor regarded the wall hanging: a scene of sacred Mount Tai. "We should meet regularly before we reach home. Our final plans must be laid."

Later, Chancellor Lee sought out the Roman. "Your Excellency." Chancellor Lee was touched by the Roman's grief. Here was a man deeply affected by the emperor's death.

"His Majesty's dead."

CHAPTER 150

MARCUS (210 BC)

The news of the emperor's death, while not unexpected, hammered Marcus.

"A group of key officials and imperial servants believe that it's imperative that the death remain a secret for the present. Chaos might erupt, and that would be dangerous for us."

Marcus looked at the impassive face. "I hadn't thought about that, Excellency."

The flat tone droned on. "The emperor named Hu Hai as his successor, and we intend to carry out his wishes."

Marcus was puzzled. "His Majesty alluded as much to me too."

"I'm glad to hear that. We'll carry on as if the emperor lives. If the news leaks, we all may die." Marcus dimly followed the argument until Little Ming's face flashed in his mind.

"His Majesty insisted that you be safeguarded."

"Thank you, sire. I'm grateful and will cooperate fully."

The party moved west, chasing the summer sun. Everything proceeded normally—until Little Ming sought her father. "Papa, the emperor's carriage stinks, and Mama says that he's dead!"

"Little Ming, His Majesty's very ill. We must not say that he died. Do you see?"

Ming didn't see, but she didn't wish to argue with her father, either. All she wanted was to have the bad smell go away. "Yes, Papa." The girl hugged her father and ran off, far away. Soon a cart of dead fish was placed behind the emperor's black vehicle.

Later, secret orders under the first emperor's seal charged Fu Su, General Tian, and subordinates with treason and demanded that they kill themselves. Fu Su took his life. General Tian was murdered by the imperial tutor's agents.

Hu Hai ascended the throne as the second Chin emperor amid a general celebration and amnesty. The royal purge continued until only three princes remained. The other task was the completion of the first emperor's mausoleum.

The deserted farm disappointed Marcus, because the stable roof needed repair, as did the toolshed. Cobwebs covered everything. Weeds were everywhere.

Fortunately, Little Ming's foster parents could work on something they knew. Even the little one helped, tying her hair in a bun and wrapping it with a turban. She swept, dusted, and ran errands. Mother Lin busied herself with the house.

Father Bing hired a laborer, and they repaired the buildings. Marcus helped them, but most of his energy went to the fields—especially the soil-rotation areas. Fortunately, they remained intact. When Father Bing finished with the building repairs, he joined Marcus in the fields.

The bustle tired all, so that they ate dinner and retired early. As the farm chores lessened, father and daughter wandered the country lanes, fished in the brook, and chased each other. The girl's lilting laugh and comedic ways eased his heart. She mimicked sheep, dogs, and cats. Marcus's special times were when he put his daughter to bed. They'd talk quietly. Invariably, her breathing would become regular and slow, and Marcus would slip out.

One late autumn day, when trees were bare and cold gusts forced people indoors, Dr. Wu rode into the compound. The fat man waddled out of his aging black carriage. "Marcus, remember the time I came here to examine your dark Indian friend?"

"Dr. Wu, how have you been? Has the emperor been interred?"

Marcus watched the triple chins animatedly fighting for the best position. "Today I'm touring the mausoleum site. Would you like to come?"

Marcus heard a noise near the corner of the house and saw blue eyes peeping out. "Come see our old friend, Little Ming." The girl hurried to her father's side and smiled shyly.

"Of course—she and I had many serious conversations on the recent trip," the doctor said. "Hi, little one."

"Hi, uncle. When will you show me the needles?"

"Let me rephrase my offer. Would you two like to go see the first emperor's tomb?"

Father and daughter looked at each other. "Tell Mama we'll have another for lunch and to pack snacks for the afternoon. Also take your new fur coat."

"Yes, Papa."

"Are you certain that she won't trouble you?"

The physician smiled. "To have her about is like taking a tonic. If you should ever tire of her, I'll take her."

When they reached the tomb, they were greeted by a sour-looking, thin man. Little Ming slid her hand into her father's.

All gawked at the massive structure. The first pit they reached contained rows of statues—all life-sized, freshly painted, and individually modeled, seemingly thousands in all. Their guide spoke in a clipped tone. "We decided to represent our peoples. There's even a barbarian for the southwest." Beady eyes regarded the barbarian.

"They all look different, Excellency. What are they made of?" Surprised by the native speech and the polite manner, the guide relaxed. "Each head was individually modeled. The terra-cotta will endure forever."

"Papa, there's Uncle Lu!" They came to a medium-sized figure posed in a martial arts stance. Indeed, it looked like Captain Lu of His Majesty's special guards, a man who taught Little Ming the rudiments of self-defense. Marcus recalled a martial-arts exhibition in which "Uncle Lu" disarmed four armed fighters with his hands. Fearless and fierce, he treated Little Ming gently.

Behind three rows of spearmen stood a team of four horses. Although stylized, the magnificent terra-cotta beasts appeared ready for action. A copper snaffle bit enclosed each animal's mouth, along with leather bridles inlaid with jade pieces.

"Although this section only has a few hundred soldiers, there are more than seven thousand figures in all. This way." They followed the guide. Another team with carriage and driver had been cast from bronze and had harnesses of gold and silver.

"If I were a bird and could fly over this army, the sight would be wonderful!" Little Ming exclaimed.

Their guide smiled. "Yes, my dear. It would give you a true sense of the scale. Come, we must look at the central vault before it closes." They set off for the hill ahead.

Dr. Wu looked down at the little one. "Little Ming, did you know that your father twice saved the first emperor's life?"

The girl looked back and forth between the bearish man and her father.

"He rescued the emperor when he was a young man," the doctor continued. "Someone tried to kill him, and your father foiled the attempt. The second time came about ten years later. At that time, both your father and I stopped an assassin who was ready to stab the monarch. Isn't he brave?"

"Papa, please tell me about it."

Prideful, musical tones teased at his heart. Marcus didn't feel quite as old. "Both your mama and I saved His Majesty's life. Uncle Wu's also a brave man."

After passing through intricately carved doors, each three paces tall, they arrived inside the central vault with a humbling view. Murals of the imperial tours and triumphs graced the chamber walls. There was Mount Tai. Marcus tightened his grip, until the child looked up at her father.

"Papa ... the sky above us." There was the scorpion, the snake ... and, of course, the dragon portrayed on the ceiling vault.

"To light each star, we've designed miniature whale-oil lamps," the guide said. "The liquid should last for five hundred years. A master artisan got the whale-oil idea from some altar along the coast."

"Papa, look at the jade cabbage piece. A grasshopper's chewing it." He squinted at the intricately crafted artifact. The jade had light green, white, and orange streaks, each artfully integrated into the carved whole.

"Exactly in the chamber's center—over here, Doctor—may be seen a likeness of the empire. Historians and geographers have spent years mapping our great land. There's the capital, the protecting ranges, and the Great River snaking along, with the Wall, marching from west to east. Over there's Langya, the Long River, and the coast." A silvery substance coursed through the river channels and out to the vast sea beyond. "To simulate water, artisans came upon mercury—difficult to collect, but worth the effort."

"What's the large boat over there?" Little Ming asked.

"His Majesty will float forever on a mercury sea, free from destructive pests." The boat would anchor near the magical isle of Penglai—home of the immortals, the place of the elixirs. "Don't touch the liquid, little girl! It's poisonous!"

Marcus pulled back his daughter's hand. "Little Ming, there's the beach, where we saw the rainbow."

When they returned to the farm, they dined on steamed mullet, stir-fry cabbage, water chestnuts, pole beans, hundred-year-old eggs, and fried rice. "This splendid meal makes my own cook seem like an amateur," the doctor said. Little Ming's mother offered another helping.

"Papa, I'm tired. I'm going to bed," Little Ming said. Dr. Wu tarried over a few cups of wine and departed.

Rays of the sun tapped insistently on Marcus's eyelids as he heard his daughter outside. Little Ming watched the yellow-winged butterfly atop the blue wildflower, then ran into his bedroom. "Papa, Papa! Let's go fishing. No hooks ... let the fish win." Marcus jumped from the bed and chased the squealing girl.

EPILOGUE
SU MA (96 BC)

Su Ma's eyes opened as he puzzled out the dream about the bearded barbarian who walked with a Chinese girl. Each carried a pole, but no hook. Twice, he had saved a man's life.

The grand historian scratched his chin. A slight pain called from below, and his spindly arms drew in. Turning onto his stomach, the little man sighed. The history stood at one hundred thirty chapters and hundreds of thousands of characters. Su Ma had never dreamed it would take so long.

Hu Hai … entombing his father's concubines … brothers murdered. Chancellor Lee should have supported Fu Su. The chancellor paid for his choice. Hu Hai stupidly revived the projects and the corvée, and peasants rebelled. General Tian, severing the earth's arteries, deserved death. Terrible civil wars! General Shang riding to the capital and torching everything … the library's priceless books!

Chancellor Lee, one of China's best administrators, implemented the centralized system, unification of the script, standardizations, rectification of the laws. For those things alone, he is a sage. Yet … why not back Fu Su? Had he done so, he'd be among the greatest.

The grand historian closed his eyes. *That bearded man and the little girl, holding hands … she smiled at me!*

978-0-595-40852-8
0-595-40852-4

Printed in the United States
94732LV00002B/174/A

9 780595 408528